This World Book Night edition was originally given on April 23, 2014 by

....

who collected it from.

....

World Book Night is a celebration of reading on April 23 when volunteers give specially chosen books to inspire a love of reading.

At The Reading Agency we believe that reading opens up opportunities for education, employment and culture and frees your imagination – in short it has the power to change your life.

Our World Book Night volunteer givers come from all over the UK and Ireland and share a passionate belief that reading is powerful and important. We work with them, our partners and other charities to give books to people who, for whatever reason, don't read for pleasure or own books.

This book is one of 20 titles, all very different, but all chosen because they are brilliant reads written by great authors. We hope it and the other World Book Night books inspire you to experience the joy of reading.

Please share your stories about being part of World Book Night. They really help us understand what works best so we know how to reach even more people who don't yet love to read. Thank you.

worldbooknight.org/feedback
feedback@worldbooknight.org

facebook.com/worldbooknight
@worldbooknight

Praise for Dreda Say Mitchell's books

'The best reflection of real-life London that I've seen in a long time . . .
A book's "voice" is what determines its greatness and Mitchell's
voice is unmistakably great.'
Lee Child on *Running Hot*

'*Killer Tune* is sharply observed, incisive and a moving story of
conflicting loyalties and unfinished business.'
Guardian

'Dreda Say Mitchell confirms her position as a hot new name in
crime writing with this taut novel.'
Elle

'Brilliant – a gripping roller-coaster for the reader'
Independent

'*Killer Tune* lays the breezy musical name-checking of Hornby's
High Fidelity over a well-crafted murder mystery'
Financial Times

'The narrative throbs with energy and has a refreshing directness.'
Sunday Telegraph

'Confidently paced tale, told in language both lyrical and salty'
Daily Mail

'Sharp-eyed, even sharper-tongued chase story . . . distinctly
different; well worth seeking out'
Literary Review

Also by Dreda Say Mitchell

Running Hot
Killer Tune
Gangster Girl (*Book 2 in the* Geezer Girls *series*)
Hit Girls (*Book 3 in the* Geezer Girls *series*)

About the author

Dreda Say Mitchell grew up in the East End of London where she
continues to live.

GeeZER GirLS

Dreda Say Mitchell

HODDER

This edition specially produced
for
World Book Night UK
2014

First published in Great Britain in 2009 by Hodder & Stoughton
An Hachette UK company

First published in paperback in 2009

A CIP catalogue record for this title
is available from the British Library

ISBN 978 0 340 93711 2

Typeset in Rotis Serif by Hewer Text UK Ltd, Edinburgh
Printed and bound in Great Britain by Clays Ltd, St Ives plc

Text printed on Bulky FSC 50gsm manufactured by Stora Enso Anjala Mill in Finland.
Paper supplied by Paper Management Services

Hodder & Stoughton policy is to use papers that are natural, renewable
and recyclable products and made from wood grown in sustainable
forests. The logging and manufacturing processes are expected to
conform to the environmental regulations of the country of origin.

Hodder & Stoughton Ltd
338 Euston Road
London NW1 3BH

www.hodder.co.uk

This one's for Anastasia. What a sister!

Big thanks to Marise and Barry for letting me nick one of the brilliant ideas from their wonderful wedding and to my agent Jane Gregory, Stephanie Glencross and to the amazing team at Hodder. Love and hugs, as always, to Tony.

And of course Tricia Burns and memories of growing up on the Berner Estate.

Any woman who's got balls bigger than a bloke is a Geezer Girl.

East London saying

now

JacKiE

one

The bride and bridesmaids stared at their guns.

Uzi.

Pistol.

Revolver.

MAC-10.

They stood in one of London's hottest clubs. On the middle floor. In a room that was two floors up from the silent dance floor, two floors down from the members-only spa. They stood in a semicircle. Around the table where the guns lay. The bride, Jackie Jarvis, dragged her gaze away from the shooters. Stared directly at her three friends. Roxy. Anna. Ollie.

Finally she broke the silence. 'Ollie's right, he's coming to get us, I know he is. And we can't take the chance that he might not come to the church.' She stopped. Her tongue did a nervous flick across her lips. 'If you want out, now's the time to say it.'

Once again, she gazed at her friends.

'I'm in,' Ollie said calmly.

'So am I,' Roxy added.

'You know me, girl.' Anna gave Jackie a half-smile. 'I'm always in.'

Jackie nodded. 'OK, this is the set-up. Anna and Roxy, there's no need for you two to be tooled up. But as soon as we hit the church you both become our eyes. Check the place over, up and down, to see if he's there.'

'And if he is?' Anna cut in.

The glow in Jackie's green eyes became grim. 'If that bastard has the brass balls to gatecrash my wedding . . .' She stopped. Eyeballed the guns. 'Me and Ollie will have no choice but to blow him away.'

They all looked at Ollie. She ran her gaze over the guns. Reached out. Picked up the double-action pistol. Shoved it inside the bouquet she held in her hand. Now they all looked at Jackie. She took a deep breath. Leaned forward. Plucked up the compact revolver.

'Anna, hide the other shooters,' Jackie commanded as she stepped back from the table. She moved quickly towards a chair. Lifted her right leg. Placed her white satin shoe on the seat. Her dress made a whooshing sound as she bunched it up. Past her ankle. Over her calf muscle. To the top of her thigh. Until her white stocking leg and electric-blue garter gleamed in the midday light. She stretched the garter with one hand. Placed the gun between it and her thigh. Shivered as the coolness of the metal settled against her skin.

'Sweet Jesus, Mother Mary and all the saints,' she whispered. Then she gently placed the garter back in place.

She moved towards the free-standing mirror, walking in the shaft of sunlight that hit the room. She gazed at her white reflection. Sighed. This should've been the happiest day of her life. The others quickly gathered around her. Stared tensely at their own reflections. They wore sky-blue A-line, above the knee, bridesmaids' dresses, and claret heels, the colours of Jackie's favourite footie team, West Ham United.

'Whatever happens,' Ollie said as her hand tightened on her bouquet. 'Always remember that we're family. We came into this together and we'll come out of it together.'

They remained silent as they stared at their collective reflections like it was the last picture they would ever take together.

'OK, ladies,' Jackie said. 'It's time to rock 'n' roll.'

They moved. Towards the door. The door opened just before they reached it. In the doorway stood the one man they all trusted. The man who had saved their lives. The man who would be giving Jackie away at the church. He gave Jackie an ecstatic, proud smile. 'Sweetheart, you look like a flamin' angel.'

Jackie's wedding dress whispered as she moved to meet him. He crooked his arm. She slid her arm into his. Smiled. He kissed her on the cheek. Then they turned. Stepped out of the door. The gun on her thigh began to warm up against her skin.

'Ready?'

Jackie nodded at the man who held her arm as they stood on the threshold of the church where the packed crowd waited inside. Her right hand tightened on his sleeve. Her left hand smoothed along her dress, feeling the outline of the gun. She took a deep breath. Held it. Stepped forward. Exhaled. The organ started to play West Ham United's theme song. The congregation turned around, watching Jackie coming down the aisle, as they began to sing.

> *'I'm forever blowing bubbles.*
> *Pretty bubbles in the air . . .'*

The song bounced with a rowdy, jubilant quality that any Hammers fanatic would be proud of. Jackie's six-year-old son, decked out in claret trousers and jacket and blue waistcoat, blew bubbles at his mum as she passed by. Jackie gave him a reassuring, shaky smile as a wet bubble burst against her veil. She quickly looked away, her gaze searching the crowd. For him. The geezer.

She checked the faces of the crowd on the left as the pulse of the singing swayed higher.

> *'They fly so high, nearly reach the sky . . .'*

Checked right.

> *'Then like my dreams they all fade and die . . .'*

She blew out a deep, low breath because there was no sign of him. Her face lit up into a cheek-popping smile. She fixed her eyes straight ahead. Onto the man she was about to marry. *Everything's gonna be alright; everything's gonna be alright*, she chanted in her head as she moved. Finally she reached her husband-to-be, as the crowd raised the roof with the song's final line.

'Pretty bubbles in the air.'

The groom lifted her veil. Touched her face. His hand fell away as Father Tom began.

'Dearly beloved . . .'

Yeah, everything was gonna be alright.

Fifteen minutes later the priest announced, 'I now pronounce you husband and wife.' Jackie stared up at her new husband, the gun at her thigh forgotten. His hand slid to her face. Pulled her forward. Gave her the biggest smacker she'd ever had. The crowd wolf-whistled and clapped. A camera flashed.

Bang.

A gunshot ripped through the air.

Someone screamed. Jackie knew it wasn't her. Her husband clung to her. Pressed her close. Then his arms fell away. He staggered back. Her head flopped down to stare at her wedding dress. To stare at the blood splashed across it. Her knees began to buckle as the blood began to spread. As she began to remember how all of this had started . . .

ten years ago

jaDE

two

A death sentence.

That's how it all started.

It took off on a Sunday, 16 December, as the plane left London's Heathrow. Touched down on Monday when it landed at General Latifi airport in the African republic of Sankura. Kicked off as thirty-three-year-old Nikki Flynn and Maxine Munro waited with the other passengers in the cramped and crowded lines at passport control.

They stood in the second line from the right, the third line from the left. Behind the young, black woman who was getting a mega-grilling at the immigration desk. Both women were decked out in classic V-line pencil skirts that clung to thighs and split to allow calf muscles to peep outside. Male officials at airports always went for a bit of leg. Distracting men was at the heart of their success in their chosen profession. Being members of what they had nicknamed the Glittering Game – the illegal importation of gems.

The sweat shone on Maxine's face as she looked nervously around, arms clenched around her middle like she was standing in the midst of a winter day.

'Shit,' Nikki said under her breath as she saw what Maxine was doing. She leaned towards her and whispered sharply, 'Cool it. You look as jumpy as a junkie facing rehab.'

The muscles in Maxine's pale cheek twitched. 'I can't help it. I've got a real bad feeling.'

Nikki's head reared back as the smell of whisky on Maxine's breath slapped her in the face. She'd told Maxine to lay off the booze. She'd tried to keep an eagle eye on her the whole flight. Maxine must've been guzzling away in the toilet like a bloody fish during happy hour. Bollocks, she didn't need this kind of aggro.

'The only bad feeling I've got is you fucking up because you're tanked out of your head all the time,' Nikki hissed. 'Just hand over your passport, smile and show your pearly-whites to the geezer behind the desk and you'll be alright.'

Maxine's hand darted into the side pocket of her shoulder bag and pulled out her asthma pump. Her hand shook as she placed the pump at her mouth and inhaled twice. Nikki shook her head as she snapped back around. She would have to do something about Maxine sooner or later. Her mate of fifteen years was becoming a friggin' liability. A total pisshead. As soon as they got out of this arse-end of a country she was going to sit her down. Lay the law down. But not now. Now they had a job to do.

The black woman at the immigration desk was still getting the third degree. Nikki hugged her black Gucci shoulder bag. Her fine fingers caressed the leather in a quick motion that matched the eagerness of her need to be reunited with her suitcase. A suitcase that had a false bottom stashed with cash that was to be used as part of the exchange for the most lucrative gems of all – diamonds. Nikki had no idea how much cash there was because their boss, Jason Nelson, always insisted on packing the cases himself.

Bang. The noise of the immigration official finally stamping the black woman's passport brought Nikki back to the present. Right, here we go, she told herself. She shook out her shoulder-length copper-red hair. Slapped on a smile. Stepped forward. Reached the desk. She leaned slightly over so that her breasts were clearly outlined against her white Lycra top. She handed her passport over. The immigration official's stone-brown eyes checked out her face. Slid from the gold chain around her neck to her breasts. Lycra and boobs never failed to be the magic combination. Nikki tilted her head to the side. Smiled some more. He ignored her smile. Turned his attention to the maroon passport and began to thumb through it. Abruptly he stopped. Flicked his head back up to look at her. She straightened her head, knowing he had found the ten-dollar bill she had discreetly folded inside her passport. She watched as he quickly grabbed the note and thrust it under some papers. The power of the mighty dollar worked every time in one of these poor countries. He stamped her passport and handed it back to her. She moved towards the bustling arrivals hall. Kept her gaze trained on the black woman who had been ahead of her in the queue, her hand anxiously playing with her necklace as she waited for Maxine. A few minutes later her friend joined her.

'I told you it would be a piece of piss,' Nikki whispered.

Twenty minutes later their baggage was loaded onto their trolleys. Nikki looked across the revolving baggage carousel and found the young black woman, who had started to move her trolley.

'Ready?' she asked Maxine. The other woman nodded. 'Let's get the fuck outta here.'

They moved their trolleys behind the black woman, across the hard floor that was the colour of congealed desert sand. Their trolleys slowed when they saw the line of soldiers waiting near the 'nothing to declare' exit. Ten of them at least. Some cradling guns. Others holding the leashes on dogs primed to attack.

'Told you I had a bad feeling,' Maxine whimpered.

Maxine's bad feeling was beginning to rub off on Nikki. Not that they hadn't seen guns before. They had, but mostly on villains posing for photos in the front rooms of their council flats. The men in the distance held them like they used them every day before they proudly took the head of the table with their wives and kids every evening.

'Just follow the usual routine and everything will be cool and dandy.'

They picked up speed. Pressed forward. The humidity built invisible walls in the air. The black woman just ahead of them reached 'nothing to declare'. A large uniformed official stepped towards her. The woman stopped, sweat running down her face. Here we go, thought Nikki triumphantly. He waved his hand at the woman, indicating she should keep moving. Bouncing bollocks, Nikki thought, that wasn't meant to happen. The black woman turned her head slightly. Looked at Nikki. Caught her eye, like she knew her. Which of course she did.

Jasmine, or Jazzy as they called her.

The third member of their crew.

Their decoy.

The set-up was simple. Jasmine always travelled in economy class – or battery-hen class as they laughingly called it – pretended to speak little English, using a false passport with a Nigerian name. A walking stereotype that officials just couldn't resist pulling over. While they searched her bags, which contained nothing illegal, Nikki and Maxine would sail through behind her.

But the set-up hadn't worked today. Jasmine turned hastily around as she wheeled her trolley away. Nikki's bad feeling turned into full-blown panic. Above her head the blades of the ceiling fan wheezed to the beat of the breath of a dying man. She and Maxine kept moving forward. The soldiers stepped towards them. Nikki plastered the smile back onto her face. Caught the eyes of one of the men. A very large man. The one she figured must be head honcho. His uniform was all-over posturing khaki green with epaulettes and gold and silver braid and SSP written in black letters on the top pocket of his shirt. She moved her gaze away from him and as they reached the customs desk, the official standing behind it held up a hand. They stopped.

Shit.

Take it nice and easy, girl, Nikki told herself. She kept smiling and looked the official directly in the eye. The man looked at the large man standing with the other soldiers. Turned back to Nikki and asked, in clipped English, 'Have you anything to declare?'

Nikki shook her head as she answered, 'No.'

The official once again looked back at the man. Then back at Nikki.

'Are you sure?'

'I said so, didn't I?'

Her tone was full of stress. She could've kicked herself for answering like that. Keep it cool, girl, nice and easy.

The official picked up a leaflet from his desk and handed it to her.

'Have you read this?'

Her eyes quickly scanned the contents. It was the usual crap you got in any country.

The things you weren't allowed to import – drugs, weapons, foodstuff . . . Her eyes flicked back up to him without finishing reading.

'Yeah, I've read this and I'm not carrying any of these things.'

The man studied her face before sighing and smiling.

'OK, you may go.'

She turned to find the man waving Maxine through as well. Thank God, because she didn't think Maxine would've got through that. The soldiers were waiting on the other side in a line, like bullies at the school gate. She kept smiling. Reached the line of gunmen. Sucked in a shallow breath. Kept moving forward. Passed two men. Five men. Seven. Her trolley hit the end of the line. Her smile pulled high as she took a long breath. Yeah, fucking yeah. She thanked God that most men the world over were exactly the same – tossers with limp dicks for brains. Her trolley was almost a metre from the exit when a large hand clamped onto her shoulder from behind. She froze. A deep voice, puffed up with politeness and confidence, said, 'Excuse me, please, English lady.'

Trembling, she turned around. The large man who she had earlier clocked as the leader of the pack stood in front of her, all his power stamped in a face she would never forget. Dark, shining, rumpled with the lines of aggressive living.

'My name is Major Omote. Do you know what the penalty for drug trafficking in Sankura is?'

Drugs? What the fuck was he going on about? They weren't drug mules.

'I don't know and I never will because I wouldn't be that stupid.'

'Culprits are bound and gagged and then shot to death in front of a large crowd at the football stadium. It's a very popular attraction.' His features were set in the stony-faced expression of a killer as he yelled, 'Search their bags.'

Nikki watched, breath crashing in her throat, as two men quickly came forward. One held tight to a spitting and snarling dog while the other held a thin metal rod, the size of a ruler, in his hand. The man with the rod yanked their cases off the trolleys. Swung them onto a long table. Although Nikki was panicking she knew it would be alright because the only thing they would find would be the cash. Besides, Jason had told them that if they got pulled up all they needed to do was offer the officials some of the cash as a 'gift' and then they would be allowed to go on their merry way.

The man with the dog brought the animal nearer to the cases. As the dog got closer he began to rear up and bark like someone had put pepper up his backside.

'Let me ask you again, English lady,' the large man addressed Nikki. 'Are you carrying any drugs?'

This time fear held Nikki's tongue. She couldn't speak. Shook her head. The large man turned to the man who held the metal rod in his hand. Nodded. The man with the rod positioned himself next to Nikki's case. Grabbed it. Flipped it upside down. He raised the rod like a dagger and stabbed it into the middle of the case. Slowly he withdrew the rod. Held it high. The last few inches of the rod were covered in a white powder. Maxine sobbed. Nikki gasped. No one had to tell her that it was either heroin or cocaine.

The mobile rang in the East London massage parlour as Jason Nelson sniffed the second line of coke that lay across the woman's naked breast. Jason was thirty, beefy, with gelled short, spiky brown hair and hazel eyes, topped six foot and was easy on the female eye. He also had a reputation for being easy with his fists. He raised his head. Closed his eyes. Enjoyed the dizziness in his mind as his body buzzed to its newest hit. The phone rang again. He reopened his eyes, his pupils enlarged and wild, and scrambled, completely clothed, off the bed. The phone rang for a third time as he plucked it off the bedside table.

'Yeah?'

'I have the women.'

A quick smile spread across Jason's face as he heard Major Omote's voice. Why oh why hadn't those three dolly birds just listened to him? That was the problem with birds, always too busy chit-chatting their brains off to listen. All they had to do was let him use their daughters for the job in Amsterdam. To sweeten them up for his request, he'd taken them out for a nice slap-up bit of nosh at that new Chinese restaurant in Whitechapel. The one that did Elvis nights every second Saturday. As the women laughed and broke their fortune cookies he'd finally got down to business. Popped the question. Nikki Flynn had cursed him and walked out. The other two had quickly followed, outrage making them wobble on their stiletto heels. Ungrateful tarts. If it weren't for him they'd still be stripping in that backwater piss-hole he owned in Bethnal Green. Of course, when the boss, Frankie Sullivan, found out the women had shown Jason the finger he went ballistic. That's when Frankie had told him to put the drugs in their suitcases instead of the gems.

Jason's mind shot back to the present as Omote carried on speaking. 'And of course, I now have the drugs as payment for our deal in Amsterdam. Tell Mr Sullivan we are aiming to complete the deal in early January. When I have dates, times and personnel I'll let you know. And the package you requested will be with you in three days.'

The line went dead. Jason's smile broadened as he moved back to the woman. He leaned over. Did the final line of C. Ruffled his finger, the one that had Killer written in gold across his ring, under his nose. Crooked the same finger towards the woman in a 'come hither' movement and stabbed it at the floor in front of him. Without speaking or smiling, the woman jumped off the bed as he punched a new number into the phone.

'It's me, boss. Everything's going to plan in Sankura.'

The woman settled herself on her knees in front of Jason.

'And the deal?' the voice on the other end of the line asked.

As Jason repeated what his contact in Sankura had told him, the woman unzipped his flies. 'All we gotta do now,' Jason continued, 'is to . . .'

'Shut the fuck up. I'm the top geezer around here so don't you fucking forget who makes all the decisions.' The man on the other end of the line stopped talking for a full half-minute. 'OK, now the women are outta the way, all we gotta do is to get our couriers ready for Amsterdam. And who are our couriers, Jason?'

The woman pushed her hand inside Jason's trousers. He let out a silent groan. It wouldn't do for the boss to find out he was getting a blowjob while he was on the blower to him.

'The dolly birds' daughters.'

'Contact Finlay. I want you both to meet me at the Dirty Dick so we chat about what we're gonna do when we get our hands on those three tarts' daughters.'

'Shit Street. Isn't that what you English people call the situation you ladies find yourselves in?'

The question flung at Nikki was asked by the Major Omote. He sat behind a wooden table, inside a box-sized room, somewhere in the airport. Lined up on the other side of the table stood Maxine and Nikki. On the table lay Maxine's inhaler and their Gucci suitcases. The secret compartments at the bottom of both cases had been ripped open. Instead of the large wads of cash they had expected there were transparent parcels bulging with white powder. Cocaine or heroin, Nikki wasn't sure what it was. What she did know was the man in front of her was right. They were stuck in the stench of Shit Street.

'I've said it a thousand times,' Nikki said, voice hoarse, pushing against the crushing humidity in the room. Her cockney accent was in full bloom, all traces of her pretending to be someone else gone. 'I don't know nothin' about that gear.'

Which was the God's honest truth. She hadn't got a fucking clue how it had got there. Their boss, Jason, always packed the cash.

'We're entitled to see the English consulate,' Nikki continued.

Major Omote threw his head back and roared with laughter. The two guards with guns standing near the door joined in his laughter. He leaned forward. Abruptly stopped laughing.

'In Sankura the only thing drug-dealing scum are entitled to is six bullets in the head. Justice in Sankura is administered very quickly, so don't be surprised if you are sentenced before you ever see your consulate.'

'I've got to get outta here,' Maxine sobbed. The air pumped out of her body in ragged breaths. She was sweating. Shaking. The same way she did when she needed the top end of a bottle in her mouth. The same way she did when she desperately needed her inhaler.

Nikki was worried about the state the other woman was in. Gently she touched Maxine's arm. Leaned close to her ear. 'Calm down, alright? We ain't done nothin' wrong so nothin' bad is gonna happen here, OK?'

Maxine silently nodded as her cries softened into quiet huffs. Nikki let go of her arm as she turned back to Omote. 'We know what our rights are, so our mouths are zipped until you get that consulate pronto.'

There was no reply, just silence. The silence was broken only by the soft sound of interrogations from other rooms. There was sobbing, pleas of innocence and occasional crashing and bashing and yells of pain. Having made his point, Omote stood up and stretched to his full height of six-three. Calmly he left the table and walked over to Nikki. He pushed his head to the side, looking her up and down like she was offering her services in a shop doorway in Soho. He had never been this close to her before. Now she could almost feel every muscle he had packed into his body.

'Aren't you wondering what happened to your friend?'

'What you chatting about?'

He looked over her shoulder. Nodded at one of the guards. The guard pulled open the door. Stood back. Someone was pushed into the room.

'Ohmygod,' Nikki called out, and covered her mouth with her hand when she saw who it was.

Jazzy.

Blood dripped from her mouth and a large bruise covered the corner of her left eye.

Nikki ran over to her and enfolded her in a huge embrace.

'What did you do to her, you bastard?' Nikki shrieked.

'Like I said, we have our own way of doing things.'

He swaggered slowly towards the two women. His large hand thrust out. Touched a strand of Nikki's hair. She felt as if a fat, brown worm was burrowing into her head. His fingers ran down the shiny, sweating skin on her neck. Played with her necklace. Suddenly, his fingers grabbed the chain and yanked it from her body.

Nikki lunged forward, shouting, 'Give that back to me.'

Omote just laughed as he shoved the necklace into his pocket. Nikki opened her mouth again. Then quickly closed it. As much as she loved that necklace she wasn't prepared to put her life on the line for it.

'I like you, tough lady,' Omote said as he ran his dark eyes over her. 'I will get your consulate. Now I've done you a favour, maybe soon you can do one for me too.' Nikki knew what the tone of his voice meant. The drunken, creepy men who had worked in the care home she'd grown up in had used it enough times when they tried to get inside her knickers.

'Take them away,' he called out to the guards.

The two guards moved. One positioned himself next to Maxine and the other next to Nikki and Jazzy. They pointed their guns at them. Maxine stumbled towards the open door, whimpering, 'I wanna go home now. I've got to go home . . .'

They were marched down a long, airless corridor. 'You alright?' Nikki asked Jazzy, her arm tight around her shoulder.

'Forget about me. What's going to happen to our girls?'

The only family they had were their fifteen-year-old daughters. Jade, Amber and Ruby. Nikki momentarily closed her eyes, picturing her daughter Jade eagerly waiting for her return so they could put up the Christmas decorations together. Since Jade had turned fifteen, a month ago, she had insisted that she could stay on her own when Nikki went away instead of staying with a neighbour. Nikki hadn't liked it but she'd let her daughter have her way. How the hell were they going to get out of this nightmare? And how the fuck had those drugs got inside their bags in the first place?

'They'll be alright.' Nikki reassured. 'What I don't get is how they figured out you were with us. How that shit got in our cases.'

Suddenly both women looked meaningfully at each other.

'You thinking what I'm thinking?' Nikki said, the blood draining from her face.

'Yeah.'

'We've been fitted up. Only one fucker could've . . .'

A shout from the guard escorting Maxine stopped Nikki's words. She looked up. Shock and dismay gripped her when she realised what was happening. Maxine was running with the speed of a wild animal. The guard next to Nikki pulled up his gun. Aimed it at Maxine. Nikki pushed Jazzy to the side. Ran in front of the guard with the gun. Kept running towards Maxine.

'Maxine,' she screamed.

Bang.

The gun went off.

three

'Still can't believe that we're gonna get our hands on those diamonds. The fucking Gates of Dawn, man, the Gates of Dawn.'

Finlay Powell's amazed statement hung in the evening air as he sat next to Jason Nelson. They sat in the shadows inside the Dirty Dick boozer in Mile End. Everyone called the Dick Turpin pub the Dirty Dick. Some claimed it got its nickname because during the war it was a knocking shop, others said it was because of the dodgy deals that went down during the reign of the previous landlord before he himself went down for life for a double-barrel murder. The place was packed, as usual, the quick-style patter of people and smoke swam in the air, while Squeeze's South London balled 'Up The Junction' played softly in the background.

Both men sat opposite their boss – thirty-year-old Frankie Sullivan. Of course, no one except Jason and Finlay knew that Frankie was the real boss of the outfit. Everyone assumed that the moniker belonged to Jason.

Frankie smiled at the amazement he heard in Finlay's voice. The Gates of Dawn were Sankura's famous diamond collection. Frankie knew that getting the diamonds was a once-in-a-lifetime opportunity. Since Sankura had descended into civil war it had been easy for Frankie, through Jason, to make contact with a high-ranking official, Major Omote, and get the ball rolling. But Omote said his people would go only as far as Amsterdam, so Frankie had to figure out a way of getting the diamonds to England.

That was when he'd hit on the blinder of an idea to use kids as couriers. Kids travelling on a trip with other children to Amsterdam were less likely to be given a thorough going-over at the airport. That was when another gem of an idea had struck him. The women who worked for him as couriers, through Jason, had daughters. Easy-peasy, all the woman had to do was say yes. But the bitches had spat in his face. No fucker did that to Frankie. So he'd set them up in Sankura, got them out of the way, and now he could do what he liked with their little girls.

'Now those three tarts are outta the way,' Jason, said, 'all we've gotta do is get their girls. And when we get 'em, we've gotta scare the fucking shit outta 'em.'

Frankie shot quietly back, 'We can't just put the frighteners on them. The last thing we need are mules transporting our gear through Heathrow who look like they're about to shit themselves.'

'So you gonna keep them banged up, twenty-four-seven, at St Nicholas until the job comes through?' Finlay asked.

St Nicholas was the care home all three men had grown up in from the age of ten. Now it was the place that Frankie ran his operation from. He knew it had been another gem of an idea because the last place the Old Bill were going to look for dodgy dealings was in a care home. Frankie twisted his lips. If only the cops knew what care homes were really like. But maybe they did and just didn't give a bollocks.

'Nah.' Frankie shook his head. 'That will turn them stir crazy. First thing we've gotta do is give them a mate who's gonna make life nice and comfy. Someone who they learn to trust.'

'Who? Fucking Father Christmas? Ho! Ho! Ho!' Jason said, chuckling, as he sniffed and wiped a finger under his nose.

Finlay was not amused. 'Shut your gob, man. All that charlie you snort is turning you into a total prick. This is the biggest job of our lives, so we ain't got time to prat around."

'Shut it, both of you, and listen,' Frankie cut in. 'I'm gonna play big brother . . .'

'You?' Jason said with an incredulous look on his face.

'Yeah, me. Remember, none of the men know that I'm the real face. They all just think that I run around after you, Jace. So it's gonna be easy to convince everyone that I'm looking after the girls. If I'm with the girls I can make sure they get properly primed for the job in Amsterdam.'

'Short of breaking their arms, how are you gonna make them work for us?' Finlay asked.

'Simple. We put them in a position where they think they're the only people who can save their old girls' lives. That's where the package arriving from Sankura in three days' time comes in. Believe me, when they see what's inside that package the only people they're gonna want to please are us. When the Amsterdam job comes up, in a couple of weeks, after the New Year, those girls are gonna be no bovver.'

'But Frankie,' Finlay said leaning back in his chair, 'I get the bit about wanting to use kids, but these girls are gonna have no experience. I still think we should be using proper couriers.'

'No way. Proper couriers want a cut and leave a trail. We'll control these girls' lives. It will be almost like they don't exist any more. Then we're gonna have to train them to be couriers . . .'

'And how you planning on doing that?'

'First of all we draw them into our world. Make them know what it feels like to be a criminal. At the same time we check that they can follow orders. So we make them do an in-house job at St Nicholas. Once the girls prove that they can work for us, they're ready for the next stage . . .'

'Which is?' Finlay carried on his line of questioning.

'The job in Amsterdam involves the girls doing it on their own, without us being there breathing down their necks. To test they can work on their own we have to give them a job to do outside of St Nicholas's walls. So Finlay, when one of your next shipments comes in tell me, because I'm gonna use the girls to deliver it. . . .'

'Are you fucking off your nut?' Jason railed, his head rearing back. 'You can't send them across London on their own. What if they do a runner and go to the Bill . . .'

'No way. Not after they see what's inside the package from Sankura.' Frankie carried on when both men nodded in agreement. 'Then all we've gotta do is train them to deal with security at an airport. All sorted.'

'You gonna run a decoy?' Finlay asked.

Frankie smiled. The decoy was his speciality. On all his oper-ations that involved airports he used a decoy, who was always black. The security at the airport just couldn't help pulling up black people and Frankie couldn't help but take advantage of the situation. Through Jason, Frankie had got the three women to run the same stunt, with Jasmine as decoy. Now Jasmine's daughter was going to follow in her old girl's footsteps and be the decoy. But this time there would be a difference. This time there had to be another black girl.

'This time I can't afford to take any chances, so I've told our contact in social services to get us another black girl. Two black girls will work much better. If one of them ain't pulled up the other one's bound to be. And then bingo, the girls with the diamonds ride on through.'

'Yihaa!' Jason said, as if he were a cowboy.

Frankie's hand whipped out of nowhere and grabbed Jason's balls under the table. Jason's face twisted with pain as Frankie applied pressure. 'I've told you to ease up on that shit you shovel up your bugle. We all need to be clear headed. If you fuck this up . . .' Frankie didn't need to finish. Jason's face paled as he remembered seeing Frankie's temper in full flight.

'Sorry, boss,' Jason said quickly as Frankie slowly removed his hand.

He eased back in the chair. 'All we've gotta do now is round those girls up.'

Finlay considered Frankie for a while. 'What if the girls don't wanna play?'

Frankie swiftly turned to Jason. 'That's where you come in, Jace. If any of them step outta line it's your job to stamp on them. Hard.'

Fifteen-year-old Jade Flynn was scared. Scared because she hadn't heard from her mum in three days. Jade was two inches above five foot, tubby, with a thick brown ponytail, sharp green eyes and freckles that took the high ground on her pale, white face. Not a stunner. Not like her beloved mum, Nikki.

It was lunchtime at Blessed Virgin Mary comprehensive school, 19 December, the last day before school broke up for the Christmas holiday. Jade's school was a ten-minute walk from the Blind Beggar pub, where Ronnie Kray had shot George Cornell back in '66. She sat on her own, well away from the other girls, because she needed to think. The low-hanging sky coughed up a wind that criss-crossed over her face and her West Ham Utd scarf. Her small hand shook as she opened her West Ham Utd lunchbox. Pulled out a packet of fags. Placed one at her lips. Lit up. Sucked hard. Got giddy as the smoke shot inside her.

All she wanted to do was belt home and sit by the blower, like she'd done yesterday and the day before, hoping that her mum would call. Hoping that her mum would be back to put up the decorations with her tonight, six days before Christmas. The estate agents that her mum worked for usually sent her abroad to look at properties at least six times a year. When her mum went away she called her every night without fail. Jade had got the first call, the one her mum always made from either Heathrow or Gatwick. Since then nothing. Not a dicky bird.

She pulled another lug of nicotine into her body. What would she do if something had happened to her mum? Really happened? Nikki Flynn was her world. There were no grandparents. No uncles. No aunts. No cousins. No bloke struttin' around their two-bed flat. The one time she'd asked Nikki why she didn't have a dad, like some of the other kids at school, her mum had harshly replied, 'We don't need no geezer giving us a load of grief and verbal and telling us when to bloody breathe.'

Jade shivered as the tears bulged in the bottom of her eyes. Bouncing bollocks, what was she gonna do if anything happened to her mum?

'Flynn,' an adult voice roared, shooting across Jade's unhappy thoughts.

Startled, Jade shot to her feet. Her lunchbox tumbled to the ground. The green of her eyes grew deeper and wider when she realised who the voice belonged to. Mrs Harris, the deputy head-teacher. Aka Battleaxe. All the girls called her Battleaxe behind her back because she was big, broad and stomped around like every student in her care was the inmate of a prison. The scowling teacher took a step closer, making Jade swallow. The spit went down her throat with a good dose of nicotine. That was when she remembered the ciggie in her hand. Shit, she knew she was going to be in a load of bovver now. Being caught 'on the puff' was an immediate three-day suspension. Battleaxe's lips tightened into a deadly line as she shifted her gaze to the cigarette and watched it like it was of one of those things the other girls whispered that Stacy Wilson let her boyfriend put in her mouth.

Jade flicked the offending object into the cold wind and pleaded, 'Miss, this ain't what it looks like. It's one of them sweetie fags . . .'

'I don't have time for your tall tales at the moment, girl. Sister Margaret Mary wishes to see you in her office.'

Jade swore under her breath. The few times she'd been inside the headmistress's office were to receive a bollocking about her behaviour. Like the time she put chewing gum on someone's chair. Like the time her maths teacher had screamed the place down when she'd left a plastic rat in her drawer. Like the time . . .

'Now, Flynn.' Battleaxe's command was a full-blown war cry.

Jade didn't need to be told twice. She picked up her lunchbox. And ran. Into the four-storey Victorian school building. Up the stairs. Stopped outside the closed office door that was located on the staircase midway between the ground and first floors. Her gaze skimmed across the bold, black lettering on the door.

Sister Margaret Mary
Headteacher
Children are an heritage of the Lord.

Jade quickly did up her top button. Tightened her red and black striped tie. Took a deep breath and knocked.

'Come in.' The command was soft.

Jade stepped inside. Fifty-three-year-old Sister Margaret Mary stood tall and thin in her black nun's habit, behind her desk, beneath a wooden crucifix on the wall. Her face was so pale that if Jade

didn't know better she'd swear that the older woman was wearing
translucent powder.

'Sister?' Jade hovered with the single word in the doorway.

'Shut the door, child.'

A frown wrinkled across Jade's forehead at her headmistress's
gentle tone. That wasn't the tone she used to tell the girls off. Quietly
Jade closed the door. Her hand tightened on the handle of her
lunchbox as she approached the desk. The light from the window
caught the cross above Sister Margaret Mary's head, casting a
distorted crucifix-shaped shadow across the wall. The nun moved
around the desk as the shadow lengthened like discarded ink down
the wall. Sister Margaret Mary reached her. The shadow crept across
the floor. The older woman stretched out one of her hands. Slipped it
into Jade's free cold palm. Softly squeezed her flesh. The shadow
seeped under the nun's habit. Touched the tips of Jade's toes.

'I'm afraid I've got some bad news. It concerns your mother. . . .'

The rest of the woman's words slammed into her as she moved her
tearful gaze to stare at the wooden cross and the crucifixion of Jesus
Christ.

four

The steel door banged shut. The loud sound echoed against Nikki's body. Made her tremble as her eyes remained firmly fixed on the cell door. She sat on the narrow bottom bunk, between a quiet Jazzy and a snivelling Maxine, who held tightly onto the inhaler Major Omote had finally let her have back. It had been three days since they'd been blindfolded, shackled and frogmarched from the airport to this maximum-security hellhole. Three days since the bastards had lined them up against the wall and taken mugshots of them. Three days since Nikki had spoken to her daughter. She closed her eyes and prayed real hard that Jade was alright. That Jade had found her black address book and contacted the only person Nikki trusted to look after her. Getting busted and facing a death sentence she could deal with; something happening to her precious Jade she could not.

Maxine's sobbing got louder, intruding on Nikki's thoughts. With an irritated tut she twisted her body furiously to the left to face the other woman and yelled, 'I've had it up to here with you making that racket, so shut it, alright. Because of you we were all nearly fucking brown bread.'

A stunned Maxine stopped mid-sob as Nikki pushed herself up. Nikki began pacing. She'd had a bellyful of Maxine's boo-hooing morning, noon and bloody night. Weeping and wailing weren't going to get them out of this jam. Nikki stopped walking. Touched the cut on her cheek where the bullet had grazed her skin. A memento from Maxine's foolish stunt three days ago at the airport.

Why she'd run after her friend she would never know. But she had and it had nearly put her six feet under.

She shivered as she remembered the sound of the gun blast. Loud, its ferocity echoing in the corridor. She'd frozen. Waiting for the bullet to bang into her body. But instead it had whizzed by her head, brushing her skin. The pain had been slight, like a bee sting. She'd almost wet herself waiting for another shot, but it never came. Instead the soldiers had rushed towards her and Maxine, yelling in a language she didn't understand, and slammed them against the wall. Pointed their guns point blank in their faces. She'd squeezed her eyes shut. Waiting. Just waiting for the trigger to be pulled. Then there was silence. An awful silence when she knew someone was weighing up whether to extinguish her life. She'd heard heavy footsteps coming towards her. She'd opened her eyes to find Major Omote himself, blocking out the light, standing in front of her. He'd looked at her. One of his large hands had moved. Touched her hair with terrifying gentleness. Then swiftly his other hand had shot out and slammed into Maxine's stomach. As Maxine groaned and crumpled to the ground, he'd whispered in Nikki's ear, 'Know why I'm letting you live, English lady? Because I've got plans for me and you. Plans as red hot as your hair.'

The way his gaze had smouldered against her she thought he was going to screw her right there against the wall. But he hadn't. Instead he'd ordered the guards to blindfold and chain them. Transport them to the main prison in Sankura's capital.

'You alright?'

Jazzy's question took Nikki out of the nightmare of three days ago and back into the nightmare of the cell. With a sigh, Nikki turned to face her mate. Despite the last three days, Jazzy still looked like exactly what she was – an incredibly attractive woman. Tall and slim with bob-cut black extensions and skin the smoothness and colour of a cup of winter-warming hot chocolate. Even the guards who came inside to leave food and water appreciated what their guns pointed at.

Nikki gave a shaky smile and nodded. 'Yeah. I'm scared shitless about what's gonna happen to my little girl.'

'She'll be alright,' Jasmine reassured her, putting an arm around her waist. 'Just like my Amber and Maxi's Ruby will be.'

Maxine began to sob again as she heard the name of her daughter.

'For crying out loud . . .' Nikki bellowed as she started to march towards her. But Jazzy tightened her arm around her waist, stopping her. 'Leave her. We're all dealing with this craphole we've fallen into in our own way. Instead of fighting each other we've got to stick together like we have all these years.'

They'd been mates since they'd met as eighteen-year-olds in the maternity ward at the London Hospital in Whitechapel. They were the only ones in the ward who'd had no visitors. No proud new fathers, no family, nobody. When they realised that they had all grown up in care homes they had bonded as if they'd been friends for years. Each one of them had decided to name their daughters after gems because their babies were the most precious people in their lives. Once they left the hospital they'd become fast friends, meeting up with each other regularly. It was Maxine who'd introduced Jazzy and Nikki to the stripping scene. She'd been stripping since she'd done a runner from the care home she lived in when she was fifteen. When their daughters were four, the owner of the club they'd worked in, Jason Nelson, had asked if they were interested in doing a little job for him. Always needing the extra cash, they had jumped at the chance. That had been their first trip abroad. Soon the stripping became a distant memory as they became Jason's permanent runners. When their daughters hit five they'd made the decision to never bring their kids when they met up because they didn't want their girls to be part of Jason's world.

'I still can't believe that Jason would set us up like this,' Jazzy said.

'You know it was him,' Nikki cut across her wearily. They'd had this conversation over and over since they'd been put in this cell. 'He's the only one who ever gets anywhere near our suitcases before a job. Now we're outta the way he don't need to ask for permission to use our girls . . .'

'But he promised he wouldn't do that. He promised that if we said no that was the end of it.' Jazzy shook her head in disbelief.

'It's never the end of it with geezers like Jason. The only two things they think about are dipping their dicks and watching their pile of poke grow. The only thing that stood in the way of him getting his fucking mitts on our girls was us. So he sets us up. Loads us up with drugs and tips off the Sankurans about our arrival. And I'll bet you a cool million that Omote is one of his mates. The drugs ain't gonna go down no plughole, they're going into Omote's pocket as payment for a job well done.'

'Fucking hell,' Maxine screamed as she shot to her feet. 'We've got to get outta here, then. Before they get our girls. Before they get my Ruby . . .'

'I know that,' Nikki yelled back. 'But since my middle name ain't Houdini there's no way we can do it right now.'

The cell echoed with Maxine's erratic breathing as she sucked furiously on her inhaler. Nikki sighed, feeling bad about yelling at her friend. She moved back to the bed and sat down beside Maxine. She put her arms around her shoulder.

'It's alright,' she crooned, as if Maxine were a baby. 'We're gonna be alright.'

A few seconds later Jazzy joined them, her arm slipping around Maxine's shoulder as well. 'Maybe that bloke from the British consulate will sort us out,' she said.

Omote had kept his promise and called the consulate. A representative had shown up yesterday. Some prissy, pinstriped suit, who looked down his public-school-educated nose at them once he heard their strong cockney accents. Threw his words at them like he was chucking food at them in the zoo. He didn't seem to care much if they were guilty or not. He found them a lawyer. A local arsehole who smelt like he brushed his teeth with rum every morning and couldn't keep his bloodshot eyes off Nikki's thrupenny bits. Two English reporters had turned up later the same day. They had checked them over like they were assessing whether they were newsworthy enough. Then the one with the notepad started writing and Nikki was sure his first sentence must've been: 'Dole-scrounging single mums with big hooters might be shot.'

'Whatever happens,' Nikki said, her fingers linking with Jazzy's, 'we've gotta remember that we're family. We got into this together and we'll get out of it together.'

The rattle of keys in the steel door made the women look up. The door creaked open to reveal Major Omote.

'Good evening, ladies.' He eased his bulk into the cell.

The women jumped up. Nikki swallowed nervously because Omote wasn't looking at the two other women; his gaze feasted on her. Two gun-toting guards marched in behind him. They strode towards Maxine and Jazzy, gesturing with their guns. As soon as they reached them they marched them towards the door. A startled Nikki cried out, 'Where are you taking them?'

'Don't worry,' Major Omote said quietly. 'I just thought each of you ladies would prefer your own private accommodation.'

Nikki rushed towards the open doorway, but he blocked her from going any farther. Stretching up on her toes she shouted over his shoulder, 'We're getting out of here, ladies. Just hold tight and we'll all be back together again soon.'

Nikki watched the terrified faces of her two mates, for what, she knew, could be the last time ever. Then the cell door slammed shut. Nikki eased back down to the balls of her feet. The tears swam across her eyes. Bollocks, no way was she crying a river in front of Omote. She tipped her head defiantly to stare up at him. His ugly mug was split into a grin.

'I kept my promise, pretty lady, to contact your consulate. Now it's time for me to find out how hot that hair of yours really is.'

Shocked, Nikki stepped back. He moved forward. Fingered his trousers. Nikki took two more steps back. He took another step forward. Pulled down his zip. Nikki's back hit the wall. He reached her. Stretched his muscular arms on either side of her head.

'Someone told me that screwing an English woman is the same as putting your dick inside a freezer. But I think that you, Nikki, are going to make this as hot as the fires of hell.'

He lowered his head. Sank his teeth into her breast. She didn't even flinch. It wasn't the first time some bloke had put his gnashers into her skin. As long as she could remember, men had been mauling their way through her life. Telling her what to do. What to wear. What to say. Scum, every last one of them. Except for . . . She winced in pain as his teeth tucked into her nipple. As his lips fastened on her flesh she began to think. She'd figured out long ago that there were only two situations when a man became senseless – when he was bombed on booze or rutting on top of some woman. The man sliding his hand up her skirt she knew would be no different. Maybe, just maybe, if she let him get his rocks off he would tell her if Jason had set them up.

Her body relaxed. Seductively, she hitched her skirt up. Pulled her knickers down.

'I suppose we should be thanking Jason for getting you into my arms, lover boy?' she whispered in his ear.

'Jason?' His voice was dazed. Yeah, she'd got him where she wanted him.

'Jason Nelson.' Her hand dipped towards his trousers. She pushed it inside.

'Come on, big boy, you can tell me. It was Jason, wasn't it?'

She pulled his cock out. Gently squeezed him. He groaned.

Her hand moved over him to the rhythm of the questions she softly fired at him. His groans became sounds of torture. He pushed her hand out of the way. Positioned himself between her thighs. Tried to push his way inside. But she tensed her muscles. He wasn't going nowhere until he told her what she wanted to know.

'Come on, you can tell me.'

His erratic breathing cut against the skin of her neck. Defeated, she knew he wasn't going to cough up. But maybe the next time. Her muscles relaxed. He shoved inside. As he began to vigorously fuck her she thought all men were scum. But there was only one man she cursed inside her head and it wasn't the one currently treating her like a slab of meat.

If you touch my Jade, I'm gonna fucking kill you, Jason Nelson.

'My mum can't be banged up.' Jade's words pounded with shocked disbelief. She sat opposite her headmistress at the round table. She had no idea how long she'd been sitting there. No idea how long since the woman across from her, a Sister of Mercy, had broken the news. Told her that her mum, her beloved Nikki, was in the slammer in some country she'd never even heard of. Sankura. Sounded like something her and her mum ordered as a side dish from the Saffron Spice Indian takeaway every Friday night.

'Would you like some water, child?'

Jade shook her head. Bloody water weren't going to do the trick. What she needed was what her mum called a granny-sized shot of gin. The one and only time she'd taken a lug of Nikki's drink of choice it had made her feel confused. Numb.

'Do you know what the Foreign Office is, child?'

Jade stared blankly at the other woman.

'They are a special part of the government. They let us know important information about the world. They rang me personally to let me know what was happening.'

'But they got it wrong because my mum said she was going to Spain on business. She always goes to the Costa del something or other on business.'

'I'm so sorry, child.'

Jade wished she'd stop bloody calling her child because she wasn't her child. She was Nikki Flynn's kid. She needed a friggin' fag real bad.

'What they holding my mum for?'

The area around Sister's mouth became pinched and tight, like she was trying to hold the words back. But the words came out anyway.

'She was detained, with two other women, trying to bring something . . .' She stopped talking, her lips smacking gently together as if looking for the right word. 'Bad into the country.'

Bad? Jade's mind spun as she remembered a programme she'd once seen about bringing illegal stuff into Britain. Endangered animals. Weird plants. Exotic food. And of course the big D. Jade shook her head. No way would Nikki get involved in that mug's game.

'Sister, do you mean booze?'

The older woman gave a heavy sigh like she was in extreme pain. For the first time she avoided looking in Jade's eyes.

'Once my mum brought too much booze back from Spain. But she promised me she wouldn't do it again.'

Sister made a quick sign of the cross and pushed out, 'It was drugs.'

Jade shot up. Her shaking legs knocked over her lunchbox. Frantically her head swung from side to side, as her finger stabbed in the air at her headmistress. She knew she shouldn't point, but it was a habit she just couldn't let go. 'No way, Sister. Not my mum. She hates the stuff. Said if she ever caught me "on the gear" she'd string me up from the nearest ganja tree . . .'

She tried to say more, but she began to cry instead. Huge, retching wails that erupted deep inside her. She felt Sister's arms fold around her. Her sobs pushed her into the softness, security and warmth of the older woman.

'I wish I could make this all better and make it go away, but I can't.' Sister's words were soothing. Caressing. Her hand moved with a lullaby softness across Jade's hair. Jade moved her head deeper into the rhythm, like she knew it was the final act of kindness from an adult she would feel for a long time.

'Who have you been staying with while your mother's been away?'

Jade's body tensed. Nikki had made her cross her heart and promise that she wouldn't say anything about taking care of herself.

'Jade, have you been home alone?' For the first time Sister's voice became classic headmistress. Disapproving. Authoritative. Wouldn't back down until she got an answer.

Jade's sobs ceased as she nodded.

'You can't remain on your own . . .'

'But I'm big enough to look out for myself.'

'We have an obligation to look after you. A duty of care. We need to find you somewhere to stay. Especially as this will all undoubtedly soon be in the press.'

Sister gently eased Jade away. Gravely looked at her. 'That means I'm going to have to call . . .'

Before she could complete her sentence the phone on the desk rang. She eased Jade back and moved to her desk. Picked up the cream-coloured phone.

'Yes . . . Put her through.'

As her headteacher spoke Jade turned her back. Bent down. Picked up her lunchbox. Opened it. Pulled out the packet of ciggies. Seconds later she was puffing furiously.

'Jade,' Sister called as she placed the phone back on its cradle.

Jade stared hard at the fag in her hand. Here we go, she thought, I'm gonna get the telling-off of my life. But she wouldn't let go of the cigarette. Couldn't let go. Slowly she turned around. Her headteacher stared at her. At the smoking sin in her hand. But instead of the harsh words Jade expected, Sister looked at her with sympathy.

'That was a very nice lady from social services called Mrs Grieves. She's a social worker. She's coming here and will make sure that you're well looked after until all this gets sorted out.'

'Sister, promise me one thing.'

The tall woman nodded once.

'Wherever they take me, you'll come and see me, won't ya? Still look out for me?' Sister smiled back. 'Of course. Are you sure there's no relatives you can stay with?'

Jade's teeth tugged at the inside of her mouth as she shook her head. Then she remembered that there was someone Nikki had told her she could contact if she found herself in a jam. Someone Jade had never met before. But the problem was this person wasn't a relative.

So she asked, 'Does it have to be someone I'm related to, Sister?'

'Yes, it has to be a family member.'

Bouncing bollocks, Jade screamed in her mind. She knew she couldn't tell Sister about this person because she wouldn't let her stay with them. So she would have to contact them herself. She knew exactly where to find their contact details – in Nikki's address book. A book her mum kept in her dressing-table drawer.

five

Jason Nelson stamped on the genitals of the man who lay sobbing on the floor. His victim screamed and rolled onto his side. Jason was dishing out a bit of old-fashioned street justice in a room on the top floor of the St Nicholas care home for children in Chingford. The room was rectangular, sparse and functional – wooden table and chairs in the middle, cooker, fridge, sink, portable music system and small colour TV. The telly was on. Volume hiked high so the children below couldn't hear the screams. Jason twisted his mouth as he looked at his bleeding victim. If there was one thing that turned his six-pack it was a bloke who couldn't take a couple of slaps. He'd learned early in life, some would say too early, that you never bawled like a baby in front of no one. No quicker way to lose respect and get branded a pussy. He crouched low beside the pussy next to him and growled, 'The next time I have to come looking for my dosh, you'll be leaving here looking like you came outta a mince machine.'

He pushed his angry, red face menacingly close to his victim. A strong smell of urine washed over his nose, making his nostrils twitch. The bloody pussy had wet himself. He was tempted to dole out a few more kicks for his literally coming in here and taking the piss. But he didn't. Instead he eased up. Looked over at the two men who stood in front of the closed door and shouted, 'One of you get this piece of crap outta here. And don't forget to use the back stairs.'

As the taller of the men rushed towards the groaning victim, the news report on the telly caught Jason's eye.

'Reports are just coming through that the three British women arrested in the African republic of Sankura have now been charged with the illegal importation of heroin. This means that all three women may be facing the death penalty. A source at the Foreign Office confirmed that a representative of the British consulate in Sankura has visited the detained women . . .'

Jason grinned. Everything was going bang according to plan. His mobile rang. Jason flipped it out of his pocket. As he listened to the female caller a smile spread across his face. He nodded a few times. Then cut the call.

'Where's Frankie?' His voice was gentle as he asked the man leaning on the door. His voice always got soft when he talked about Frankie. He knew the other men didn't get it. And they didn't need to understand who Frankie really was. Their job was to follow orders.

'Dunno,' the other man answered as his body shot forward like that of a soldier receiving his commanding officer.

'Dunno?' Jason yelled. 'What the fuck do you think I'm paying you for? To stand around and look at my ugly mug all day? He's gotta be close by because he's taking care of our newest guests. Get him in here pronto because I've got a job for him.'

Frankie had picked up Maxine and Jasmine's daughters that morning. Now the call had come through that Nikki's daughter was ready to be reeled in.

Frankie Sullivan sat calmly in the neighbouring room. It was kitted out as a bedroom, with four beds, a single window, wardrobe, three-drawer dressing table, wire-brushed tan floorboards and its own private bathroom. Frankie wasn't alone. On one of the single beds sat two girls. Amber and Ruby. Jasmine Craig's and Maxine Munro's fifteen-year-old daughters. The newest residents of the St Nicholas care home.

'Is this gonna be our new crib until our mums come back?' one of the girls asked. The black one. Amber, Jasmine's girl. She was a dead ringer for her mum. Slim face, lively eyes, with her shoulder-length black corkscrew extensions, with beetroot-coloured highlights, pinned high with a gold scrunchie and a skin tone a few shades darker than her name. Her long legs, in black jeans, hung over the bed. Her arms were crossed over her tracksuit top like she wanted to remind people she could be a tough girl when she wanted to.

He smiled at her. 'Yeah.'

She couldn't take her eyes off him and he knew what she saw. What every other woman saw. A man who resembled an artist's image of an angel. Fair skin, soft summer-blue eyes, twin dimples and sparkling golden hair that most women wanted to run their fingers through as they held him lovingly against their breast. He got that hair from his mum. Except hers had become dirty blonde, always swinging in the air as she raised her hand, letting him know that the only touch he would ever get from her was from the buckle end of a belt. The only mark that marred his beauty was a tiny, old scar, at the corner of his right eyebrow, a lasting gift from his bitch of a mum.

'Is it nice here?' Amber asked him, leaning forward, her gold-ringed fingers making easy-going gestures in the air.

'Nice' wasn't a word that anyone used to describe St Nicholas. He should know. He'd lived here with Jason and Finlay when they were kids. More like survived, he corrected himself. There was no point bursting the girl's bubble yet. She'd learn the truth soon enough. And the truth was that Mr Miller, the man who ran the home, turned a blind eye to Frankie's criminal comings and goings on the fourth floor. And he would keep his eyes closed as long as Frankie kept mentioning those photographs of Mr Miller and those young boys. Photographs that would land sweet old Mr Miller, who last year had been honoured by the mayor for services to the community, in the slammer quicker than anyone could say nonce.

'When's my mum coming home?'

Frankie switched his gaze to the other girl, as her question hung in the air. Ruby. Maxine Munro's girl. Her voice was thin and as high as than of a squeaking mouse. She wasn't that much shorter then Amber, but her fragile, bony body made her seem much smaller. On her tight, pale face were perched a pair of nondescript glasses framed by her loose, brown hair. One of her hands clung tightly onto an asthma inhaler while her other hand knotted in the blue duvet. She reminded Frankie of a tortoise who couldn't wait to shove her head back inside her shell.

Frankie leaned forward. Remembering he was posing as the girls' guardian angel, he pulled a fake, soothing smile onto his face. 'We'll talk about your mum later tonight. So for now . . .'

The door burst open. Amber and Ruby scrambled back onto their beds. Frankie shot out of his chair. His hands balled into fists by his side. His hands uncurled when he saw who it was. Billy 'Motor Mouth' Baker, whose voice he'd heard with Jason coming through the wall next door.

'There's no need to frighten the ladies,' Frankie said as his fists uncurled.

Billy spread his legs. Folded his arms across his chest. His eyes swept over Frankie from head to toe, like Frankie was a bag of rubbish. Finally his contemptuous eyes blazed onto Frankie's face as he said, 'Who do you think you are? The fucking boss or something? You're just everyone's run-around boy. You ain't even got a real bloke or a geezer's job. You're just a chimp, so move your arse because Mr Nelson wants you next door.'

Billy smeared him with a final dirty look. Turned and left.

Rage stained Frankie's cheeks. So that's what they called him behind his back – 'run-around boy'. Mr Nelson's gofer. If Mr Nelson wants a package picking up, get Frankie. If Mr Nelson needs ferrying around town, get Frankie. If Mr Nelson needs the blood licked off his Italian leather shoes, get Frankie. Frankie's lips twisted into a tight smile. If the men knew who he really was they would be shitting themselves with maximum respect.

He'd started in the biz at the bottom of the slagheap, at twelve years old, as a runner for a local face. That was how he'd learnt his trade, listening and watching the way the big players turned a trick, including the times they made prats of themselves and fell flat on their faces. At nineteen he'd been ready to break free and set up his own firm. Of course, no one, except his two boyhood mates, knew that he was the face. People assumed that it was Jason. He'd seen too many major players go down in handcuffs because the Old Bill knew exactly how they worked. No way was that going to happen to him.

Best way to ensure success was to remain in the shadows and let someone else take the heat. And Jason, being the heavy-footed thug he was, just loved the feel of the limelight on his skin. His outfit had started small, specialising in knock-off gear. Then had come the drugs, the gems, moving his operation from local to national to international. Now the Amsterdam job was going to send him global. Frankie turned back to the girls, his dimples deep in his cheeks. 'I'm trusting both of you to guard my seat.'

Both girls said nothing. Just stared at him with, he suspected, the same look that had frozen their faces when they'd found out their mums weren't coming home.

He left the room. Closed the door quietly behind him. He took three steps forward and reached the room on the left. Grasped the handle. Pushed the door. As he stepped inside, Jason shot to his feet and said, 'The call's just come through that our last little gem is waiting to be collected.'

'Where the bloody hell is it?' Jade muttered to herself, as she tried to find her mum's address book.

She was on her knees in front of the dressing table in her mum's bedroom. Her hand frantically moved inside the top drawer. Her mum's undies drawer.

'Are you nearly ready, dear? Our car will be here soon,' the social worker, Mrs Grieves, called from downstairs.

Her hand stopped. She twisted her head fearfully towards the closed door. She knew she wasn't meant to be in here. Mrs Grieves had warned her not to touch any of her mum's things just in case the Old Bill needed to do a search.

It had been just over two hours since the social worker had taken charge of her life in Sister Margaret Mary's office. Under two hours since they had both left the school. Just over an hour since they had entered Jade's home so she could pack. Jade lived in Manny Shinwell House in Poplar in East London. Of course, it wasn't really a house. Not like the houses in the books the teachers made her read at school with their pretty gardens where flowers and happiness grew all year round. Manny Shinwell House was a tower block.

Fourteen floors of tough bruised brick. They lived on the eighth floor. Corner flat. A maisonette. High enough to peep at the rapid-moving high-rise, glass-and-steel developments on the Isle of Dogs. Low enough to see the goings-on in Chrisp Street Market.

'Did you hear me, dear?'

'Yeah, yeah. Five more minutes, miss, that's all I need.'

Now her hand began to move with a speed a pickpocket would have been proud of. Thirty seconds later she raised her head, breathing heavily; the only thing in her hand was a cassette of Soft Cell's album *Non Stop Erotic Cabaret*, which featured her mum's all-time favourite song, 'Tainted Love'. She placed the cassette on the floor.

Then slammed the drawer shut. She pulled open the middle drawer. It was filled with paper – letters, bills and envelopes.

'You alright up there, dear?'

Startled, Jade looked towards the door. The voice was closer, like Mrs Grieves was standing at the foot of the stairs.

'Everything's cool, miss,' she answered as her hand started to move frantically through the contents of the drawer.

'Do you need some help, dear?'

The social worker's voice was followed by another creak. Jade knew she was coming up the stairs. She speeded up her search. Started to fling paper out of the drawer and onto the floor. Finally she gazed at the empty drawer.

Nothing.

Another stair creaked. Jade shuffled back on her knees. She grasped the handle of the next drawer. Wrenched it open. Gasped when she saw what was inside. Piles of loose cash – tenners, twenties, fifties, even hundred-pound notes. Bouncing bollocks. What the hell was her mum doing with all this spare cash?

But she didn't have time to ponder her question as she heard Mrs Grieves's breathing joining the creak of every step she took. Jade's hands dived inside the drawer. Into the money. Her hands moved left. Moved right. Still no little black book. Panting, her hands shuffled in a wild dance. Suddenly they stopped as she felt something hard in the left-hand corner. Her fingertips pulled it forward.

Bingo. Her mum's address book. She shoved her hands behind her back at the same time as Mrs Grieves opened the bedroom door.

The landlord of the Dirty Dick let out a low wolf whistle as the black woman came through the pub door. Legs up to her gold-looped earrings, trim and tall, with brunette braided extensions that were a shade lighter than her skin. She wheeled a suitcase behind her as if she'd come straight from the airport. He stopped polishing the bar and pulled himself straight. Gave her a smile. She didn't smile back, but spoke with a soft African accent. 'I'm looking for a Jason Nelson.'

The landlord ran a curious look over her. She didn't seem like Jason's usual type.

'He ain't here, babe.'

The skin on her face tightened at the 'babe'.

'Tell him to come now,' she ordered, then wheeled her suitcase and herself towards the nearest table.

'Hang on, love, I don't get on the blower until . . .'

'Just tell him that his package from Sankura has arrived.'

The social worker stood in the doorway and looked at Jade suspiciously. Mrs Grieves was a small sparrow of a woman, with the cuts of life indented on her shrivelled face and faded eyes that sparkled only every Friday and Saturday night at bingo.

Jade stared at the older woman from the vantage point of her knees. Her pose and expression mirrored exactly what her school report claimed that she was – a reckless, mischievous child.

'What on earth are you doing?' the older woman demanded, showing her thin, sliced teeth stained with tobacco. The older woman's eyes settled on the piles of paper scattered on the floor.

Jade sprang to her feet, her hands remaining behind her back.

'This is your mother's room, isn't it? I told you not to come in here.' Mrs Grieves's words came in a rush as she pushed herself into the room. The red heat of rage spread across her cheeks. 'What have you got behind your back?'

'I just wanted to get this,' Jade answered as her tears began to fall.

One of her hands came out from behind her back, clutching a rectangular object. She showed what she was holding. The Soft Cell cassette she'd found in the dressing-table drawer.

'My mum loved this. "Tainted Love" is her favourite.'

'I know you're upset, dear, but our driver's waiting. Get your stuff together and I'll see you downstairs.'

Mrs Grieves turned and left the room. As soon as the woman disappeared Jade stopped crying. She rushed over to her holdall. Picked it up and slung the handle over her shoulder. Then she picked up her lunchbox. Opened it. Her hand moved to her back pocket. She pulled out the black book she'd hidden there just before Mrs Grieves had entered the room. She opened it and began to flick through, searching for the M page.

'We need to leave now.' The older woman's voice was hard.

She knew M was only a couple of pages away.

'Now.' The voice was a frantic reminder of Battleaxe at school.

She'd look later. She slipped Nikki's address book inside her lunchbox, next to her packet of fags, and her first communion candle. And the other thing the social worker had told her to pack – her passport.

six

They took the lift to the ground floor. Exited Manny Shinwell House using the back door. Passed a group of run-of-the-mill boys-on-the-block who were too busy practising the latest poses and patter to notice the anxiety in Jade's eyes. She kept her lunchbox tight to her side like it was a new body part. Soon they entered the car park, packed with vehicles, most belonging to the Chrisp Street market stallholders. The churning wind carried tiny drops of rain. The sky was the colour of trouble overhead.

'There's the car,' Mrs Grieves said.

Leaning against the bonnet was a tall man in an open wool overcoat, having a smoke. He flicked the fag. Turned in their direction just as the sun came through above. Gobsmacked, Jade felt her mouth fall open when she saw his face. It was what the girls at school called 'a bit of awright' – pop-star quality and teen-heartbreaker good looks. The sunlight that surrounded him made him look like he was already a pin-up on her wall.

'Come on, dear.' Only when the older woman spoke did Jade realise that she'd stopped walking. She sighed as she picked up her feet, catching a glimpse of her distorted reflection in the shiny, greased puddles created by the rain. They reached the car. Jade blushed as the man pushed himself straight and gave her a killer smile. She caught the colour of his eyes and couldn't look away. A blue so deep that she felt she was drowning in them. Her blush deepened and she swallowed as she finally looked away. Mrs Grieves opened the front passenger door and said, 'In you get.'

She felt the tears burning her eyes, the back of her nose. Bouncing bollocks, no way was she going to start blubbing again. She sniffed as she lowered her head and got into the passenger seat. Placed her bag on the floor between her legs. Wrapped her arms baby-tight around the lunchbox in her lap.

The ends of Frankie's blonde hair blew in the breeze as he walked towards Mrs Grieves. He made sure that his back was to the car so Nikki's daughter couldn't see what he was going to do next. Without speaking to the social worker he jammed his hand into the top inside pocket of his coat. Pulled out a bulging, brown envelope. Handed it to the woman. Her hand trembled as she took it. Frankie had seen that shaking before. On his mum, shivering from Sunday to Sunday, after years of drowning in drink. But it wasn't his business to tell this pitiful woman that she needed her own care worker.

Besides, him and Mrs Grieves had a history. She had become his social worker after he'd done a runner from the first care home they'd placed him in. After the police had found him sleeping rough in an abandoned car, they'd placed him in St Nicholas with Mrs Grieves as his care worker. Care worker my arse, he thought. She'd been too busy boozing her life away to take much interest in the kids in her care. He'd told her all those years ago what was really happening to him, Jason and Finlay in that place, but she hadn't given a toss. It was only accidentally, years later, that he'd discovered she had a massive debt with a casino up West. He'd purchased her debt and now she did anything he asked her to. But he didn't want her to think he was a total heartless bastard, so he always gave her a bit of pin money when she did a job.

Frankie lowered his voice. 'Don't forget to make sure you lose all three case files. And if any nosy bastard asks, tell them the girls are at one of those respectable care homes, like St Anne's. Don't forget I still need one more girl. And don't forget she's gotta be black.'

Mrs Grieves slipped the envelope into her bag as she answered, 'It's going to be hard for me to find one straight away because I won't be in the office over Christmas. I'm being shifted to the airport to look after any refugees or asylum seekers. . . .'

Frankie's hard stare made Mrs Grieves's words dry up.

'You know what's gonna happen if I don't get that girl . . .'

Business over, Frankie smiled as he made his way to Nikki's daughter in the car.

Nerves crawled up Jade's spine as the driver's door was pulled open. Cold air danced inside as the man settled his long body into the seat. The tang of tobacco and aftershave shifted towards her. Her arm tensed around her lunchbox. A sharp rap at the window made her look up. Mrs Grieves was bent over, peering through the window, her bony fingers digging into the leather of her shoulder bag.

'Well, this is goodbye for now, Jade.'

Jade's eyes bulged big with alarm. 'But miss, ain't you coming?'

The social worker's lips tightened as she straightened. Stepped back. The door lock clicked down. Startled, Jade swung around to face the man in the car. Her lunchbox nearly toppled from her lap when his hand shot out towards her.

Horrified, Jade stared at the offered hand. No adult had ever invited her to shake their hand before.

'Everyone just calls me Frankie,' the man next to her said as he pushed his hand out farther. His cockney accent was low, light, filled with the smoke he'd been inhaling a few minutes ago.

'Go on, babe.' He laughed. 'Shake it. It ain't the big, bad wolf.'

Jade rubbed her lips together as she continued to look nervously at him. Before she shook his hand she needed to try and figure out what type of man this Frankie was. Nikki had told her there were two kinds of blokes in this life – gents and geezers. Nikki said she couldn't say much about gents because not many of them had crossed her path, but geezers, now those she could write the rule book on. Jade shuddered as she heard her mum's words in her mind – 'All geezers are interested in is impressing their mates, getting bladdered, wearing gold until it pops out of their eye sockets and making your life hell. Geezers use their knuckles not their brains.'

Jade flicked her mind back to the bloke beside her. He gave her a reassuring grin. Finally her hand moved out of her lap and took his palm. His skin felt rough, but secure. He gave her hand a gentle shake.

'Now that weren't hard, was it?' His hand dropped away as his grin grew.

She shook her head as she blushed.

'Now I know you must be wondering why that nice Mrs Grieves ain't tagging along with us for the ride, but she's got a bit of an emergency. You packed your passport?' Jade nodded. 'So where we going?'

'To a place called St Nicholas . . .'

'Ain't he the saint that looks out for all the kids?'

'Right on, babe. St Nicholas is this big house which looks after girls and boys who've lost their mums and dads . . .'

'I ain't lost my mum.' Jade vigorously shook her head. 'She's coming back to me . . .'

'I know,' Frankie reassured softly. 'I knew your mum. . . .'

'What?' Jade shot back at him. Her mum hadn't ever mentioned knowing a Frankie.

'We used to work together. She's a great girl, that's how I know she'd want you to be well taken care of. She's gonna feel much better if word gets to her that you're being well looked after in a place like St Nicholas.'

Jade's face sagged as she thought of her mum locked up in a tiny cell. Frankie caught the look on her face. 'Really sorry to hear about your old girl. But don't you worry, babe, I'm gonna make sure that you're properly sorted out.'

He reached over and put the radio on. Blondie's 'Hanging On The Telephone' swept into the car. As Frankie started the engine, he softly sang along with Debbie Harry. Jade stared up at Manny Shinwell House one last time. She'd be back. Wouldn't she? With her mum?

*　　*　　*

Frankie felt like the dog's bollocks as he drove Nikki's daughter to St Nicholas. Everything was going bang on plan. Once he got Jade settled with the other girls he would be ready to get them to work for him, just like their old ladies used to.

Frankie whistled as his motor swung past the late-night-closing corner shop into St Nicholas's driveway. The care home was located well away from any of the neighbouring houses, on its own near a large green field where the fog often drifted in the morning in winter.

'Welcome to St Nicholas,' Frankie said to Jade.

As he cut the engine, out of nowhere a police siren blared behind the car.

Jason was coked as high as a balloon when he entered the Dirty Dick boozer later that afternoon. He saw the black woman straight away, sitting at a table sipping a drink. He swaggered over, the ends of his wool coat flapping behind him. The woman looked up at him. He gave her the once-over. She was a pretty sort, but he didn't go with black birds.

He pulled up a chair. 'You got it?'

The woman opened her Prada bag and dug inside. She pulled out an A4-sized beige envelope and pushed it across the table to him. As he plucked it up the woman stood up and grabbed the handle of her suitcase.

'Hang on a minute, I've gotta check that the right merchandise is inside.' Jason couldn't be sure, but he thought she stared back at him with the same look his old man would give his mum before he clouted her one.

'I've done my part.'

And with that she left. Jason quickly opened the envelope. Pulled out what was inside. He whistled as he stared at the contents. Frankie was right – when the girls saw this lot they would do anything to help their mums.

Frankie waited tensely in the car as the siren continued to scream behind. Shit, he hoped this wasn't a load of aggro. He would bet his life they weren't after him, but the Old Bill were like cockroaches, often appearing when he least expected them. He let out a long sigh of relief when the police car whizzed past them to stop at the front of the house.

'What's going on?' Jade asked, peering through the windscreen.

Frankie didn't answer. Instead he remained in the car to see what the Bill were doing at the home. Two coppers jumped out of the car, one of them holding the arm of a tall, thin, teenage boy. An average-sized older man stepped out of the main door of the house, his frosty white beard, hair and cap making Jade think he was a dead ringer for Captain Birds Eye, but without the smile and twinkle in his eye. He rushed down the stairs as the policeman thrust the boy forward. Captain Birds Eye looked well pissed off, Jade decided. The police nodded at the man and jumped back inside their car. As the car drove away, the man grabbed the boy by the front of his T-shirt and backhanded him twice across the face. Jade gasped, horrified at what was happening. The man dragged the boy by his ear into the house. The door slammed behind them. 'I ain't staying here,' Jade said to Frankie.

'Relax,' he told her. 'That ain't gonna happen to you. I've got somewhere special for you to stay. What you've gotta understand about St Nicholas is that it's got some troubled kids in it, the type your old lady wouldn't want you hanging around with. That's why, while you're here, you ain't gonna have nothing to do with the other kids. That boy was most probably lifted by the cops because he was doing something bad.'

'But that man whacked him one.'

'Don't worry about that geezer, Mr Miller, because you ain't gonna have nothing to do with him. He runs the home, but I'm gonna be the one looking after you. Get your gear together and let's go.'

Jade got out and stared at her new home. It looked like one of those fuck-off houses she'd seen in books. Tall, with a red roof and white-framed windows with the late afternoon shadow of the nearby trees swaying against its brick walls.

Frankie took Jade's bag, leaving her with her lunchbox. She walked with Frankie towards the back of the house There was a garden with a long brick building at the bottom and a swing in the middle of the trimmed lawn. They stopped at the bottom of a wrought-iron staircase that led to a landing at the top of the house.

Abruptly Frankie turned to her. Startled, she jumped back. Face solemn and serious, he said, 'Whatever happens, just remember you can always come to me. I'll look after you.'

She gazed at him strangely, a shiver shooting through her bloodstream. She didn't like what he was saying. Like there was something scary waiting behind the door at the top of the landing.

They walked up the stairs. Reached the landing door, which was rusty from years of being battered by the rain. Frankie grabbed the long handle. The door fussed and creaked as he pulled it open. He heaved his arm, settling the handle of Jade's bag more securely on his shoulder. Jade's eyes darted around her. Quickly she tightened her hand on her lunchbox and followed Frankie. She entered a corridor that was long and thin with light shooting in from a window planted in the wall directly facing her. Frankie stopped at the first room he reached on the left. His hand grasped the round handle. Opened the door. But instead of walking inside he leaned back, grinned at Jade and said, 'After you, milady.'

She stepped anxiously forward. Past Frankie. Through the doorway. Into the room. She halted, surprised to see two other girls sitting on separate beds.

'Hi, girls,' Frankie said, as he dropped Jade's bag at her feet. 'This is Jade. She's your new roommate. While you lot shake hands, I've got a few odds and ends to sort out.'

He stopped talking, his face becoming drop-dead serious. 'And make sure you stay put until I get back.'

Jade eyed up the two other girls with suspicion. She wasn't in the mood to make new mates. December 19 was already turning into one of the worst days of her life. Both girls continued to sit on their beds. The white one looked how Jade felt – uptight and plain scared. She stared uncertainly at Jade, over the computer magazine she held in her hand. Then her grey eyes, behind her glasses, flickered wildly, like smoke, from Jade to the door, from the door back to Jade, as if she expected someone to burst in and start slapping her up. The black girl, on the other hand, lounged back, midway through painting her nails fluorescent pink. Her brown face was relaxed, limbs loose, cultivating an air that told the world she was all that and a bag of chips. She gazed at Jade with dark, friendly eyes.

'I'm Amber, and my girl over there,' she pointed her finger at the other girl, using a cockney-Caribbean accent that some of the street-smart kids on Jade's estate loved to use, 'is Ruby.'

As soon as Jade heard their names she knew who they were. Amber and Ruby, her mum's mates' daughters. She'd never met them but had heard Nikki drop their names around at home every so often. What the f'ing hell were they doing here as well?

'Your mum's doing bird as well, ain't she?' Amber said.

'My mum ain't no drug pusher,' Jade replied defensively, splashes of red anger singeing her cheeks.

She picked up her bag and marched over to the empty bed with the yellow duvet.

'Take a chill pill, girl. There's no need to dog me out,' Amber shot back. 'I never said she was no drugs bunny. All I'm saying is she got busted with our mums, didn't she? They were in the same line of business.'

Jade looked at the other girl with stunned surprise and said, 'You mean that both your mums worked at the estate agent's as well?'

'Estate agent?' Amber asked in a baffled tone. She twisted the lid of the bottle of nail polish. Slung it on the duvet as she slid her long body to sit on the corner of her bed.

'I think what Amber is trying to say is we're all in the same boat,' Ruby said quickly, fixing her eyes fully onto Jade.

Jade noticed that her voice was different to hers and Amber's. She had what old Mrs Singer, Jade's next-door neighbour in Manny Shinwell House, bitched to anyone with an ear her snob of a daughter had – a bit of culture. Jade dumped her bag on the floor. Sat heavily on the bed. Cuddled her faithful lunchbox in her lap.

'Your mum was Nikki Flynn, weren't she?' Amber continued.

'*Is*. My mum *is*, not *was*.' Jade stabbed her finger at the other girl on the words *is* and *was*. 'She's still bloody breathing. And she's been fitted up on bogus charges.'

'You don't know, do you?' Ruby said in the same quiet voice.

'What are you chatting about?' Jade threw back, already fed up with the company of her new roommates. Roommates – more like bloody morons.

'What did your mum tell you she was up to?' Amber asked.

'She weren't up to nothing. All she did was go to work one day and never come home.'

'We aren't saying that your mother was a bad person. It's just there are things you obviously don't know,' Ruby said.

Jade was taking a strong dislike to Miss La-di-da and her flippin' fancy accent.

'The only thing I need to know, darlin', is that my mum is the best. She worked her guts out for that upmarket estate agent, who did a load of deals abroad.'

'Our mums were involved in the deal-making business alright,' Amber said, all the cockiness gone from her voice. 'But they had nothing to do with flogging people houses. OK, this is it, straight up, girl, have you ever heard of the glittering game?'

Jade gave the tall black girl a confused look. The glittering game? Sounded like some daytime game show to keep OAPs happy until they kicked the bucket.

'Gem smuggling,' Ruby said quietly. 'Our mothers took money abroad and exchanged it for jewels, mainly diamonds . . .'

'You've both got a flippin' screw loose because no way in hell was my Nikki involved in shit like that.' Jade's voice tailed off as an image of the drawer full of money she'd found in her mum's dressing table flashed in her mind.

'Shall I tell you how I know?' Amber jumped in. 'My mum never lied to me. We had this deal that we were always straight up with each other. From day one she told me what she was doing and who she was doing it with. She said that she worked for this geezer called Jason.'

The words hit Jade like bullets flying in the air. She rubbed her hand over her forehead. She heard a noise from across the room.

Looked up to find Miss La-di-da coming towards her. Ruby reached her and sat on her right side. As Jade inhaled in spurts of disbelief, Ruby began speaking. 'I didn't believe it either until I overheard my mother on the phone a week before she left for Sankura. She was talking to your mother about their next deal. The last deal they were going to do. Collecting diamonds in a country called Sankura.'

'What you saying?' Jade flung out, her finger stabbing in the air again. 'My mum's as bent as a nine-pound note?'

'No.' Amber stood up as she spoke. She moved towards Jade's bed. Sat on her left side. 'Whatever went down went wrong,' Amber continued. 'I know my mum and no way in fucking hell would she get involved in a fool's game like drugs.'

'Maybe we should tell the police . . . ?' Ruby started.

'What are you, stupid or something?' Amber's indignant response filled the air. 'If we tell Five-O what our mums have really been up to I bet you a tenner that they'll be down the nick as soon their plane touches down in Heathrow.'

'So what are we going to do?'

Amber considered Ruby's question. 'Ain't nothing we can do except sit tight. Besides, we ain't got much alternative because on the radio I heard that . . .' She closed her mouth and for the first time Jade saw fear in Amber's eyes.

'What did you hear?' Jade's voice was small. Frightened of what the reply would be. Amber took a deep breath. 'I heard that they might stick 'em on death row.'

Ruby gasped. The blood drained away from Jade's face. Jade shook with the enormity of what she'd been told. Death was for old people. Wasn't it? Not her beautiful mum. No way could they kill Nikki. No way. She wasn't gonna let it happen.

She reached for her lunchbox. Opened it. Pulled out Nikki's address book. Shot to her feet. Began briskly walking to the door.

'Where are you going?' Amber asked, standing up to her full five-nine. 'You can't just bounce outta here. Frankie said to keep our skins inside the four walls of this room.'

'Well, Frankie ain't here and I've got a call to make.'

She opened the door and waltzed out into the corridor. Her hand shook as she flicked through the book. She stopped when she came to M. Scanned the page until she found the name she was after.

Miss Misty McKenzie.

seven

'Sweet Jesus, Mother Mary and all the saints, deliver me,' Jade mouthed as she made her way downstairs.

She was shit scared. Her heart boom-boxed like crazy. She made a quick sign of the cross as she reached the next landing. No one in sight. She continued, her hand gripping the banister. When she hit the second floor was when she heard the voices of children. Muffled, coming from somewhere below. Finally she reached the hallway, which was big, wide, with black and white floor tiles. Two teenage girls stood with their back to her, one of them pinning a piece of paper to the large noticeboard next to the main door. Jade rushed over to them. Sensing her presence, the girls turned around. Jade's eye caught the information on the paper they were pinning to the board.

January
Trip to Amsterdam

Jade flicked her eyes away from the notice to the girls and asked, 'Is there a telephone anywhere?'

The girls looked at her as if she'd just landed from outer space. Finally one of them shook her head.

'Shit,' Jade let out. 'There's gotta be one here somewhere.'

Two closed rooms were on her left and right. She moved towards the one on the right. As she got closer the voices of the children got louder. She clasped the handle. Began to turn. Click. She eased forward as the door opened. Inside were at least twenty children sitting around three long tables, eating. The children's chatter instantly stopped when they saw her.

'You're not meant to be in here,' an aggressive voice shouted behind her.

Startled, she turned around to find the man she'd identified earlier as looking like Captain Birds Eye looking daggers at her. She remembered that Frankie had said that the man's name was Mr Miller. Jade cringed back when she remembered how he'd slapped the boy silly in front of the house. No way was she going to let this man put his hands on her.

'Mr Miller, can you help me?' she asked.

'Get back up to the fourth floor now.' He waved his hands at her like he was shooing sheep.

Fuck you, she wanted to yell at him. But instead she brazenly said, 'I need to use the blower.'

The eyes of the watching, silent children burned her back.

'Get. Back. Upstairs.' The fury of the man's words pushed into her face along with his stale breath.

The words were out before she could seize them back. 'Up yours, mister.'

She darted around him as she heard a few chuckles coming from the children. His hand swiped out, but she was too quick. She dashed for the front door.

'You can't go outside,' he shouted, barrelling towards her.

'Watch me,' she taunted.

'You can't because Frankie . . .' His words stopped. Hung in the air like poison. Intrigued, she turned to look at him. The expression on his face was pure terror. So he was shitting himself over Frankie. She quickly realised that Frankie must've told him to make sure they were alright. Well looked after. What a gent.

'Frankie said I could use the blower.' She told the lie swiftly and quickly. 'And if you don't let me, I'm off out onto the street to find one. And what's Frankie gonna say if something happens to me?' The last sentence she said slowly, the words grating like a screw turning.

She watched the indecision play the 'should I or shouldn't I?' game on his face.

'Follow me,' he finally said.

Jade stuck a satisfied grin on her chops as she followed him down the hall. They entered a small office near the kitchen in the back. The room was cluttered, with a desk teeming with piles of wayward papers and files. But Jade had eyes only for one thing – the black telephone perched on the corner.

'Five minutes,' the man ordered, then was gone.

She wasted no time as she leafed through Nikki's address book. She found Miss Misty McKenzie's number. Folded the left-hand corner of the page. Tapped the number out quickly. Held the receiver to her face. Shoved the address book into her tracksuit hip pocket. At the other end the phone rang. Once. Twice. 'Come on,' she ground out anxiously. Three times. The line connected.

'Hello?' she called out.

'Who . . . ?' the person on the other end started.

But she never heard the end of the sentence because a finger clamped onto the phone, cutting the line dead.

Jade knew she was in deep bovver just looking at the finger on the receiver. Big and chunky from muscle, not fat. Its centrepiece a ring. The type of gold ring that had a word carved in box letters in the metal across the front. Usually a sentimental word like Mum or Love. This ring said Killer. The man was huge and wide, with spiked, gelled brown hair, strange-looking pupils and a white face painted with the most terrifying picture of anger she'd ever seen in her young life.

'What the fuck are you doing?' the man screamed, as he shoved his face into her space.

She gagged on the lick of alcohol coming off his breath. The receiver slipped from her fingers. She shuffled frantically backwards until the solid barrier of the French windows stopped her. That was when he made his move. Came at her with his fists swinging like hammers at his side. One of his hands shot out. Sank into her tracksuit top like it was paper. Dragged her forward. Hoisted her until her shocked green eyes were level with his face. Her little legs kicked with the fury of fishes at the end of the line.

'Who you been fucking calling?' he stormed, his breath dragon-hot in her face.

Jade stared with shock at the stranger, unable to answer. The only sound coming from her mouth was the uncontrollable motorised moan of her breathing

He jerked her closer. 'In three seconds my fist is gonna be bouncing off your jaw if you don't start spilling about who the fuck you were on the blower to.

'One . . .' His shout was dramatic.

Her breathing got louder, but she wasn't gonna tell him.

'Two . . .' His tone dropped to a snarl, telling her he meant business.

Her huge, jagged sobs tore up the room.

But she wasn't gonna tell him.

'Three . . .' He yelled the final digit.

Jade snapped her eyes shut.

She wasn't gonna tell him.

She cringed, waiting for the blow. But it never came. Instead she felt the man tighten his fist in her clothes. Her eyes bounced back open. He hauled her closer. Swore violently in her face. Then he did the last thing she was expecting; he dropped her. She hit the wooden floor, arms, legs and emotions all twisted. As she scrambled desperately backwards, on her bottom, his hand swiped at her. She screamed as it grabbed her ponytail. He wrenched her hair high. She continued to scream as he dragged her towards the open doorway. Her bottom scraped and slid against the floor as they hit the hallway. The children, standing crammed in the dining-hall doorway, watched the scene fretfully. But no one moved to help Jade.

'What the fuck are you lot looking at?' Jason bellowed at the watching children. They shot back into the room.

Thick tears streamed down Jade's face as the pain in her head intensified. She let out a breath of relief as the man's hand left her hair. But her relief was short lived because he reached down and locked his arms around her middle. With a grunt he hauled her shaking body high into the air. Then he took the stairs two at a time.

'Let me go,' Jade yelled, her legs kicking in the air.

But he ignored her as he continued the journey up into the building. They reached the fourth floor, but his pace didn't let up. He carried her struggling body towards the room she'd left five minutes ago. His harsh breathing echoed in the corridor as he raised his foot and kicked the door open. The two girls inside shot to their feet, their faces paralysed with surprise and fear. The man threw Jade onto the floor. She landed on her front, her head hitting the ground. As she groaned in pain, his hand grabbed the back of her tracksuit. Flipped her onto her back. Crouched over her, he growled, 'One last time, bitch, who the fuck were you calling?'

Jade didn't even think about what she was going to do next. She just did it. Her foot came up and connected with his balls. She quickly scrambled away as he moaned and tipped onto his knees. Jade shot to her feet. Wobbled as the pain in her head tipped the room one way, then the other. She dragged in hulking breaths of air. Twisted around. Looked wildly around the room. She found the figures of Amber and Ruby shock-still beside their beds.

'Come on,' she shouted at them. 'We've gotta get outta . . .' But before she could finish the sentence a hand grabbed her clothing from behind. Dragged her backwards. Then she was lifted and slung onto her back, on the bed she had sat on earlier. As her body rocked with the motion of her landing, her eyes momentarily closed. Hot, furious breath on her face made her reopen them. She gasped as the man's murderous face blocked out anything else.

'I'm gonna make sure, cunt, that you never kick another man in the family jewels again.'

One of his hands reached for something behind her head. Move, move, move, she chanted at herself in her head. But her body felt too heavy. Then all her thoughts stopped when she saw what was in his hand. A pillow.

She heard one of the girls start to sob. She tried to move. But it was too late. The pillow was shoved over her face. Instinct made her close her eyes. The ridges of his fingers pressed hard over her face through the pillow. Her arms flayed in the air. Her legs kicked up. The pressure increased. Fuck, she couldn't breathe. In her mind she screamed for her mum. Her access to oxygen slipped away. Her legs and arms became heavy. She tried desperately to keep them moving. Once. Twice. There was no third time. Her limbs fell flat onto the bed.

'What the fuck's going on?' She heard the question in the distance.

Nikki. The name screamed in her mind one final time. Then everything went black.

'Jee-zuus.'

Frankie's yell matched the motion of his body as he propelled himself from the doorway towards Jason and Jade on the bed. He couldn't believe what he was seeing. Sure, he'd told Jason to keep the girls in line, but the stupid fucker was trying to kill one. That wasn't part of the plan.

Frankie reached the bed. He swore harshly under his breath as he grabbed the other man by the back of his jacket and slung him on the floor. Frankie's breathing hammered in the air as he fell on his knees. Ripped the pillow from the still girl's face.

'Shiiit,' he blasted out when he saw the blue tinge of her mouth, the deathly pale colour of her face.

He ran his eyes rapidly over the rest of her body. Abruptly stopped at her chest. No rise. No fall. She wasn't breathing. He rested two fingers on her pulse. Kept them there for a full half-minute. Then he twisted his head around. Caught the eye of every other person in the room. Ruby. Amber. Jason.

Finally, he spoke, his words dropping like freezing air into the room.

'I think she might be dead.'

Major Omote let out a rumbling grunt as he sagged between the thighs of Nikki Flynn. The sweat dropped from his forehead. His gaping mouth caught the oxygen as he adjusted back to the regular beat of his breathing. He leaned over to kiss her dry lips. She twisted her head to the side so that his mouth caught the line of her jaw. He scoffed at her defiance. Gave her breast one final, twisting grope. Stood up and over her, showing off the mountain of a man he was. Zipped up his flies. This was the third time he'd been at her since he'd screwed her for the first time that morning. Nikki stared up at the cracked ceiling. Waves of disgust washed over her. She'd kill for a shower just to get the stench of this man off her skin. But she knew that a shower wouldn't be able to cleanse away the memories. At least she was still alive. With a defeated sigh, she swung her legs over the side of the bunk. Buttoned her blouse. Then she asked him the same question she always did after he screwed her.

'Did Jason Nelson fit me up?'

He stopped fixing his gun holster to his waist as his dark eyes bore into her. 'Like I told you this morning, I have never heard of such a person.' He returned his attention to the holster. Buckled it around his taut, muscular body.

'Well, who set me up, then?'

'Sometimes it's best if things remain in the shadows.' He still didn't look at her.

'I don't need fucking riddles . . .'

He finally looked at her. Her words halted when she saw the coldness gripping his face.

'Look,' she pleaded, softening her tone. 'I just need to know who did this to me.'

'What is the point? You will never see them again.'

'Whatcha mean?' A frown slashed across her forehead. 'When I get out of here . . .' Her voice trailed off as a pant of fear exploded from her. 'I am getting out of here?'

He spread his legs. Gazed at her with pity or contempt, she wasn't sure. His hand moved to the back pocket of his trousers. Pulled out a folded piece of white paper. 'Your lawyer asked me to give you this.' He threw it at her. It landed by her on the bed.

She grabbed it. Unfolded it. Read.

'By the authority of the Sankuran supreme court, Nikki Flynn has been charged with the illegal importation of heroin. It is the judgement of this court that Nikki Flynn be sentenced to death . . .'

The word death swam in front of her. The letters got bigger. Bolder. Darker. A wave of dizziness pulled her forward. Shit, she was going to fall over. All that time he'd been fucking her with her death warrant in his pocket, ready to screw up her life as well. Bastard. The fury drove her to her feet as she yelled out, 'You can't sentence me to death without a trial.'

'As I've told you in the past, we do things differently in Sankura. We don't believe in long trials that will cost the government lots of money or see the need to have the defendant in the dock. All the judges need to see is the evidence presented by your lawyer. Nice and quick, just like the execution. But there's no need to get too upset . . .'

'You cunt . . .' She advanced towards him. Raised her hand. But his own large hand grabbed her wrist.

The cell door was thrust open. An agitated soldier stood in the doorway and said in Sankuran, 'Major . . .'

'What is it?'

'Information, sir, that the rebels will attack the National Bank tonight.'

He let go of Nikki. Shoved her away. She tried to stay upright, but she couldn't keep her balance. The onslaught of emotions pulled her to the floor. Her face crumpled as the tears came.

'Nikki.'

The major's hard command made Nikki raise her tear-streaked face. The expression she read on his face startled her. Compassion.

'We will talk later,' was all he said. Then he was gone.

What was the point of talking later? Nikki bellowed in her mind. They were still going to drag her kicking and screaming outta here to kill her. She was never going to see her beloved Jade again.

Frankie quickly pinched Jade's nose. Covered her mouth with his. Pumped two long breaths into her still body. He pulled his mouth away from hers. Clamped his hands, one over the other, onto her chest. Pressed down. Once. Twice. Kept going until he reached ten. But her body didn't move. He swore as he tore his hands away and went back to her mouth. Two more breaths. Back to her chest. Ten more compressions. She still wasn't moving. He went back to her mouth. On his second breath, her chest jacked high into the air. He pulled his mouth away. Her green eyes sprang open as she let out a series of hard, choking coughs.

'That's it, little one,' Frankie whispered. 'Breathe.' He swung his head around, calling out, 'Someone get some water.'

But no one moved. Jason stared back at him, crouched on the floor, his eyes still bright from his last drug hit. Ruby stood bollocks scared and pinned to the wall, the sound of her wheezing breath tipping into the room as she sucked hard on her inhaler. Amber stood next to her, shock cemented across her face.

'Water. Next. Door,' Frankie yelled at Amber.

Wide eyed, the girl scarpered across and out of the room. Frankie turned swiftly back to the gasping girl on the bed. Gently he raised her, until she was in a sitting position. 'That's it, easy breaths,' he coaxed.

As he spoke, Jason slowly raised himself to his feet and moved towards Frankie. Sensing his approach, Frankie turned towards him. If it weren't for the presence of the girls, Frankie would bitch-slap him into the back end of tomorrow. But instead he sent Jason a look loaded with meaning. A reminder that in front of the girls they had to assume their roles. Jason as top geezer. Frankie as foot soldier.

'I'm really sorry, boss,' Frankie mumbled. 'I didn't mean to rough you up, but I know that you said that you needed the girls. *All* of the girls.'

Jason puffed his chest out. 'I thought I told you to make sure they stayed put upstairs? I found the bitch on the blower downstairs holding an address book . . .'

'An address book?' Frankie interrupted, giving Jade a sharp look.

'That's right,' Jason continued. 'She needed to be taught a lesson. Taught who's boss.' With that he reached into his jacket. Pulled out a beige A4-sized envelope. Dropped it on the bed beside Frankie. 'Make sure this lot understand the shit their old ladies are in.'

He threw a final look at the terrified Jade. She cringed back on the bed. Frankie cuddled her close, his hands running down her body and over her trouser pockets. With a snarl Jason turned towards the door. Opened it. But instead of pushing outside, he turned back around to face Frankie. 'Don't push your luck, Frankie, because if you ever touch me again, it will be your head I'm banging on death's door. And don't get soft over these bitches.' With his words of warning hanging in the air, he left. Frankie continued to soothe Jade as one of his hands left her and moved with a flash to his back pocket. A few seconds later, a breathless Amber rushed back in, with a mug of water. She handed it to Frankie. Then stepped well back. Frankie clasped the back of Jade's head, as he raised the cup to her lips. Slowly she began to sip. Finally she moved her mouth away from the cup.

'That geezer,' she croaked frantically between high-kicking breaths, 'tried to top me.'

'Jason just got a bit moody. . . .'

'That was Jason?' The disbelieving interruption came from Amber. 'That's the guy our mums work for? You work for him as well, don't you?'

Frankie opened his mouth, but before he could answer Amber's quickfire questions, Jade knocked his hand away and started to clamber unsteadily off the bed. Frankie grabbed her arm in a bruising grip. She tried to shake his hand free, but he wouldn't let go.

'I'm going to the Old Bill . . .'

'You can't do that.'

'As soon as you let me go, I'm gonna leg it . . .'

'No you ain't. And you wanna know why?'

He released her hand and quickly reached for the envelope Jason had dropped on the bed. She was transfixed by the movement of his hand as he opened it. Reached inside. Pulled something out. Gently placed it on the bed between her and him. Jade gasped when she saw what is was.

In a shaky voice she said, 'It's my mum's necklace.'

eight

Jade swallowed hard as she reached for the necklace. A fine gold chain with a heart-shaped locket on the front. She picked it up. The chain was broken. She quickly opened the locket. She shot a sharp breath into the room when she saw the photo inside. A picture of her when she was eight dressed all in fluffy white for her first Holy Communion. Her mum never went anywhere without it. The last time she'd seen Nikki wear it was just before her mum left to get her flight to Sankura.

Jade's hand clutched the chain as she raised her tear-filled eyes to Frankie. 'How did you get my mum's chain? She never goes anywhere without it.'

But he didn't answer her. Instead he reached for the opened envelope. Stood up. Swung his head around the room. Caught each girl with his intense blue eyes. Ruby still against the wall. Amber marooned by the dressing table. And finally Jade, still pulling the life back into her body. Then he spoke. 'I think we need to make ourselves comfy next door. See, the thing is, girls, it's time we had a little chat. A chat about how you're gonna help to save your mums' lives.'

'How did you get my mum's necklace?'

Jade still held her mum's chain as she sat with the other two girls facing Frankie at the table. And between them, on the table, sat the envelope. Frankie tilted his head. A lock of blond hair flopped across his forehead, deepening his boyish good looks. 'One of Jason's mates in Sankura sent it to him . . .'

'But how did he get?' Jade persisted.

Frankie pushed his head straight. Looked directly into her gleaming, green eyes. 'One of the bad men in Sankura ripped . . .' Frankie's voice rolled, long and hard, over the last word. '. . . it from her neck.'

The girls all gasped.

Jade's voice shook as she asked, 'She ain't . . . ?'

'Dead?' Frankie quickly supplied. Jade rapidly nodded her head. Frankie gave her a grave look. 'No. Well, she weren't the last we heard.' His tongue flicked out. Moistened his bottom lip. 'But I'll be straight up with you, girls, things ain't looking too bright for your old ladies.'

Suddenly his hand reached for the envelope. He picked it up. Pushed his hand inside. Slowly his hand came out holding three photos. He laid them on the table. Flipped each around, so the girls could see them.

'Ohmygod,' Amber said as she and the others stared at the photos.

Individual close-up shots of their mums' faces. The first one showed Nikki with blood running down from a cut on her face. The next showed an exhausted Jasmine, with bruises next to her mouth and left eye. The last was Maxine. Her skin was unmarked, but the scared, battered expression she threw at the camera told its own terrifying tale.

'I ain't trying to scare you.' At the sound of Frankie's voice, the girls pulled their gazes away from the pictures to stare helplessly at him. 'But if we don't do something soon I think your mums are gonna be brown bread.'

'But what about the Foreign Office?' Ruby piped up, speaking for the first time. 'I thought it was their job to make sure British citizens weren't abused.'

Frankie stretched his hands across the table. Locked his long fingers together. 'What you gotta understand is that when you get banged up abroad it ain't like being held at Her Majesty's pleasure. Here we believe in innocent until proven guilty. Other countries have their own way of doing things. Sankura ain't no different. You just have to look at those pictures to know that your mums ain't at no tea party.'

'But if we show these pictures to the Foreign Office surely they'll help our mums?' Ruby continued.

'The Foreign Office know full well how prisoners are treated in Sankura and so far they've done dick about it. And the Old Bill ain't gonna do shit either.'

'But if no one's gonna help get them out . . .' Jade started.

'Who said no one's gonna help them?'

The girls all looked at Frankie with a collective expression of surprise.

'Who?' Amber's body sprang to alert in her chair.

'Jason.'

Jade pushed herself half out of her chair as the words erupted from her mouth. 'I ain't having nothin' to do with that head case . . .'

'Sit down,' Frankie threw at her. When she didn't move he added. 'Please.' Jade reluctantly resumed her seat.

'Jason feels well bad about what happened to your mums, especially as they were working for him at the time. He's got some contacts in Sankura. Important contacts. People that can make things swing the right way for your old girls. One of his mates sent him the photos and Nikki's necklace. His people in Sankura are saying that they can get your mums outta the poke, so Jason's gonna pull every string at his fingertips. But . . .' He left the word hanging in the air. Took in their expectant faces. 'No one in this world is prepared to do anything for nothing. The only way Jason's mates are gonna help is if he greases a few palms.'

'But we don't have no dosh,' Jade said.

'Nor does Jason. We can get some cash, but it all depends on you girls.'

'What you chatting about?' Amber said.

'You girls are gonna have to earn that money. All you've gotta do is a few jobs . . .'

'Jobs?' Jade jumped in. 'What sorta jobs?'

'What the jobs are don't matter for now. The important thing is Jason needs an answer ASAP. His people in Sankura are getting impatient. They want their money or they ain't doing dick to help your mums. So what's it to be, girls? You gonna help your mums or you gonna let 'em swing?'

The girls shifted and looked uncertainly at each other.

'Can me and the girls have a chat about it?' Jade asked.

The side of Frankie's mouth flipped into a lopsided smile. 'Of course you can. But remember that any minute now your mums could be six feet under, so we ain't got time to waste. You got one minute.' Frankie picked himself up and left the room.

The girls moved their chairs closer together.

'Are you alright?' Amber asked, touching Jade's arm. 'My eyes nearly bugged outta my skull when Jason started flippin' and slammed that pillow over your face.'

'If Frankie hadn't been there . . .' Jade shivered as her words trailed off.

'What are we going to do?' Ruby's voice was strained and stressed.

As Jade flicked her eyes away from Ruby, Amber reached for the photo of her mum. She ran her thumb caressingly over her mum's features. 'We ain't got no choice,' she replied softly. 'Jason might be a twenty-four-carat arsehole, but he's the only one who's gonna do the business for our mums. So far no one else has said they will.'

'What you saying?' Jade rushed out. 'That we gotta do what he wants?'

Amber flicked her eyes away from the picture towards Jade. 'From where I'm sitting, girl, it don't look like we've got much choice. Anyway, if Jason was telling porkies Frankie would've told us, wouldn't he? I mean, he did save your neck from that whack job.'

Before they could say anything else, Frankie re-entered the room. Leaned casually up against the wall. Folded his arms. 'So what's it to be, girls?'

Jade looked nervously at the other two. Finally Amber and Ruby both gave her short, uncertain nods.

She gave him the answer he was looking for. 'Alright, we'll do it.'

But Frankie didn't speak. Didn't push off the wall. Instead he pinned Jade with a hard blue-eyed stare. Moved his hand to his back trouser pocket. Pulled something out. Displayed it between his fingers in the air.

'Hey, how did you get that?' Jade said in shock as she stared at her mother's address book.

'The five-finger discount . . .' He stopped when he saw the puzzled look on her face. 'Don't worry about it, it's a little trick I learned along the road. I got it out of your pocket while I was helping you on the bed. This belongs to your mum?'

She hesitated for a split second, then nodded.

'Did you manage to connect to any of the names in the book?' She shook her head.

'Jason can't help you if you're on the blower to people he don't know.' His voice dipped to a husky whisper as he added, 'I don't know.'

A tight silence filled the air. 'I'm gonna keep this safe for you.' Frankie shoved the book into the inside pocket of his jacket. 'And when your mum comes back I'll give it to you. Deal?'

Reluctantly Jade nodded.

Frankie pushed off the wall in a smooth motion. Walked towards the table. When he reached it he started gathering the photos together and placed them back into the envelope. Jade's hand quickly clenched around Nikki's necklace. She didn't want to give it back. She raised pleading eyes to Frankie. He met her gaze and nodded his head. She pushed the necklace into her trouser pocket.

'So what jobs do you want us to do?' Amber asked.

'Don't worry about that for now. You'll soon know what you've gotta do.'

With that he left them alone. Jade gave it half a minute before she lunged for the door.

'What the arse are you playing at?' Amber called out as she marched towards Jade.

Jade twisted her head around to face the other girl at the same time as her hand grabbed the door handle. 'Getting outta here . . .'

Amber's hand slammed over Jade's on the handle. 'You need to clean the wax outta your ears, girl. Didn't you hear what Frankie said? Didn't you see those photos? You might not give a toss about your mum, but you ain't putting no noose around my mum's neck.'

The girls stared hard at each other, their fury sizzling in the space between them.

'You better let go of my hand.' Each word twisted slowly out of Jade's mouth with anger.

'Whatever,' Amber threw back defiantly, tightening her grip.

Jade tried to move her hand, but Amber wouldn't let go. They began to struggle. Amber's free hand came up. She slammed it into the smaller girl's shoulder, pushing her against the door. Jade wobbled on her feet, taken completely by surprise by Amber's attack. Her face scrunched into a mad mask as she raised her arm. Swung it back and whacked the other girl in the face. Amber cried out as she staggered back, finally letting go of the door. The taller girl's hand came up to touch her throbbing cheek. Seeing her chance, Jade turned back to the door. As her hand reached out again for the handle, she felt fingers, like claws, grip her tracksuit top from behind. Amber spun her around. The taller girl's arm was raised, ready to administer retribution, and she shouted, 'I'm gonna slap the fat outta you, girl . . .'

'Stop it. Please stop brawling like dogs in the street,' another voice screamed out.

Both girls' gazes shot across the room. They'd forgotten all about Ruby. The hysterical girl sank onto her bed with her hands clamped over her ears. Her head dipped low as her sobs grew louder. Jade forgot about her mission to leave and rushed over to the fragile girl. She shoved herself onto the bed beside Ruby. Placed a comforting arm around her shoulder.

Jade rocked her as she soothed, 'Everything's gonna be alright. Our mums will be back before you know it.'

Amber slowly sauntered across the room. Plonked herself on the bed, on the other side of Ruby. She eased her arm above the crying girl's shoulders. Hesitated because she knew that if she dropped her arm it would be on top of Jade's. The same arm that had just slapped her silly. She swallowed her pride and let her arm fall. Jade and Amber peered at each other across Ruby.

'I didn't mean to slap you,' Jade apologised quietly.

'And I shouldn't have pushed you.'

The girls continued to stare at each other. Suddenly a quick smile passed between them.

'I don't really look like no dog in the street, do I?' Amber asked, clearly more insulted by Ruby's earlier comment than Jade's slap.

Jade laughed as she shook her head.

'You ain't the only one who wants to roll outta here,' Amber said, her face back to serious. 'But if we do, who's gonna get the money to send to Jason's people in Sankura?'

'What type of jobs do you think we'll have to do to get the money to sort out our mums in Sankura?' Jade asked.

'Dunno.'

Suddenly Ruby gazed at Jade with shining eyes and mumbled, 'Have you ever thought about what you would do if your mum died?'

Jade stared at Ruby with an expression that plainly said the other girl was giving her a massive dose of earache. 'It's a stupid question because it ain't gonna happen.'

'But what if it does?' Ruby persisted. 'What if they never come back? What if . . .'

'Ain't you got any happy pills you can scoff?' Amber said.

'I used to think my mum wanted to die,' Ruby said in a rush.

'With a kid like you, I ain't bloody surprised,' Amber mumbled under her breath. Jade caught Amber's glance. They rolled their eyes at each other.

Ruby carried on speaking. 'She was always drinking, especially if she didn't have a boyfriend. She was always happy if she had a man on her arm. I remember one day she didn't get out of bed. So I went upstairs and she was lying on her bed, still in her clothes, with an empty bottle of vodka by her side. I couldn't get her up. I thought she was dead.'

'Fucking hell, what did you do?' Jade whispered.

Ruby shrugged her shoulders, her hands clenching into fists. 'Didn't have a clue what to do. So I went downstairs. Made a cheese sandwich and put the telly on.'

'Dimbat, why didn't you call 999?' Amber said.

'Because I was frightened they might take her away. I was scared that I'd be all on my own.'

Her words hung in the air. Made Jade shiver. Got her thinking about what Nikki would be doing on Christmas Day. In a cell. No decorations. No Christmas tree. No turkey. Nobody.

'Jade, you alright, girl?' Amber asked.

Jade gazed at the other girl. 'Yeah.' She took a deep breath. 'Yeah.' She turned to stare at Ruby. 'You've gotta snap out of this shit,' Jade coaxed. 'They ain't gonna die, so stop rabbiting on about it. Frankie's told us how we can help get them home, so that's what we're gonna do. Any job that Jason wants us to do, we're gonna do it.'

Suddenly Jade got up and moved across the room to her bed, where her lunchbox lay. She opened it and took out the candle her parish priest had given her at her first Holy Communion seven years ago. It was long, stout and white with a turquoise panel on one side featuring a bright red cross and an angel, holding its wings out, at the top. She took out her lighter.

Jade saw the other two girls staring at her with puzzled expressions. She started walking again, this time towards the dressing table. When she reached it she carefully positioned the candle in front of the mirror. Stood it between Amber's large collection of make-up and her Polaroid camera and Ruby's hairbrush, so it rose up like a white icon. She felt the girls' warmth touch her and knew they were on either side of her.

'What you doing?' Amber asked.

'At my church people light candles and say a special prayer for the people they love. So I'm gonna say a special prayer for my mum,' Jade answered, as she reached into her trouser pocket. She pulled out Nikki's broken necklace. Arranged it around the candle.

'Does it work?' It was Ruby's voice this time.

'Of course it works, you just light it.'

'No. I mean does the prayer work?'

'Yeah.'

'Can you say a prayer for mine and Amber's mothers as well?'

Jade flicked her head sideways to look at the other girl. She gave her a quick smile and nodded.

Her finger flicked the lighter's wheel. Ignited the flame. She stretched forward and lit the candle. She felt Amber's arm curled around her waist. Then Ruby's arm settled over her shoulder. They stood there, in the silence of their room, watching the flame flicker. 'Just like our mums are together,' Jade said, 'we've gotta stick together. Like we're a family.'

Then she dipped her head, closed her eyes and said a silent prayer for their mums.

Frankie smiled as his motor drove away from St Nicholas. He knew he had the girls eating out of his hand. He should feel sorry for them, believing that they could help those stupid bitches they called mums. But he didn't. Any softness he felt for anyone else had long ago been beaten out of him by his own mum during his childhood. Then he thought about his own five-year-old daughter, Daisy. She was the only one that he allowed into his heart. Doing the Amsterdam job was going to net him mega-bucks. Put his face forever on the underworld map. And if that meant fucking up the lives of three women and their daughters, so be it.

His mobile rang, dragging him back to the present.

'Yeah?'

'It's Jason. Just heard from Omote in Sankura. The job's on the sixth of January. He'll send us details nearer the time. Plus I'll tell you what I just heard on the news . . .'

Frankie's smile broadened as he listened to Jason. After Jason had finished he said, 'Good. It's time to put the girls to work. We get them ready. Tonight . . .'

nine

'I can't breathe.'

The words shot out of Jade's mouth as she catapulted up from her bed later that night. The sweat lay thick against her forehead as she took deep, lunging breaths. She'd been dreaming that the pillow was back over her face. As her breathing became easier, she searched through the dark to see if she'd woken the others up. Both Amber and Ruby were soundly asleep. Jade threw the duvet back, revealing her West Ham Utd jim-jams. Quietly she got out of the bed. Dropped to her knees and searched under the bed for her lunchbox. She took out a fag and the lighter and tiptoed towards the window. She knew that Ruby had asthma, but she needed a puff badly. She partially opened the window. Stuck her head outside. Lit up. Sucked in hard.

Her gaze roamed over the garden. It stopped, surprised, at the lights shining from the building at the bottom of the garden. She wondered who was up, what they were doing. Then she wondered about her mum. What she was doing. What other people were doing to her. The smoke flip-flopped deep in her throat as she remembered the photo Frankie had shown her of Nikki. All bloody and bruised, with an expression she'd never seen her mum wear before. She rubbed her forehead, trying to get rid of the image from her mind. But it wouldn't leave her.

As she smoked frantically down to the butt, the door of the building in the garden opened. Her eyes widened when she saw two men come outside. One was buckling his belt as the other shoved his arms through his coat. Suddenly the man with the coat looked up at her at the window. Jade shuffled quickly back. Dipped down low. Waited. Then she heard the sound of sobbing coming from the garden. She knew she shouldn't do it, but she couldn't help herself. Slowly she raised her head. Peeped back outside. Two young girls followed behind the men, one with her arm around the other, who was softly crying. A chill ran through Jade. Her arm snaked out, closing the window. She stepped well back. She didn't know what was going on in the garden and decided she didn't want to know. She had her own problems to deal with. She made her way back to her bed. Stared hard at the pillow. Felt Jason pressing hard against her face. She picked the pillow up. Slung it under the bed. Got back under the duvet. Five minutes later she finally fell into a restful sleep.

But as 19 December faded into the next day her eyes shot open when she felt the hand against her skin.

'Jade?' a voice called beside her.

She began to breathe in an easy motion when she recognised who it was.

Frankie.

She twisted her head and saw him crouched by the bed, his hand clasped around her arm. His face was bathed in the shadows created by the dark.

'Frankie, you nearly give me a heart attack. What's going on?' she asked drowsily. His hand dropped from her arm and she sat up.

'You need to get up,' he said softly.

Frankie pulled himself to his full height. As she raised her confused gaze up to him she noticed Amber and Ruby already standing besides their beds. What the hell's bells was going on? She stifled a yawn as she threw the duvet back. Eased out of the bed. Stood nervously by the bedside, not sure what to do.

'Ladies, you need to follow me,' Frankie said as he turned his back and started to move towards the door.

'What time is it?' Amber's voice was groggy as she followed him.

'Don't worry about the time, just come on.'

But Jade didn't move. Instead she shivered in the cooling late night air.

'Can we get dressed?' she asked.

But when Frankie didn't answer she quickly moved to catch up with the others.

'What's all this about?' she whispered, folding her arms across her middle, tucking the warmth from her body around herself.

'Ain't got a clue, girl,' Amber responded.

Frankie reached the door. Opened it. Disappeared into the dark corridor. The girls trudged behind him. Frankie stopped outside the room next door. The girls stopped in a line behind him. Jade, Amber, Ruby. Frankie opened the door. Moved inside. Jade peered over his shoulder into the dark room. She hesitated. Her gut clenched, her shoulders hunched.

'Jade, go on,' Ruby urged behind her.

Jade took a step. Then another. The third took her well inside the room. She swung her gaze around, trying to adjust to the dark. The black blinds were drawn over the two windows.

She twisted her head towards Frankie and said, 'Frankie, what the heck . . . ?'

Abruptly the door banged shut. The vibration echoed in the room. Jade twisted around at the same time as the other two girls did. Standing on the left-hand side of the door was a shadowy figure. She couldn't see his face, but she knew it was a man because of the aftershave in the air. The man's hand flipped sideways. Touched something on the wall. The light sprang on, bathing the room in bright artificial colour. Jade took one look at the man by the door and nearly toppled backwards. Arms folded, standing by the closed door, was Jason Nelson.

'Great to see you again, ladies,' Jason said.

He hitched himself off the wall. Took two strides towards them. Stopped like he was posing for them, all big and large. He looked at Jade as if he were looking at her hung upside down in a butcher's crowded window. Amber and Ruby moved instinctively towards Jade as if she were their leader. Jade grabbed for Amber's and Ruby's hands. Found them. Held on tight.

'Girls, you need to park your bums.' Jason gestured towards the chairs around the table. 'Because I've got something to show you.'

The girls huddled closer together. Passed worried looks between each other.

'Now,' Jason growled.

The girls quickly shot onto the chairs. Jason nodded at Frankie. Frankie moved towards the small telly. Pressed the 'on' button. He flicked through the channels until he found a twenty-four-hour news station. As Frankie stepped away from the telly, the confused girls kept watching while the female newsreader read the latest news.

After two minutes of not understanding what was going on, Jade's gaze leaped to Frankie as she said, 'I don't get . . . ?'

'Shut it,' Jason shouted, making Jade quake in her chair. 'Just fucking keep your mince pies on the box.'

She quickly did what she was told. Kept watching. And watching. Then the next item came on. What she heard was to change her life for ever.

'Breaking news. The Foreign Office has confirmed that the three English women arrested in Sankura for the importation of heroin have been sentenced to death . . .'

On the other side of the world, in Sankura, fifteen-year-old Grace's hands tensed around her M-16. She was crouched on her haunches. Wrapped in the silence and shadows of midnight. The last in line of the Sankura rebel forces. The Jaguars of Justice, or the JJs, as the population called them, had been embroiled in a fierce war with the government for the last five years. The JJs claimed that they were fighting for democracy and freedom, but everyone knew that the real battle was over the control of the country's most lucrative export – diamonds. Grace had joined their ranks three years ago. Not that she'd been given much choice. When the JJs had raided her village and killed the adults, including her parents, she and the other terrified, crying children had been lined up in front of a freshly dug trench with guns pointed at them and given two choices – death or the life of a rebel foot soldier. Not all the children had made the same choice she had. Her hand tightened on her gun.

She and the other rebels were concealed in the alley facing the National Bank. The bank was housed in a neoclassical building that dated from colonial times on the city's main street. Their mission was simple. Grab the national treasure, which was a diamond collection called 'The Gates of Dawn', so named because the veins of blue and red lines inside the stones reminded people of the peaceful beginning of a new day. Popular rumour had it that the diamonds were long gone. Some said they'd been looted by the British when they'd left. Others were of the opinion that various leaders of the country had helped themselves to the collection over the years and they were now safely tucked away in Switzerland. The rebels' leader, Commander 'Smith', knew better. He had a man on the inside in a position to know. That guy had assured him that some of diamonds were still there, stored in shoeboxes on metal racks in the most secure of the vaults. It went without saying that the bank was the mostly securely guarded place in the whole country with the possible exception of the presidential palace itself. A detachment of soldiers was on permanent guard and overall security was in the hands of the State Security Police, the SSP. There was a popular joke on the streets of Sankura: 'One of my parents has been detained by the SSP – the other one is also dead . . .' Renowned for their arbitrary and brutal violence, the SSP were allowed to pretty much do what they liked. Even the army and the president were afraid of them. So Grace didn't need to be told to kill any of the SSP bastards who got in her way.

A finger tapped her shoulder. She looked up at Moses, the soldier in front of her. Moses had become her saviour, appointing himself as her guardian, making sure that she dressed in a way that made the other rebels forget she was a girl.

'This will make your aim strong,' he said as he held his hand out to her.

She looked at the object clasped between two of his fingers. A joint. She knew it would be cannabis laced with cocaine because that's what the Jaguars used on a regular basis, especially when they plunged into a new operation. A joint would be passed down the line of rebels, each hoping that an inhalation would make them breathe courage. She shook her head as she always did when she was offered any drugs. She wasn't going to become doped and duped like the other children, pumped high on short-lived heaven and hopelessness. Moses shrugged his shoulders. Chucked the joint onto the ground and mashed it with the toe of his boot. He spun back around. Grace did the same. The human line became taut. Alert. Waiting.

A few minutes later at the front their leader raised his hand, the signal that the waiting was over. His hand shot down. A stray dog howled into the night. The Jaguars started to move.

It wasn't long before the four guards at the front of the bank saw them. Before they could reach for their guns the rebels' gunfire traumatised the night. The guards fell quickly. Grace aimed her gun at the street lights. Blew them out. The darkness intensified. An explosion ripped the air as two grenades blew the bank doors open. A hand grabbed the scruff of her neck. Stunned, she looked up to find Moses behind her. He dragged her across the street, firing blindly at the guards rushing outside. They bumped into dead bodies, nearly cut in half by machine-gun fire. Flew up the steps. Moses let her go. They both rushed inside, firing at the same time.

The inside of the bank was filled with grey smoke and bodies and blood scattered everywhere. A large picture of the president hung on the opposite wall. Grace sprayed bullets across it. The picture crashed to the floor. She smiled. A shot whizzed over her head. Quickly she crouched down. Rolled across the floor until she found herself behind a large desk. Swung her gun around. No one. She kept low, waiting. Then she found her opponent. His head peeping out from behind a concrete pillar as he took aim at her. She blew his brains out with a single shot to the head. The noise intensified as more rebels streamed in, shooting and yelling at the same time.

'Follow me,' Moses said, his face a glaze of violent sweat.

They kept firing as they moved. Reached a stairwell. Moses took the lead as they rushed down. Below a man charged out. Moses shot him. Another came from the same direction. Grace took him down. Suddenly a rifle butt caught Grace in the ribs. As she fell, Moses raised his weapon and ended the life of the man standing over Grace with his finger on the trigger. Moses quickly helped her up. They reached the bottom of the stairs. Jerked their guns around.

'There it is,' Moses said.

His gun pointed at a large, thick metal door. The vault.

'How are we going to get in?' Grace asked, breathing hard.

'Easy,' Moses said, grinning. 'Commander Smith's inside contact left it open and the safety deposit boxes unlocked for us.'

They ran towards it. Moses kicked it with his boot. The door swung open. They jumped inside. The place was empty except for a wall filled with safety deposit boxes.

'Let's do this before the others arrive,' Moses said, moving forward.

'Do what?' Grace shot back.

'Take as much as we can for ourselves, of course.'

She looked at Moses, shocked. Couldn't believe what he was saying. Abruptly he grabbed her by the front of her shirt. 'In this life the only person who looks after you is yourself.'

He let her go. 'You start at that end.' Moses pointed to the far row of deposit boxes. 'And I'll start here. If Commander Smith asks any questions, we tell him that we found it like this.'

Grace didn't need to be told twice. She began pulling out and rifling through boxes, stuffing dollars, sterling, yen and jewellery into her pockets. She rattled one slightly rusty tin and heard stones inside. The tin was marked with an official coat of arms, dating back to colonial times. Prising the lid off, she found a fistful of large, roughly cut diamonds. From the blue and red veins in them no one had to tell her that they were the Gates of Dawn. There were only three, which meant that most of the collection had indeed already been looted. She swung her head around to shout at Moses. Then stopped. 'The only person who looks after you is yourself' – wasn't that what Moses had just told her? She twisted back to the box. Back to the diamonds. She turned her back, so Moses couldn't see what she was doing. Grabbed a diamond. Shoved it down the front of her trousers. Used a finger to push it inside a place only she and her mother had seen. She gritted her teeth with the sudden pain. Grabbed two more diamonds and did the same thing.

A burst of gunfire echoed outside on the stairs.

'Get away from the boxes,' Moses yelled.

As the words left his mouth a group of rebels filed inside. They began laughing, jumping and shooting their guns into the ceiling when they saw the safety deposit boxes. Grace moved awkwardly to the back wall. Another group suddenly burst in, yelling in panic-stricken voices, 'It's the SSP, it's the SSP!'

One of them toppled over as bullets riddled into him from someone shooting outside. A canister, moving with a slow hiss, rolled into the vault. A cloud billowed out of it. Grace felt it in her nostrils and the back of her throat first, a stinging irritation followed by the burning of her eyes and shortness of breath. She'd seen street disturbances broken up with tear gas before. The SSP burst in, wearing gas masks, and the battle began. The only issue for Grace was how to stay alive. As bullets banged around her she dropped on to the floor, coughing. Shit, she wasn't going to make it. Then the idea came to her. In the chaos no one noticed what she did. She grabbed and dragged Moses' fallen body towards her. Lay flat on the floor. Pulled his body over her face and upper body to block the gas. Shut her eyes. Played dead. And prayed. For ten minutes she lay there, death making its presence felt all around her.

Finally the gunfire ceased, replaced by the forlorn music of agonising groans in the air. She felt figures roaming around her, up and down the length of the vault. From their regimented strides, vibrating against the floor, she knew it was the SSP. She felt a shadow move over her. Heard someone next to her on the floor plead, 'No.' Bang. The man next to her didn't cry out any more. The shadow fell away. Another bang. Grace knew what was happening. The SSP were shooting any survivors in the head. She held her breath. Lay completely still. Bang.

'You idiots, stop killing them,' a rough voice shouted. 'Major Omote wants to make an example of them. Round them up and take them to the prison.'

The groans and moans grew louder as any survivors were heaved to their feet. Grace waited until there was only silence. She opened an eye. Gulped oxygen into her body when she realised it was just her and a stack of dead bodies. She winced as she felt the diamonds inside her body. She wasn't sure how she was going to get out, but she'd come this far and somehow she was going to make it. She flung Moses' corpse off her. Began to stand up. As she did an SSP materialised in the doorway. Without hesitation he aimed his gun at her.

'They can't kill them, can they, Frankie?' Jade asked, her head shaking with denial as she continued to stare at the telly.

Anger pumped through her. An anger so great it made her small body heave and tremble. No one, including God, was going to take her mum away from her. Over her dead body.

Huge wheezing next to her made her swiftly turn her head. Ruby was clutching her chest as she gulped lungfuls of air. The girl's face had become so red that Jade thought she was going to topple over.

'What the fuck's the matter with her?' Jason asked harshly as he moved towards the table.

'She needs her inhaler,' Amber pumped out quickly.

Jade half rose as she said, 'I'll get it . . .'

'No, you keep your fanny where it is,' Frankie cut in. 'I'll fetch it.'

As Frankie left the room Jade eased back down into her seat. She placed an arm around Ruby's shaking shoulders, gently rocking her, saying over and over, 'It's gonna be alright, it's gonna be alright.'

She lifted her head. Caught the shattered expression in Amber's eyes that said nothing was going to be alright ever again. They stayed like that until Frankie came back. He hunched down on his knees beside the distressed girl as he passed her the inhaler. She gazed back at him with red, tear-streaked eyes as she grabbed it quickly, taking deep sucks on it. Soon her breathing eased. Calmed down. Fell back into place.

'Right,' Jason said, as he stepped back. 'Now we've got the drama outta the way, we need to have a chat, because as you can see, your old ladies are one step away from being yesterday's news.' He stopped to look over at Frankie. 'Sling your hook for fifteen minutes.'

Frankie pitched off the wall, his hands moving frantically in front of him. 'But Jason . . .'

Jason made a savage sound. 'Now.'

Frankie's hands fell to his side. He swallowed. Gave the girls one final look and left. The girls stared at the man they feared most in the world, hearts beating madly.

'I know Frankie's been telling you that I'm doing everything to get your old girls out of deep shit. I know he's told you that my people in Sankura want paying. So I've got some jobs lined up for you to do. The most important job is the one in Amsterdam . . .'

'Amsterdam?' Jade called out.

'Stop fucking interrupting me. I don't like little girls with big gobs.'

Jade stiffened in her seat with wire-tight tension.

'Let's get the first job started so we can begin that cash flow,' Jason said.

He intensified his gaze at the girls, a little smile licking at his lips. He folded his arms and said a single word.

'Strip.'

ten

'Wait.'

Grace shouted the command, thrusting her hands in surrender in the air, as she watched the soldier with the gun pointed at her heart. He looked at her and advanced forward.

'I can make you rich, sir,' she belted out.

She knew she had no alternative but to offer him a good old-fashioned bribe. That was how Sankura had been operating for years. 'One country, one people,' was the strapline of Sankura's constitution, but most said it should be 'You scratch my back and I'll scratch yours'.

He kept coming. She made her decision. Took her chance. Slowly she dropped her arms. Undid her trousers. Let them drop to the floor. His nostrils flared when he saw her nude lower body. She winced as she pushed her fingers inside herself. Pulled out a diamond. Raised it in the air so that he saw it.

'This, kind man, is for you.' She held it out to him.

He stopped in front of her. Inspected what was in her hand. He lowered his gun as he took it.

'One of the Gates of Dawn,' she whispered seductively.

He sucked in his breath at her words.

'All I ask in return, sir, is that you find a way to get me out of Sankura. I beg you.'

He flipped his head at her. She quickly refastened her trousers. Dug into her pockets and pulled out the cash and jewellery she'd found in the safety deposit boxes. She handed them to him. He took them. Shoved the items and the diamond in his own pockets. Raised his gun. Grace cringed because she feared that her gamble maybe hadn't paid off. But instead of shooting her, he grabbed her by the collar and marched her upstairs.

The graveyard. That was what most Sankurans called the main prison in the capital. Most prisoners went inside and were never seen again. She remembered hearing one story of a man who had been arrested. After not being heard of for one year, his family had eventually given him a funeral. Seven years later, he had turned up, after years of being lost in the prison system. He was the only lucky one she had heard about. The nickname resounded in Grace's head as she took her final step into the bowels of the prison. Fear walked with her because she thought that the soldier had bought her here to murder her.

'Keep moving,' the soldier beside her said as he prodded her with his gun.

She quickened her pace, trembling as she moved deeper along the musty corridor. The stone walls leaked with the sweat of heat and a green-tinged moisture. They passed a cell door at the same time as a scream ricocheted inside. Grace shivered, but kept moving. Finally they stopped outside another cell door with a guard posted outside. Grace dipped her head low to avoid the guard's eyes. The soldier quickly pulled the guard aside and whispered rapidly in his ear. Grace raised her head as the guard ran a speculative gaze over her. He looked back at the soldier. Nodded his head. Moved back to the cell and began to open the door. As the guard pushed the door open hard footsteps sounded at the entrance of the corridor. Grace and the two men quickly turned around to find a soldier standing at the head of the steps.

'What's going on down there?' His voice echoed harshly against the walls.

The soldier next to Grace swore softly. Then called back, 'Nothing, sir.'

The superior officer moved quickly to meet them.

'You aren't meant to be here,' the officer blasted at the soldier. 'Everyone knows that Major Omote has strictly forbidden anyone to come down here except himself.'

The soldier swallowed. 'I'm sorry, sir, but after I found this rebel I realised that she was a girl. I felt bad about putting her with the men. I have a daughter myself . . .'

'A girl, you say,' the officer cut in. His eyes ran slowly over Grace. His tongue flicked out and ran across his bottom lip. Grace quickly dipped her head again.

'Both of you leave,' the officer shouted.

'But, sir,' the guard started. 'Major Omote has instructed that I stay here at all times.'

Uncertainty rippled across the officer's face. He gave the guard a sharp look. 'Come back in half an hour.'

Both men scurried away, leaving Grace and the officer alone. With the footsteps of the men still ringing on the stairs, the man made his move. He pushed the fifteen-year-old into the open cell. She heard a sound behind her as she tumbled to the cell floor.

'What the fuck's going on?' a voice said in English.

She understood English but hadn't let any of the rebels know. She had learned long ago to never give anyone any information they didn't ask for.

'Shut up, bitch,' the man said to whoever was behind Grace.

Then he fell on top of Grace and began to rip at her clothes. She thought about fighting, but didn't. She'd seen what happened to women who fought during their rapes. The image of a girl not much older than herself, who'd been raped during a raid last year, flashed through her mind. The soldier had got tired of the girl's struggles and had slit her throat from ear to ear. As she lay dying the soldier had raped her anyway. Maybe, just maybe, if she gave this man what he wanted he would spare her life.

'Get off that kid now,' screamed the voice behind her.

Then she heard footsteps and saw an arm smash down against the man's back. The man twisted around with murder in his eyes. As he raised himself up, a voice roared from the doorway, 'What is going on?'

The man toppled backwards. From her position on the floor, Grace saw a pair of black boots. Her gaze trailed up the figure of a powerfully built soldier, wearing all the regalia of his rank on his shirt.

'I asked a question,' the newcomer continued.

'He was trying to rape her.'

Grace swung her head to the side to find the owner of the voice. Once again her gaze skidded upwards, stopping in shocked surprise. Standing beside her was a white woman with hair so red she thought the sun had set in the cell.

Strip.

The word hung in the air.

Stunned, the girls let out a collective gasp.

'I said get naked.' Jason's voice was louder. Harder.

'I don't want to,' Ruby croaked, vigorously shaking her head, as more tears streamed down her face.

'Well, well, well.' Jason shifted the position of his legs. The left inched back, the right inched forward. Classic fighter's stance, ready to do battle. 'I think we need to clear the air in here.'

Then he moved towards one of the windows. Yanked up the black blind. Hiked the window wide open. Jets of unwelcome cold air flooded into the room, but it didn't cool the atmosphere inside. He flipped around. One side of his face tilted up into a nasty grin. Then he began to move again. Large, menacing steps towards the girls. Their protective instinct made them shoot out of their chairs and shuffle back. He kept moving. They kept moving. Until their backs touched the wall. He reached them. Flicked his gaze over each of them. Without warning his arm shot out. Grabbed Ruby by the arm. Dragged her forward. She screamed. Struggled. Sobbed. His free arm locked around her waist. Lifted her high. Bastard, Jade thought. No way was he going to do to Ruby what he'd done to her earlier that day. She raised her furious green-eyed gaze to his face. Began to heave herself forward, but the look in his steamed-up hazel eyes stopped her, along with the chill of his words. 'You move and the next time you see her it will be face up in a pine box paid for by the state.'

Jade stopped moving. Collapsed back against the wall. Watched helplessly as he carried a hysterical Ruby towards the window. He shifted her sideways. Held her immobile for a second just so they understood what he was about to do. Then he did it. He shoved her head and shoulders out of the window.

The wind gushed through Ruby's hair as she stared down at the ground. Ruby screamed, but the wind swallowed the sound.

'Perhaps you haven't got a decent view, then?' Jason growled. 'Let's make things a bit clearer . . .'

He tipped her upper body out of the window. Her glasses nose-dived from her face, smashing into the ground below. Without her glasses, the world appeared out of focus, a mass of blurred lines and colours. With a grunt, Jason took a firm grip of her ankles. Ruby screamed again into the anonymous wind as she dangled out of the window. Her arms flapped in the air as her body swayed and crashed into the brickwork of the building. Her chin banged against the hard surface, making her teeth bite into her tongue. Blood burst into her mouth. As her head moved sideways, the textured brickwork zig-zagged across her chin, scraping against her skin. The air whooshed from her mouth as the pain reverberated across her face. Inside her head.

As Jason shifted his legs, one of his feet skidded out of control to the side. One of his hands released one of Ruby's ankles so he could steady himself.

'Whoops! Butterfingers!' he called out.

Half of Ruby's body rocketed to the side and dropped a few inches as she was left floundering in the air by one ankle. Now she started to cry because she knew she was going to die.

Jason twisted his upper body back towards Jade and Amber, his face reddened from the effort of holding Ruby.

'If I get any lip from anyone, shit starts to happen. Lovely Ruby here don't wanna be spending Christmas tucked up in a hospital bed or in the dead house, now, does she?'

'We'll do what you say,' Jade yelled.

She followed her words by urgently tugging at her pyjama top. She quickly yanked it over her head. Amber swiftly followed what she did. Jade stopped when she was down to her bra and knickers.

She might be shitting herself, but she'd be fucked if she was letting some geezer see her in her birthday suit. He'd have to ask again if he wanted the lot off. She straightened. Looked back at him with hooded, defiant eyes.

Jason pulled Ruby back into the room. Let her go as easily as he'd caught her. She crumpled in shock to the floor, filling the room with the sound of huge breaths and shattered cries. Both Jade and Amber gasped when they saw Ruby's face. Her chin was scraped raw and blood seeped out of her mouth. Tears rolled from her wild, grey eyes.

Jason stepped over Ruby. Crooked his finger at Jade and Amber. Uncertainly they moved towards him. Stopped a few steps away from him. He slowly circled them until he reached their backs. Jade almost jumped when she felt his hand against her skin. His cold fingertips ran slowly along her neck. Across her collarbone. Her body tensed as his fingers slid to her breast.

'Nothing like breaking in young meat,' he whispered in her ear as his fingers found her nipple.

A ripple of fear shot through Jade. She knew she had to help her mum, but she'd be fucked if she was letting some man take advantage of her. She raised her hand, intending to slap his fingers from her flesh, but as she neared her target, his fingers jumped up and caught her hand. She groaned as he tightened his grip. He leaned into her ear. Whispered, 'Don't forget what you promised. You'd do anything to get your mum back.'

He held onto her hand for a few seconds. Then stepped back.

'What's been going on?' They all turned around towards the voice behind them.

Frankie stood in the doorway. In his hand he held a bundle of clothing. He swung a surprised gaze at Ruby on the floor. Then towards the almost naked Jade and Amber.

'Give the girls their new uniforms,' Jason instructed.

Frankie did as he was told and handed Jade and Amber the clothing he had in his hands. Black overalls. He looked at the devastated figure of Ruby.

'Don't worry about that one,' Jason said. 'She's a bit knackered after kindly giving us an open-air performance. Leave her. Get the bag.'

As Jade and Amber struggled into the overalls, Frankie got the holdall by the door.

When the girls were finished, Jason said, 'Sit down.'

They both took a seat. Jason nodded at Frankie. Frankie moved forward with the bag. Put it on the table. Unzipped it. Picked it up by its bottom. Tipped it upside down. The contents scattered onto the table. Hundreds of small, sky-blue pills rolled onto the table along with small transparent plastic bags. Jade and Amber gazed at the pills with fretful eyes.

'Know what these are, girls?' Jason said.

Amber answered him. 'Bumblebees.'

'You what?'

'Bumblebees. Ecstasy. E tabs.'

'No way,' Jade said, swinging her head in rapid denial. 'My mum would kill me if . . .'

Jason didn't let her finish. 'Your mum ain't gonna kill you. You know why? Because she'll be dead if you don't do what you're told. How the bloody hell do you think we're gonna make cash to get your mum home? Stand on a street corner with a cap in our hand?'

'Jason's right,' Frankie threw out softly. 'The people in Sankura want their money like now and the only way to whip up that kind of dosh is drugs.' When Jade flinched at the D word he savagely added, 'I know you don't like it. I don't like it. But if we don't do this your mums are not coming back.'

'All you've got to do,' Jason said, 'is put five in each bag. The overalls are to make sure you ain't tempted to take any when you go. When you leave the overalls stay behind. You've got three hours max to do it.' He swung around to Ruby. 'That includes you, stupid cow.'

He flicked his wrist up. Checked the time on his watch. 'Frankie, I'm outta here. Make sure that the job gets done.'

As soon as the door closed Frankie asked, 'Did he hurt you?'

Jade and Amber didn't answer him. Instead they ran over to a traumatised Ruby. As they put their arms around her Jade told him what had happened.

'I'm sorry, girls, I didn't know that was gonna happen.'

Jade didn't reply. She didn't know who to believe any more.

'Let's wash her face,' Amber said.

They helped Ruby to her feet and towards the sink. Ruby started crying again as they bathed away the blood.

'Have you got another pair of glasses?' Jade asked gently.

A still-sobbing Ruby nodded.

Suddenly Jade turned around. Looked directly at Frankie. 'Do you know how old we are?' she asked him, her voice quivering. He didn't answer her, just started straight back into her eyes. 'We're fifteen. We don't wanna be drug dealers. Can't we do something else?'

He held her gaze as the wind picked up speed and laced through the room. 'I know that you're most probably cursing me out as a scumbag in your mind because I'm making you do something you think dirty and illegal. But I'll tell you this much, Jade Flynn.' His finger came up and affectionately rubbed the tip of her nose. 'Whatever happens, I'll always look out for all of you.'

For the next ten minutes Frankie taught them how to pack pills. As the girls shook and trembled Frankie put on the radio. The mournful sound of Jeff Buckley's 'Hallelujah' filled the room. He closed the window. Pulled down the blind.

Four hours later, the girls were back in their room. An exhausted Amber and Ruby were fast asleep. Jade was not. She was on her knees in front of her Holy Communion candle, its flame flickering strongly. Her hands were clasped tightly around her mum's necklace, like it was a rosary bead. And she prayed. Prayed for forgiveness for being involved in drugs. Prayed that her mum wasn't already dead. Prayed that the world hadn't forgotten about three fifteen-year-old girls.

eleven

'I used to hold my little girl like this.'

Grace listened to Nikki, as the woman held her in her arms on Christmas Day. Nikki had held her like this for the last five days. As Nikki's hand caressed her closely cropped hair, her mind zipped back to the events of five days ago. The large soldier, who she later learned was the feared Major Omote, had been furious that the other man had dared to come into the cell. He'd pulled out his pistol, ready to blast the man's brains all over the walls, but Nikki had restrained him. Reminded him that a child was present. He'd laughed at that, saying that Grace hadn't been a child since the day she'd picked up a gun. And he was right. She couldn't remember what innocence felt like. So the major had spared the man's life and told him to get out. After that Nikki had persuaded him to leave Grace in the cell. If she hadn't seen it with her own eyes she wouldn't have believed it, but a tender look had passed over Omote's face as he gazed at Nikki. He'd nodded and left them alone.

Nikki had used halting English and gestures to tell Grace her name and communicate with her. She'd kept the knowledge that she understood English to herself. She'd learned it at the small village school from the two English teachers who had come for five years, then stopped coming once the fighting consumed the country. If she told Nikki, the older woman might start offloading her pain and Grace had more than enough pain in her life without having to deal with someone else's.

But she would be forever grateful to Nikki for the nights. The nights were heaven. Grace knew that Nikki was dreaming of holding her daughter, but she took the comfort because no one had done that to her in three years. Sure, some of the children would huddle together against the mountain cold in the rebels' camp, but that was survival, not love.

Keys rattled in the door, dragging Grace back to the present. The fifteen-year-old girl pushed herself out of Nikki's arms. Flew to her feet at the same time as Nikki did. The door was shoved open. Incredulously Grace watched the same soldier she'd given the diamond to walk into the cell holding a gun. She'd long given up hope that he would help her.

'You,' he shouted at Grace, pointing his gun at her.

She held back for a second. Then she moved towards him with tiny, hesitant steps. He gestured with his gun towards the open doorway. Quickly she obeyed his unsaid instruction and stepped outside. He followed her, but didn't lock the door.

'You leave now,' he whispered.

Grace wanted to shout out 'Hallelujah!'

'Where?'

'I will take you to a car. Someone will give you clothes, papers and a ticket to England. They will drop you at the airport. Then you're on your own.'

She reached for his hand. Grabbed it. Kissed it. A Sankuran gesture of respect and gratitude. As she let go of his hand, he grabbed the front of her shirt. Slammed her against the wall. He leaned down into her, his breath settling on her face.

'If I hear that you've mentioned me, if you get caught, I'll make sure you never see the sun set again.'

He let her go. She breathed heavily, pushing herself off the wall. Kept her eyes down, not out of respect, but so he couldn't see the menacing look in her eyes as she silently cursed his children and grandchildren.

She turned back to the cell.

'You must go now.' His words were sharp.

'Yes, sir, but I must say goodbye to the English woman.'

He snorted with disgust, but he didn't stop her. She eased back into the cell. Nikki was sitting down once again. Grace leaned against the wall. Pulled off her boot. Tipped it over. Out rolled one of the two diamonds she'd expelled from her body and hidden in her boot when Nikki was asleep. She shoved her boot back on and rushed over to Nikki. Ran her palm softly over the woman's arm and said, 'Nikki.'

The English woman looked up, the whites of her eyes as red as her once glorious hair.

'For you,' she said, and held out the diamond.

Nikki stared at it and then raised her gaze to Grace in confusion.

'Give this to guard Nikki,' Grace said. She desperately tried to think of what the English word for bribe was, but she didn't know it. 'He will help you.'

Nikki slowly took it, but the confusion still raged in her eyes.

'Hope dies last of all,' Grace said in Sankuran, remembering a saying the elders had taught the village children.

She turned her back on the woman. Rushed for the door. Rushed out of a hellhole that had once been her beloved country. Rushed towards a one-way ticket that was a chance to recapture whatever youth was still left in her life.

'OK, girls, it's time for a break,' Frankie said.

The girls relaxed back into their chairs. They'd been packing pills for a week now. Even two days ago, when it was Christmas Day. They never went downstairs because Frankie said they had to stay put on the top floor. They cooked their meals at the small kitchen unit in it in the same room they packed the Es. If they needed to go out Frankie took them for a spin.

'Right,' Frankie said, stretching. 'I'm off for a quick puff.'

Jade scrambled up and quickly followed him. She needed a smoke as well. They ended up sitting side by side, outside on the back stairs, overlooking the garden. The light in the building in the garden burned bright.

'What footie team do you support?' Jade asked Frankie.

Frankie gave her a little smile. 'The Gunners, of course.' His finger rubbed the tip of her nose. Jade blushed. She liked it when he did that to her nose because it made her feel safe. Loved.

'How can you support Arsenal? The best team in the world is West Ham. My mum used to take me to matches.'

A companionable silence fell between them as Jade flicked her butt into the garden. Watched it arc in the air, then dive to earth. 'Did Jason teach you that little trick?'

Jade knew that maybe she shouldn't have asked him the question, but she liked Frankie. Liked his quiet voice, the way his blue eyes twinkled when he smiled. But most of all she liked it that he acted like a protective wall between them and that bully-boy Jason. The girls had nicknamed Jason The Geezer. They hadn't seen him since that awful night he'd hung Ruby out of the window.

'What trick?'

'You know, the one you did when you took my mum's address book without me noticing.'

'Nah. Learned that one from my mum.'

'Can you teach me?'

The breeze ruffled his hair as he thought about his answer. 'Alright, why not.'

He turned around and said, 'OK, try and take something out of my pocket without me feeling it.'

As soon as her hand touched his pocket his hand slammed over hers. 'Got ya.'

Frankie turned around to face her. 'See, I knew when you were going to roll me because I knew when you were coming. Here.' He handed her his wallet. 'Put that in your pocket.'

She did what he asked.

'Shit,' he swore, as he tripped and fell on her. His hands grasped her trying to keep his balance.

'You alright, Frankie?'

Suddenly he straightened and looked at her with a mischievous gleam in his eye. 'Of course I'm alright. Know why? Because I've got . . .' He held the wallet that he'd given her in the air. '. . . this.' Jade looked at him, astonished. 'First rule of dipping is distraction.'

'Dipping?'

'Your fingers dip.' His hand moved down. 'And lift.' His hand came up. 'All you've got to do is distract someone. Bump them, chat to them, ask them a question. And then let your hands do the talking. That's how I got your address book. You were too busy crying. It gave me a reason to touch you. So, as I'm comforting you, my hands do their nifty five-finger discount. Life's all about distraction and deception.'

Distraction and deception. The words ran around Jade's mind. As she opened her mouth to speak she saw the door of the building in the garden open. Just as on the first occasion she'd seen it, she saw two men come outside. She couldn't be sure, but they looked like two different men. This time a younger girl and a boy followed them.

'What's that building for?' she asked Frankie.

A startled gasp flew out of Jade's mouth as Frankie grabbed her arm. In a low, tight voice he warned, 'Don't let me ever see you or the others near that place.'

Jade trembled as his fingers dug into her skin. Quickly she nodded. Slowly Frankie let go of her arm. She opened her mouth to ask another question but the grim look on his face told her she would be asking one question too many.

Four days later, on New Year's Eve, the woman at the passport control desk at Heathrow held out her hand.

Grace swayed with dizziness and dehydration as she handed over her false passport. She leaned her weight on her right foot because her other foot was sore where the diamond rested in her shoe. She had made it through the security and passport control at General Latifi airport. Through the cramped eleven-hour flight. And now, she prayed, she would make it through immigration at the other end.

The woman took her passport. Opened it. Flicked through it until she got to the photo at the back. The photo was of someone else, another young girl, but the man who gave Grace the passport said it would be no problem as all white people thought all black people looked alike. The woman flicked her gaze back and forth between the photo and Grace's face. Grace cast her eyes down, swallowing convulsively. Sweat dotted her nose and forehead. She couldn't get caught now. Not after having come all this way.

'What's your name?' the woman suddenly asked her.

Grace tipped her head up slightly. Said the name that was in the passport.

'Age?'

'Fif . . .' Grace clawed the word back, realising her mistake. 'Eighteen.'

The woman eased back in her chair. Snapped the passport shut. She turned her head and nodded to a uniformed man who stood next to the wall. He quickly moved towards the desk. Towards Grace. She swung her head, around desperately, like a caged animal. Shuffled back. Her legs wobbled. The room started to spin. She began falling. She collapsed, in a dead faint, onto the floor.

Grace woke up in a room somewhere in the airport. The bright light hurt her eyes as she stared at the plain white ceiling. She swallowed, letting out a gasp of pain because it felt like she was swallowing glass.

'She's waking up,' a female voice said.

Grace looked in the direction of the voice to find a uniformed man and woman standing close by her. Her heart immediately started going like a train, scared that the adults were the police and might beat her up like the police did to those they arrested in Sankura.

'It's alright,' the woman softly reassured her, resting her hand on Grace's shoulder. But Grace still pulled herself into a sitting position. Her legs flicked down. Only then did she realise that her shoes were gone. Where was the diamond? she frantically thought.

'My . . . shoe,' she croaked out.

A look passed between the man and woman. For the first time the man spoke. 'Your shoe half fell off when you fainted, so we took it off. We found this.' He held out his hand. Grace gasped when she saw the diamond. Her diamond.

'How old are you?' the man asked.

She told them the truth. 'Fifteen.'

'What's your name?'

Grace's lips clamped together. She wasn't going to be telling anyone her name because she was terrified they might find out what she had been in Sankura.

The man persisted with his questions. 'Did you come here with other people? Some adults?'

Grace shook her head.

The man turned to the woman. 'Right, it looks like we've got an unaccompanied minor.'

That made Grace tense. Unaccompanied minor? The words bounced fretfully in her head. She didn't know what that meant. Maybe they would send her to prison? Did England have prisons like the Graveyard?

'We need to get the duty social worker down here.'

The man moved away and took out his mobile. Rapidly spoke into it.

'She's coming over,' he told the woman.

They gave Grace a glass of water and waited in silence for the social worker. Finally the door opened. A small woman walked into the room.

'Hello. I'm the duty social worker.' She peered at Grace with a tight, tiny smile. 'My name is Patricia Grieves.'

Frankie was looking at a snap of himself and his daughter when the call came through. Daisy. The photograph showed him and her on Southend beach last summer. They were posed on their knees, his arm around her shoulder, next to three sandcastles she'd made. Funny, but that Jade reminded him of his little girl – tough and vulnerable both at the same time. He knew he was treading on dangerous ground, but he couldn't help it, he was starting to like Nikki's daughter.

He answered his phone.

'Yeah?'

'It's me.' Mrs Grieves.

'Good news, I hope?'

'I've got the black girl for you.'

'Is she clean?'

'No family. A new arrival. The only people who know she's here are immigration and they will have long forgotten her by now. They came straight to me, which means no papers, no trail. I'll bring her over later.'

'Fit her up with an emergency passport.'

He smiled as he cut the call. Now he had all the girls, all he had to do was make sure they were primed and ready for the job in Amsterdam in six days' time.

New Year's Eve found the girls doing what they did every night, packing Es. But tonight was slightly different. For the first time they were on their own, no Frankie.

'I need a friggin' fag,' Jade said as she stretched her hands up and yawned. 'I know, I know,' she continued lazily, catching the look Ruby aimed her way, over her glasses.

'You've got asthma, yeah, yeah, yeah.'

'What was that?' Amber jerked up straight in her chair, as she peered from side to side.

'What?' Jade asked.

'I heard something.'

'I didn't hear nothing.'

'Nah, I definitely heard something,' Amber persisted as she got up.

Her gaze roamed around the room. Searching. The window. The bathroom door. The dressing table. The main door. The floor near the door. Her gaze skidded to a stop.

'What's that?' She pointed her long finger at something white on the floor near the door.

As Amber briskly walked over and dropped to the floor, the other two got up. Amber swivelled around as Jade and Ruby reached her crouched figure.

'It's a bit of paper,' she told them.

The paper was folded. Amber eased up as she began to open it.

'It's a note from someone.' She ran her eyes eagerly over it. 'It says, "We're going raving tonight. If you want to come meet us at the bottom of the stairs at ten."' She raised her head. 'Who the heck is us?'

Jade and Ruby threw her blank looks. Suddenly Jade leaned forward. Opened the door. Stepped outside. The other girls crammed behind her as she looked left. And right. No one.

She came back inside and closed the door.

'It must be from the other kids,' Ruby said as she pushed her glasses up her nose. 'It is New year's Eve, they must be going out somewhere.'

'But we can't go nowhere without Jason or Frankie's say-so,' Jade said.

Ruby nodded her head in agreement.

Amber cocked her hip to the side. 'Well, I ain't staying here like a damned caged fool. I'm off out raving as well. And I've got something that's gonna make sure I have a whack-a-do of a good time.'

The other two looked at her, confused. Amber lowered the zip on her overall. Her finger dug into her belly button and pulled something out. She held it up. Both Jade and Ruby gasped when they saw it. One of Jason's E tabs.

'Are you flamin' bonkers?' Jade's voice ripped through the air. 'He'll batter you if he finds you've been nicking from his stash.'

'Well, he ain't gonna find out, is he? Unless, that is, your big gob starts motoring.' Jade pointed her finger at the other girl. 'Amber, one of these days . . .'

'Come on, lighten up. All I need to know, girlfriends, is are you coming with me to meet the others, yes or no?'

She popped the pill into her mouth. Swallowed as she defiantly gazed at Jade and Ruby.

twelve

Forty-five minutes later the girls went downstairs. They were tarted up to the eyeballs, with a mix and match of clothes they'd all packed, because Amber said they needed to look old enough if they were going to a club. Amber wore a little black number, Jade hipsters and a crop-belly top and Ruby stone-washed denims that were ripped at the knees. As they'd guessed, at the foot of the steps, in the cold air, stood a group of kids. Two girls and three boys, all teenagers like the girls. Jade immediately recognised one of the boys as the one the cops had brought back to St Nicholas the day she'd arrived. The slap he'd received from Mr Miller was still evident in the fading bruise on his cheek.

'Alright, people?' Amber greeted the group. 'What's occurring . . . ?' Amber carried on talking and Jade looked at her, worried. Since taking the E Amber's mouth and mind had moved a mile a minute – while they got dressed, while they put on their make-up, while she grabbed her camera, and now as she introduced the girls to the other kids. Finally Amber stopped talking. The other kids looked at her as if she had just taken them through a whirlwind.

The boy Jade recognised stepped forward. 'I'm Sam.' He then introduced the other children. 'We usually sneak out to go raving,' the boy said. 'And thought you might wanna go with us since it's News Year's Eve.'

Amber gave him a slow, flirty smile. 'You got that right. So where we heading?'

The boy's eyes lit up as he gave Amber a long, lazy look. 'This club we usually hang out at.'

One of the girls dug into her metallic blue shoulder bag. Pulled out a bottle of vodka. Tipped it to her lips and swallowed. Then she waved the bottle, offering it around.

Jade's eyes nearly bulged out of her head when she saw Ruby eagerly reach for it. As she swallowed she let out a small choking sound, but managed to push the liquid down. The bottle went around the group. Jade was the only one to shake her head. Instead she whipped out her packet of fags and offered them around.

Amber suddenly pulled the Polaroid camera from her bag and announced, 'Can someone take a snap of me and my mates?'

One of the girls took the camera. Jade, Amber and Ruby gathered together, arms around each other, and shouted out, 'Sweet dreams.' The camera flashed.

'Right,' Sam said, as he pushed himself closer to Amber. 'We've gotta be back before one just in case the men . . .' His words clipped to a stop. A haunted expression covered his eyes as he flicked them over his friends. One of the girls shook her head.

'What men?' Jade asked.

'Nothing.'" Sam's voice was sharp. 'We've just gotta be back before one.'

With that the group briskly walked away from St Nicholas as the bottle was passed around again. This time Jade took a slug and prayed that Frankie or, God forbid, The Geezer never found out they were gone.

'This is sooo great,' Amber said, as she did a double spin on the dance floor. 'You wanna hear my heartbeat. Boom! Boom! Boom! It feels triple cool.'

Jade gazed at the other girl as they grooved on the dance floor.

Ignite. That was the name of the club the kids took them to. It was a one-minute walk from Walthamstow Dogs. The place was more interested in collecting the exorbitant entrance fee than checking IDs. Amber and Jade danced near the other girls and boys, under the striking strawberry and lilac light, as Donna Summer's 'I Feel Love' purred around them. Ruby sat in the corner, as she'd done for the last hour, drinking. Jade and Amber had tried to coax her towards the dance floor but she'd shaken her head, looking petrified.

Jade looked up at Amber, worried. Since they'd arrived, Amber had hit the dance floor like a woman possessed. No tune was too trashy to get down with. Jade knew it was the E tab she'd taken most probably making her behave that way. But she didn't like seeing Amber this out of control.

'Maybe we should park our bums for a while?' Jade said.

Amber threw her an incredulous look. 'Stop fluffing your feathers, girl. Feel the beat. Feel the rhythm. Feel . . . the . . . groove.' Amber's voice ended in a long whoooo sound as she spun around.

Out of nowhere, a voice asked, 'Wanna dance?'

Both girls turned to find a pissed-out-of-his-box Sam standing next to them, looking eagerly up at Amber.

Amber smiled at him, but held her still-gyrating body back. 'No thanks.'

Sam ran his hand up Amber's bare arm.

'Get off the merchandise, man,' Amber said, as she shook his hand off. 'I said I don't wanna play doubles with you.'

'Come on . . .'

'I don't fancy you or any other boys, get it?'

The boy wobbled as he threw Amber a dirty look. Then sulked away.

'Creep,' Jade muttered. She turned back to Amber. 'You alright?'

The other girl nodded. Then she took a long slug of water from her bottle. She'd explained to Jade that if you were doing Es you had to drink heaps of water.

'Have you ever had a boyfriend?' Jade asked as they started dancing again.

'I had one once . . .'

'Oh yeah?'

'His name was Billy. Billy Love . . .'

'You're making it up.'

'I swear on my life that's what he was called.'

'And did he live up to his name?'

Amber scoffed. 'Nah. Kept trying to interfere with my raspberry ripples. Totally grossed me out.' Suddenly Amber's face became serious as the track playing came to an end. The crush of people around them manoeuvred themselves into new positions. Amber cuddled close to Jade and said, 'Can you keep a secret?'

Curiosity filled Jade as she nodded. The tip of Amber's tongue sneaked out of her mouth. Ran over her deep red bottom lip. A new track hit the dance floor as she said, 'I kissed someone once.'

Jade drew in a deep breath, her curiosity rising. 'Oh yeah? What was it like?'

Amber inhaled deeply as her face split into a grin. 'Total . . . big . . . time . . . heaven.'

'Did you use tongues?' Jade's tone was half fascinated, half disgusted.

Amber nodded, laughing.

'No boy's ever kissed me before.'

The smile vanished from Amber's face. 'See, that's my secret. It weren't a boy.'

Jade stopped moving. Stared at Amber with complete astonishment. Amber grabbed Jade's arm in a punishing grip. 'You ain't gonna tell no one, are you?'

Dumbfounded, Jade shook her head.

Amber slowly let go of her arm. A silly grin settled on her face. 'Her name was Mitzie Stuart. One minute we're dancing at the school disco, the next we're outside doing the cha-cha-cha . . .'

'Here . . . comes . . . the . . . New . . . Year . . .' the DJ shouted, cutting off the music and across Amber's words. 'Three . . . two . . . one.' The crowd shouted out, 'Happy New Year!'

'Happy New Year,' the girls belted out at each other at the same time. They gave each other a tight hug. Then Jade remembered what Amber had just revealed to her. She quickly stepped away. Instead of being offended, Amber laughed. 'Don't worry, girl, ain't no way in hell I'd fancy you. I like my ladies well stacked on top.' Her hands gestured in front of her chest. 'You get me?'

Both girls started to giggle.

From nowhere, one of the other girls appeared. 'Time to hop it.'

Amber and Jade nodded. They rushed over to the table Ruby was sitting at. They found her leaning back, looking up with a dazed expression on her face and a nearly empty glass in front of her.

'Ruby, you alright?' Jade asked, concerned at the flushed features of the other girl.

Ruby hiccupped. Giggled. Amber leaned towards her. Sniffed.

'She ain't . . . ?' Jade began, disbelievingly.

'Yes, she is,' Amber cut her off. 'She's totally P-I-S-S-E-D.'

Jason's hands tightened around the kneeling blonde's throat. She gagged and choked as she sucked him off. Jason pressed harder against her windpipe and smiled. He liked his sex the way he lived his life – rough. The woman's tongue went at him like his donger was on the end of a lollipop stick. Fuck, what a way to bring in the new year. He groaned. Leaned over the desk and snorted another line of charlie. His mobile rang. He pulled the phone off the desk. Looked at the name on the screen. Frankie.

'Yeah?'

'Finlay phoned. One of his shipments has come in. After New Year we get the girls to deliver it to check that they can operate without us . . .'

'Still think this is a dumb idea, boss, to let those girls loose around London, especially as there's only six days to Amsterdam.'

'Leave the thinking to me. Just do what you're told. Oh yeah, I've got the other girl.'

1.33.

That was the time the girls and the others got back to St Nicholas. A full moon was on high alert in the sky. The air was filled with frost.

'Thanks for asking us out,' Jade whispered in the driveway of the home.

'The Spice Girls are shit,' Ruby yelled out in a slurred raucous voice.

The drunk girl was propped between Amber and Jade.

'Sh,' Jade warned. 'Keep a lid on it.'

Ruby ignored her and continued her rant. 'Girl power, my arse. I mean that Ginger Spice looks about fifty years old.' She tottered with the final word. Wobbled and almost fell onto Jade.

'Sounds like your mate's big trap's gonna get us caught,' Sam said, his eyes flickering fretfully to the front door. 'So we'd better scarper.' His eyes flashed up at Amber. 'Maybe we can go out another time.'

'Maybe,' Amber replied.

The girls dragged a protesting Ruby in the direction of the back stairs as the others quickly scrambled towards a window they'd left open downstairs. As the girls melted into the shadows around the corner, behind a young tree, the front door was suddenly flung open. The girls froze. Turned back around. Jade immediately clamped a hand over Ruby's mouth. Through the space between two branches, they watched an angry Mr Miller standing in the doorway.

'Where the fucking hell have you been?' he blasted at the children.

Without waiting for a reply, he leaped forward and backhanded Sam in the face. Sam let out a terrified cry. The man grabbed the front of the boy's jacket. Slapped him again. And again. And again, until the boy's mouth was bleeding on both sides.

'I lost valuable money because of you lot tonight. My friends came to see you, but you weren't there. Get inside the house now,' he screamed.

As the children obeyed his command, in a rush of tears and legs, his hand whipped out and grabbed Sam.

'Go up to my room.'

Sam let out a shaking sob as he dashed into the house. The man slowly pulled off his belt as he followed him.

'Shit,' Amber said as she watched the empty space where the man and children had been. Her fingertips touched her lips as if she were trying to keep from vomiting. Jade's head moved from side to side in horror at what she'd just seen. The chill wind picked up speed around them.

'I should've let him dance with me,' Amber said.

Jade said nothing, not sure how to deal with the other girl's regret.

'What do you think he meant by the kids having lost him lots of money because his mates came around?'

Jade was tempted to tell her about the building in the garden. But she didn't. Their job was to help their mums and get out of St Nicholas as quickly as possible. Instead she said, 'We'd better shift ourselves upstairs.'

She let go of Ruby's mouth. They started to move. Reached the stairs at the same time as Ruby began ranting and raving again.

'You're gonna wake the whole flamin' house up,' Jade said.

They yanked her quickly upstairs. Got inside the building. Quietly closed the door. Ruby stared at Jade, her gaze flickering over the other girl as if she were seeing her for the first time in her life. 'You fancy Frankie, don't you?'

A pink stain spread across Jade's face.

'I've had enough of this,' Amber said, and yanked Ruby's arm, drawing her into the corridor.

'Fancies Frankie. Sounds funny, doesn't it?' Ruby giggled at the end. 'Jade fancies Frankie. Jade fancies Frankie. Jade fancies . . .'

Her last word was choked back with a strangled noise as Jade covered her mouth with her hand.

'I'm only gonna take my mitt off if you promise to keep it zipped.' Ruby gave her head a quick nod. As Jade eased her hand away, a terrifying scream echoed from somewhere downstairs. The girls froze. The scream came again. And again. Then silence.

Jade and Amber looked at each other. Neither girl said anything, but they knew they were thinking the same thing. Without anyone having to tell them, they knew the screams belonged to Sam.

'Evil fucker,' Jade muttered, as she thought of the wicked Mr Miller.

'I want to lie down,' Ruby slurred.

Both the other girls ignored her. They tightened their arms around her and briskly walked into the shadows towards their room. As they neared it, they noticed a beam of light coming from underneath the door.

'I thought we switched the light off,' Jade whispered to Amber in surprise.

'We did.'

'Can I lie down now?'

'Shut it,' Jade whispered furiously.

Both Jade and Amber looked at the door.

'Maybe we left it on?' Jade finally said.

Amber shrugged her shoulders. 'Dunno.'

They began to move again. Reached the door. Jade let go of Ruby's arm. She grasped the door handle. Twisted it. Pushed it slowly open.

'Want to sleep,' Ruby mumbled, as if she had marbles in her mouth.

Jade moved forward. Across the threshold. Into the light. Her eyes zoomed around the room. Skidded to a halt when she saw someone lounging back in a chair by the dressing table.

Frankie.

But her breath caught in her throat when she realised he wasn't alone.

'I'm waiting.'

Frankie's voice was hard as he looked at Jade and Amber standing in the doorway with Ruby propped between them. Jade swung her gaze between him and the black girl sitting on the bed. The girl wore a baseball cap, hand-me-down clothes and a compelling and un-settling gaze in her black eyes that made Jade's heart bounce. 'For the second time, ladies, where the friggin' hell have you all been?' Frankie stood up and each of the girls doubted that Ruby was the only one pissed in the room.

'We just wanted to be like everyone else celebrating the new year,' Amber said in a tiny voice.

Frankie's arms waved at them as he said, 'All you had to do was ask me. I would've taken you out for a night on the tiles.'

Jade and Amber looked at him, shame-faced.

'From the state of Ruby, I'd say you had a blinder of a time.'

Ruby's hand shot to her mouth as she choked, 'I'm going to chuck up.'

Frankie pointed at Amber. 'You go and help her.'

Amber swiftly dragged Ruby to the bathroom. The room was silent as Frankie gazed at Jade. She gazed back at him. Frankie let out a sigh, the anger leaving him. He walked slowly towards her. Her head dipped low.

'Look me in the eye.'

Her head slowly tipped up. Held his intense blue eyes.

'Don't you trust me? I thought we were mates.'

Jade said nothing. Instead her teeth ground into her bottom lip.

'Amber doing a bunk I can understand. But you? You don't live for the moment like her.' He tapped his finger to the side of his head. 'You've got a brain . . .'

As if on cue, Amber and Ruby staggered out of the bathroom. Ruby's face looked pasty and pale.

'You alright?' Frankie asked softly as he walked towards her.

She nodded, but bubbles of tears were bright in her eyes.

'Hop it.' Frankie pointed to Ruby's bed. 'It's beddy-bye time for you, little Miss Ruby.'

She moved over to her bed. As she got her nightclothes ready Frankie moved towards the bed where the new girl sat and said, 'This is your new roommate . . .'

'New roommate?' Amber and Jade replied together.

'She's new to this country and don't speak the lingo. I want you to look out for her. Sort her out.'

Jade took a step forward. 'But why ain't she with the others downstairs? I thought we were all together because Jason's helping our mums.'

'I just do what I'm told. I don't ask any questions. Neither should you. She won't tell no one what her name is so give her a name. You know, something like Tinkle Bell. Gotta run.'

He moved towards the still-open door. Turned back around.

'Don't forget what I said. Look after her. I'll see you tomorrow. Jason wants you to start a new job for him the day after today.'

And with that he was gone.

'Do I look like a babysitter?' Amber folded her arms as she checked out the new girl.

'Have a heart. She looks lost. Bet she ain't got a mum or dad.'

Amber sashayed towards the girl, who kept looking at her. 'My name is Amber,' she said loudly and slowly.

'She ain't deaf, idiot, she just can't speak English,' Jade said as she joined Amber by the girl's bed. 'My name is Jade. And that total mess,' she pointed at Ruby, who was snug under her duvet, 'is Ruby.'

Grace's stare moved from Amber to Jade. From Jade to Amber. Her head dropped to her hands lying in her lap.

'So what we gonna call her?' Amber asked.

'Can't call her Tinkle Bell, that's for sure. Me, you and Ruby have all got names that are the same as jewellery – Jade, Amber, Ruby. Maybe we should do the same with her.'

'What, like diamond?'

'Yeah, but that ain't no girl's name.'

'What about Crystal?'

'Nah, she don't look like no Crystal.'

They spent the next few minutes going through names.

Pearl – no.

Jet – no.

Sapphire – a definite no-no.

'I've got it,' Jade said triumphantly. 'What about Opal?'

'That's a sweetie. Opal Fruits.'

'I know, but she looks like an Opal.'

Amber studied the seated girl. 'Maybe. Yeah, maybe you're right.'

Jade gazed at the new girl and pointed at her. 'You . . . Opal.'

The new girl just gazed back at her blankly.

'Say . . . my . . . name . . . is . . . Opal.'

The other girl finally raised her dark eyes and quietly repeated, 'Opal.'

'What do you think this new job's gonna be?' Amber suddenly asked.

'Dunno,' Jade replied. 'We'll soon find out.'

Grace pretended to sleep as she secretly watched the fat girl praying in front of a candle. She tried to remember the fat girl's name. Jade, yes, that was what the girl had said she was called. Jade and the other girl, the black one with the jewellery and laughter in her voice, had fussed over her like she was a newborn baby as they got her bed ready. Then they had tucked her in, pulling the blood-coloured duvet to her chin. The taller girl had jumped straight into bed, completely naked, but the other one had gone over to the dressing table and lit a candle. Then she had dropped to her knees, clasped her hands together and started praying. At first, Grace had closed her eyes, feeling she was intruding on Jade's privacy. But her eyes had burst back open when she'd heard the girl mumble the name Nikki. Funny they should both know someone called Nikki. It must be a popular name in England. Her mind zoomed back to the cell in Sankura. She wondered if Nikki was alive or dead. Prayed that Nikki had understood what she had to do with the diamond she'd given her. Prayed that Nikki clung onto her words – 'Hope dies last of all.'

Jade sprang to her feet, making Grace snap her eyes shut. She heard Jade's footsteps as she padded across the room. The rustle of her duvet, then the movement of springs as she got into bed. Grace shifted to her side, curled into a ball, reopened her eyes. She didn't know what this place was, but at least she wasn't lying on a hard floor for the night. She was so tired. Exhaustion was like a living man pressing down on her life, pinning her to the softness and warmth of the bed. The type of warmth and softness that made her feel safe. A security she hadn't felt in years. But she knew she couldn't get attached to this place. At some time in the future she would have to leave. Find her own way. But without her diamond she didn't have anything to barter for money. Besides, wasn't it her mother who always said, 'When you are lost never walk fast.' No, she would only leave when she had her strength back and had learned as much as she could about her new country. Only then would she begin the next journey in her life.

And now the other girls had given her a new name. Opal. She didn't much like it, but maybe that was what she needed to start to forget her past, a new name. A new beginning.

Opal.

thirteen

'I've told you to stop pinching the soddin' gear,' Jade snapped at Amber as the other girl swiped up an E from the table.

It was the morning of the second day of January, and while the world got into the swing of the new year, the girls felt anything but comfortable about their new life. Jade shoved herself to her feet and glared at Amber. 'My Nikki ain't dying in no prison cell in Sankura just because you decided . . .'

'Nikki?'

Jade spun around, knowing that it was Opal who had spoken. Although Ruby had taken Opal under her wing, trying to teach the new girl English, Jade had rarely heard her speak. Opal looked at her now with confusion kicking inside her eyes. But before Jade could say anything, Amber shot back at her, 'Who the fuck do you think you are? My mum or something?'

Amber defiantly grabbed another E. She looked Jade square in the eye. She popped it with slow insolence into her mouth.

'I'm warning you,' Jade growled, the heat of anger gliding up her face.

'I ain't jackshit scared of you.' Then Amber stuck her tongue out, the pill balanced just behind the tip, and said, with the hard-edged taunt of a playground chant, 'Why don't you come and get it?'

Jade flew at her, five foot two of bristling anger, ready to slog it out. She reached Amber. Jade's hands rolled into fists by her side. Amber pushed her chest out. Then her throat bobbed as she swallowed. Jade's hands erupted forward.

'You two need to knock it off,' a stern voice said behind them.

Both girls twisted around to find Frankie standing in the doorway. His hair was darkened and damp from a dose of rain, but his blue eyes were as bright as ever. In his right hand he held a holdall. Black and zipped tight. He shifted into the room and closed the door at the same time as Jade's hands fell back to her side. The girls stared at each other, scared that Frankie might have heard what they were arguing about. But his features didn't show that he had.

'We need to get ready for that new job Jason wants you to do, so sit down.'

The girls quickly did what he asked. Frankie pulled up a seat as well. He did a quick circuit of their faces. Then placed his bag on the table. He glanced at Opal and said, 'How's she getting on?'

'Very well,' Ruby piped up proudly. 'I've been teaching her English. I'll get her to tell you her new name.' Ruby turned to Opal and slowly said, 'Say . . . my . . . name . . . is . . . Opal.'

Opal stared at Ruby, her eyebrows crinkling together. She turned to Frankie and said, face completely blank, 'Jackshit.'

A deafening silence filled the room. Then Frankie tipped back his head and laughed. 'I don't recommend that you become a teacher in the future,' he said to the mortified girl.

Ruby glared at Amber across the table. Amber just lifted her shoulders in a what-you-gonna-do-about-it shrug.

'OK, girls, like I told you on New Year's Eve, Jason wants you to do a new job for him. This one's gonna really up the amount of dosh we send to Jason's mates in Sankura. Then we'll be ready to do the big job in Amsterdam in four days. Today's job involves you helping one of Jason's mates move some gear across town. So we're gonna have to go and meet Jason's mate.'

Frankie opened his bag. Pulled out items of clothes and threw them on the table.

'You're gonna need to wear these for the job.'

They stared at the clothing. White blouses, sky-blue ties and navy-blue V-necks and skirts and small straw hats with blue ribbons tied around.

Ruby turned to Frankie, frowning, and said, 'These look a bit like my school uniform.'

'Got it in one,' Frankie replied. 'See, if you wear school uniforms when you move the stuff the Old Bill will leave you alone. They'll just think you're like all the other kids going home from school.' He stood up. 'Right, girls, you need to get your fannies into gear now because the people in Sankura are getting impatient for their lolly.'

Nikki's daughter.

That was all Opal could think of as she dressed with the others in the clothes Frankie gave them. She secretly glanced at Jade, who was moaning with Amber about their appearance as they checked themselves over in the dressing-table mirror. She still couldn't believe it. Nikki's daughter. She zipped the skirt up. But it must be true because she knew there wouldn't be any other Nikkis in Sankura's main prison. She straightened the stupid hat the white man had given her on her head. Now she had a problem – should she tell Jade she'd met her mother or not? If she did tell her she'd blow her cover and let on that she could speak English.

'Ruby, bring her over here.'

Opal's head shot in Amber's direction because she knew she was referring to her. 'Look at the state of her hat. And I'm sure she's never done a tie in her life.'

As Ruby moved towards her, Opal pinched the inside of her mouth with her small teeth. Should she or shouldn't she? As Ruby gently took her arm she made her decision. Her teeth let go of her skin. She clamped her lips together. No, she wouldn't say anything, but she made another vow. As long as she stayed with the group she would protect the back of the daughter of the woman who had saved her from being raped.

'This is it, girls.'

Frankie's words hung in the air as the girls stared up at the music shop off Denmark Street in Soho. It was situated in a narrow street, between a second-hand bookstore and a door advertising the services of a Swedish model.

'This looks well fresh,' Amber gushed, as she stared at the shop.

Over the entrance hung a sign with the solitary word 'Finlay's' composed of bass clefs. The frontage was decked out in plush burgundy velvet and glittered with every kind of brass, bronze and silver instrument – saxophones, clarinets, trombones, tubas and other exotics that the girls had never seen before. The shop was too cool to put prices in the window but they could see that things of that quality didn't come cheap.

Frankie pushed the door and the girls made their way inside. The shop was a blend of highly polished floors and white-tiled walls, lined with photos of musical greats. There seemed to be hundreds of instruments for sale and various serious-looking musos were inspecting them, although whether they were there to buy or just to admire, it was hard to tell. Pride of place, though, went to an original 1950s Wurlizter jukebox. As Jade closed the door, shutting out the world, the Wurlitzer burst into life, playing Gloria Jones's Northern Soul version of 'Tainted Love'.

Jade stood still for a few seconds, basking in the beat of her mum's favourite song.

'Come on,' Frankie whispered in her ear, snapping her back to the present.

Her gaze roamed around the shop, until it stopped at a black man behind a desk at the back. His face was a rich mahogany brown and sported a goatee beard at one end and short, spiky dreads at the other. Despite the dim light, he wore wrap-around shades. He was dressed in a purple suit, yellow shirt and paisley tie. The outfit shouldn't have worked, but it did. He seemed to be holding two conversations at once – one on a landline and the other on a mobile. On the landline he seemed to be a Jamaican, on the mobile he was using black cockney.

'Don't give me GBH ear-style on the dog and bone, man. When I've got it, you'll get it – you know what I mean?'

He ended both conversations when he noticed Frankie and the girls moving towards him. He stood up, revealing his impressive six-foot-plus frame. He leaned on his back foot and spread his arms wide, in an extravagant gesture.

'Hey, bro,' he let out as he pulled Frankie into his embrace.

Once he let go of Frankie, his gaze settled on the girls. He gave them a quick once-over.

'These my people?' he asked Frankie.

'Let's chat in the back.'

The girls followed the men into the back of the building. The corridor was dim and enclosed. A shiver ran up Jade's spine. Finally they stopped at a white door with a frosted-glass panel. Finlay opened it. They stepped inside. A studio. The room was square and small, with a large glass window with a view into the engineering room, and littered with free-standing mics, a drum kit and four black instrument cases propped up against a side wall.

'Wo! Wo! Wo!' Amber beamed with dizzy delight as she spun around. 'Is this a studio?'

Finlay proudly sauntered over to her. 'I like a lady with taste.'

Amber looked back at him shyly.

'Let's get down to business,' Finlay said, as he turned around and moved towards the wall where the four instrument cases were. 'Gather around,' he instructed the girls.

He picked up one of the cases, which was about the right size to hold a clarinet.

'Each one of you are gonna take one of these to a mate of mine, who hangs out in Peckham.'

'In South London?' Jade asked.

'Well, it ain't on the moon, girl,' he cut in impatiently. His hand dipped into his inside pocket. He pulled out a folded piece of paper. 'Now Peckham ain't the easiest place to get to. That's the problem with South London, no bloody Tube. So you're gonna need to get a couple of trains and a bus to Peckham High Street. Here's a map . . .'

'Aren't you coming with us, Frankie?' Ruby asked. Her arm was tightly linked with the silent Opal's.

'No,' Frankie answered. 'This is a job we trust you lot to do on your own.'

Finlay carried on with the instructions. 'It also tells you how to get to the meeting place, a café, where you're gonna meet my man Dave. Just settle yourselves at a table and wait for him to drop in. He takes the cases, you say bye-bye and go straight back to St Nicholas. Easy.' He casually held out the paper, between two fingers, towards Amber. 'I'm giving this to you, babe.'

As Amber's hand came out to pluck it from his fingers, Finlay's other hand whipped out and caught it in a punishing grip. She let out a yelp of pain as his grip tightened. 'If I get a whiff that any of you have been poking your beaks inside these cases, know what I'm gonna do?' His gaze ran slowly over each girl. 'I'm gonna nail your hand to the table, take one of these cases and use it to beat you on your hand until every last finger is broken, you get me, people?'

He let go of Amber's hand. Without warning, Finlay whipped off his sunglasses. Jade sucked in her breath when she saw his eyes. Dark, and cold, as if something had been decaying in them for a long time.

Amber, Jade and Ruby trembled as they nodded at him. Only Opal didn't respond.

'You taking the piss?' Finlay growled at Opal, stepping menacingly closer to her.

'She don't understand the lingo,' Frankie explained. 'She's just arrived on the last boat.'

Tension sizzled in the air as Finlay continued to look at her. Then he stepped back.

Eased his shades back onto his face.

'Choose a case.'

The girls quickly did as he asked. Jade was surprised at how heavy the case felt. Her mind started to wonder what was inside.

'Everyone understand what they've gotta do?' Frankie asked.

The three girls nodded.

'Who you meeting, girls?' Finlay asked.

'Dave,' the girls shot back in unison.

'Where you going?'

'Peckham.'

'Good.' Frankie said. 'Don't forget your old girls are depending on you. And I'm trusting you to be out and about on your own.'

The girls hooked the handles over their shoulders and set off, with no idea what they were carrying on their backs, to a part of London none of them had ever been to before.

The 36 bus dropped them on Peckham High Street and accelerated away – and who could blame it? Jade thought. She didn't like the look of Peckham, not one bit. There was a certain grim honesty about it. Other places might pretend to be on their way up or suggest 'regeneration' was riding into town some day soon. In the heart of SE15, though, there was no pretence; we're poor, it said, some of us live on the wrong side of the law, and if you want to make something outta it, make sure you've got the weapons to back you up.

They followed the directions of Finlay's map, moving quickly as the rain kicked in and nosedived around them. Past a few chain stores that were clinging on as evidence of their 'commitment' to the 'community'. Past mini-marts that had the larger members of the owner's family riding shotgun by the counter. Past pubs that had notices on their doors pleading with the punters not to deal drugs on the premises and vain warnings about CCTV.

'The café should be at the end down here,' Amber said, pointing to the end of the street.

The rain turned nasty, heaving and bouncing back against blocked drains as they passed an off-licence with a grille on its counter. A group of schoolkids tumbled out of the door. They caught sight of the girls, pointed at their hats and started jeering and laughing.

'Wankers,' Amber yelled back, giving them the finger.

'Don't do that. They might come after us,' Ruby pleaded.

'Do I look like I need your permission to breathe?'

But Ruby was right, Amber's taunt provoked a wagon-load of trouble.

'Oi! What you got in them cases?' one of the jeering gang shouted.

'Just keep moving,' Jade ordered, her footsteps getting faster.

The girls kept their faces forward. Kept moving. Didn't look back. But they heard the Peckham kids' footsteps behind them. With each of their footsteps came more insults.

The girls moved faster. The gang moved faster. Suddenly the footsteps behind them motored into a rushed rhythm.

'Bloody scarper to the caff,' Jade screamed.

The girls ran as the gang chased them. Passers-by stopped to watch, but no one intervened, as if they had seen it all before. The sign for Glen's Grill loomed in the distance. The world passed the girls in a whirl as the footsteps beat closer to them. The café got nearer. Ruby screamed. Jade jerked around. One of the boys had caught the collar of Ruby's coat. Jade rushed back towards Ruby. Reached her and the boy. Jade flipped the case off her back. Swung it high and whacked the boy on his arm. As he stumbled back, she grabbed Ruby and dragged her forward. Ran. Her breathing pulsed madly out of her mouth. She looked up to see Amber already at the café. Urgent fingers tangled in the flying strands of her hair. She cried out but didn't stop. The force of her forward movement made the fingers slip from her hair. Amber and the café got closer. And closer. Finally she reached the café. Amber jerked the door open and the girls tumbled inside. Banged the door shut. They leaned on the door, breathing heavily. The customers inside gave them curious looks, but soon dipped their heads back down into their own lives. The girls turned around and watched from the window as the gang outside swore and retreated.

'Shit, that was close,' Amber said between heaving breaths.

'I thought there was more of them,' Jade said, still gazing after the retreating figures.

'Where's Opal?' Ruby cried, her hand clutching her inhaler.

The girls looked at each other and realised that Opal wasn't with them.

Opal had run in the opposite direction to the girls and the gang, but some of the Peckham kids had followed her. Her hat almost flew off as she picked up speed. Her heart beat furiously as she took a left. They kept coming. When she twisted, they twisted.

When she turned, they turned. She dived into an alley. Ran. Skidded to a halt when she realised that her route was cut off by a tall, large wire fence. She ran towards it, chest heaving. Her gaze skidded up its length. No way was she going to be able to climb it. Not with the case. Swiftly she turned around when she heard footsteps behind her. The kids moved towards her, a menacing line of three. Two boys and one girl.

'We asked what you had in your case, bitch?' one of the boys shouted.

'I bet we could flog it for some dosh,' the girl said.

Opal stared the largest one in the eye. Big boy, sloppy school tie and large hands.

She bent down and placed the case on the ground. She pulled herself tall. Relaxed her back into the fence. Big boy smiled as he and his friends advanced towards her.

'We should go and look for her,' Ruby said anxiously.

They had been sat at a table in the café for seven minutes and still these was no sign of Opal. Glen's Grill was the usual greasy-spoon eat-your-grub-quickly-and-get-on-with-your-life type of joint. No thrills inside, just anonymous, tired tables and worn chairs.

'We can't,' Jade replied. 'Finlay's mate Dave will be here soon and wondering where we are.'

'But she doesn't speak English,' Ruby persisted. 'She might be lost. Or they might have found her.'

Guilt began to eat away at Jade. Ruby was right, they needed to find Opal.

'Alright, this is what we're gonna do,' Jade whispered as she leaned across the table.

'I'm gonna hit the streets and look for her. You two stay here with the cases and when Dave comes give them to him . . .'

'But we've only got three cases,' Amber jumped in. 'He's gonna want to know where the other one is.'

'I know that,' Jade replied in a hard voice. 'I ain't stupid. You'll just have to tell him there were only three.'

'But Jason's gonna go ballistic . . .' Amber carried on.

'I know,' Jade said, standing up. 'We'll just have to deal with that when it happens.' She pushed her chair back. Headed for the door. As her hand reached for the handle, the door swung open.

'Opal,' she cried out as the other girl staggered, head down, inside.

Jade let out a long sigh of relief when she realised that Opal still had her case. Her relief was short-lived when Opal slowly raised her head. She gasped when she saw her face. A raised jagged cut, with congealed blood, split both her lips, and three fingerprints of blood were under her left eye mixed with her tears.

'Opal,' Ruby cried as she rushed from the table towards the door.

Ruby stopped short when she too caught the damage done to Opal's face. She threw her arms around the other girl, giving her a firm hug. Her teeth twisted into her bottom lip as she stroked Opal's hair.

'You OK?' she continued softly as she led Opal towards the toilets. 'I'm going to clean you up.'

Instead of sitting down, Jade angrily opened the door.

'Where you going?' Amber said, leaping out of her chair and rushing to catch up with Jade.

Jade swung around, a furious light setting her green eyes on fire. 'Bastards. They ain't getting away with this. I'm gonna find 'em and take 'em all on.'

Amber caught her arm, shut the door and dragged her back to the table. 'You can't do that. We've got business to take care of . . .'

Before she could finish the door opened again. The girls knew instantly that it was Dave. He looked like what Jade's mum called a classic dodgy geezer – rough, barrel-chested and with hands that looked like they did his talking for him. He found them easily.

'You got it?' he asked, his hand squeezing his nose, the same way that Jason's did. Amber and Jade passed him the instrument cases. He hooked the straps of the cases over his shoulders.

Then his eyes glided over the girls. 'I thought there were meant to be four of you?'

A worried look passed between the two girls. Finally Jade spoke. 'The others are in the Ladies.'

He sent them a telling look. Then he gave them a brisk nod and was gone.

'Wheeew!' Amber let out, wiping her fingers across her forehead. 'That was close. Thank God Opal still had the case because whatever was inside we still delivered to Dave. Didn't we?'

fourteen

That night Jade never finished her prayers because the door was kicked in. Startled, she clutched her palms to her chest as she twisted around. A puffed-up Jason stood in the doorway.

'Get your fucking arses up,' he yelled as he stomped into the room.

As Jade trembled to her feet, the other three girls shot out of bed. Amber quickly grabbed a long T-shirt and slipped it on. The girls stood shaking, looking at him. His gaze swept over them. Without warning he rushed at Jade. As the others gasped, he slammed her into the wall. 'Where the fuck is it?'

Too shocked to speak, Jade stared back at him, her eyes squinting in pain. His arm jacked, sideways, under her throat. 'I said where is it?'

'I don't know what you're going on about,' she squeaked.

'The fucking cases . . .'

'But we gave them to Dave . . .'

'He got the cases alright, but one of them was flippin' empty.'

The girls all sucked in their breath as they looked at Opal. He hiked his arm deeper into Jade's windpipe. Small choking sounds stabbed out of her mouth.

'Alright,' Amber yelled. 'I'll tell you what happened.'

Jason eased back the pressure of his arm, but didn't look around. 'I'm waiting.'

'These mad kids started chasing us, so we scarpered to the caff, except Opal, who got lost. But she found her way back to the café. You should've seen her face, those nutters roughed her up. They must've nicked what was inside her case. She don't speak English, so she couldn't tell us. We didn't know the case was empty, so we give it to Dave . . .'

Jason cut her off and growled. 'You stupid bitches.' Abruptly he let Jade go. She leaned back into the wall, taking huge gulps of air into her body.

'Fuck with me, will ya?' he snarled at all of them. 'We're going for a ride.'

The girls shuffled, terrified, out of the room in their nightclothes and bare feet.

Jade knew it was a stupid move, but she had to ask. 'Jason, where we going?'

For over an hour, Jason had been motoring through London's dark streets like a maniac. He flicked his head towards her, his face lit with disbelief and scorn. Abruptly one of his hands came off the wheel. Reached out towards her like he was getting ready to push her out of the car.

'Watch out,' Amber screamed from the back.

Jason's hand shot back as he twisted his head back towards the windscreen. He swore as the car headed towards a zebra crossing with a drunken man weaving on it. Jason jammed his hand back on the wheel and hit the black-and-white stripes at the same time. Frantically he shifted the wheel through his fingers. The car lunged, pushing its occupants to the right. Both Amber and Ruby let out piercing screams. The car swerved around the man on the crossing.

'Tosser,' the man shouted, raising his hand in the classic wanker sign.

'What did he fucking call me?' Jason screamed.

The car swerved to a stop. Swearing like a man who'd just discovered he had a tongue, Jason jumped out of the car. Ran to the boot of the car and took out a car jack. He charged across to the man on the crossing. When he reached him, he yelled, 'Fucking tosser, am I?' He raised the jack and hit the terrified man a vicious blow in the face. The man dropped. The petrified girls watched as Jason crashed the tool, again and again, into the fallen man's body.

'Let's do a runner,' Jade said, her hand reaching for the door handle.

'We can't,' Amber cried. 'We ain't got nothin' on our feet. Where would we go? You can't even contact your mum's mate because Frankie's got your address book. I'm scared if he catches us I'll end up like Sam.'

Before Jade could respond, Jason turned back to the car. His body heaved with deep lungeing breaths as the jack hung limply by his side. He got back in the driver's seat. He dropped the jack next to Jade's legs on the floor. She cringed as she gazed down at it; it was covered with blood.

'See, that's what happens when someone fucks me off,' Jason growled. 'If one of you opens your two-bit gob again it will be you on those black-and-white stripes being battered to death.'

Half an hour later Jason's wheels began to slow as they entered a back street. He turned off the ignition.

'Get out,' he yelled.

Jade peered at the street, through the windscreen, and realised where they were.

Finlay's music shop looked different in the dark. The backstreet in which it stood now looked like what people said Soho once was and some claim still is. Trouble.

'Inside.'

The girls quickly obeyed Jason's command. They stepped into the main room, which was bathed in a darkness that covered the glitz and glamour they had once admired. Their bare feet stumbled when they heard the click of the lock in the front door behind them.

'Right, get in the back,' Jason said as he overtook them and led the way.

As they shuffled deeper into the dark corridor they heard two male voices arguing, coming from the studio. Jason pushed the studio door wide. He grabbed each girl in turn and shoved them inside. In the dimly lit room stood Finlay and another man, who they had never seen before. The unknown man was of medium height, white and had hands that could knock a person out cold with one slug.

'Didn't I tell you girls that if any of you fucked with my gear I was gonna break every bone in your fingers?' Finlay roared.

The girls shook, terrified, beside each other.

'They're claiming that some likely lads mugged off the new girl and took it,' Jason said.

'But how come she had the case still?'

Jason flicked his head to the side and looked down at Opal. 'Yeah, how come you still had the case?'

Opal pushed her head down.

'Looks like your little African bird maybe ain't singing you the right song,' Finlay said, hard faced.

Jade, Ruby and Amber gasped as Finlay grabbed Opal's arm and dragged her towards the unknown man.

Jade quickly jumped in, 'Leave her alone. It ain't her fault that Peckham is a jungle. I'm sure you can get more drugs . . .'

'Drugs?' Finlay growled. 'Go and open one of those cases.' He pointed to one of the cases against the wall.

Jade didn't want to go, but she knew she had no choice. Slowly she moved her freezing feet across the room towards the cases. Nervously, she picked one up. She flicked open one silver clasp. Then the other. Slowly lifted back the lid.

'Ohmygod,' she squealed when she saw what was inside.

The case dropped from her hand. Onto the floor clattered four handguns. Shock rocked through Jade because she'd never seen a gun in real life before.

'That look like fucking drugs to you?' Finlay tightened his grip on Opal's arm.

'Those guns are masterpieces, so where's my shooters?' the un-named man yelled at Opal.

She just stared back at him, eyes wide and flicking.

'Ain't no point chatting to her, she don't know the lingo,' Jason said in disgust.

Finlay's fingers pinched into the skin around her mouth. She winced and eased up on her toes as the shape of her mouth twisted and distorted. Finlay looked deep into her eyes and said, 'Can't speak English, that's what they all say when they come here. Push a fucking giro under their noses and you've never heard people talk English so quick in your life. I'll get her lips flapping.'

He let go of her face. Shoved her into a chair. He turned and left the room. Soon he was back, this time with a large, square can in his hand. He leaned over Opal and smiled. Then he raised the can. Unscrewed the lid. Petrol fumes swept the air. He heaved the can back and splashed the liquid over Opal. Her right side. Her left. Eventually he tipped it over her head. He chucked the can on the floor.

He pulled out a bright, yellow lighter from his jeans pocket. The others girls gasped when they realised what he planned to do. Finlay crouched down beside Opal. Ran his finger over the tip of the lighter. 'So what happened to the guns?'

Opal hunched her shoulders, shivering and shaking her head, but she said nothing. With one stroke Finlay ignited the flame. The sound of Ruby's crying tore through the air. Opal stared straight ahead. She stopped shivering.

Jade's hands folded over her mouth to stop her own screams. Without thinking of the consequences she ran forward.

'Oi! Where you going?' Jason yelled.

She ignored him. Kept moving. Finlay flicked his head around just as she reached him. His hand snaked out to grab her, but she swayed out of his reach. She pushed herself in front of Opal and finally the screams inside her came out as words.

'Leave her alone. Just leave her alone. Frankie told me to look out for her and that's what I'm gonna do.'

Finlay reared back on his heels and said, 'Frankie said what?'

Finlay looked back at Jason. Jason looked at him. Then they began to laugh. High and wild.

'Frankie said . . .' Finlay echoed.

His laughter cut off. He pushed his attention back to the two girls. He reignited the flame. Moved it slowly towards them.

'You can't do nothin' to us,' Jade screamed out.

'And why's that?'

'Someone will miss us.'

'Like fucking who? You notice anyone come knocking at the door looking for you lot? No one gives a shit about any of you. As far as they're concerned you're the kids of three women who took their clothes off for any bloke with a wallet and then got their just desserts selling gear abroad. They can't even be bothered to report it in the news any more, that's how much they think about your old girls. East End scum, that's what they think your mums are. And they're not interested in you lot because you're not cute enough to look good in the papers or the telly. Only one who stood a chance was Amber, but she's the wrong shade, you get me? And as for your little friend there, illegals don't even register on the somebody scale. So when you're smoking brown bread don't even expect a priest to be standing at your graveside . . .'

His rant was interrupted by a sharp knock on the window connecting with the engineer's room. Everyone looked up. The outline of a figure shrouded in shadows could be seen.

'Is that . . . ?' Jason asked.

'Yeah,' Finlay replied as he eased up. 'Right, the girls know fuck all.' He looked at the girls. Swore. Then said to Jason, 'Get these teenage divs outta here before I really mess them up.'

The girls followed Jason down the street. The cold and debris on the ground dug into their bare feet. Ruby's arm clung tightly to Opal and Jade held Amber's hand. The dark had started to fade. They squinted as a car's headlights shot on, reflecting bright in the rain-soaked road. Its engine revved up. It began to move. It got closer. They got closer. They reached the mouth of the street at the same time as the car juddered to a halt. Jade held onto Amber's arm, frightened. No more geezers, please, she chanted in her head. Tentatively she moved forward. Took that turn. Breathed an incredible sigh of relief when she spotted Frankie's motor.

Jason strolled to the driver's side of the car. Leaned down as Frankie rolled down the window.

'Get 'em back to St Nicholas pronto.'

Then Jason was gone, a shadow disappearing into the aggravated early morning light. Once the girls were inside the car, with Jade in the passenger seat, Frankie asked, 'What happened?'

In a haunting and halting voice Jade told him.

'Frankie, how can you stand working with a geezer like that?'

'Don't forget your mums worked for him as well. No one ever looked out for me apart from Jason. No teachers, no social workers, nobody. I owe him.'

Jade bowed her head as the truth of his words sank in. 'Finlay said that no one gives a monkey about us.' Her chest heaved. She placed a hand over her heart as fast, silent tears came. She didn't realise that Frankie had pulled the car over until she felt his arms around her. Her head pressed against his chest.

'You're wrong, you know,' he whispered. 'I care.'

He held her like that for a few minutes, soothing her, making her feel safe again. Finally he eased her forward. Stared into her eyes. She gave him a little smile.

'I'm taking you lot out and about tomorrow.'

'Where? Are we going to Amsterdam?' Jade asked, as she sniffed.

He smiled at Jade. 'No, that's in four days' time. What's one of the best places to spend Saturday afternoon?'

Saturday afternoon? Jade thought incredulously. Opal had just been nearly burned to death and Frankie wanted to chat about Saturday afternoon. She stared back at him with a have-you-gone-off-your-rocker look.

'No need to look at me like that. Alright, I'll let you. I'm taking you and the others to a footie match . . .'

'You're not taking me to . . . ?' Jade gushed, feeling a mad wave of excitement.

'Yes I am. Tomorrow, we're off to Upton Park to see West Ham kick arse, just like you used to with your old mum.'

The girls put Opal in the shower. Fussed over her as they scrubbed and rinsed the petrol from her body.

'Right, all done,' Amber announced.

Opal raised her head as Jade wrapped a towel around her.

'Let's get you to bed, then,' Ruby said, reaching for her.

But Opal shook her head and pointed to the toilet. Ruby looked at her, confused, then her mouth shaped into an 'o' when she realised what Opal wanted.

'OK, let's give her some privacy,' Ruby said.

A few seconds later Opal was alone in the bathroom. She moved to the door. Gently turned the lock. Then she turned to the sink and dropped to her knees. Her hand felt inside the hollow of the sink's porcelain stand. She pulled out the gun that she'd hidden there. A gun that had once lived inside a clarinet case. As she handled the gun she recalled what had really happened earlier that day . . .

fifteen

The big boy and the other two thugs advanced on her.

'Step back,' Big Boy shouted to his friends. 'I'll do her with one hand tied behind my back.'

His friends laughed as he suddenly picked up his cocky stride and moved forward. Opal dug her eyes into him. Waited for him to reach her. As he raised his fist, her foot flicked out and up. Smashed into his privates with such force that he fell with a roar of excruciating pain. The next boy stormed towards her. He flung a wild punch at her, which glanced off her cheek. She ducked. Came up as he lost his balance, his foot kicking the violin case. As he rolled onto his back her foot banged into his ribs. The third teenager, the girl, was already bolting out of the alley by the time Opal stood straight. She took in deep breaths as she remembered the lieutenant in the rebel army who had been in charge of teaching the new recruits hand-to-hand combat. *'Always fight dirty because the enemy is never an honourable man.'*

His words resounded in her head as she watched the girl finally disappear. She felt the heat of the bruise beginning to grow and burn on her face. She touched it. She'd had worse. She looked around for the instrument case. Found it, tumbled open on its front. She crouched down. Grabbed the handle. Pulled it over. Her breath caught in her throat when she saw what was on the floor. Three guns. Now she realised what they had been delivering in the cases. She twisted her mouth with disgust. Then her mouth relaxed. Maybe this wasn't such a bad thing. A gun gave you protection. Made you feel safe. And she didn't feel safe in this crazy city called London. A groan from one of the boys made her spin around. She shot up. Moved towards him. Looked down at him. She raised her foot again and stamped on his hand. He screamed. She moved to the other side and did the same to his other hand. That would teach him to raise his fists to a female. She moved to the other boy, who was still languishing on the ground, and meted out the same punishment.

Calmly she moved back to the guns. Picked them up. Picked up the case. Closed it. She knew it would cause trouble, but she had no alternative. As she passed the big boy she leaned down and dipped three of her fingers in some of his blood and pressed her bloody fingertips under the bruise on her face. That would make it look like someone had really beaten her up. She raised herself up and began to walk towards a large steel bin against a wall in the middle of the alley. She lifted the lid and dropped two of the guns inside. She gave her full attention to the remaining gun in her hand. She quickly unlocked the chamber. Grinned when she saw that it was completely loaded. She pulled off her hat. Placed the gun on the crown of her head and securely jammed her hat back into place.

She began to move forward, then abruptly stopped. Suddenly she realised that this was her chance. To keep walking. Away from the St Nicholas care home. Away from the evil drugs they packed at night. If there was one thing her time in the rebel army had taught her, that was walking. Sometimes they would walk for miles and miles across hills, deserts, mountains. Now here was her chance to use that skill again. But what if she walked away and messed it all up for Nikki? And Jason stopped helping the others? What about her vow to protect Nikki's daughter? Could she really sleep at night with all of that as her bedfellow?

'*If you burn a house, can you conceal the smoke?*' was what her grandmother had once said after she'd eaten a mango without permission, with juice still around her mouth. No, she might walk away, but she wouldn't be able to sleep easy at night. A promise was a promise.

Decision made, she ran to meet the others at the café and prayed that Dave didn't inspect the cases.

*   *   *

Opal shivered in the growing chill of the bathroom. Stared at the loaded gun in her hand. The man in the studio had been right. The gun was a masterpiece. Old-style, eight-round handgun with, she suspected, a solid gold handle. Moses, her self-appointed guardian in the army, had taught her about guns. Pistols, revolvers, pump-action, double-action, shotguns, machine guns. She stood up, shaking off the memories. Placed the gun back in its hiding place. Finlay and Jason were bad men and in her heart she knew that Frankie was bad too. She wasn't taken in by his smiles and bright blue eyes. Only one thing would protect her and the others – the gun.

'There's something bloody wacky about that African kid,' Jason said.

He sat with Finlay and Frankie in Finlay's studio as the third day of January began to creep over London.

'She's just a kid in a foreign country, 'Frankie replied, stretching out his legs. 'Most probably shitting herself after what happened today.'

'Nah,' Jason persisted. 'Did you see her eyes? I didn't see no fear in her face. Now that ain't natural.'

'Don't matter if she's wacky or not,' Frankie replied. 'Because tomorrow her and the others will understand exactly what they've gotta do in Amsterdam in three days' time.'

'I'm forever blowing bubbles.
Pretty bubbles in the air.
They fly so high, nearly reach the sky.
Then like my dreams, they all fade and die . . .'

Jade sang West Ham's song as Frankie's motor parked up near Upton Park, the home of the football club. The others sat in the back, while Jade was in the passenger seat.

'Do you have to keep singing that tune? It ain't got no bass,' Amber said scornfully.

Jade twisted her head and just grinned at the other girl. 'Like you would say, Amber, take a chill pill, girl.'

Amber just kissed her teeth at that. Jade couldn't believe how happy she felt. She'd loved going to matches with her mum. Happy memories washed over her.

They all got out of the car. The girls looked around curiously. Of course, Jade had seen it all before. In the streets surrounding Upton Park, the residents were preparing for the match. The 1970s had seen running battles on the neighbouring streets between rival supporters and the police – plus any other likely lad from the East End who was up for a ruck. Those days were long gone, but some people had long memories and had pulled the curtains on their homes and gone shopping for the afternoon. Asian shopkeepers had brought in extra hands to enhance their security and the pubs had posted warnings about drunkenness and disorderly behaviour.

'I need you lot to do me a favour,' Frankie said as he moved towards the back of his car.

The girls looked at him curiously as he opened the boot and fished inside. He pulled out two rucksacks. Plain, black, nothing special.

'Jade and Ruby,' he called, holding the bags out towards them.

The girls took them without asking any questions, but their curiosity deepened. They didn't place them on their backs, just held them in their hands. Frankie got out two more identical bags and passed them to the two remaining girls.

'Come here,' he commanded softly.

He gathered the girls around until they stood in a circle. He placed his arms around the two girls on either side of him, Jade and Ruby, like they were his best mates. His voice dropped to a whisper. 'I've got a top job I need you to do for me. I need you to look after these bags. They're real important, OK? You don't open them and you don't let anyone else get their grubby mitts on them. Understand?' His eyes did a circuit, landing on each of them. The girls didn't move. Didn't say a thing. 'Is that clear?'

Frankie's voice hardened.

The girls rapidly nodded their heads. Frankie leaned back. Shook his natural cheeky smile back onto his face. 'Come on, ladies,' he said brightly. 'We've got a footie match to go to.'

'What do you reckon is in the bag?' Jade whispered to Amber, as they followed Frankie.

'We've done drugs and guns, so the next step must be a cut-up dead body.'

Jade gave Amber a startled look, then tightened her lips when she realised the other girl was joking.

Soon they were part of the broad river of claret-and-blue fans drifting towards the ground. Some of the men had children on their shoulders and there were more women than in former times, but it was still very 1970s nonetheless, very, very white and very, very male. Suddenly, without any prompting, the fans raised their hands above their heads and began chanting. They were suggesting that rival fans didn't have sexual partners at the moment.

Jade walked beside Frankie and Amber, while Ruby and Opal followed behind. Opal's eyes darted around, and by the fretful look in them the others could tell she wasn't enjoying the crowd. Ruby slipped her arm around her shoulder, pulling her close.

'This is like a bloody madhouse,' Amber muttered to Jade.

Jade turned a shining, bright face towards her. 'This is flamin' fantastic.'

She waved her arms in the air and joined in the chanting. Amber just rolled her eyes at her.

When the ground came into sight, Frankie stopped the girls.

'Right,' he started. 'I've gotta go and meet Jason because we're meeting someone who's connected to Jason's people in Sankura, which means I'm gonna miss the first half of the match. But you girls go in and have a good time and I'll catch up with you later.'

The girls looked back at him, alarmed.

'But we don't know where to go or what to do,' Amber said.

'Jade does, don't you, babe?' Reluctantly Jade nodded. Frankie tweaked Jade's nose, making her blush. 'This is Jade's old stomping ground.' His hand thrust into his inside pocket at the same time as West Ham's fans called out allegations about a rival player's wife and her preferences in the bedroom.

Frankie's hand came out holding the girls' tickets. 'Right, it's simple.' He handed each girl a ticket. 'You go up to the turnstiles, hand over your tickets and ask a steward where you go and sit. All the seats are marked, it couldn't be simpler.' He gave them one of his dazzling smiles. Said, 'Catch you later,' and weaved his way through the crowd away from them.

The girls were soon lost in the sea of people that packed more closely together as they approached the turnstiles. The police stood impassively by walls or sat on horses.

The girls soon entered the ground. A few minutes later they found their seats, four seats, near the end of the row, with a spare seat on each side. The girls placed their bags in their laps. The terraces filled up as the girls watched the crowd grow in front and behind them. The players came out. The referee blew his whistle. The match kicked off.

Jade soon joined in with the movement of the crowd, rising and falling, cheering and jeering, with the ebb and flow of the game. Ruby and Amber soon joined in. The only one who remained seated was Opal, who remained uncomfortable and tense. The opposing team were from the west of England, so there were soon plenty of arrogant cockney chants about combine harvesters, straw in people's hair and men marrying their own sisters.

'Ferti-lizer! Ferti-lizer Ferti-lizer! Ferti-lizer!' the crowd screamed at the opposing team.

Then West Ham scored. The crowd went ballistic, rising up like a tidal wave, roaring and cheering, jabbing their fingers at the opposing fans and screaming abuse at the country bumpkins who'd had the terrible bad luck not to be from London. The forty-five minutes passed in no time.

'This is better than going to a concert,' Amber said, her face gleaming with pleasure and excitement.

Jade looked tickled pink that Amber was having such a blinding time. 'Maybe Frankie could fix us up with a season ticket, he knows people, doesn't he?'

'Excuse me, ladies.'

Surprised, the girls looked sideways to find two men standing by the spare seat at the end of their row. Jade gulped when she saw the size of the men. They looked as big and as wide as human skyscrapers. They wore suits and ties and had ID tags hanging from their lapels.

'We're security,' one of the man continued slowly.

The men dropped their gazes. Settled them on the girls' bags.

Jade's arms instinctively wrapped themselves around the bag in her lap. One of the men pushed past them until he reached the spare seat beside Amber, then he sat down in it. The other man sat in the seat at the beginning of the row, next to Jade.

'Right,' the man next to Jade said. 'What have you got in your bags?'

Jade's heartbeat galloped inside her chest as her hands tightened on the rucksack. She waited for one of the others to speak, but no one said anything.

Finally Jade lied, 'Just some packed lunch that our mums gave us.'

'We need to take your bags,' the man next to Amber said.

Ruby began to raise her bag, ready to hand it over, but Jade's arm came up and grabbed hers. Frankie had told them not to give the bags to anyone.

'We ain't giving them to you,' Jade defiantly said. 'Ain't that right, everyone?'

The others girls all said 'yes' and held onto their bags. The hand of the man next to Jade flashed out and he grabbed her bag. She heaved the bag close to her chest and began to struggle with him.

'Let go of the bag,' he growled.

'No way,' she answered.

'Right,' the man said, standing up. 'You lot are coming with us.'

The girls stood up, conscious of the eyes of other people on them. They followed the man down the steps. Into the corridor downstairs. Past the crowds, heading for the loos and refreshments. Towards a closed door.

'We're gonna take you inside that room and search all of you, if you don't give us the bags.'

The girls looked at each other indecisively. Jade was the first to shake her head and the others quickly followed her action.

'Right, I warned you,' the man said as his hand reached for the door handle. Slowly he opened it. 'Inside,' he ordered.

'Maybe we should give him the bags?' Ruby asked, her voice wobbling.

'No, we can't,' Jade hissed. 'Because Fr . . .' She stopped speaking.

'I don't wanna get searched,' Amber said. 'Here . . .' She held out her bag to the other security man.

'Amber,' Jade screamed. But it was too late, the man already had the bag.

'You might as well give me the others,' the man said.

Slowly, one by one, the girls handed over their bags.

'Inside, the lot of you,' the man holding the door open said.

The girls shuffled past, with Jade taking the lead.

'What the heck is going on?' Jade said as she realised where she was. She was standing outside the football ground. Her words dried up when she realised who waited for her, with his arms folded.

Frankie.

And when he saw that Jade no longer had her bag, his face turned a furious red.

sixteen

'That was totally fucked up,' Frankie blasted.

The girls were back at St Nicholas. They stood in a tense line in front of Frankie.

'I told you not to let anyone get those bags,' Frankie continued in a stern voice.

'But they were security . . .' Jade lashed back.

'I don't care if they were the fucking Queen and her corgis. You had your instructions, which were pretty simple – don't let no one near those bags.'

Jade's teeth nipped into her bottom lip as fear rolled over her. She'd never seen Frankie this angry before.

'Sit down,' he ordered.

Each girl grabbed a chair. Frankie hunkered down in a chair as well, opposite them.

'Alright, I'll be straight up with you,' he said. 'That was a test.'

'A test?' Amber asked.

'To see how well you operated under pressure with security. Those geezers who nabbed you weren't real security, they were my mates. I doshed them up to give you a rough time.'

'But why?' This time the question came from Ruby.

'You all know that the most crucial part of getting the money to the people in Sankura is the job in Amsterdam in three days' time. Mr Miller and the other kids are gonna be with you on this trip to Amsterdam. Now this job is gonna net the people in Sankura a wagon-load of cash. But there won't be no dosh if you lot muck up at immigration . . .'

'Immigration?' Amber piped in.

Ruby gave her an exasperated look. 'When you visit another country you have to go through passport control and immigration. They check your papers and sometimes your luggage . . .'

'I ain't stupid,' Amber retorted furiously. 'I do know what immigration is. My mum told me all about it when she and the others used to smuggle diamonds through the airport.'

'Diamonds?' The word shot out of Opal's mouth.

The others looked at her as if she had two heads. Opal tightened her lips and dipped her head down.

Frankie's hand whipped down and grabbed one of the bags he'd given the girls, which was at the foot of the table, and slammed it onto the tabletop.

'When you go to Amsterdam each of you will have a bag. You'll be carrying stuff just like you did today at the footie match. You'll be given instructions to meet someone in Amsterdam. When you meet this person you will exchange your bag with another bag they will give you. The bag they give you will look exactly the same as the one you carried from England. Then all you've gotta do is bring the bag back. But . . .'

The girls looked expectantly at him.

'It ain't as easy as it sounds. If you get stopped and searched by immigration they'll find the gear. Which means that there'll be no money going to Sankura. Which means your old ladies will be fucked. So it's real important that you understand how you behave if someone stops you.'

Suddenly he thrust out of his chair. The girls looked up at him. 'Who fancies themselves as a bit of an actor?'

Amber's hand immediately shoved into the air. 'Come here,' he told her.

The girl nervously followed his instructions. 'Alright. This is what we're gonna do,' Frankie started. 'I'm gonna pretend to be someone in security at the airport. And Amber, you're gonna be a passenger coming back with her bag. OK?'

Amber nodded.

'Madam, why were you in Amsterdam?'

Amber's tongue nervously flicked against her lip.

'First problem,' Frankie said, giving Amber no time to speak. 'You never show them that you're shitting yourself. A classic sign of nerves is when people rub their tongue against their lip. It means that your mouth is dry, which means you must be as nervous as fuck. Always keep your body relaxed and make sure you look them in the eye. So look me in the eye, babe.'

Amber stared back at him. But her eyes were unsteady. Moving from side to side.

'No, no, no. Keep your eyes steady.' Frankie waited until Amber did what he asked.

'That's it. Good girl. Let's start again.'

Frankie repeated his question. Amber looked him straight in the eye and answered, 'Well, I come on this plane, didn't I, and I was sorta on a trip thingamajig . . .'

'Stop,' Frankie ordered.

A deep sigh pushed out of Amber's mouth.

'First of all, your voice sounds like you've just finished running the London marathon. Always keep it nice and slow and calm. Let the tone of your voice tell them that you've got nothing to hide. And you can't be saying shit like you just did to them. Always have your story worked out. Something like, "I've been on a trip with the people from the home I live in." Simple. Now let's try again.'

So they tried again. 'Great.' Frankie gave Amber a big encouraging smile. 'Let's just say I'm still suspicious of you, so I say, "What's in your bag?"'

Amber thrust her hip to the side, 'Dunno mate. Someone gave it to me.'

Frankie threw his hands in the air.

'But that's true,' Amber shouted.

Frankie pushed his hand into his hair. 'I know it's true, you know it's true, but they don't know that and that's how it's gotta stay. You just say, 'It's full of things that I bought in your wonderful city, sir. Amsterdam is a fantastic place.' See, that way you pretend that there's nothing funny in your bag and you big-up his city. So, let's try again and this time keep your body nice and straight and respectful.'

They practised three more times until Frankie was satisfied with the results. He finally let Amber retake her seat.

'What I want each of you to do is to practise each night together. We've got three more days before you lot hit Amsterdam. Don't forget that if you mess up and get caught, the Dutch police will sling you in the slammer. And you know what that means? It's your mums who are gonna pay the price.'

So they practised what they had to do for the Amsterdam job. The night before the trip, Frankie delivered the rucksacks. The girls all sat around the table in the room where they packed the Es. On the table next to the bags was a map, a bundle of guilders, secured with an elastic band, and a mobile phone.

'These,' he pointed to the bags, 'are the same ones that you had at the footie match. Inside are magazines because it's gonna look strange to Security at Heathrow if you go through with sod-all in your bags.'

He picked up the map. 'Now this is a map of Amsterdam city centre. When you get off the plane I want you to travel with Mr Miller and the rest of the kids to the city centre, but then go your own way. The map is just in case you get lost or need to find somewhere.'

His gaze settled on the phone. 'Jade, I want you to carry this. Our contact in Amsterdam will ring you and tell you where to meet them. I don't know what time it will be, so keep the mobile in a place you can hear it. The cash is in case you need to get a taxi. Does everyone understand?'

All the girls nodded, except Opal.

'Make sure you get a good night's kip. I want you lot up and ready downstairs with the other kids in the morning bright and early at eight. Make sure you keep this,' he touched his mouth, 'zipped around the other kids.'

Then he instructed Jade to put the bags and other items some-where. She stashed them in a pile under the dressing table.

Frankie stood up. 'If this all goes nice and smooth, I guarantee that your mums will be back in a couple of days.'

As soon as Frankie left, Amber shoved an E in her mouth.

'You're totally crazy, you are,' Jade said to the other girl, shaking her head. 'You better not take any of that shit with you tomorrow because if you get searched at Heathrow and they find them, Jason's gonna make sure you're dead meat.'

After the others went to bed, Jade prayed hard that the job would go bang as planned. The thought of seeing Nikki again sent a thrill through her.

As she got up and blew the candle out, an anguished moan echoed from the other side of the room. She stopped. Scanned her eyes through the dark in the direction of the noise. It came again. It was definitely coming from either Ruby or Amber's bed. Jade groaned. Not fucking Ruby crying her eyes out again.

'What's that?' Ruby's voice called through the dark.

Jade swung her head towards Amber's bed, realising where the moans were coming from. She ran across the room to Amber. She found her flat on her back, covers pushed aside, her hands clutching her stomach as she groaned loudly, convulsed in pain.

'Amber, what is it?' Jade asked as she dropped to her knees beside the bed.

The other girl opened her mouth to answer, but instead of words a fountain of pain gushed out.

Jade turned sharply towards Ruby. 'Get the light on now.'

Ruby galloped out of bed. The light hit. Revealed Amber. The breath stuck in Jade's throat when she saw the other girl. Amber's face was awash with sweat and tears, her head bobbing erratically from side to side. The pain skinned her lips back and fired her eyes into liquid jet pools. One hand tore into the white sheet while the other balled and twisted into her tummy.

'Amber?' Jade leaned her face closer with her question.

Suddenly the middle section of Amber's body arched into the air. She let out a powerful scream. Her convulsion and scream pushed

Jade back. Then Amber's body collapsed back down. Her head lolled listlessly to the side. Jade gingerly touched Amber's forehead.

'What's wrong with her?' Ruby asked, now standing on the other side of the bed.

'Shit, I dunno.' Jade's voice was frantic. Helpless.

Opal stepped forward. Crouched by Jade. Peered hard into Amber's listless eyes. Opal twisted her head back towards Jade. She pinched two fingers together and hurriedly moved them to her open mouth as if she were eating.

'What is she doing?' Ruby asked.

'Fuck knows,' Jade answered.

But Jade carried on looking as the other girl continued with her mime.

'Shit, the E tabs,' Jade said, realising what Opal was trying to tell them. 'I bloody well told her this would get her one day.' She flicked her head towards Ruby. 'I think she's taken too many, either that or they were a bad lot.'

'Does that mean she's going to die?' Ruby said slowly as her hand clutched her chest. 'Shit,' Jade cried. 'We need to sort this out. The job's only hours away. Fucking hell, if we don't get her moving and Jason finds out, he's gonna slaughter us. And our mums . . .' She knew she was getting hysterical, but the thought of what might happen if they didn't help Amber was too horrible to bear.

'I saw this on the telly once,' Ruby cut in. 'We need to turn her onto her side.'

The other girls helped her move Amber.

'Now what do we do?' Ruby said.

'Dunno.' Jade's breathing was coming hard. 'We've got no choice, we're gonna have to get help.'

'Where from?' Ruby replied.

Suddenly Jade legged it it to the window. Pulled up the blind. Her gaze found the building in the garden. She let out a breath of relief when she saw the lights were on.

'I'll be back,' she shot at Ruby and Opal as she ran for the door.

She ran down the corridor. Down the outside stairs. Across the damp grass in the garden. Finally she reached the building at the back. She could hear voices and noises inside. Thank God, she thought. She grabbed the handle and pushed the heavy door. Her eyes bulged when she saw what was happening inside. One of the girls, who had sneaked out with them on New Year's Eve, was on her knees in front of a short man with his trousers around his ankles. Jade's hand clamped over her mouth in horror when she saw what the girl was doing with her mouth. Grunts coming from the other side of the room caught her attention. On a bed, two bodies moved together. Near the bed, fixed to the wall, were manacles and chains.

'What the hell . . . ?' one of the occupants of the bed said.

The two faces of the people on the bed swung towards Jade. She gulped when she saw the faces of Mr Miller and Sam.

'Sorry . . . Sorry . . .' The words tumbled out of Jade's mouth as she trembled, backing away.

She twisted around. And ran like there were flames licking at her feet. Her mind rocked in horror at what she'd seen. Men were taking kids into that building and . . . and . . . her mind couldn't finish the sentence. As she neared the steps, a hand clamped down on her shoulder from behind. She jumped. Screamed. Terrified as the hand twisted her around. A furious Mr Miller, wearing boxer shorts, stared at her.

'What were you doing coming here?'

'Please just get Frankie,' she said, batting his hand off her shoulder.

'Why the bloody hell should I?'

'If you don't get him one of us ain't gonna make the trip tomorrow.'

The man swore. 'Get back up to the fourth floor and I'll get him.'

Jade dashed back upstairs. She slammed the door shut. Leaned back on it and began to cry. She didn't want to stay in this evil place any more. Then she remembered Amber. She pulled herself straight and ran back to the room. Ruby and Opal were still gathered around Amber.

'Did you get someone?' Ruby asked.

Jade wanted to tell them what she'd seen in the garden, but she knew it would freak Ruby right out. So instead she nodded her head and said, 'Frankie's coming.'

'He'd better get here soon because I don't know how long she's going to last.'

'What's going on?' Frankie asked as he came through the door twenty minutes later. His face was pale and his hair tangled as if he'd rushed through the streets of London. The girls were sat on the bed next to Amber. Tight and tiny breaths blew from her exhausted body. He strode towards them. He looked down at Amber. Shook his head. Crouched by the bed. Touched Amber's forehead.

'She feels like shit,' he said as his hand fell away.

Silence.

'What's she eaten?' he asked.

All the girls avoided his gaze. Bent their heads.

'It is something she's eaten, ain't it?'

Silence.

'What's going on here, ladies?'

Silence.

Finally Jade raised her head and answered, 'She's been nabbing the pills.'

'What pills?'

'The Es.'

Frankie shot to his feet. 'You're fucking kidding me.'

Frankie couldn't believe what he was hearing. If the girl wasn't so sick he would stand her up and bitch-slap that lying mouth clean off her face. Because she couldn't keep her tea-leafing hands off his gear she might screw his operation up. He knew he could do it with just one black girl as the decoy, but two would make it safer. No, he was gonna have to get Amber back on her feet.

Without warning, he grabbed Jade by the arm. Hauled her to her feet. She stared into his face. His face was mottled and swollen with mounting rage.

'This can't be happening hours away from the job in Amsterdam.' His fingers dug deeper into her arm. 'How long has she been taking that shit?'

'From the beginning. I told her to knock it on the head. . . .'

He hauled Jade closer and whispered, 'Of all the people, I'd have expected you to tell me. I thought we were mates?'

Abruptly he let Jade go. Ran his hand through his hair as the anger shot from his mouth. 'She's gonna need to get her stomach cleaned out . . .'

'You mean take her to a hospital?' Ruby asked with relief.

'No.' Frankie looked at each girl in turn. 'We're gonna have to get that shit out of her stomach ourselves.'

seventeen

All the girls looked at him, shocked. Frankie tore off his jacket.
Rolled up his sleeves. 'There should be a basin, next door, under the
sink, and check the cupboard to see if there's a bottle of oil,' he
ordered Jade.

Less than a minute later Jade was back with a green bowl and a
bottle of vegetable oil.

'Give me the oil.'

Jade gave it to him. He unscrewed the top and tipped a generous
amount of oil over two of his fingers.

'Right, you and you.' He pointed at Ruby and Opal. 'Lean her head
over the bed.'

The girls shifted Amber until Ruby was holding her head over the
bed.

'And you.' He pointed at Jade. 'Hold the basin under her mouth.'

Jade got on her knees in position. Frankie knelt by Jade. He
grabbed Amber's jaw and opened her slack mouth. Slowly he pushed
his oiled fingers down her throat. His fingers whipped out as Amber
began to gag. But she didn't vomit. He pushed his fingers into her
throat once more. Once again she gagged, but didn't vomit.

'Shit,' Frankie exploded, as he reared back on his knees. He wiped
the sweat from his forehead. Turned to Ruby. 'Fill a glass with warm
water next door and pour loads of salt in it and find a can opener.'
Ruby nodded and ran out of the room. Frankie turned to Jade. 'Get a
couple of quid from my jacket and run to the shop at the corner and
buy some cat food . . .'

Cat food, Jade thought in confusion.

'But the shop will be shut.'

Frankie flicked his wrist up and checked the time on his watch. 'It shuts at ten. You've got two minutes.'

Jade ran through the dark streets, knowing that her friend's life depended on it. She almost tripped when her foot hit a can she hadn't seen. The can clattered along the ground as she motored forward. She twisted into the main street. Saw the shop, but it was bathed in darkness. Shit, she was too late, it was already shut. Then she saw a figure coming out of the doorway.

'Yesss!' she screamed, running forward.

She reached the figure, an older man, with keys in his hand and wearing a flat cap.

'Mister . . .'

'Kid, I'm shut.'

'Please, mister, all I want is a tin of cat food.'

'Cat food?' He gave her a suspicious look. 'Have you been drinking, young lady . . . ?'

Jade did the one thing her mum had taught her that men hated – she started bawling her head off.

'Please, please, mister,' she said between sobs.

'Alright, alright.' He pointed his finger at her. 'You stay put.'

Her eyes dried quickly as the man went and came back in less than half a minute. He handed over a small can of cat food.

'Thanks,' she said, taking the tin. She offered him a quid, but he waved his hands at her, saying, 'Just get yourself home.' As she ran, she heard him mutter, 'St Nicholas, the patron saint of kids, what a soddin' joke . . .'

'Open it up,' Frankie shouted at Jade as soon as she came back.

The opener Ruby had brought back from next door was on the table, next to the glass of salt water. Jade quickly did what Frankie asked. Jade reared back, her stomach rolling when the smell hit her. It smelt like rotten meat that had been decaying in the heat of the sun for days.

'Help me take her into the bathroom,' Frankie told Ruby and Opal. 'Jade, you bring the salt water and cat food.'

They lifted Amber from the bed and tried to get her to walk, but her legs collapsed under her. Frankie scooped her into his arms. When they entered the bathroom, he settled her, on her knees, by the edge of the bath.

'You two,' he instructed Ruby and Opal again. 'Hold her up so she doesn't fall.'

As the girls settled on either side of Amber, he told Jade, 'Listen carefully, this is what we're gonna do. I'm gonna make her drink the salt water and when I tell you hold the cat food under her nose.'

Jade handed him the glass. He tipped Amber's head back. Opened her mouth. Tipped a good amount of salt water into her mouth. Then used his other hand to clamp her mouth shut. Amber jerked as she swallowed the water. Her eyes bulged as it went down. Frankie tipped her head forward. 'Now,' he shouted at Jade.

She rushed forward. Placed the can under Amber's nose. Amber's eyes widened even more when the revolting smell hit her nostrils. A choking sound came out of her mouth as her stomach convulsed. Her cheeks bulged as she began to vomit into the bath. Over and over she was sick into the bath. Then she sagged wearily against Ruby. 'We do it again until what she chucks up looks clear,' Frankie said.

So for the next fifteen minutes, they used salt water and cat food to clean the poison out of Amber's system. Finally Frankie told them to take a floppy Amber back to her bed.

'Make sure she's on her side,' he told the girls. 'And you lot are gonna have to take it in turns to stay up because you need to keep feeding her water.'

Frankie swayed as he found a chair. He pulled a packet of fags from his pocket. Lit up. Took two strong puffs.

'Is she gonna be alright?' Jade asked from her kneeling position next to Amber's bed. He gazed at them, with steady eyes, through the gliding smoke. 'She better had be because if all four of you ain't ready to hit the road to Amsterdam later on, not only are your old ladies gonna be fucked, but you will be as well.'

'You ain't gonna grass us up to Jason?' Jade pleaded.

Frankie said nothing for a few seconds. 'I don't want to, but if she ain't up come the morning light, I ain't gonna have much choice.'

Opal sprang to her feet.

'Where the heck is she going?' Frankie asked.

Opal started moving to the bathroom like she didn't understand.

'She's just going to the Ladies,' she heard Jade answer Frankie.

She kept moving. Reached the door. Pulled it open. Stepped inside. The room reeked of Amber's vomit. Quietly she closed and locked the door. Now she moved quickly. Towards the porcelain stand of the sink. She stretched inside and pulled out the gun. She sat on the edge of the bath. Checked how many bullets were in the gun. Eight.

Enough to plug four slugs each into Frankie and Jason.

If the men tried to fuck them up, she would be ready.

She placed the gun back in its hiding place.

'She'll be alright,' Frankie said, just after six in the morning.

He'd stayed with the girls while the night changed to morning. As he'd instructed, the girls took it in turns to stay up and look after Amber.

He looked down at a sleeping Amber and knew that the worst had passed. He still couldn't believe that she'd had the nerve of the Devil to nick his gear. Thank God he knew about the cat food and salt water trick. He'd learned that one off his bitch of a mum. She always kept a tin of cat food in the cupboard for those times she got so boozed up she needed to pump her tummy clean. But of course she'd been too bladdered to do it, so from the age of five, he'd had to help her.

'Get her up,' he told a tired Jade. 'And get her washed and ready. Then you all need to get ready. Mr Miller and the others will be waiting downstairs for you at seven.'

Jade helped a shaking Amber get ready in the bathroom.

'I didn't mean to make trouble,' Amber croaked.

'It don't matter,' Jade whispered back as she helped put Amber's pullover on.

Suddenly Amber's hand grabbed the other girl's arm. She stared at Jade with tears filling her eyes. 'I only took them because I was scared. I miss my mum.'

Amber's hand trembled as it dropped from Jade's arm. A shaking smile danced across Jade's lips as she pushed her hand into Amber's hair and gently soothed the other girl. 'I know. We're all shitting it. But it don't matter now because it's all gonna be over soon. Our mums are coming home and don't you forget it.'

The plane took off from Heathrow at eleven. Touched down at Schiphol airport at three minutes before midday. The girls detached themselves from the rest of the group when they hit the city centre and strolled by the canal, anxiously waiting for the phone call that would kick off the job. The call came through as the girls were drifting towards the red-light district.

The others looked at Jade. Anxiously she pulled the mobile out of her pocket.

'Yeah?'

The voice that replied was a woman's, with an accent that reminded Jade of Opal's. 'Take the first taxi that comes along and tell it to take you to the McDonald's on the Haag Straat.'

The line went dead.

The others all peered at Jade. As she opened her mouth to tell them what the instructions had been, she saw a taxi coming their way. She leapt to the kerb and stuck out her hand.

'What you doing?' Amber asked, her voice still sounding very croaky from her ordeal the previous night.

Jade ignored her as the taxi slowed down. The driver wound down the window. He wore a baseball cap low over his face and shades.

'McDonald's. The Haag Straat.'

The driver nodded.

'Come on, you lot,' Jade instructed, opening one of the doors.

The others piled in behind her. None of them took their rucksacks from their backs. Jade gazed nervously at the others. Then she spoke. 'We're on.'

*   *   *

'Amber, how you holding up?' Jade asked about five minutes into the journey.

'I feel like crap, but I'm OK.'

Amber pulled out her bottle of water and took a long pull.

'We'll be home before you . . .'

'This ain't right,' Ruby cut across Jade's words. Her face peered out of the window.

'What you chatting on about?' Jade threw back.

Ruby's face whipped back to face the others in the taxi. 'I've just seen a sign that said Haag Straat, but we're going in the opposite direction.'

Suddenly the locks on the door clicked. Startled, the girls all looked at each other. Jade leaned over to the transparent partition that divided the back from the driver.

'Hold up, mister, you're going the wrong way.'

No response. She banged against the partition, but the driver still didn't respond.

'Jade, what's going on?' This time the anxious question was asked by Amber.

'I don't know.' Jade's answer was frantic. 'Try the doors.'

Opal and Ruby fought with the door handles, but couldn't open them. Suddenly Jade pulled off her bag. Swung it at the window nearest to her, but the glass didn't break. Then she realised that it must be shatterproof. Shit.

'What we gonna do?' a terrified Amber asked.

Jade's body jacked back deep into her seat, her chest heaving. 'We're stuck. There ain't nothin' we can do. But whatever the driver's got up his sleeve, there's only one of him and four of us.'

The taxi drove out beyond the city limits. The girls sat on the edge of their seats, in the back. The taxi did a sharp left into a street dominated by a four-storey car park. It shot down a ramp into the underground section of the car park. The light faded as the taxi pitched the girls into the dark.

'Right,' Jade whispered. 'This is what we're gonna do. As soon as the doors are opened we do a runner.'

The others nodded back. There were only a few cars in the car park. The taxi eased into a bay beside a black jeep with tinted windows. The engine died. The girls' heartbeats slammed inside their chests. But the locks on the doors remained down.

A door slammed somewhere outside. The click of heels sounded against the concrete floor. Jade peered desperately outside, but she couldn't see who it was. Then the passenger door of the taxi was pulled open.

The girls were startled to see a young black woman take the passenger seat in the taxi. The woman turned to face them. She was small and wore a red Arsenal baseball cap, black jeans and sweatshirt and a long leather coat.

'I hope the ride here didn't frighten you,' the woman said softly as she smiled. Jade realised that the voice was the same as the woman's on the phone. 'But let me reassure you that there is no need to be scared. I just like to do things my way. Let's step out of the car, so we can conclude our business.'

The doors were unlocked. Jade and the others got out of the car with their bags. The woman walked towards the back end of the black jeep.

'Nice wheels,' Amber said, glowing, showing her old animation for the first time that day. The woman responded with a slight nod of appreciation. She opened the back of the jeep. Turned back to them and said, 'Give me your bags.'

Each girl handed their bag over. The woman placed the bags inside the jeep. Her hand came back out holding identical-looking bags.

'Which of you are Jade and Ruby?'

Surprised that the woman knew their names, both girls nodded. She passed each one a bag. Then she turned back to the jeep and pulled out two other bags, once again identical to the ones the girls had brought. She passed them to Opal and Ruby. Suddenly Opal started to speak to the woman in a language Jade had never heard before. The woman threw Opal a startled look. Then she spoke back to Opal in the same language. Opal pressed on with more words. The woman replied. Whatever Opal asked next made the woman's mouth momentarily clam up.

'Please,' Opal begged, taking a step closer to the woman.

The woman looked at her for a few seconds, then she nodded her head and replied in a quickfire voice. Whatever she said made Opal gasp. Opal quickly flashed her eyes over the others. Stopped at Jade. The expression on Opal's face made Jade shiver.

'What's going on?' Amber whispered.

Jade shrugged her shoulders.

Opal spoke to the woman one more time. This time a hard look covered the woman's face. She didn't speak. Opal nodded her head as if the woman had answered. The woman quickly moved away from Opal towards the driver's side of the car. She slipped inside. Closed the door. The girls stepped back. The noise of the engine rumbled in the air. The woman lowered the window. Pushed her head out and said, 'The taxi will take you to the airport. Tell my friend in London that Major Omote said it was good doing business with him.'

Opal drew in a sharp, audible breath when the woman said 'Major Omote'. The car roared off, leaving the girls, with their new bags, staring after it.

'Opal,' Ruby addressed the other girl. 'What . . . were . . . you . . . talking . . . about?'

Opal dipped her head down like she couldn't bear to look Ruby in the eye. She didn't answer the question.

'My bag feels well heavy,' Amber said. 'Wonder what's in it?'

'Ain't our business,' Jade said. 'Come on, we need to make tracks to the airport.'

Opal was still reeling from the shock of what the woman had told her as the taxi took them to the airport. She would have to tell the others, but that meant revealing that she spoke English. She couldn't do that. Not yet. Now she knew the truth she wished that she had brought the gun with her.

The mobile that Jade carried began to ring, cutting off Opal's thoughts.

*   *   *

'Yeah?' Jade said.

'It's Frankie. Did you make the exchange?'

'Yeah. It was a bit weird, though . . .'

'Forget that, all that matters is that it's done. Right, listen up. Put the mobile on speakerphone so the others can hear.'

Jade followed his instructions, placing the phone on her lap.

'Well done, ladies, the first part of the operation is complete. When you get to the airport head for the departure hall, where the other kids and Mr Miller will be waiting for you. Then you'll be ready to go through passport control and security. Don't forget how I told you to behave. Remember, you're part of a group of kids so they're unlikely to stop you. Now you need to listen carefully. There are two things you've gotta do. First thing is, Jade, dump the mobile at the airport. Pull it apart and chuck it in a bin. When you get in line I want you to be in this order – Amber and Opal. Jade and Ruby. If any of you get pulled over I want you to get as mouthy as hell.' The line went dead.

eighteen

Against a background noise of jet engines accelerating, braking and climbing into the sky above, the girls stood at passport control in departures. The mobile was long gone, in a bin in the toilets. The girls stood in line with the other children, in the order Frankie had told them to be. Amber, Opal, Jade and Ruby. The line moved. They got closer. Ruby accidentally caught the eye of one of the cops, who held a submachine gun. Heart beating like the clappers, she hurriedly looked away.

'Ruby,' Jade whispered urgently, when she saw what the other girl was doing. 'Stop looking jumpy. Cool it, alright.'

Ruby swallowed, not answering. She pulled out her inhaler, put it to her lips and nervously inhaled. She knew she shouldn't do it, but she couldn't help herself; she turned to look at the cop again. She almost cried out because he was still giving her the eye.

'They know,' she whispered frantically to Jade, her hand tightening around her inhaler. 'We're going to get caught and flung into prison.'

Her statement spooked Jade. 'What are you rabbiting on about?'

'The cops are staring at me.'

Jade's heartbeat galloped in her chest. Bouncing bollocks, what were they going to do if Ruby was right? They both turned to look back at the cop at the same time. He wasn't staring at Ruby any more.

Jade leaned close to Ruby's ear. 'You've gotta stay calm or we're all gonna get nicked.'

Jade turned back to the front just as Amber reached the desk at passport control. The woman behind the desk remained stony faced as she took Amber's passport. The woman flicked to the back of the passport. Her eyes rolled up to study Amber's face. Then she looked down, as if she was reading something on her computer screen. She looked back up and over Amber's shoulder at Opal. Then she stared back at Amber and gave her the third degree.

'Did you pack these bags yourselves?'

Amber tried desperately to remember what Frankie had taught them. Remain calm. Give the woman a steady look in the eye. Although she was still feeling weak from the night before, she carried out Frankie's instructions perfectly by saying 'yes' with a smile.

'Not carrying much, are you?'

The unexpected question made Amber bite her lip.

'No.'

The woman looked deep into Amber's eyes. Then she handed back the passport with not another word. Amber moved to join the security line for the baggage check as Opal stepped up to the desk. Mr Miller appeared at her side, from where he'd been hovering, near a security guard, supervising the line of children.

'She doesn't speak English,' he explained to the woman.

The woman gave Opal's passport the once-over and handed it back. The woman dealt with Jade's and Ruby's passports equally quickly. As they moved away, the woman picked up a walkie-talkie on her desk and whispered into it.

The girls were back in their order in the line for the baggage check. The children ahead of Amber and Opal began to put their bags on the conveyor belt for the X-ray machine. Amber's turn soon came. As she began to remove her bag, a security officer appeared, accompanied by another man in plain clothes, blocking Amber's way.

'Excuse me, ladies.' He addressed both Amber and Opal. 'Could you step this way, please?'

Mr Miller ran forward and asked, 'What's going on? We're going to miss our flight.'

'We can delay the flight for ten minutes. But we must speak with these two girls. This won't take a moment . . .' Then he added '. . . hopefully.'

Amber and Opal were marched away, towards a long table against a wall. Amber anxiously looked back at Jade.

'I told you they knew,' Ruby whispered to Jade as they approached the security barrier.

'Just shut it,' Jade rasped back.

She was shitting herself. Amber and Opal had been pulled up and she knew that it was going to be her and Ruby next. She reached the X-ray machine. Her hands shook as she pulled the bag off her back. She looked into the eyes of the security woman standing near by. Smiled. Used one hand to start placing the bag on the machine. She anxiously watched as the bag slid onto the belt. It started to move. As the bag slipped out of view, a voice yelled out, 'This is racist.'

Jade and the security woman looked in the direction of the shout. They stared at a vocal Amber standing at the table with Opal and the two security men.

'You're only doing this because we're black.'

The man whose job it was to check the X-ray machine stood up to watch. Jade's bag came out the other end.

'Quick, Ruby,' Jade whispered to her, seeing that the man was distracted. 'Sling your bag on.'

A sweating Ruby followed her instruction. The girls pushed their way through to the other side. Jade breathed a grateful sigh when she saw her and Ruby's bags waiting at the end of the moving belt. They grabbed them. As they moved to join the other children, Ruby asked, 'What about Opal and Amber?'

'We ain't leaving without them.'

'I'm sorry for this further check ladies,' the plainclothed security man said to Opal and Amber.

Amber's voice got louder. 'Just because we're black you think we're running drugs? That's what this is about really, ain't it?'

The man looked very uncomfortable, but he replied, 'Not at all. This is just a routine security check.'

'Then how come we were the only ones pulled out from all the other kids? I'll tell you why, because of our brown faces. Everyone told me not to come on the trip because Holland's a racist country.'

The man looked upset by her accusation, but he nodded at the other security man, instructing him to search their bags.

Amber's heart thumped as their bags were turned out on the table. She knew that they were going to find whatever Frankie's contact had put in their bags. The contents of both bags were spread out – teen magazines, sweets, make-up and cans of fizzy drinks. Amber's eyes zoomed in on the drinks. That was where whatever the gear was must be hidden. Her anxiety level hit the top of the scale when she saw the dogs and their handler. Two of them, decked out in coats like they were ready for a winter walk.

The dogs jumped on the table and sniffed around the contents and inside the now empty bags. They checked everything. Then they went round again to be sure they hadn't missed anything. When they were satisfied there wasn't the telltale odour of drugs, they jumped off the table and stood to attention.

Amber sent Opal a curious look. There was nothing in their bags? What the fuck was going on?

The dogs were directed to use their talents to sniff the girls' clothes. Knowing that the mutts would find sweet FA on them, Amber got cocky and bold. She spread her arms wide, looked directly into the dog's eyes and said, 'Bring it on, Rover.'

When the dogs had no more luck, one of the staff whispered something to the plainclothes man in Dutch. He shook his head, and replied in English, 'Body search? I don't think that will be necessary.'

He turned to the girls and pretended it was all in a day's work, 'OK. Well, enjoy your flight . . .'

A shaken Amber caught his eye and said with a sneer, 'Klu Klux Klan . . .'

'They should be high in the sky, on their way back now,' Frankie said, eyeballing his watch.

He sat with Jason and Finlay playing cards at the table where the girls packed the drugs. The TV hummed in the background. Frankie smiled as he placed his poker hand on the table. As Finlay went to lay his hand down, he caught the breaking news headline running across the bottom of the TV screen.

'Shit,' he yelled, jumping up, his eyes glued to the screen.

Frankie twisted around to the telly and nearly fell out of his chair when he saw the headline. He swiftly took out his mobile as he continued to stare at the headline with disbelief. The call connected. He swung angrily away from the telly.

'Omote, I told you to make this a reality tomorrow.'

'Tomorrow, today – in a place like Sankura these things can sometimes mean the same thing,' Major Omote replied.

'I get it, so now you're already spending the cash you made from the drugs you don't give a fuck?'

'Yes, the adoration of money has always done terrible things to my memory. Be satisfied, my friend, that it has been done as you asked. Anything else is not my problem.'

The line went dead.

'Cunt,' Frankie raged as he hurled the phone at the TV. His chest elevated in anger. Then his breathing slowed. Became easy. Still gazing at the telly he said, 'Plans have changed. I can't afford for anything to go tits up if the girls see that news report.' He jumped up. 'When that plane lands I want you both to be there to pick the girls up.'

Opal and Amber rushed past security, knowing that their flight must've been called. Amber checked the departures monitor to see what gate their flight was at. When she found it she grabbed Opal's hand and said, 'We need to rush.' When they finally reached the gate, they found an anxious Jade and Ruby waiting for them.

'Thank God,' Jade said. 'What happened?'

'I'll explain on the plane,' Amber said, as they rushed forward. 'But we didn't have nothing in our bags.'

'What?' a startled Jade asked.

'Dunno what's going on here, girl, but our bags were alright, which means you and Ruby must be carrying the hard stuff.'

Open mouthed, Jade and Ruby stared back at her.

They got on the plane and braved the dirty looks of the other passengers, who blamed them for the delay, and a nervous-looking Mr Miller. Exhausted, the girls threw themselves into their seats, in the row at the back of the plane.

'So you think me and Ruby are the carriers?' Jade asked Amber.

'Must be. Don't worry, though, you've done the hard bit. All you and Ruby have got to do is go through the "nothing to declare" channel at Heathrow. That should be a piece of piss.'

Jade prayed that she was right as the plane took off. Ten minutes into the flight Amber said, 'I don't feel too good.'

Ruby took out the water from Amber's bag. Helped her to drink. Noticing the sweat on Amber's face, Jade pulled out the free newspaper in the pocket of her seat, intending to fan Amber and help cool her down. As she folded the newspaper, the headline on the front caught her eye.

'Ohmygod,' shot out of her mouth after she had read it.

The newspaper fluttered into her lap.

'What is it?' Amber asked.

Jade tried to speak, but couldn't. Amber grabbed the newspaper. Read: 'Brits Executed in Africa . . .'

nineteen

Jade's fingers pressed tight against her lips because she knew she was going to scream. She could feel the sound coming up from her belly. The newspaper must've got it wrong. Frankie had promised them that their mums were coming home.

The sound was banging inside her chest.

Her beloved Nikki was dead. Wasn't coming home. Wouldn't ever read her a bedtime story. They wouldn't ever dance around the room together to Nikki's favourite track, 'Tainted Love'.

The sound was pushing against the back of her throat.

'Does that mean my mum isn't coming home?' a dazed Ruby stuttered.

Jade swiftly looked at her, but knew that if she answered the scream would come diving out of her mouth. Ruby's face crumbled as she began to sob. As her sobs grew louder people turned around to stare at her. Opal pulled her into a hard embrace, muffling her grief. Suddenly Jade felt Amber's head slip onto her shoulder as the other girl sobbed softly and muttered, 'What we gonna do? What we gonna do?' Jade leaned her head against the other girl's as her own tears began to fall.

An anxious Mr Miller appeared. 'Is everything OK?'

OK? The word swam in Jade's mind. She looked back at him. Was he fucking nuts? How could everything be OK when her mum was dead? Then she looked at him in a completely different light. He was a friend of The Geezer's, wasn't he? What if Jason had known all along what was going to happen? Jade pushed her head straight. Held back her tears.

'Everything's cool. It's just their time of the month, you know what I mean?'

Mr Miller gave them one last anxious look, then was gone.

'Right, you lot,' she said to the others. 'We ain't got time to cry, not now anyway. Dry your eyes, we've gotta talk.'

The others looked at her. The only one who remained composed was Opal.

'Do you think Jason knew about this?' Jade whispered.

'He said he was helping our mums,' a distraught Ruby replied.

'But do we believe him?' Jade shot back.

Amber answered. 'What, you think that he knew that our mums were gonna get killed all this time and he's been using us to make money for him? Bring back whatever goodies you and Ruby have got in your bags?'

'But what if his friends in Sankura tried to help but couldn't stop the . . .' Ruby's voice faltered. 'The execution?'

'He . . . never . . . going . . . to . . . help . . . you.'

Stunned, they all looked across at Opal as they heard her halting, deeply accented voice.

'Bloody hell, you speak English,' a stunned Jade said.

Opal nodded.

'Why didn't you tell me?' Ruby said.

'How do you know Jason weren't gonna help us?' Jade jumped in, pushing Ruby's question aside.

Opal let out a heavy sigh. Then she spoke slowly, trying to remember as much English as possible. 'The woman . . . Amsterdam . . . from Sankura. I ask her if your mothers OK. She tell me they already dead. . .'

'Why didn't you flamin' well tell us?' Jade raged.

The words caught in Opal's throat. She knew how hurt her friends were, but she had to tell them the truth. 'I do not want . . . to be one to tell you.'

Silence greeted her words.

'But that don't mean that Jason's been stringing us along from the get-go.' Amber broke the silence.

'I tell the woman . . . the English man who send us was looking after your mothers. Why he don't save them? I ask her why his people no save your mothers in Sankura? She say what people in Sankura? She tell me no more.'

'Are you sure?' Jade asked.

Opal reluctantly nodded.

'Bastard, bastard, bastard,' Jade ranted. Her breath was heavy and laboured for a few seconds. Then she turned to the others and said, 'OK, listen up, everyone, this is what we're gonna do. We're gonna find out what's in mine and Ruby's bags.'

The girls were crammed tight into the toilet cubicle. Jade shoved the toilet lid down. She nodded at Ruby. The other girl knew what to do. She placed her bag on the toilet seat. Unzipped it. Pulled the flaps back so that the others could see.

'It's a pair of lady's heels,' Amber said in disbelief.

The shoes were mega-high-heeled purple velvet Pradas. Around the ankle, on both shoes, were what looked liked two diamanté baubles. Each bauble had a striking red and blue vein running through it.

'I don't get it,' Ruby said.

They opened Jade's bag next. Once again it was a pair of lady's shoes. Gucci this time – leopard skin, with silver six-inch heels, each with two large baubles, the same as the other pair, positioned around the toe.

As Opal looked from one pair to the other she sucked in her breath.

'What is it?' Jade asked.

Opal picked up the one of the shoes and pointed to the jewellery on the front. 'These diamonds.' The others girls gasped. Ruby put her hand over her mouth. Opal carried on speaking. 'Called Gates of Dawn. From Sankura.'

'You are having a laugh?' Jade said, rearing back.

A terrified Ruby asked, 'What are we going to do with them?'

Opal looked at each girl in turn and said, 'I'll tell you what we do now . . .'

The girls were back in their seats, the plane coming in to land. Their plan was formed and they were already executing it.

'Finished,' Ruby said, raising her head. In her hand she held a note she'd written.

'Put in bag,' Opal instructed.

Ruby placed the handwritten note on top of the Prada shoes. She read the note one last time before she closed the bag.

Diamonds.

Jason Nelson.

London gangster.

St Nicholas home for lost girls and boys.'

'Put under seat,' Opal told Ruby.

Ruby stashed the bag under the seat in front of her.

'Are we sure we don't wanna leave this bag as well?' Jade asked, her arms tightening around the rucksack.

'No,' Opal replied. 'We take with us.'

The plane taxied to a halt and the rush to get off began. But the girls remained in their seats. Opal scanned the darkness outside. She immediately realised that their plane was the one docked nearest to the perimeter fence. She saw the trailers forming below to collect baggage from the hold and ship it into the terminal. One of the trailers was only half filled and had no one in it.

'Can you see that thing?' She didn't have the English to explain what it was. The others followed her pointing finger.

'The buggy?' Ruby asked.

Opal nodded. 'We go downstairs and get to it . . .'

'You're nuts,' Jade shot back, with a vigorous shake of her head.

'Trust me.'

'And what are we meant to do when we get in it?' Amber said.

'Don't worry. I will sort out.'

Finally the girls got up, Jade clutching her bag. Amber and Opal had dumped their bags in the overhead locker. They reached the flight attendant, who wore a glue-fixed smile. 'Thank you for travelling with us . . .'

'Ain't we going down the stairs?' Jade asked, realising that the woman was standing at the mouth of a gangway.

The woman's smile broadened. 'No. This will take you straight into the building.'

'Excuse me, miss,' Ruby interrupted. 'But I think someone left a bag at the back, under the seat.'

As the woman went to thank Ruby, the girls were already moving past her.

'What the fuck are we gonna do now?' Jade said. 'We ain't gonna be able to get to the buggy. This is gonna take us into the airport. And what if Jason is waiting for us?'

None of the others answered. They just kept walking. A few minutes later they exited the gangway and reached a steel staircase. Ruby panted heavily as they descended to the next level, following the other passengers. They stopped when the other passengers charged on ahead, following the signs for immigration control.

'What now?' Amber asked.

'Go down,' Opal answered, pointing to the remaining steps.

They flew down the stairs until they reached the ground floor.

'There,' Opal said.

The others followed her finger, which pointed at a steel door tucked into the wall to the side. A sign that read 'Staff Only' was on the front.

'We go there,' Opal ordered, already marching towards the door.

The others followed. Reached the door. Jade leaned forward. Pushed the handle down. Inched the door forward. A blast of chilled wind pushed inside as the girls stared at the aircraft stationed on the tarmac. The only other people on the tarmac were a few baggage handlers, their buggies already moving towards the terminal, and a few marshallers in the distance. Opal scanned the plane they'd just disembarked from. Next to it the half-filled trailer was still stationed.

Opal whispered, 'No run. Walk slow.'

They began to move with Opal, slowly towards the trailer. Nerves crawled up each girl as they waited for someone to shout at them. But no one did. Finally they reached the trailer. Once again Opal gave them instructions. 'Inside. Get down.'

As Opal clambered in the front the others jumped in the back, among the luggage, and crouched down.

'How we gonna drive it?' Jade whispered frantically, the rucksack still on her back. Opal didn't answer because she was stunned that the keys were still in the ignition. Moses had taught her many skills in the rebel army, including how to drive so she could steal vehicles. She twisted the keys. The engine coughed into life. The trailer juddered, struggling to cope with its luggage and additional passengers as Opal drove at maximum speed, about 20 mph. She kept moving forward. For one minute. Two minutes. Three. Thirty seconds through the third minute a voice yelled out, 'Where you taking that?'

That was when they heard pounding footsteps in the distance behind them.

Frankie sat in his 4 × 4 in a well-known plane-watchers' haunt, in a small wood, adjacent to the airport's perimeter fence. It was a risky thing to do but there was no way he was going to take the far riskier option of going into the airport itself. Finlay and Jason were both inside, waiting for the girls to appear in the arrivals hall. His mobile rang. He pulled it quickly from his pocket, a smile gliding onto his face. It must be Finlay and Jason with news that they had the girls.

But he was wrong. It wasn't his partners in crime, it was fucking Miller.

The smile dropped clean off his face as he listened. 'What do you mean, you've lost them?'

He listened tensely. Cut in, 'Right, get out of there pronto before the Old Bill connect you to them.'

Fuck.

He pulled out a fag, deciding what to do next.

'Get bags out,' Opal screamed, thinking they would get to the fence quicker with less weight.

The girls twisted around and began to shove the luggage onto the tarmac. As they threw it out, they saw a group of baggage handlers and security people running after them. As they approached the wire fence, Opal screamed, 'Get down.'

The other girls dived down as Opal sped the trailer towards the fence. She rammed the vehicle into the fence. The fence buckled, but didn't break. She revved the engine and directed the trailer backwards. Rammed it forward again. But the fence remained intact.

'What we gonna fucking do?' Jade screamed.

Frankie was as mad as hell after getting the call from Mr Miller. Fuck, the girls had his merchandise. His mobile rang again and he knew that it was more bad news.

It was Finlay.

'It's all kicking off in here. There's security running all over the place.'

'Shit. What's it about?'

'No one's saying – but I did hear some security guys mention the flight from Amsterdam . . . Frankie? You listening?'

Frankie didn't answer because he was no longer listening. The phone slipped away from his face because he couldn't believe what he was seeing, about a quarter of a mile in the distance, on the other side of the airport fence.

'We climb fence,' Opal ordered.

The girls clambered out of the vehicle. Farther along the fence airport security officers were running towards them on foot. The girls lunged for the fence and began to climb.

'My inhaler,' Ruby screamed as her inhaler hit the ground.

Jade looked sideways at her and yelled, 'Leave it.'

The engine of a vehicle revved somewhere in the distance on the other side of the fence. But the girls didn't pay it any attention as the security officers got closer. The girls climbed higher.

Suddenly the girls screamed as the fence wobbled violently. Jade's gaze flew downwards to find a 4 × 4 reversed into the opposite side of the fence. The vehicle skidded backwards. Bolted forward. Rammed into the fence once more. The girls shook against the fence as if a megawatt of electricity had gone into the wire they clung onto. The running footsteps of the security guards got louder.

The 4 × 4 moved back and forward one more time. Its towbar tore part of the fence away.

'Quick,' a voice shouted from the driver's side of the car.

The girls all looked down, startled to see Frankie sitting in the car. They dropped down from the fence, as the wild, erratic noise of a police siren sounded in the distance. They scrambled through the opening he had made. Frankie leaned over the driver's seat and opened the back door. Whether from shock at seeing him or fear of what he might be about to do, they hesitated.

'Look,' a terrified Ruby shouted.

The girls looked in the direction she was staring at. They all gasped when they saw that the cops running towards them were unslinging their weapons.

Frankie very quietly said, 'No matter what you think I might do, it can't be any worse than what they're gonna do when they catch you – now get in . . .'

twenty

The girls jolted in the back as Frankie's motor screeched with acceleration. Frankie knew that within minutes the make and registration number of his wheels would be the number-one priority for every armed cop on the Metropolitan patch and on all the neighbouring forces. But Frankie wasn't Frankie for nothing; he was always one jump ahead. On any major operation he always had a back-up motor, parked five or ten miles away in an area where there were no prying eyes or cameras. A car that wouldn't get you noticed. A car that was delivered by a mate who managed one of Gatwick's long-term car parks. The owners of this one were away in sunny Cyprus for three weeks and when they got back their motor would be back exactly where they'd parked it.

As soon as Frankie hit a side road, he did a neat J-turn. The 4×4 carved up the road as the sounds of police sirens screamed in the opposite direction. Then he slowed and drove steadily to the fringes of a newly built but as yet unoccupied estate about seven or eight miles from the airport in Hounslow. He pulled up behind a second-hand car in the shadow of some trees and newly built walls. He switched the engine off. Lowered all the windows. Turned to the girls.

'You do what I tell you, unless you want the Old Bill to nab you.'

The girls' ragged breathing filled the car as they stared back at him, obviously scared out of their wits. Finally Jade, still clutching her rucksack, threw him a tense nod.

'Outta the motor.'

The girls jumped out quickly, followed by Frankie. He ran to the other car.

'Get in,' he yelled at the girls.

As the girls rushed to follow his instruction he called out, 'Not you, Jade. You're the front with me.'

She shot him a surprised look, but didn't argue.

'Give me your airline ticket,' Frankie demanded, holding out his hand towards her. Jackie looked puzzled by his request.

'You want the boys in blue to track us down?' Frankie shot out at her.

Jackie swallowed as she dug into her jacket pocket and pulled out the ticket. As soon as she handed it to him Frankie rushed to the back of the waiting car. Opened the boot. Took out a can of petrol. He rushed back to the 4 × 4 and began to splash petrol all over it – front, back, sides. He threw the empty can onto the driver's seat. Took out a box of matches. Threw them onto the driver's seat as well.

He yelled back at the girls, 'Get down.'

The girls dived down onto the other car's floor. As they hit the floor Opal said, 'No tell him I speak English.' The others girls all nodded.

Frankie took out a lighter. He ignited the flame. Touched it to Jackie's airline ticket. He lobbed the blazing ticket into the 4 × 4. He pelted back towards the other motor as the car burst into flames. Then the fire hit the engine. Bang. The 4 × 4 exploded into violent, high-kicking orange and yellow flames. The force knocked Frankie to the ground. He lay dazed for a few seconds. Then he shoved himself back onto his feet. Got into the driver's seat of the second car. The girls were still crouched on the floor.

'Get up. If anyone stops us, we've been out to a kids' party.'

'Where we going?' Jade's voice was tight and, Frankie couldn't be sure, it sounded angry.

He didn't answer her. Just locked all the doors. Then he drove along the side roads to the A4. Back to London.

Jade was the one who finally broke the silence as Frankie drove.

'Our mums are dead.'

Frankie gave her a quick sideways look. 'I know you don't believe me, but I didn't know nothin' about what was gonna happen to your mums.'

'I don't fucking believe you,' Jade blasted back at him.

'You said you were our mate,' Amber joined in.

'I've always been upfront with you girls that I work for Jason. I've never hidden that. But I ain't in his close circle. I ain't . . .'

'Then what were you doing at the airport? I don't . . .' Jade's voice juddered to a halt as Frankie slammed hard on the brakes. The car stopped. The girls all looked at Frankie as if he had finally lost his mind. Frankie twisted to where the girls sat in the back, leaned across Jade and flung open the passenger door.

'Go on, then, go,' he said calmly.

Each girl hesitated as they kept looking at him. 'I ain't keeping you here. If you don't wanna believe me that's fine.' The silence lengthened in the car. 'I don't need to tell you what a big, bad world it is out there if you ain't got no one looking out for your back. And when the cops pick you up, as they will, they'll sling you into one of them youth offenders trash bins, where kids like you are bullied, beaten, even raped. They make St Nicholas look like flamin' Butlins.'

Still no one moved.

'I'm Jason's runaround boy. He made me stay with his car while he went to pick you up with Finlay. But when I saw you lot climbing over the fence, I just couldn't leave you. I had to get you out of there. If I was out to get you, why didn't I just leave you to the cops and do a runner? Why don't I just kill you now I've got you all safely in the car?'

On hearing his last words, Jade gasped along with the others. Silence pulsed in the car. Jade didn't know what to believe any more. Could she believe him? Couldn't she? Her mind was a total mess.

'Anyway,' Frankie quietly added, 'I'm as fucked as you lot now.'

'What do you mean?' This time it was Ruby who spoke.

'Not only have I torched Jason's wheels, but I've also nicked his back-up motor. When he hears what I've done he's gonna put me out of action for life. So like it or not, we're in this together and I wanna think that we're gonna get out of this together. But that's up to you.'

The silence pressed down even more.

'What do you think?' Jade whispered to Amber.

'I don't know who to trust any more.'

'Ruby?' Jade said.

'I want to, but . . .'

Jade was about to ask Opal when she caught the look of warning in the other girl's eyes. Then she remembered that they'd agreed not to reveal that Opal spoke English.

'And if I'm not mistaken,' Frankie said, abruptly 'you've still got some of Jason's merchandise in that bag. He's gonna take this town apart looking for it. I'm the only person who can help you get away.'

'Alright, Frankie.' Jade had made their decision. 'Say we go with you, how the hell are you gonna get us out of this shit?'

'Easy. We get your gear and I take you someplace to lay low for a while.'

'But our stuff's at St Nicholas,' an alarmed Amber put in.

'I know. Jason and Finlay are still trying to get out of Heathrow. We'll get back there long before they do. When they get back we'll be long gone.' Frankie flipped down the rear-view mirror. Checked out the anxious girls in the back. 'Trust me, ladies.'

'I ain't going in there,' Jade said, as her hand clutched the bag to her chest.

The girls stood with Frankie outside the long building in the garden. Not a soul had moved from inside St Nicholas when Frankie had driven up. The place was shrouded in the dying evening light, making it easy for them to move undetected to the garden.

Jade stared at Frankie with revulsion. 'I know what happens in there.'

The colour of Frankie's face was stark white, which surprised Jade. 'I'm sorry you had to find out, but we ain't got no choice. You can't go inside the house. All the other kids and Mr Miller must know by now that the Bill are after you, so you can't let them clock you. This is the only place you can hide out while I get your gear.'

Frankie quietly opened the door. Flicked the light on. The girls stepped inside. A chill ran through Jade as her mind zoomed back to what she'd witnessed in here.

'What is this place?' Amber asked, her gaze taking in the two beds and the chains and manacles on the wall.

'I'll tell you later,' Jade replied.

'I'll be fifteen minutes tops,' Frankie said, giving them one of his dazzling smiles.

Then he was gone.

'Don't sit on none of those beds,' Jade warned the others.

'What did you see in here?' Amber asked Jade.

Jade gulped and then quickly told the others what she'd seen. The other girls reared back in disgust, the fear growing inside them.

Without warning Opal started heading for the door.

'Where you going?' Jade shot out.

'Toilet. Upstairs . . .'

'You're off your head,' Amber said. 'You can't do that.'

'I'm coming with you,' Jade said. 'Frankie won't know where to find my lunchbox under the bed. And there ain't no way I'm leaving without that.'

'But . . .' an anxious Ruby said.

Jade threw the bag at Amber as she said, 'We'll come back with Frankie.'

Jade and Opal ran out of the door as quick as the wind rushing in the night.

They took the back stairs quietly. Reached the top. Jade pushed open the door. On tiptoe the girls made their way along the corridor. It was bathed in an intense dark that was solid and uncomfortable. They reached their room. Jade was surprised that there was no light trickling from under the door. Maybe Frankie had already left and gone out the front way? She gripped the handle and turned it. Both girls pushed inside.

Opal marched briskly to the bathroom. As she disappeared, Jade headed straight for her bed. Dropped to her knees. Stretched her arm out and searched. Seconds later she had the handle of her lunchbox in her hand. She pulled it out. As she got to her feet her gaze flicked across the bed. Across her T-shirt, folded where she'd left it.

She did a double-take. Puzzled, she stared hard at the T-shirt. Frankie should've packed it. Her gaze swung around the room. To the dressing table. The other girls' beds. Everything was in exactly the same place as that morning. Nothing had been taken. Briskly she walked over to the wardrobe. Opened it. All their clothes were still inside. Why hadn't Frankie taken them?

What if Jason had somehow got hold of Frankie?

Shit. She jumped back from the wardrobe. She needed to get out of here. Get the others out of here. She walked on tiptoe to the dressing table. Grabbed the candle, Nikki's necklace and the photo of her, Amber and Ruby on New Year's Eve which was stuck to the mirror. She opened her lunchbox and shoved the items inside. She turned around at the same time as Opal came out of the bathroom.

'We need to get out. Now,' she mouthed at the other girl.

The girls eased back into the corridor. As they began to move away, the door of the room next door clicked open.

The girls couldn't move. The shock of the situation held them still. Then they heard voices tangled in a fierce argument coming from the room next door. Voices that belonged to Finlay and Jason. Shit, they must have Frankie in there, Jade thought.

'We go,' Opal whispered fiercely.

But Jade couldn't. She couldn't leave Frankie to face the music on his own. She slid along the wall, as Opal mouthed, 'No.'

But she didn't stop. Not until she stood flush with the open door. That was when she heard the words that made her run.

Finlay's voice. 'You're the boss, Frankie, so what we gonna do with them four bitches?'

Jade didn't wait to hear any more. She slid slowly along the wall. Grabbed Opal's hand and ran. Out of the door. Down the stairs with her lunchbox beating in the air. Frankie wasn't a mate, he was a geezer. The Geezer.

The geezer who had made them pack drugs.

The geezer who had made them transport guns.

The geezer who hadn't helped their mums.

The geezer who was going to make it his business, she was sure, that they never reached sixteen if they didn't get out of here.

The girls hightailed it across the grass. Banged open the door of the building in the garden.

'We've gotta leg it.' Jade's words puffed out of her heaving chest.

'What you chatting about?' Amber said, the urgency in Jade's voice making her stand up.

'Now,' she roared.

'But Frankie's getting our stuff.'

'Frankie's the . . .'

'What am I?' a cool voice said behind Jade and Opal.

twenty-one

Jade twisted around to find Frankie. The horror of her discovery pushed her farther into the room, along with Opal.

'What's up?' he asked as he stepped into the room. He closed the door behind him.

Both girls kept moving backwards until they stood with the others.

'Nothin',' Jade replied. She swallowed. 'We were just waiting for you.' Her words came out as if they were sticking to the surface of her tongue.

His mouth softened as he swept a casual gaze over them. When he reached Jade he stared harder at her. When he saw the lunchbox quivering in her hand his blue eyes shot to her face as he quietly asked, 'Where did you get that from? You didn't have that before.'

She clutched the box tight to her side. Tried to speak but the words wouldn't leave her mouth.

'Oh.' He made the sound like it was a lover's caress in the night. 'Tut, tut, tut. I get it.'

He half turned towards the door. Touched the key in the lock. Twisted. Click. The door locked. He turned so he faced them full-on again. Frankie leaned casually against the door. 'Childhood can be such a bummer sometimes. You know why?' His arms dropped to the side at the end of the question.

Jade was too frightened to even shake her head. But he didn't wait for an answer, just carried on. 'Because adults are always telling big porkies. One lie after another, you can't trust 'em, you know.

Remember, Jade, when I taught you to pick a pocket? Do you remember what I said?' Jade couldn't respond. 'Life's all about distraction and deception.'

The fingers of his left hand began to drum against the door.

'So what happened, Jade? Did you go upstairs looking for that little friend in your hand? Trouble is you didn't just find that, did you? You found me having a little chinwag with my ole pals Finlay and Jason.' The beat of his fingers got faster.

'What's going on?'

Jade wasn't sure who asked the question. But it didn't matter. Both Amber and Ruby had a right to know.

'He's the Geezer,' she answered.

'No, Jason is.' Amber's voice was adamant.

'No he ain't. *He* is.'

Both girls gave a collective gasp of horror. They shuffled closer to Jade. Ruby hooked her hand around Opal's arm, the one with her hand in her pocket, and pulled her with them.

Suddenly he kicked his body off the door. The girls catapulted back. But he didn't move towards them. Instead his hand jammed into his pocket. Ruby screamed, her hand releasing Opal's arm, when she saw his movement. His hand came out of his pocket at the same time as Opal's came out of hers.

He held a mobile phone.

Opal held a gun.

Frankie, Ruby, Amber and Jade all stared at Opal in shock. She ignored the other girls and levelled the gun at his chest. Never taking her eyes off his face, she took three steps towards Frankie. Stopped when there was a distance of half a metre between them.

'Drop. The. Phone.' She said each word separately.

The phone dived from Frankie's hand.

'Well, well, well, our little refugee speaks the Queen's English.'

She took a half-step towards him. Waved the gun at him and commanded, 'Move into room.'

He followed the wave of her gun. As he did what she said, the other girls shot over towards the door.

Frankie curled his lip at Opal. 'So you had the gun all this time. All that bollocks bullshit about being attacked in Peckham. I should've let Finlay make you burn, baby, when I had the chance.'

She took easy, confident steps towards him. Once again she stopped when there was half a metre between them.

Opal widened the stance of her feet as she spoke. 'Mrs Grieves not know I was child soldier?' She heard the gasp of the girls behind her. Saw the look of amazed shock in Frankie's eyes. She took a full step towards him. Straightened her back. Steadied her hand. With a sudden move she pulled the gun down. Pointed it at his right thigh.

'Bang, bang, Frankie.'

Pulled the trigger. Frankie screamed. The girls screamed. He hit the floor. Jade hit the key in the door. As her shaking hands twisted the key it tumbled out and fell to the ground. As the other girls scrambled to help her, Opal stepped closer to Frankie. Looked down at him moaning as he clutched the bleeding hole in his leg. Calmly she aimed the gun higher, just above the first bullet hole. Pulled the trigger. His upper body jerked up in pain. His scream bounced around the room.

Opal crouched by his side. Felt in his trousers pockets. Came out empty. Felt in his jacket pocket. Came out holding his car keys and a wad of cash. She turned her back on him and moved towards the girls. They scattered back with fear when they saw her. Saw the gun. She reached the door. Squatted and picked up Frankie's phone.

Reached across and picked up the door key. She stood. Put the key in the door. Turned. Opened the door.

But she was stopped by Jade's panicking voice. 'We need my mum's address book. He took it off me. He might have it on him.'

Opal calmly turned back. Walked back to Frankie, who was slowly losing consciousness. Crouched down and once again began to search through his pockets. Finally her hand came out holding a small black book. She held it in the air.

'That's it,' Jade said.

When Opal reached the door she glanced at the terrified girls and said, 'Let's get out of here.'

                    *   *   *

They moved quickly in the darkness until they reached Frankie's motor.

Opal immediately went for the driver's seat.

'How did you learn to drive?' Amber asked in a rush.

'The same way I learned to kill – quickly.'

Each girl gave Opal a shocked stare. They still couldn't believe what she'd been before she came to England.

'I'll get in the front with Opal, you two get in the back,' Jade told Ruby and Amber, breaking the silence.

As they got into the car, Opal passed Jade the phone and address book.

Opal turned the ignition. The engine growled. The car shot off into the dark.

'So where we going?' Ruby piped up nervously from the back.

Without answering Jade furiously leafed through her mum's address book. She grabbed the phone. Punched in the numbers.

'Who you phoning?' Amber asked behind Jade.

'Someone I tried to call when I first got to St Nicholas. A mate of my mum's.' Jade's face became pale when no one picked up at the other end. *Come on, come on, come on*, thumped in her head.

The line clicked. Connected. A hard breath of relief shot out of Jade's mouth.

'I'm looking for Miss Misty McKenzie.'

'Ain't we all, love,' a husky voice replied.

Then there was a long drag, as if the person on the other line was partway through a smoke.

'But does she live here?'

'Who wants to know?'

'But does she live there?'

'Look, Midnight Fairy, I don't wanna see your birth certificate, but I need to know who you are. Misty don't like mystery callers.'

'Alright. Just tell her that it's Nikki's girl . . .'

There was a gasp on the other end. 'Is that you, Jade? It's Misty. I heard what happened to your mum.'

'I can't explain now but we're in a wagon-load of bovver and need to come over to you.'

'You on foot?'

'No, we got wheels.'

'Get to the nearest Tube station. Ditch the motor. Then get the train to King's Cross. Listen carefully because this is where I live . . .'

Jason checked his watch for the fifth time in five minutes.

'He's taking his bloody time,' he said to Finlay.

They'd been waiting for Frankie for a good half-hour.

'Cool it, man,' Finlay replied. 'Frankie's most probably getting rid of the girls. If there's a problemo he'll give us a little tinkle.'

But Jason wasn't convinced. He began pacing. Hooked his thumb under the blind to check out of the window.

'Hold up,' he said. 'Frankie's motor ain't there.' He spun around to the other man.

'This don't feel right.'

'Maybe he decided to dispose of the girls somewhere else?'

'Nah, he would've let us know.'

Jason jerked his mobile from his inside pocket. Punched in some numbers. Waited for the phone to connect.

'Look, there's a station,' Jade called out.

They all peered hard out of the windows.

'It's Blackhorse Road,' Ruby said.

The car swung closer at the same time as the phone in Jade's lap began to ring. Jade tensed against the seat. Tilted her head down and stared at the phone as if it were a grenade in her lap.

It rang again.

Still looking at it, she said, 'Shall I answer it?'

'No,' Amber answered, leaning forward. 'It might be Frankie.'

'But it might be your mum's friend,' Ruby said.

The phone rang again. Jade rubbed her palms up and down her thighs, near the phone, but not touching it.

The ring came again.

She picked it up. Placed it to her face. Pressed the connect button.

'Hello?'

'Who the fucking hell are you?' came the explosive answer.

The phone tumbled out of Jade's hand.

'It's Jason.'

Opal cut the engine. The car juddered to a halt. The girls didn't think twice, they scrambled out of the car and belted towards the Underground station.

Jason turned towards Finlay.

'That was one of them bitch girls.'

'How come they've got Frankie's mobile?'

'Frankie never lets anyone touch his business line.'

They stared at each other. Then they rushed for the door.

Frankie came to. Gritted his teeth as the pain lanced through him. Then he remembered why he was lying flat on his back on a cold floor. One of those bitches had pumped lead into his leg. The bitches had some of his diamonds. Slowly he began to wriggle his body across the floor. He stopped when his head touched the back wall. Using his hands, he slid his body up until his back rested against the wall. The sweat dripped from his forehead as the pain made him close his eyes.

He reopened his eyes. Scanned the floor, looking for the mobile that he'd dropped. He swore viciously when he saw it was gone. How the fuck was he going to contact Finlay and Jason?

His hand shot into his jacket pocket. Pulled out a packet of fags. Popped one in his mouth. He felt into his jacket again. Found his lighter. Lit up. Pulled in hard. Finally gazed down at the damage done to his leg. Two small holes and blood deepening the colour of his trousers. He was still bleeding but not badly. No way was he going to get up on his . . .

The door shot open. He tensed. Relaxed when he saw the large figures of Finlay and Jason burst into the room.

'Fucking hell.'

Both men spoke at the same time. They rushed over to him. Crouched down.

'What happened?' Jason asked.

'What the fuck do you think happened?' Frankie blasted back. 'That African bitch had the gun from Finlay's shipment all the time and conveniently used it to stop me in my tracks.'

'But how . . . ?' Finlay started, confused.

'The next time we use Mrs Grieves make sure to tell her no child soldiers.'

He ignored the stunned expressions on both their faces and continued. 'Get me upstairs. Then phone our doctor and tell her to get her arse over here pronto. Those bitches have still got my merchandise so we need to track them down ASAP.'

'London's a big place, boss, so how are we gonna do that?' Finlay said.

'I don't fucking care how you do it. Just find 'em.' Then Frankie started bellowing.

'No one, no one, treats me like a ten-quid pussy and gets away with it.'

'This feels well creepy,' Amber said as she shivered.

They stood opposite the ghostly façade of St Pancras station, beside a café that pumped out sickly smells and the Pet Shop Boys' 'West End Girls'. The café door swung open. The girls swiftly turned around. Two women in high heels, miniskirts, flesh busting out of the seams of their Lycra tops and cigarette smoke chopping out of their mouths walked out of the entrance. Halfway through a deep suck on her fag one of the women noticed the girls. She whipped the fag from her chops and yelled, 'Oi! Get your fucking skinny arses off of our patch.'

The girls staggered back at the ferocity of her words. Jade shuddered. She hustled the others along, following Miss Misty McKenzie's directions. For the next seven minutes they kept their heads down as they passed gangs, toms, drunks and nuts and rushed through blowing takeaway wrappers, blasted lives and dirty rain. Jade thought Amber was right – King's Cross looked like a total fleapit. It was a walking directory of reasons to move to the country. And didn't they have HMP Pentonville down one road and Holloway Prison down another? Or were they the estates some of the residents lived on? No wonder King's Cross station had so many Tube lines intersecting at it – because there were so many reasons to get out of the neighbouring streets.

Finally they reached the canal.

'She says she lives on the third boat down there.'

They started walking again. They passed the first boat. The second. As they neared the third they saw two figures, moving like silhouettes, as if they were doing some disjointed night dance. But as they got closer they realised it was a man and a woman and from their voices they weren't engaged in a relaxing pastime but an old-fashioned ding-dong.

'Go on, shoo, I've told you to piss off,' the woman yelled, her arm moving to the rhythm of her words.

The woman's back was to them. She was slim, her tall body elevated higher by long heels and even longer legs. Her glossy, brunette hair was cut to her chin and bobbed in the air. The light from the lamp post gave them a half-view of the man's face. He was more distinguished, several inches shorter than the woman and holding a hat in his hand.

'But I love you,' he pleaded.

'Love? Is that what you tell your wife, Monday to Friday, and me at the weekend? Go on, sling your hook.'

'But I . . .'

Suddenly the woman dipped down and wobbled as she reached for one of her shoes.

She pulled it off. 'I'll give you bloody love,' she shouted as she shook her shoe in the air.

Then she pelted it straight at the man. He ducked. The shoe sailed over his head. He made the mistake of pushing his head back up.

'Love hurts, ain't that what they say?' The woman yelled as her second shoe hurtled through the air. This time she made a direct hit and the shoe slammed into his forehead. He staggered back with the force of the impact.

'Now sod off.'

The man swivelled around and strode away. The girls shifted to the side as he passed them. As the woman stared after him her gaze stopped when she noticed the girls. She stepped forward, wincing as her stockinged feet gingerly trod on the concrete. The girls stood immobile, waiting for her to reach them. When she did, she let out an 'ouch', and twisted her foot up to inspect it. She pulled a can ring from under her foot.

'Bloody toms and the trash they leave,' she muttered.

She straightened and gave the girls a direct glare. 'Now who you lot looking for?'

'We're looking for a Misty . . .'

'Oh, Jesus, Mary and Josephine,' the woman gasped, covering her mouth with her hand. She looked directly at Jade. Her hand fell away, revealing the sad expression that covered her face.

'You're Jade.'

Jade nodded.

The woman held her arms out wide. 'Come and give ol' Misty a big, fat, juicy hug.'

Without hesitation Jade flew forward. The woman engulfed her in her embrace. As Jade sank deeper into the human warmth offered her she stopped when she realised that the woman's chest felt hard. Confused, she pulled her face away. Looked up and saw a few bristles on the woman's chin. An Adam's apple. She shook herself sharply away from the person holding her and asked, 'Are you a geezer?'

twenty-two

Was she a geezer?

The question rocked in Misty McKenzie's mind as she watched Nikki's daughter. Blimey, it had been donkey's years since anyone had asked her that question. Most people knew what she was. If you'd caught her a decade ago, you could have slapped the geezer label on her forehead because she'd certainly lived the life of one, albeit reluctantly. Back then she had definitely been a him, the youngest brother of one of East London's hardest underworld families from the Ashbury Estate, or Trash City, as most people called it. He'd grown up rough and fast, with only one type of life marked out for him – that of a hard man. His brothers had put it about with their fists, but he'd tried to live a little less drastically, a little less violently. So he'd chosen the life of a bouncer. No one had guessed that the bouncer flexing his muscles most Saturday nights would boot troublemakers with feet with painted toenails. Misty had always loved the aroma and drama of women's clothes and cosmetics. Loved running his hands over his mum's and nan's clothes. The first time he'd ever been kitted out in a suit as a ten-year-old, he'd stared at the drab colours and thought, Was this it? Were these the type of colours he'd have to wear for the rest of his days? And from that day forward he'd tried his mum's clothes on, dabbled in her make-up. Always done in secret. That is until he met Nikki Flynn.

They'd worked at the same club, some deadbeat dive in Shoreditch, him handling the traffic on the door, her stripping on the stage. She'd caught him trying on her lipstick. Instead of freaking out, she'd shaken that curtain of red hair behind her shoulder and calmly said, 'Wrong shade, mate. You need regal red, not princess pink.' And that was how he and Nikki Flynn had become fast friends. She'd taken him shopping, shown him how to apply make-up, introduced him to a salon that specialised in sorting out blokes like him. Soon he'd left the life of a geezer behind and become Miss Misty McKenzie, drag act extraordinaire. A *her*. 'Course, the family had freaked out. But, to her surprise, instead of pushing her out, all her eldest brother Charlie had said was, 'Just make sure when you come around here you don't wear none of that shit.' Misty suspected that they'd known for years what *he* was. Mind you, Misty had never been interested in literally changing sex, only ever in showing the world who she physically was.

She had a lot to be thankful to Nikki Flynn for. It might sound a bit dramatic but Nikki had saved her life.

Misty looked down at the small girl. Gave her a trembling smile. 'I ain't no geezer, but I am the person who's gonna sort you and your mates out. So step aboard *Miss Josephine*.'

Miss Josephine was three cabins of floating nostalgia. She was an old model that looked days away from being committed to a junk yard. They sat inside her main cabin, which was past its best years but clean and well looked after. It had the standard table and comfy chairs, but also little touches that demonstrated how much Misty loved it – the old-time record player, the large, floppy-leafed green plants, the framed photos on the wall, the three rugs on the floor.

'I didn't mean to be rude or nothin' outside,' Jade said, her fingers fluttering nervously in her lap; she was still feeling very confused by the person sitting opposite her. Misty sat in a wicker chair, her bare feet curved beneath her thighs.

'Don't worry about it, babe.'

'What do we call you?' Jade asked, embarrassed. 'Mister or Missus?'

Misty gave a little chuckle. 'Neither. I answer to Miss or plain ol' Misty. We'll have a chat about me later, but for now let's talk about you and your friends.' Her fingers looped solemnly together in her lap. 'I'm sorry about what's happened to your mums. I only knew Nikki and she was a cracker of a woman.'

The girls all looked uneasily at each other, but remained silent.

'You said you were in a bit of bovver.'

Slowly Jade began to tell her about their lives at St Nicholas. Misty sat with a stunned look on her face when Jade finished. She couldn't believe what she'd just heard. Drugs? Gun running? Gem smuggling? Attempted suffocation? People being hung out of the window? Child soldiers?

Then another thought occurred to her. 'So you lot were the ones I saw on the late news crawling over the fence at Heathrow?'

The girls all nodded.

'Bloody hell, girls, you certainly know how to wake a girl up.' Misty paused for a minute, then asked, 'How do you like boats?'

The girls all gave her the same confused look.

She unfolded her feet. Rested them on the floor. Leaned forward. 'See, the thing is, girls, you're all gonna have to stop here with me. This Frankie sounds like a Rottweiler who's lost his bone, so he'll come after you, especially if one of you put a few slugs in him. And the Bill will be all over London hunting you. So how do you feel like kipping with me for a while?'

'Won't social services come looking for us?' Ruby asked.

Misty shook her head. 'I don't think so. That Mrs Grieves will most probably put it about that once you heard about your mums you all run away. Besides, I've met too many fifteen-year-olds who run away from the care system straight to London's nightlife and no one ever comes looking for them. The care system looks after you until you're sixteen years old and then it washes its hands of you. So when you're fifteen you're too near the age when they don't have to sort you out any more. As far as they're concerned you've done them a favour. So what do you say, girls, to coming and keeping me and *Miss Josephine* company?'

The girls all looked at each other. Amber was the first to nod, making the decision for them.

'Alright,' Jade said. 'But we ain't got nothin' to pay you with . . .'

'Yes we have,' Opal cut in.

Opal stretched her hand out to Amber, indicating she wanted the rucksack. She got up and took it from the confused-looking girl. Unzipped it as she made her way to the table in the middle. She pushed her hand inside. Pulled out the Gucci shoes. Placed them on the table. Hunched down. Pointed a finger at one of the gems on the shoes.

'These are diamonds.'

'Get outta here,' Misty said.

'That's why Frankie coming after us. He want diamonds back.'

Silence sizzled in the room. Finally Misty broke it. 'How much are they worth?'

'Commander in my army say . . .' Opal stopped talking. Wet her lips with the tip of her tongue. 'One million pounds each.'

Everyone gasped.

'You are joking?' Misty said, dazed. Her eyes quickly swung across each diamond. Counted. Four. 'That means four million nicker is sitting on my Auntie Glad's second-hand table.'

Opal kept her eyes on Misty. 'We sell, buy ourselves new life.'

No one said anything. They just kept looking at the diamonds. Looking at the temptation of a new life.

'Can you help us sell, Misty?'

Misty started chewing her bottom lip. Her lipstick settled against her teeth. She moved. Began pacing, hand chopping through her hair. Suddenly she stopped. Turned back to them. 'I ain't been involved in that world for years, but yeah, I can get it sorted. Your Frankie will be expecting them to be fenced straight away, so we're gonna have to sit on 'em for a while. At least a good six months. After that a bloke I know will be able to shift 'em for us.' She looked at each one of the girls in turn and asked, 'Does everyone want me to do this?'

The girls all gazed at each other, indecision stamped across their faces. Finally Jade spoke. 'I know this is wrong, they don't belong to us, but it's gonna help us make a new start. I'm in if everyone else is.'

Again silence gripped the room.

'I'm in.' They all looked shocked that it was Ruby who'd made the next move. 'I know it's wrong as well and it's bad, but the one thing

I've learned is that no one is going to take care of us, we have to do it for ourselves.'

Sadness spread across Misty's face. Sorrow that these girls had had to grow up well before their time.

'What about you?' Jade asked Amber.

'Now my mum ain't coming back,' her voice was quiet, 'I've got to look out for myself. Yeah.' She nodded her head with the force of her decision. 'I'm in.'

'Alright, ladies,' Misty said, moving towards them. 'That means you all need to be fitted with new IDs. My big brother Charlie will be able to get all that organised.' She studied them for a few seconds. 'Your appearances will have to go through a mega-makeover. Stand up and shift yourselves into a line.'

Slowly they did what she asked. She stood in front of them, rubbing the knuckle of her forefinger under her chin.

'You,' she pointed at Amber, 'we're gonna get rid of the little-girl reggae look and go for uptown R ' 'n' B beauty. Nice long hair and even longer legs. Blue contacts to change the colour of your eyes.'

Misty took a sidestep. Gave Ruby the once-over. She twisted her mouth as her finger tapped her lip.

'Got it.' Her finger shot off her lip and pointed at Ruby. 'We're gonna get rid of the I-change-my-knickers-every-day-goody-two-shoes look.' The girls giggled. 'And make you go ever so slightly punk. Spiky short hair and rebel make-up. Fatten you up a bit as well.'

Ruby gazed back at her doubtfully.

'And you.' She swung her arm at Opal, taking a sliding step to stand in front of the girl. 'We'll keep the hair short, stick a pair of glasses on you and make you look like one of them young, gifted and black sisters.

'And finally, my lady Jade.' Misty waved her hand like it was a wand. 'Diet, diet, diet. Suck that puppy fat outta you, give you a short pixie cut and dye that hair. Now what colour?'

'Red.'

'Carrot?' Misty looked back at her like she was losing it big time. 'I don't think . . .'

'I want the same colour as Nikki's.'

A deathly silence filled the cabin. The fun flowed out of Misty. She folded her arms around her middle.

'Sure. I understand. Hey, why not? I mean, you don't much look like her, if you don't mind me saying, so no one should recognise you. This Frankie gonna be on the warpath trying to track you down, so come morning light we're outta here. But he's gonna keep hunting you, so even when your IDs are sorted we're gonna have to lay low.'

Opal's gun dangled from Misty's hand, over the side of the boat. Misty stared at the canal, two hours after she'd managed to get the girls asleep.

'Nikki, Nikki, Nikki, why didn't you listen to me, babe?' She whispered into the cold wind.

But Nikki had been the kind of woman who'd listened to advice, but not always taken it. Misty knew why she'd got involved in the underworld – so her precious Jade could have a better life than the one she'd started out with

'I'll tell you this much, Nikki, darling, I'm gonna look after Jade and her friends.'

She dropped the gun into the freezing water below.

Jade got up two hours after everyone was asleep. She tugged her lunchbox off the shelf she'd placed it on. Knelt on the floor. Opened it. Pulled out the stub that was all that was left of her Holy Communion candle. She took out her lighter and lit it. The flame burned bright. She heard a noise behind her and swiftly turned. Opal was on her knees on the floor, her little body shaking, her hand gripping her mouth. Then Jade saw the tears running freely down her face. It was the first time she'd seen Opal show any type of emotion. Jade opened her arms. Opal moved into them. Jade squeezed tight.

'What's your real name?' Jade whispered.

'Grace.'

Jade rocked the other girl as she watched the flame. But she didn't pray. She was never praying again. What was the point? God hadn't been listening to her. Instead she reached across to her lunchbox on the floor next to her. With one hand she took out her Walkman. Found the earphones. Placed one in her ear. The other in Opal's. Pressed 'play'. She closed her eyes, rocking Opal to the sad refrain of 'Tainted Love'. She slipped into sleep, still holding Opal, at the same time as the candle blew out.

twenty-three

The next day Jason got nicked. The news sent Frankie into over-drive. Not only had the girls done a runner with some of his diamonds, but a source at the nick Jason had been taken to told him a rucksack with a note had been left on the plane, putting Jason slam bang in the shit. Frankie wasn't worried about Jason being held too long because he knew that Jason's lawyer would tear the credibility of the note to shreds and have him back on the street in no time. But still, Frankie didn't need that kind of heat. And if that wasn't enough, to top it all, two vanloads of cops had turned up at St Nicholas. After they had searched the outbuilding in the garden the police had arrested Mr Miller and all the other adults who worked in the care home.

Frankie had put the word out, but no one could find those bitches. With Jason locked up he knew the law were going to be sniffing around, which meant the heat was too strong to keep hunting the girls. He knew that it was only a matter of time before his name got chucked into the frame. It was time for him to sort out this mess. Time for him to let the men and the rest of London know who the real face running this outfit was.

Five days later, while *Miss Josephine* was docked on the River Lea in Hoddersdon in Hertfordshire, Misty called the girls together to show them their new IDs.

'These are your National Insurance cards with your new names on. I've tried to get you names that start with the same initial as your old names because with a brain like mine, I'll only get all your names mixed up. Anyway, I thought you might like that.' Misty passed the papers out. Each girl read her new name.

Jade Flynn became Jackie Jarvis.

Amber Craig became Anna Crane.

Ruby Munro became Roxy Malone.

Opal became Olivia Dean.

Jade stretched out both her arms. The others understood what she wanted them to do. They linked hands.

'We're gonna be alright,' Jade said. 'You know why? Because we're a family now.'

ten years later

JacKiE

twenty-four

'Straight up, the stupid cow starts doing herself with a leg of lamb, topped with mint sauce.'

Billy 'Motor Mouth' Baker laughed out loud after telling his joke in the Dirty Dick boozer that Saturday night. Billy loved to talk. Everyone said that his non-stop gob was going to get him into trouble one day. And they were right. He should've kept it well and truly zipped tonight, two weeks before his boss, Frankie Sullivan, was due to stand trial for tax evasion.

The Clash's 'London Calling' rocked in the background as Billy sat with a group of seven people at two round tables. The tables shook on their legs as the laughter of the people around them erupted.

'Is it true that Frankie Sullivan's empire is gonna fall around his ears next Friday?' someone asked.

An expectant silence fell across the table. Made Billy feel he was the main geezer. He picked up his pint glass. Raised it to his mouth. Swallowed.

'We won't tell if you don't, Billy,' a female voice softly coaxed.

Billy knew he should keep it shut. If there was one thing that Frankie Sullivan couldn't stand it was a yakker. Business should always stay indoors. He looked around both tables. He'd had a jar with each one of them before. These were his mates. No one was going to grass him up.

He slipped on his most menacing gangster-number-one face and said, 'Well, I say this, now the Bill have got their snout well and truly

in Frankie's business, they ain't gonna leave him alone until all he's
left with is the shirt on his back.'

The circle seemed to grow tighter as more questions were fired his
way. But Billy laughed and stood up at the same time as the woman
who had egged him on to confide in the group went to the Ladies.

He nodded to the group. 'If I don't get home my old lady will be
wondering where her shag's gone.'

As soon as she reached the toilet the woman pulled out her mobile.

'His mouth's moving quicker than a virgin dick inside a tom. He's
on his way out.'

Billy staggered into the blustering night breeze. As he walked he
began to whistle the current number-one tune. He turned into the
narrow, dark street where he'd parked his motor. A swift kick hit him
between his legs from behind. He toppled backwards, groaning. He
looked up at the same time as a baseball bat whacked him across the
mouth. Two of his front teeth loosened, filling his mouth with blood,
as he slipped into unconsciousness.

Billy knew he was fucked as soon as his eyes opened and he saw
Frankie Sullivan standing over him. Billy was naked and trussed up
like a Christmas turkey, lying on a large piece of plastic in a tiny
cabin on a boat moving along the River Thames. His mouth was held
wide open by some kind of contraption so he couldn't speak. His
eyes looked wild with fear as he gazed terrified at his boss.

'This is what happens to people who can't keep their gobs shut,'
Frankie said softly. He held his arm out to the side. Another man stepped
out of the shadows. Jason Nelson. He placed a metal object into
Frankie's hand. Billy's eyes ran manically over the object, not able
to process what was going on. Frankie crouched down beside him. His
hand pressed a button on the object he held. A blue and orange flame
ignited. Billy nearly pissed himself when he realised what it was. A
blowtorch. Jason suddenly knelt down behind Billy. Grabbed his head.
Shoved it upward. Frankie leaned towards Billy, the flame getting closer
to Billy's mouth. He shoved the flame inside. Billy screamed as the fire lit

up his tongue and the inside of his mouth. His tongue exploded in a fountain of blood. Blood spurted onto his face, onto the floor. Then his mouth erupted into flame. His screams and the smell of burnt flesh filled the cabin. Frankie stood up and watched Billy's head burn. Ten minutes later Billy was dead, his face completely unrecognisable.

'Get rid of his teeth and hands and then cut him up and feed him to the fish,' Frankie instructed the two men standing in the shadows near the door.

Jason and Frankie stepped back, beginning to peel off their bloody clothing.

'From now on make sure that the men know to keep it buttoned. If this happens again, it's gonna be your tongue that hits the dirt,' Frankie spat out.

As Jason nodded, Frankie's mobile went off. He answered it. It was Finlay.

'I've got the info you need on the judge . . .'

Frankie smiled as the boat drifted past one of London's hottest clubs – the Shim-Sham-Shimmy.

'Right, get your gear and get out.'

Jackie Jarvis winced at the furious words coming from inside Misty's office in the Shim-Sham-Shimmy club. She knew there was a real ole ding-dong going on inside. Physically she had changed completely from the plump Jade who'd landed on Misty's boat ten years earlier. She was still small, but now slim, with a face still dominated by huge green eyes, but topped with coral-coloured, pixie-cut hair and a chin that thrust out, projecting to the world a feisty don't-f-with-me English bulldog image.

She stood at the top of the glossy steel spiral staircase that led to Misty's office. Below, the dance floor was packed with punters letting off steam to a new club remix of Grace Jones's 'Slave To The Rhythm'. Sometimes she still couldn't believe that this club belonged to her and the others.

Her mind zoomed back ten years. The sale of the diamonds had raked in a cool four million. Misty had fenced the diamonds through some contacts in the underworld. The sale had been completed abroad so that Frankie would be less likely to trace the transaction. To keep those sniffing around off the scent, Misty had put it about town that she'd come up trumps on the lottery. They'd agreed that there was no way they could put the money in a bank because it would get people asking awkward questions; instead some of the money was invested in property and the rest in the one thing that Misty had always wanted – her own club on the banks of the River Thames. So they'd gone on the hunt, looking for the right place to become their club. Five months later they'd found it, a run-down building, full of dust, broken windows and with part of its roof missing, in Wapping. The building had been like that for years and the owners, London Transport, had been keen for someone to take it off their hands. It took them nearly a year to transform that tired-looking building into the Shim-Sham-Shimmy club, filled with people decked out in their party clobber, high on music, having a blast every night of the week. They were all equal partners in the club, but the girls were silent partners. Jackie and Anna were the only ones who took an active role, Anna helping Misty with the entertainment side of the biz and Jackie in charge of the bar staff and the cleaners. Roxy and Ollie had little to do with the club, Roxy content to devote herself to married life and her computer analyst job and Ollie living an unobtrusive existence working in a charity helping asylum seekers and refugees.

Remaining in London had always been a risk, but the girls had said that the only place they'd felt safe was with Misty, and Misty had said that the day she left London permanently would be the day she was put six feet under. So they'd lain low on Misty's boat for a year, travelling along England's waterways. At the same time Misty had spread rumours, through her brothers, that the girls had scarpered abroad with their ill-gotten gains. The girls had turned into successful women, living lives finally free of Frankie Sullivan and the St Nicholas care home.

The shouting inside Misty's office got louder, dragging Jackie back to the present. With a sigh, she opened the door and stepped inside.

*   *   *

Misty's office was rectangular, a good size, painted in eye-blinding white and yellow – floor, walls, door, phone, even the furniture. Misty said that when people came into her office she wanted them to imagine they were stepping onto the sunny side of the street. The only other colour was provided by a large, framed photograph of David Bowie with his arm casually around guitarist Mick Ronson's shoulder as they sang 'Starman'.

On one side of the office stood a tearful Stacey, the club's young singer, and Misty McKenzie. Misty was decked out in a butt-hugging, long shimmering dress – the colour of which Jackie had never had the heart to tell Misty reminded her of a blue rinse – which stopped just before it hit the floor, allowing her metallic purple heels to peep through. Long, soft cotton gloves covered half her arms and she wore a black wig that was a throwback to Diana Ross in her Supreme days. Misty might be kicking forty plus – she'd always been a bit hazy with the girls about her age – but she hadn't changed much since that night in King's Cross ten years earlier. Maybe a few more creases around her eyes, but it was the same ol' Misty.

A thunderous-faced Anna Crane, who had once been Amber Craig, faced Misty and the club's singer. Ten years ago, as a teenager, Amber might've been a knockout, but now, in her new guise as Anna, she'd become a raving beauty. The bronze glow of her long face and the ready smile on her ripe lips, her finely arched eyebrows and blue eyes, which most people didn't realise were thanks to contact lenses, drew people in. Her thick black hair swirled beneath her shoulder blades. She dressed like a celeb expecting the paparazzi to burst through the door and always wore four-inch heels to make sure she topped six foot.

Anna moved angrily towards Stacey, her chest heaving with the force of the words she'd just spoken.

'I won't do it again,' Stacey pleaded, taking a step closer to Anna.

'You're damn right you won't because you ain't getting the chance, girl. I've warned you in the past about turning up sauced out of your skull,' Anna countered.

Misty stepped between the two women. 'Look, sweetheart.' Misty directed his words at the young singer. 'Anna's already given you untold chances. I think if you're gonna stay with us we need to have a bit of a chinwag with your manager. We took you on without meeting him, but I think it's time we brought him into the picture.'

Relieved, Stacey nodded.

'Why don't we go to the dressing room so you can give me your manager's details? He's based in Soho, ain't he?'

Stacey quickly nodded again as she headed for the door and rushed out as if the hounds of hell were after her. The rhythm of the music downstairs pulsed into the room. Misty followed, but Anna's words held her back.

'You're such a soft touch.'

'I can't help it if my heart is made of the purest gold,' Misty replied defensively.

'Alright, you sort it out. Lay the law down to her manager and make him understand that the next time she gets blotto she'll be flying through the air because my foot has kicked her arse outta the door.'

Misty gave a quick nod and was gone.

Anna continued to stare hard at the closed door. Then she moved towards the window to watch the crowds downstairs. 'I wish she didn't treat this as if it were a charity.' Jackie moved to stand beside her.

'Let's not forget it's because of her charity that we're standing here today.'

'Yeah, but she's gotta understand that this is a business. It's taken us years to put the Shim-Sham-Shimmy on London's map.'

As Jackie opened her mouth to speak, a wave of dizziness swept her. She wobbled on her feet.

'You alright?' Anna asked as her hand steadied Jackie.

'Yeah,' Jackie quickly answered. Her fingertips caught the gold chain around her neck. Nikki's necklace. She'd had it repaired and wore it always. 'I've been feeling a bit rough lately.'

'Must be nerves about the wedding next week.' Anna chuckled. 'Look,' she suddenly said, her voice lighting up with excitement as she peered through the window. Her finger pointed downstairs. 'There's Ollie.'

Jackie's eyes danced through the crowd until she found Olivia's – or Ollie as they called her for short – figure moving around the side of the dance floor.

'Come on,' Anna began, heading for the door. 'Let's go and join her to chat about all those delicious plans we've made for your hen night next Friday and the big day on Saturday. I still can't believe that you're tying the knot.'

Arm in arm they made their way downstairs, all thoughts of Stacey and her manager pushed out of their minds.

They found Ollie seated at their usual table in the VIP lounge. Jackie leaned down and gave Ollie a tight hug. There was little left of Opal, the child soldier who had turned up in their life on New Year's Day ten years earlier. She had ditched the baseball cap in favour of a small, finger-combed Afro, Michael Caine-style designer glasses and large looped silver earrings. Unlike Anna's her clothing was simple, usually standard jeans, T-shirt and leather jacket. She was still the quietest member of the group, the gentleness and strength stamped on her face growing more intense with age.

As the two other women seated themselves beside her, a breathless voice called out, 'Really sorry I'm late.'

They looked up to find Roxy rushing towards them. Ruby's transformation into Roxy Malone had turned her into a chubby, buttermilk blonde, who had ditched the glasses for contacts and wore clothes that were best described as middle-of-the-road nice. Tonight she wore a tailored blue skirt suit that fitted with her chosen life as a computer analyst for a City firm in the day and a childless housewife come evening. She'd married one of her work colleagues, Martin, five years earlier.

Roxy did a mad rush around the table, dropping a kiss on each of her friends' cheeks. Jackie instantly smelt the mint spray on her breath and knew it was to disguise the booze she secretly downed every day. Jackie knew that Roxy would be shocked to find out that they all knew about the flask of Smirnoff vodka she carried in her bag.

'Traffic was an absolute nightmare,' Roxy said as she plonked herself into a chair, stretching her arms across the table. 'London's unbelievable. It's a wonder anyone can move around at all. I tell you . . .' She continued talking, in a voice that was still high and squeaky, as the others sighed. They were used to her rabbiting on about nothing and everything. Chatter, chatter, chatter. Sometimes it was hard to get her to stop.

'What happened to your arm?' Ollie asked abruptly, in her quiet accented voice. Jackie and Anna followed the direction of Ollie's gaze. The exposed lower part of Roxy's arm showed a ring of deep, red bruises that resembled fingerprints. Roxy quickly whipped her arms off the table and laid them tightly in her lap. Her eyes darted nervously around. 'You know what the trains are like in the morning. A real animal house. Some man pushed me out of the way to get a seat.' The veins in her throat grew with each word.

'He's still fucking hitting you, ain't he?' Jackie spat out.

Three years into Roxy's marriage, Jackie and the others had begun to notice the bruises on the exposed parts of Roxy's body, which usually meant her throat and arms, but never on her face. At first they'd swallowed Roxy's tales of being accident prone, but it hadn't taken them long to realise that her beloved Martin, Mr Respectable Middle Class, was frequently decking her one. As much as the others had tried to persuade her to leave him she wouldn't go, always insisting that Martin was sorry and loved her.

'You've gotta get out of there, Roxy, before he really shits you up,' Anna said.

Roxy pulled out her asthma pump. Inhaled twice. 'It's all going to be OK now because we're seeing a counsellor . . .'

Jackie stabbed her finger at Roxy as she furiously cut in, 'He don't need no fucking counsellor, babe, he needs to be locked up twenty-four-seven and the key chucked away. If he's still going at you after my wedding I'm gonna come around and sort him out.'

Before Roxy could answer, a voice softly asked, 'Ladies?' They looked up to find Gio, who ran the bar, standing next to their table. 'What can I tempt you with?' His eyes settled boldly on Ollie. She caught the gaze of his caramel eyes, then hastily looked away and dipped her head low. The others didn't need to see her face to know that she was blushing like it was a sizzling summer's day. Gio had the hots for her. They knew it. She knew it. Gio was what Anna called 'a classic piece of manhood' and just couldn't understand why Ollie didn't take what was on offer.

'Bottle of your best vintage fizz,' Anna answered.

'Plus a double vodka and Coke,' Roxy added.

Gio smiled, nodded, gave Ollie one last lingering look, then was gone.

'Why don't you put that man outta his misery?' Anna asked, looking directly at Ollie.

'He's a walking sex machine. No one has got a bad word to say about him.'

'Anna's right,' Jackie chipped in. 'He's a real love. You wanna read what the graffiti say about him in the Ladies. He's got a wagon-load of women after him, but he won't even glance their way because those big brown eyes of his are too busy touching you up and down.'

Ollie let out a tiny sigh but said nothing.

'Go on,' Roxy joined in, flicking her fingers through her fringe, moving her hair out of her eye. Her sleeve eased back, revealing the bruises on her arm. 'For once in your life let someone take care of you.'

Ollie ran a knowing glance over Roxy and said, 'Like Martin takes care of you with his fists every day?'

A strained silence descended on the table. Roxy pulled her sleeve tightly over the marks on her arm at the same time as Anna's mobile began to ring. Anna's eyes lit up as she pulled out the phone.

'Hey, babe . . .' she said, voice all dreamy and soft.

She carried on talking as the others watched her. Jackie smiled, knowing it was Anna's latest girlfriend. The only one she'd never let them meet. Anna had been upfront about her sexuality since she'd hit eighteen. And, as she'd put it, 'If anyone didn't like it they could sit on this' – she'd shown them the finger. From that day forward Anna had revealed herself to be a complete tart in her pursuit of the ultimate sexual pleasure. She loved women and didn't care who knew about it. Many a man had followed her progress across the dance floor with regret as she grooved with her latest lady. But whoever her latest shag was she was keeping to herself. Jackie suspected that Anna was in love for the first time in her life.

'See you on Monday for lunch?' Anna ended the call.

'Are you bringing this phantom woman to the wedding?' Jackie asked.

Anna giggled. 'I might. I might not. Forget about my love life. I think we've all forgotten what we're doing here. We're meant to be organising Jackie's hen night for next Friday, so let's get happy, people.'

A waitress interrupted, bringing their drinks. As the women drank their excited talk spilled across the table.

'Alright, this is the plan,' Anna said, taking charge. 'A mate of mine can guarantee us some male strippers – you know, the ones that put pink fluorescent rings on their you-know-whats as their finale piece . . .'

'I've already told you I don't want none of that malarkey at my do. I just wanna keep it simple. Us lot, Misty, music and loads of booze,' Jackie cut in.

Roxy signalled for another vodka and Coke as she said in a slurred voice, 'Don't be so boor-ring. How can you have a hen night without a prime bit of meat stuck in your face?'

Everyone, apart from Jackie, chuckled. 'The only meat I'm interested in marinating is my man's.' Jackie shook her head. Raised her champagne flute to her lips and sipped. 'I just want it be a family affair. My last night of being single, I don't want no strangers there.' She stopped. Took a deep breath. Her voice was soft as she continued. 'I want my hen night to be a celebration of the people I love most in the world. Without you lot and Misty I wouldn't be tying the knot next Saturday.'

A thoughtful silence tightened around them. Each one of them thinking of what might have been if they hadn't contacted Misty ten years ago.

Anna's resigned, cheerful voice broke the silence. 'Alright, have it your way, but I'm telling you I've heard that those strippers hit a maximum ten every time on you hetero girls' clitometre.'

They all roared with laughter. Anna's face lit up when Abba's 'Dancing Queen' hit the dance floor. She sprang to her feet and shouted, 'Come on, you lot, let's show this crowd what real dancing looks like.'

Laughing, the others followed her to the dance floor. A deep smile spread across Jackie's face as they all began to groove in a circle. This was the life. Mates. Music. And next Saturday, matrimony. She let out a high-pitched laugh as she did a mad half-spin. Yeah, life was bloody good. And there was only one way her life was going – up!

twenty-five

'Silly cows,' Misty muttered with affection as she stared through the office window at her four girls gyrating madly on the dance floor.

She raised the glass, with its final layer of G&T sloshing at the bottom, to her red-painted lips. She loved those girls and always would She moved away from the window and walked to her desk. Wearily she placed the glass on the desktop as she sat down. She riffled through the desk until she found what she was looking for. A photograph. It showed Anna, Jackie and Roxy, ten years ago, when they were Amber, Jade and Ruby, all dressed up, ready to celebrate New Year's Eve. Misty knew she should've thrown the picture away as they'd all agreed to destroy anything that linked them to the fifteen-year-old girls who'd lived at St Nicholas. But for some reason she hadn't been able to let the picture go. Maybe it was because it was the last snapshot of them before they'd had to change their lives? Maybe it was because she didn't want them to regret not having any great memories when they got older and nostalgia crept into their lives?

As she'd predicted, if anyone had come looking for the girls all those years ago they never found them. *Miss Josephine* had been the ideal place to hide out. Mind you, she'd never told the girls that Frankie had nearly got close two years after they'd started the club. A man had turned up looking for Misty, asking questions. Of course, Misty had played the innocent, saying she didn't have a clue about no girls. The man had never mentioned Frankie's name, but Misty knew it must have been him who had sent him sniffing around.

She placed the photo back in the drawer. Picked up the card with Stacey's manager's details on it. Kicked off her purple heels. Shoved her feet onto the desk as she dialled the number.

'Is that Stacey Long's manager? This is Misty McKenzie from the Shim-Sham-Shimmy club. I'm really sorry to be bothering you so late, but the thing is I think we need to meet up to discuss Stacey. She's a great kid and singer, but she's developed a slight crease in her contract that needs ironing out.'

Misty listened as she wiggled the tiredness from her toes. 'I'm glad you agree. Why don't you come down to the club on Monday? Let's say at one.'

The bastards were out to get him.

The words slammed through Frankie Sullivan's mind as he moved towards the window of his penthouse office on the Isle of Dogs. His eyes squinted in a face that had changed very little in the last ten years. Sure, there were a few more lines, a couple of stray grey hairs, but what could a bloke expect after building up one of London's toughest criminal empires?

He leaned forward. Opened the catch on the window. Pushed. Cast his eyes over the city's darkness. Inhaled. Strong and deep. His breathing became easier, as it always did when he savoured the sounds and tastes of London. This was his city. His manor. It had taken him years to carve his name into its granite. After those four bitches had ripped him off, ten years ago, and left that bag full of diamonds on the plane, which finally brought him onto the Bill's radar, he had made sure he'd kept a stranglehold on his business. Of course, the Bill had had to let Jason go through lack of evidence, but they had tried every which way they could to try to bring him down, although they'd never been able to make anything stick. That was until now. Next Friday he was in court on tax evasion charges. But his brief had warned that if they found him guilty it might be the Bill's first step in trying to strip him bare of everything he'd ever made. No, that wasn't how it was going to be played out. No way. Not while he still had a lick of breath in his body. He was prepared do anything to stop it. Anything.

The only option left to him was to dig up any dirt on the judge who was trying his case and pile the pressure on. Push the judge so far into her own dock she had no alternative but to rule that Frankie ran a legitimate operation. Game over.

'What did you find out about Her Worship Cynthia Gray-Hammond?'

Frankie directed his question at the two men who sat at his desk behind him – Jason Nelson and Finlay Powell. They were still together, just like they'd been all those years ago growing up at St Nicholas. If it was possible Finlay had become more flash with age – designer suits of all colours and shades, two gold studs in his ears and a new mobile phone every time he stepped outside his front door. Frankie shifted his eyes to Jason with distaste. All the money they had netted over the years should have made Jason into a professional man. Instead he'd became coarser, louder, with twenty pounds of excess fat sloshing around his middle and always yakking in a voice filled with the tone of an arrogant drinker and cokehead.

Frankie winced as a wave of pain shot through his right leg as he moved to join his friends. He sucked in a harsh breath, the intense spurt of oxygen whizzing his mind back to the days at St Nicholas. Back to that teenage bitch who'd pumped two slugs into him, leaving him with this legacy of pain. If he ever got his hands on her he'd push the nozzle of a piece into her mouth, watch the fear twist in her black eyes and blow whatever life she'd been living for the last ten years out the back of her head.

'The old leg giving you a bit of gyp again?'

Jason's question pulled Frankie back to the present as he sat down. He threw the other man a sharp, heated look. Both Finlay and Jason knew better than to ever mention anything to do with his leg. It got him mad. Real mad.

'I got this new bird,' Jason carried on, oblivious to the warning in Frankie's glare. 'A real young 'un, in one of my massage parlours, who will sort that leg of yours out. Fucking hell,' he swung his head from side to side like he was regaling an audience down the pub, 'she's got hands that'll make you feel like a newborn baby.' Jason bellowed with laughter.

'Shut the fuck up, man, and stop performing like a tit.' Finlay swung towards Jason. He kissed his teeth. 'We're up to our chops in shit and all you can chat about is some tart with healing hands.'

'Sorry, Frankie, no harm intended, mate.'

Frankie ignored the apology as he leaned back in the black leather chair and repeated, 'What did you find out about the judge?'

'Sod all,' Finlay replied as he spun a document folder, clockwise, across the table towards Frankie. The colour of the folder blended into the shade of the desk, which was a former butcher's block. Frankie had purchased it as a reminder to all three of them what they needed to do sometimes to stay on top.

'She's bloody Snow White,' Finlay continued. 'Couldn't find one speck of dirt on her lady bitch the judge.'

Frankie stabbed his forefinger on the folder. 'Let me be the judge of that.' He should've laughed at the word 'judge' but didn't.

He opened the folder. The first page held a large photo of a woman with a steel-grey bob and borders of deep wrinkles around her eyes which said she was well on her way to sixty. Her face was set into a stern, icy pose. Definitely a woman who didn't let people off the hook. Frankie shifted the photo to the side as he read the next sheet of information.

Name: Cynthia Gray-Hammond
Age: 58
Occupation: QC
Home: 14 Primrose Square, Chelsea
Education: St Bernadette's private school for girls, Oxford University and the LSE
Family: Son and sister. Husband deceased
Leisure: Bridge, the Mayflower Club and cooking

'What do we know about her time at school and university?' Frankie finally asked, keeping his eyes on the paper.

'No drugs, no raving. Little Miss Judge was a good little girl.'

'What about the husband?'

'Nothing there either. Get this for a fucking fairy tale.' Finlay rolled his eyes in a dramatic gesture. 'They were *in love*. So it was a total shock when he was kidnapped in Colombia four years ago.'

'Kidnapped?' Frankie's voice was sharp as he lifted his eyes to Finlay.

'Yeah. He was the big chief of some company and got nabbed on his way to dinner one night. The five-figure ransom was paid, but didn't stop his body turning up minus its head.'

'Any other blokes since then?'

'The judge is keeping her pussy sealed to the world.'

Family: Son . . . Frankie ran his eyes over the information. Did it again. And again. 'What do we know about her boy?'

'Name's Daniel, but everyone name checks him as Danny. Fifteen years old and at some boarding school on the other side of town. And she loves him to bits. Apparently he's the spitting image of her old man.'

Frankie's finger came up and rubbed the scar next to his left eyebrow as he remembered another little boy who'd been the spit of his old man.

'I'll teach you to look at me with his eyes, Frankie Sullivan,' his mum had yelled.

Then she raised her hand, swung the belt through the air and brought it down with all her might across his nine-year-old face. The leather caught him under the chin. Quickly he tried to cover his face, but it was too late. The next blow caught him at the corner of his left eye. His screams had brought the neighbours thumping at the door.

'Fuck off,' his old lady continued to yell at the door. 'Ain't right Johnny bloody Sullivan's face has got the brass nerve to keep looking at me every day, not after what he done.'

The next thing he remembered was the breaking down of the door. That night he'd been taken away for good.

'The son.' Frankie's voice was faint, his mind locked inside his memories, his fingers locked down on the sheet of paper. His eyes shone bright as he gazed at the bewildered expressions on his two friends' faces. 'That's her weakness.'

'Back up one minute, boss. Tell me you ain't thinking of what I think you're thinking.' Finlay leaned over the desk. 'Bro, you outta your fucking tree? You can't be thinking of snatching him?'

Frankie tilted his head to the side as he spoke. 'Look, if we can get her darling little boy we can play a little game with the right honourable judge. It's a game where both parties have something the other one wants. She's got a stronghold over my assets and I've got the stranglehold on her son. The rules are simple. She says there's nothing dodgy about my finances and I let her kid go. Simple.'

'I get where you're coming from.' Anxiety joined the bewilderment in Finlay's voice. 'But we're talking about a woman who's always walked on the right side of the street. What's to stop goody-two-shoes from blabbing to the Old Bill? Fucking hell, you'd be doing serious bird for the rest of your days.'

'She won't . . .'

'It's too risky. How can you be so sure she won't?' Jason finally joined the debate. Frankie pulled his head straight, with a grim expression on his face. 'When the good judge looks at her son she sees her beloved dead husband. That's what she loves, it's his face. When she receives a close-up photo of his face, mouth and eyes covered tight with duct tape and a nine-millimetre stuck in his temple, do you think she's gonna risk going to the police? Do you think she's gonna risk losing the one living connection she has to her husband? Risk another member of her family being kidnapped and turning up dead?'

'OK.' Finlay shuffled back in his chair. 'Say you're right and she decides not to go to them, what's stopping her from contacting the filth once her kid's back in her loving embrace?'

'Easy. We outsource the work. We get someone else to do the snatch on our behalf. So if the Old Bill come knocking at our gates they're gonna be pissing in the wind because they'll have to show us what evidence they've got connecting us to the deed. And if we've outsourced the work there ain't gonna be a trail leading back to us. And by then it's too late, the judge has ruled in my favour.'

Frankie flicked his gaze between his two friends as they mulled over his idea.

'So who've you got in mind to do it?' Jason asked. 'It ain't like the old days, you just can't trust the fuckers on the street any more. All they're interested in is lining their pockets with as much bread and honey as they can. You give the job to one of them and they'll take our dosh and shop us to the Bill as well in the blink of an eye.'

'I know that. I just ain't sussed out who it will be. But whoever it is has got to be an outsider. Someone who the Old Bill wouldn't figure out in a million years would be involved in this kind of shit.'

'What time did I tell you to get back home?'

Roxy heard her husband's voice as soon as she shut the front door. She knew that she might be pissed to kingdom come but that didn't stop the fear she felt every time she came home. She found him waiting in the darkness at the top of the stairs of their five-bedroom house in Greenwich. She stared back at him, frightened out of her wits as she flattened her back against the front door.

'We just got talking about Jackie's wedding. I . . . I . . . I . . .'

'I asked you a question.' Each word was slow, matching the steps he now took down the stairs.

'Martin, please . . .' She cringed against the door.

The man she'd pledged her life to five years ago ignored her plea as he stepped into the hall. He stopped. Ran his gaze insolently over her.

'Please,' his voice mimicked hers.

His hands moved to his waist. Worked quickly at the buckle of his belt. Pulled the belt from its resting place around his trousers. Doubled it in his hand. Shook it as he moved slowly towards her. Roxy filled the decreasing distance between them with huge, aching sobs. She slid broken and helpless down onto the carpet. He reached her. Raised the belt high. Held it. Then it swung down in an arch of anger, seeking flesh. It landed with a direct hit across her stomach and waist. Her body jerked back in pain as she screamed. And in the midst of her scream she called out a single name. Maxine.

The name of her mother.

'Wanna come up for a cuppa?' Jackie asked Ollie.

They stood in the midnight shadows of the stairs of the block they both lived in – Ernest Bevin House, nicknamed Ernie by all its residents. It was a four-storey purpose-built block on the south side of Hackney, a few minutes' walk from the Regent's Canal and a couple of bus stops away from the City. Misty could never understand why Jackie and Ollie didn't live in one of the plush apartments overlooking the canal instead of a council block. All Jackie had said in response was that she needed to live somewhere that reminded her of Manny Shinwell House, with people below and above her. She still needed to feel she was part of a community. Both she and Ollie had intended to keep their heads down, their noses to themselves, but soon Jackie had begun to do favours for some of the other residents.

'Do you mind babysitting my Chantelle while I'm out?'

'Will you come with me to the council building because I've been waiting two weeks solid for them to repair my hot water?'

'Know anyone who can sort my cheating husband out because he's been seeing some tart?'

Before she knew it people saw her as the voice of the block. What the other residents didn't realise was that between them Jackie and Ollie owned seven other flats in the block. They both rented them out to the local authority as a place for teenagers leaving care and refugee families.

Ollie shook her head. Jackie squeezed her mate's hand. 'You might not need them one day.'

They both knew what *them* were. The heavy-duty sleeping pills that Ollie took to help her sleep and escape the nightmares she still had about her time in the rebel army. Ollie said nothing, just let her face stay closed. Jackie leaned over and kissed her on the cheek.

'See ya tomorrow,' she whispered. She turned and made her way to her home.

Ollie stepped into the chilled darkness of her one-bedroom flat and closed the door behind her. The tiredness tingled in her bones as she leaned back against the door. Maybe, just maybe, the tiredness would tumble her into a natural sleep tonight. Without the nightmares. Without the pills. She hovered at the partially opened door of her bedroom as she did every night. And the feeling was always the same. She was frightened to take that step forward. Frightened to lie on the bed and close her eyes. Frightened that the only images waiting for her were a haunting replay of the life she'd once lived. Plus, after all these years, she still hadn't told Jackie that she'd known her mother. What was the point in telling her? She'd only get upset all over again. And Ollie wasn't going to add more pain to Jackie's life.

Ollie knew she should get help. Put herself into therapy. But she hadn't and as the years passed the nightmares got deeper. Longer. That was why she couldn't see Gio, even though she fancied the bollocks off him. The others, she knew, would be shocked to find out she'd never had a boyfriend. How the hell was she going to explain that she'd once killed people for her daily bread?

She pushed the door. Stepped inside. Moved to the bed. Sat down. Looked at the small side table that held three items. A small digital clock, a black-bound Bible and a bottle of heavy-duty sleeping pills. She eased fully clothed onto the blue duvet. Closed her eyes.

Tipped helter-skelter into a nightmare. Of fire. Of bullets. Of broken and twisted bodies. Of her last night in Sankura sharing a cell with Nikki Flynn. Of Frankie Sullivan's blood oozing down his trousers as she blasted him in the leg.

Ollie bellowed with outrage as she shot up. Fingertip-sized rivers of sweat carved into her face. Dripped into her eyes. Her body shook as if the bed were a blanket of ice. Her hands searched wildly for her bottle of pills. She tipped a single pill into the palm of her hand. Stared at it and cried harder. Cried because the only peace she got in the night came from a flat red pill that was the same colour as the blood of the first person she'd ever killed.

twenty-six

What the bloody hell is that? Jackie asked herself as she crept along her hallway. The noise came again, this time louder, shooting from under the door of the sitting room. She shook her head from side to side when she realised what it was. Giggles. A man and a boy. Her son Ryan and husband-to-be Elijah 'Schoolboy' Campbell. Even without looking she knew what they would be up to – Ryan practising his part in the end-of-year performance for the drama school he attended on Saturdays.

She moved to the door, pushed it slightly open and gazed at the two most important people in her life. Ryan was in his jim-jams, reciting lines from *Oliver Twist*. He was the product of a six-night stand. At eighteen, like most other girls basking in the first thrill of womanhood, she'd set out looking for love. And what a total disaster that had been. Instead of finding Romeo she'd got all gooey-eyed over some lowlife wannabe geezer. Jimmy Burke. Six foot of flashing teeth, gold chains up to the eyeballs and non-stop chat. When she announced she was up the duff he'd lived up to the unique qualities of his surname and pissed off as quick as his fast grin came and went. Misty, as usual, had picked up the pieces, provided a shoulder to cry on and offered to find her a discreet clinic. But her Catholic upbringing had reared its head, reminding her of the consequences of eternal damnation. So she'd had her baby two months before her nineteenth birthday. Cried real hard when she held him in her arms for the first time and realised he had Nikki's flame-coloured hair.

Jackie pushed the door wide and entered the room. Ryan and Schoolboy shot around. Schoolboy was a medium-sized black man, with a strong thirty-two-year-old brown face, shoulder-length locks that were neatly tied back and dimples that could make Jackie's heart swell as wide as the Mile End Road.

'You,' she pointed a finger at Ryan, who stood just in front of the telly, which was on low, 'should be in bed. And you,' her finger swivelled to point at Schoolboy, 'should know better.'

Schoolboy grinned back at her, the two dimples she loved so much digging into his cheeks. He raised his hand and shrugged his shoulders. 'You know us boys, when the cat's away . . .'

Jackie turned her stern-mummy eyes to Ryan. 'Hop it.'

Jackie ruffled his hair as he skipped past her and left the room. As soon as the door closed Schoolboy stretched out his hand and she walked into his embrace. She melted into the warmth and scent of this man, who Misty said she was nuts to hook up with. But only she understood that she and Schoolboy were kindred spirits. One of a kind. The former bad boy of the block and the woman with one too many secrets. Secrets she hadn't shared with him. She had come close many times to telling him, but each time she'd stopped herself, worried by what he'd think. Worried that the only man she'd ever stuck on a pedestal, next to Misty, would turn and walk the other way.

'You look like you're sleeping on your feet, babe. A heavy night at the Triple S?' His question pulled Jackie away from her turbulent thoughts.

Before she could answer him he manoeuvred her to the soft two-seater sofa and pulled her upper body across him as he sat down. She snuggled deep into him as she answered his question.

'The usual. Anna doing her nut because one of the singers is playing up. Roxy pissed out of her brainbox. Gio trying everything, short of waving his knob in her face, to get Ollie's attention.'

'Two weeks left and you're all mine, morning, noon and night.' His hand stroked her hair.

'You're sure you still wanna do this?' She drew imaginary tiny, shy circles on his chest.

'Can't think of anything better than to spend the rest of my respectable life with my favourite girl.'

Favourite girl. Just hearing him say that gave her a thrill. More than if he'd said I love you; adore you; I'll give you the sun, moon and stars and all that bollocks. He was her favourite girl and she was his favourite boy. Simple. They'd both come through life the hard way. Seen and done things that would make other people shudder. Guilt started eating at her as she thought about the secrets she hadn't told him. What would he say if he knew what had really happened while she was in St Nicholas? That her given name was Jade Flynn? Maybe she should do it now while she was wrapped in the tenderness of his arms.

She tipped her head back to look at him with anxiety deepening the green of her eyes and quietly asked, 'What's the worst thing you could find out about someone?'

'They've got *The Sound of Music* in their DVD collection.'

She giggled and rested her head back on his chest. But the smile soon dropped away as she felt the steady rhythm of his heartbeat.

'I'm being dead serious.'

'You know where I've come from and it ain't pretty, so who the fuck am I to judge anyone else?'

'But just say someone did . . .'

'I ain't a complete doughnut, Jack,' he cut her off. 'I know you've got secrets. So have I. Shit, if I told you half the stuff I'd done you'd be flogging that wedding dress to the Oxfam shop quicker than you can say "I do".' His hand left her hair. Settled into the small of her back. Pulled her tighter against him. 'I love you. There ain't anyone like you. And if I was a praying man I'd be on my knees every day thanking the Almighty that a decent girl like you took a one-time scumbag like me into her life.'

A decent girl. The phrase echoed in her mind. She couldn't tell him, she just couldn't do it. Not now. Maybe never. She burrowed deep into his body, let the security of his love help her banish the memories of the past. Suddenly she pushed him, making him fall onto his back. Eased her upper body straight. Wiggled forward until her knees were either side of his hips.

'Why don't I just remind you how good I am at taking you into my life.'

She met his eyes. Their lips touched and the loving started. Her head reared to the side as she groaned. Her glazed eyes caught the TV screen. Caught the news. Caught the headline, in white type, at the bottom of the screen: 'Frank Sullivan first to be prosecuted by the new Criminal Assets Recovery Agency?'

Jackie stopped moving. Stopped breathing. Frank Sullivan. Frankie. Over the years she had heard bits and pieces about him. Knew that his empire had grown and he was considered one of the leading lights of London's underworld. A man to be feared.

'You alright, girl?'

Dazed, she swiftly turned to face Schoolboy. His eyes darted towards the television and then back to his face.

'Yeah, sure,' she mumbled.

But she wasn't alright. Slowly she moved off him and sat limply beside him.

'Jack?'

She felt him push himself into a sitting position. His arm moved across her shoulders.

'I'm fine.' Two of her fingers rubbed Nikki's necklace. 'Just tired. Do me a big favour, make me a nice cuppa.'

'Your wish is my command, Milady.'

But she didn't laugh at his attempt at a joke. How could she with fucking Frankie Sullivan camped in her head? She heard Schoolboy leave the room. Quickly she turned back to the box. The news item was still on, but now with film of Frankie, wearing shades, getting into a car outside a building somewhere in London. She just sat there and stared at the screen. A minute later, the news item changed, to reports of the previous month's military coup in Sankura. Jackie pressed her lips together, tight and hard. If anyone ever tried to force her son to live the type of life Frankie had made her live, she wouldn't hesitate to do it. She'd kill them.

twenty-seven

Balls.

She was late. A flustered Misty checked her watch again. Thirteen minutes late for the meeting with Stacey's manager. Monday was already proving to be a killer of a day. The club was such a popular venue that sometimes Misty thought they took on too much. Private parties, stag nights, hen nights. A smile lit her lips as she thought about the one hen night she didn't mind happening in the club on Friday next week. And later tonight she had to be with Jackie, watching Ryan's performance in the latest production of the Saturday drama school he attended. She checked her watch again. Balls, balls, balls. Rushed up the steps to her office, taking them two at a time, no mean feat in the new 1950s four-inch spike-heeled red satin peep-toe shoes she was breaking in.

The office door was already open. Her visitor already waiting inside. The sight of the black man, bound in a sheet of sunlight, made Misty stop on the threshold. *Oh, very nice*, she mused as she ran an appreciative gaze over the man who stood with his back to her. Six foot at least, Misty guessed, with a tailor-made deep blue designer suit fitted over his muscular frame. The tang of the man's tobacco and high-priced cologne had already staked its claim inside the room.

'So sorry to keep you waiting,' Misty apologised in a low tone.

Stacey's manager flipped around. Misty's tongue did a double flick over her top lip. *Oh, very, very, very nice.* The man's front view didn't disappoint. A solid brown face, with sharp cheekbones and sharper goatee, and a lover-man smile. The way he held his body, legs slightly apart, arms half loose, half ready by his side, with the flash of a gold chain peeping from his polo shirt, told Misty this was a man's man. A geezer. Shame. But what the heck, no harm dreaming.

Misty introduced herself, extending a hand as she came into the room. The man's smile broadened as he clasped Misty's acrylic-nailed fingers.

'My girls call me Mr Powell. But you can call me Finlay.'

'Nice outfit you've got here. The Shim-Sham-Shimmy is quite a legend.'

Finlay settled himself more deeply into the chair, near the photocopier, as he spoke to Misty from the other side of the desk. Misty threw back a smile and ruffled her neck from side to side with pride at the compliment.

'I'm surprised you haven't blessed us with your company before.'

'I'm a bit old school to be burning the midnight oil.'

Misty gave Finlay a slow, appreciative once-over. 'Oh, you look just the right age from where I'm sitting. I bet you're a real goer late at night.'

Misty raised her eyebrow at the other man knowing, that Finlay's response would show the kind of man he was. Over the years Misty's cheeky comments had raised a variety of responses – some men went ballistic, beating their chest, others rushed on talking as if nothing had been said, some cackled with laughter and took the compliment and others . . . well, they saw Misty later on to see if she could follow through on her words. Stacey's manager threw his head back and cackled with gushing, mellow laughter.

'I like a man . . .' Finlay stopped and corrected himself when he caught Misty's raised eyebrow. 'Sorry, a girl, who ain't afraid of the skin she walks in. So tell me, what's the hullabaloo with my girl Stacey?'

Misty fixed a serious expression onto her face. 'Stacey's a fantastic girl, with a cracking pair of tonsils, but . . .' She sighed. Rubbed a finger across her top lip. 'But the long and short of it is she's been behind the mic one too many times totally arseholed. We've warned her in the past and she'll stop for a while, but then the girl is back at it again.'

'You sure we're chatting about my girl Stacey?'

Misty nodded, leaning back into the comfort of her chair. Finlay sat there, still nodding his head in disbelief. 'I've known that kid since before she started putting lipstick on. Poor girl's home life was total trash, so I took her under my wing. I've been looking after girls in this business for donkey's years, and let me tell you, Stacey is one of the best. The first time I heard that girl's voice I nearly cried like I'd just come out of my momma's womb. Do you wanna terminate her contract? Is that why I'm here?'

'I don't wanna have to do that, especially now I know she's got a manager who cares about her.' Misty slipped a seductive smile onto her face 'I really like you, Finlay. Any man who looks after young girls the way you obviously do must have a good heart under all that manly flesh.'

Finlay's face crinkled as he smiled. 'I understand your position. Your place has got a reputation to protect. When my Stacey gets up on the stage she becomes the face of this Shim-Sham-Shimmy. You can't afford for punters to be thinking this is some shebeen on the waterfront.'

'You're her manager and we want to keep her, but something's got to give.'

'Why don't we bring Stacey in here for a little sit-down, wave her contract in her face and remind her that dreams for girls from her corner of the world sometimes come true but once in a lifetime. I didn't bring a copy of her contract – any chance you've got one?'

'Yeah, yeah, sure,' Misty said as her right hand reached for the top left-hand drawer of her desk. She began to empty the contents of the drawer onto the desk. 'Why can't you ever find anything when you want it? Sod's law it will be right at the bottom.' Misty continued to grumble as she placed item after item onto the desk.

Brown A4 envelope.

Scissors.

Photo.

Fluorescent lime-green G-string.

Misty's hand wavered on the G-string on top of the pile as she realised what she'd placed on the desk. She pushed her head up and looked at Finlay with a mischievous smile. 'Oops.' She winked at him. 'I use it to clean the windows.'

She snatched at the underwear. The fast movement of her hand tipped the pile onto the floor. Mortified, Misty lunged to the floor, desperately trying to gather the items together. As her hand reached for the photo she felt a shadow move over her. She flicked her head up to find Finlay crouching down.

'Let me do that,' Finlay offered, reaching for the photo. Misty's arm flopped back as the other man picked up the picture. Finlay started to pass it to Misty, but stopped when he caught the faces in the photo. Three teenage girls. Two white, one black. Dressed to the nines, ready for a late-night rave. Slowly, Finlay raised himself up. Stood to his full immense height, in the afternoon sun, the photo in his hand.

'Nice girls,' he said quietly. His eyes moved from the photo to Misty. 'Friends of yours?'

'No.' Misty's reply was as rapid as the movement of her legs as she stood up. She didn't like the look on Finlay's face. Shit, she hoped he wasn't one of those kiddie-fiddlers. Finlay smiled. Held the photo out to her. Misty almost grabbed the photo out of his hand. Slammed it back into the drawer. 'Just a picture from way back. Fans. Can't even remember when it was.' Misty's words were strung together like she'd just finished doing twenty laps around the room.

When she looked up, Finlay was back, cool and relaxed, in his seat. 'Forget about the contract,' Finlay said. 'Look, I think it might be better for me and Stacey to have a two-way chat on our own. You go and get her and then I'll make her understand what her future holds.'

'Great idea,' Misty replied, shaking any worries that she had about Finlay from her mind. 'I'll be back in a jiffy,' she added, back to her flirtatious tone.

Misty tottered towards the door. Past Finlay, who had his lover-man smile welded to his face.

*   *   *

The sunshine died in the room as the smile peeled off Finlay's face. Well, fuck me. He couldn't believe it, just couldn't believe who he'd seen in that photograph. Abruptly he got up. Swung a furtive glance towards the closed door. Then he moved. Three long strides, that was all it took to reach the other side of the desk. He stood in the invisible shadow of Misty's perfume as he stared at the drawer. He flicked his gaze back at the door. Flicked it back to the drawer. His hand reached out. Pulled. Rummaged through the contents until he found what he was looking for. Gently he lifted it out. Stared hard at it. The faces of three of those four fifteen-year-old bitches stared – smiling – back at him. As he started to move away he noticed a wad of papers, stapled together, peeping out of the drawer. He drew the document out. Flicked through it. Then he realised what he was looking at – the ownership papers of the club. He rushed to the last pages until he saw the names and signatures.

Misty McKenzie
Anna Crane
Roxy Malone
Olivia Dean
Jackie Jarvis.

He rushed over to the photocopier and quickly made a copy of the photo and the last pages of the ownership document. He rushed back to the desk. Put back the photo and papers. Tucked the photocopies into his inside jacket pocket.

I saw Frankie.
The words kicked inside Jackie's mind. She stared at a talking Anna as they sat at the club's bar, but didn't hear her mate's words. They were both hitched high on diner-style teardrop-based bar stools, with kettledrum seats the colour of the kind of lipstick mums always told their daughters only loose women wore. Jackie's hand was moulded around a thin glass of pineapple juice that sat on top of a Doris Day and Rock Hudson *Pillow Talk* drinks mat.
'Hell-lo! Earth to Jackie!'

'Uh?' Jackie answered, dazed, staring at Anna, who waved her hands frantically in front of her face.

'Have you heard a word I've just said?'

'Sorry, did you say something?'

'Say something?' Anna shuffled her long legs onto a strut of the bar stool. 'I've only been chatting on for the last five minutes like a damn fool. I asked if you're feeling nervous about the dress rehearsal tomorrow?'

'I . . .' Jackie's mouth snapped shut. It took her a few seconds to open her mouth again. 'I saw Frankie.'

The cockiness and blood fell from Anna's face. Her feet dropped from the stool. Click, her heels hit the floor. She stood up as if an invisible hand in her back had propelled her off the stool. She took a clumsy step to the side, nearly bumping into Misty and Stacey as they hurried by. Then she took a step towards Jackie. Leaned next to her on the bar.

'Where?' Anna's voice was frantic. 'Did he recognise you?'

'I didn't see him in the flesh . . .'

'I don't get it.'

'I saw him last night on the box. On the news. Looks like the Old Bill are trying to close his operation down by sucking him dry.'

'You mean he's finally gonna get screwed?' A smile crinkled the corners of Anna's mouth. 'And in public?'

'Can you imagine it?' Jackie carried on her friend's get-him-in-the-balls riff. 'The once high and mighty Frankie Sullivan broke, begging for loose change outside Mile End station?'

They looked at each other and laughed real hard. Jackie was the first to stop.

'Just wish our mums were here to see him finally get his balls cut off.'

'Do you think we should tell Roxy and Ollie?' Anna whispered.

Jackie shook her head. 'What's the point? It might just freak 'em out.'

A grinning Anna leaned over the bar and yelled, 'Oi, Gio.' The man turned around.

'Two glasses of your best bubbly.'

'What you doing?' Jackie asked.

'We're celebrating,' Anna answered as Gio placed two flutes, decorated with red hearts, in front of them and filled them up.

Both women picked up a glass. Held them out to each other.

'Never thought I'd say this,' Anna started. 'But here's to the Old Bill for doing a fucking good job of sweeping the scum off London's streets.' She took a slug of champagne and then quickly placed her glass on the bar. 'I'm outta here. I'm meeting my lady for lunch.'

Anna might be grinning from ear to ear, but Jackie couldn't shake the bad feeling she had had since Frankie had stepped back into her life on Saturday night.

By the time Misty returned with Stacey, Finlay was back in his chair. Relaxed. Legs folded, right over left, smile tilted on his face. The only difference was he now wore his purple-tinted Dolce and Gabbana shades so no one could see his eyes.

'Hi, baby,' Finlay greeted Stacey as he stood up. When he reached her, he slipped his arm around her shoulder. He twisted his head towards Misty and asked, 'Any chance of those blinds coming down so me and my girl can have some privacy?'

'No worries,' Misty said as she moved to grant Finlay's request.

When Misty was finished the sun only peeped through, branding the room in thick lines of light like the bars of a prison cell. The lack of light tightened the walls, making the room appear much smaller than it was.

'I'll leave you two to it,' Misty said as she moved towards the door. As she reached the threshold she spun back on her spiked heels, gave Finlay a generous smile and said, 'You ever decide you need company to remind yourself what burning the midnight oil feels like, you just let me know.' She let out a light, frothy laugh. Then closed the door.

Finlay's body and hand moved so fast that Stacey never saw what was coming. His hand shot off her shoulder in a deadly arc towards her throat. She squealed. He tightened his grip so that it was the last sound she made for a while. He dipped his head so that his chin rested in the crest of her neck. His nostrils flared as he smelt the tang of her high-street perfume and fear. His hot breath and words crashed against her ear. 'You need to listen up and listen good, girl. See, this is the thing, Stacey, if I give you a little squeeze you're gonna have a sore throat.' His fingers pushed against her windpipe. 'Now if I push down just a bit harder,' he followed his words through with the action, 'you might not be able to jar with your mates for a couple of days. Now if I did this . . .' His forearm slid across her throat. Locked into place. He heaved in a deep breath that rumbled in his chest like a boxer preparing for his next big swing. Stepped back, yanking her off her feet. The young woman began choking. Twisting. 'You might never sing again.' Using his arm, he swung her to the left. Swung her to the right. 'But I don't wanna destroy my girl's chance at a decent life. And let's face it, Stacey, girl, this is your only chance because you're piss poor at everything else. Don't forget where I found you – on your back with those dirty old men playing ping-pong between your legs at St Nicholas. Don't forget it was me who picked you up and taught you how to walk straight again.'

Slowly he lowered the terrified girl to the floor. Removed his arm. Stacey staggered, her hand rubbing her throat as she dragged in hulking shots of oxygen. She shook. Wobbled. Began to cry. Finlay placed his hands on her shoulders. Instinctively her shoulder jerked up, her head lowered. He twisted her so that she faced him. He moved his hand to the inside pocket of his jacket. Felt the edges of the photograph. His fingers skipped behind it and pulled out a handkerchief.

'Let's get rid of those tears.' His tone was as soft as if Misty were back in the room. Slowly she raised her face and looked at him. He placed the handkerchief on her face. Traced a path of tears that ran from her cheek to her chin. He used a finger to tip her face up and said, 'Now you know ol' Finlay hates jacking up on his girls.'

She nodded quickly.

'But we're alright now, ain't we?' he finished with a large beaming smile.

Once again she nodded. But this time she wrapped her arms around her middle as if to hold back the shaking. Finlay reached back inside his pocket and withdrew the photocopied picture. He shoved it in front of her face. 'You ever clapped eyes on this lot before?'

Terror still blazing on her face, Stacey rapidly shook her head.

'Tell me about this Anna. What's she like?'

'She runs the entertainment . . .'

He cut across her impatiently. 'I mean, what does she look like? Tall, blonde, black, white, short, fat, thin, that kind of shit.'

'Black. Tall. All the blokes fancy her . . .'

'You sure her name's Anna?'

'Yeah, yeah.'

He grabbed Stacey's arm again. She winced with the tightness of his hold. 'Who does she hang with?'

'I dunno.'

Finlay slammed Stacey into him. 'Don't make me get reacquainted with that throat of yours.'

Stacey shook as she spoke. 'She's always with Jackie, who keeps the club tidy . . .'

'What does she look like?'

'Small, slim with green eyes. She's getting married next week, Saturday, I've got an invitation to the wedding. She's having a dress rehearsal tomorrow . . .'

'Green eyes.' Finlay muttered to himself. 'What about Olivia Dean?'

'Dunno. But Anna and Jackie do have a mate who has an accent like my dad's African one and another mate who likes a bit of a guzzle. They have a girl's night in every month at the club.'

'And let me guess.' Finlay slowly let Stacey go. Gazed at the photo. 'Two are white and two are black.' He sent Stacey a menacing look. 'First thing you do when you get your arse indoors tonight is find that wedding invitation and give me a bell with the address of the church.'

He grabbed her arm and marched her towards the window near the door. With his other hand he hiked up the blind, giving them a clear view of the bar area below.

'Can you see any of those women?'

Stacey stretched her neck, looking around. She stopped when she saw Jackie sitting at the bar.

'That's Jackie.'

Finlay took a long, hard look at the woman, still not sure if it was Jade Flynn.

'Shit, she might clock me when I leave,' he murmured.

He pushed himself away from the window. His large hand clamped onto Stacey's shoulder, as hard as the glare he gave her. 'When I roll outta here you're gonna be bouncing right ahead of me, got that?'

'And then what?'

'Don't ask fucking Looney Tune questions.' He raised his palm like he was going to backhand her. But then he remembered that the blind was up. His hand dropped to his side. 'Just do what you're told. And while we're on the subject, if I ever hear that you've been trippin' standing in the spotlight I've paid for, the only use for your throat will be on your knees in a back alley with some lowlife with his trousers around his ankles, you get me, girl?'

A minute later, Finlay and Stacey were downstairs. Finlay pulled his handkerchief from his pocket, placed it over his face, pretending to sneeze, as he passed Jackie Jarvis.

twenty-eight

'Sorry to keep you waiting,' Frankie's lawyer called out as she stepped into the room. He turned to face her. Bell Dream had bob-cut blonde hair with grey threads and snappy brown eyes, a veteran of the courtroom and a hard player. Everyone said that she was the best. He'd even heard that she was a raving dyke and didn't give a toss about who knew it.

'I'm paying you by the hour,' he snapped. 'So don't keep me waiting again.'

She gave him a smile as they both sat down. Yeah, that was why he liked Bell Dream, nothing fazed her.

'Do you know what the first rule of growing up in the East End is?' Frankie asked as he took a seat.

Bell Dream shook her head.

'Keep that,' he tapped his mouth, 'shut. Second rule is never beat about the bush, so tell me, am I gonna get done or not?'

Bell linked her fingers together on the desk. Gave him a frank and open stare. 'Your case should be a simple one about tax evasion. But it is not. If the judge finds you guilty that may not be a problem. She may just give you a hefty fine and you'll be on your way. But if she finds you guilty and indicates in her summing-up statement that there's a lot more to your finances than meets the eye she effectively gives the police the green light to start proceedings against you in trying to seize your assets.'

Bell eased back in her chair. 'You're not just a case, you're *the case*. The one that they're going to try to prove that crime doesn't pay. Previous criminal assets recovery agencies have been complete shambles. Instead of confiscating the assets of suspected criminals, millions in public money went down the drain. The last agency became such a public embarrassment they had no alternative but to lock its doors, but they didn't throw away the key. Instead they're using it to unlock a new organisation whose primary aim is to prove a point. They're doing everything in their power to make sure, to paraphrase a former home secretary, that they get "flash guys in flash cars". And if you're found guilty of tax evasion I suspect that you are going to become the first case for the new Criminal Assets Recovery Agency.'

'So what's gonna happen when I go to court next Friday?'

Bell gave him a penetrating look. 'I'll be honest with you, it isn't looking like it's going to be the best day of your life.'

Frankie swore.

'They've amassed a significant amount of evidence against you in relation to tax evasion. But as I've said, the tax evasion has given them the opportunity to delve deeper into your finances. They are leaving no stone unturned. And, as I have explained to you in the past, the choice of judge selected to preside over your case, in my opinion, has been no accident. Judge Cynthia Gray-Hammond is not known to have a courtroom full of lots of hugging and bonding. She's known as being one of the toughest in the business. If she finds against you, you can be pretty sure that she'll give the thumbs-up to the police to make sure the next time you're in court the only thing you'll be leaving with is the shirt on your back.'

'Ain't I paying you to get this sorted out?' The fury of his words pushed him forward.

Bell plastered a reassuring smile onto her face. 'Let's not be gloomy before we've been bitten.'

Frankie stood up, deciding that the meeting was over.

'Come over to my home on Tuesday with an update.'

Frankie left without shaking her hand. So Judge Cynthia Gray-Hammond thought she was a tough old bird, Frankie thought. We'll see how tough she is after I get my mitts on her boy.

*   *   *

Finlay pulled the handkerchief and sunglasses from his face as he exited the club. He took sharp, driving steps in the dense pouring rain towards his ride. He jumped into the driver's seat. Closed the door. An ugly smile reshaped his lips. He pulled the photograph from his pocket. A clap of thunder boomed overhead. He dropped the photo into his lap. Pulled out his mobile. Punched in Frankie's number.

Frankie was standing by the lift near his lawyer's office when Finlay's call came through.

'It's me . . .'

'This had better mean that you've got someone to do the job.'

Finlay laughed. 'I've done better than that, boss. Meet me at the Dirty Dick because you'll never believe who I think I've got in the car with me.'

Finlay cut the call at the same time as Frankie's lift arrived. Head down, Frankie stepped forward as he shoved his mobile into his pocket. He just missed knocking into the woman who stepped out of the lift, her head down as her hand riffled inside her shoulder bag.

'Sorry,' Anna mumbled vaguely to whoever was stepping into the lift as she stepped out.

She didn't lift her head as she fumbled inside her bag, looking for her lippy and compact. She stopped once she found them. Retouched her lips. She wanted to look hot for Bell. She still couldn't believe how she felt about her. The woman was the other arm of the law, a lawyer, for fuck's sake. Plus she had at least twenty years on her. But Bell must've put a spell on her because Anna loved her to bits.

After Bell's PA had buzzed her to say that her lunchtime appointment was here, Anna approached Bell's door. She shook her hair back. Settled a cat-that-got-the-cream smile on her chops. Did her catwalk high-kickin' strut into her lover's office.

'Been missing me?' she whispered to Bell, who was sitting behind her desk.

Bell swung back in her chair. 'I've got the toughest case of my life on my hands. And I get the felling that it's slipping away from me.

And you know how much I hate losing. Why do you people from East London always give me such a hard time?'

Anna threw Bell a sexy smile as she moved towards her. She used a foot to push aside Bell's briefcase, so that she could perch on the desk. She pushed her hand into the other woman's blonde, silver-streaked hair, which stopped at the shoulder. Ran her fingers through its length. Let the pads of her fingers rub against the arched shaped neck and perfume-sprayed pulse.

'If I had a couple of hours I could show you what a real hard time this East Ender could give you . . .'

'Happy birthday, bro,' a voice said next to him.

Frankie looked up to find a grim-faced Finlay pushing his body into a chair at the table he was sitting at in the Dirty Dick.

'What are you going on about? It ain't my birthday.'

'It is now.' Finlay pulled the photo from his pocket and shoved it across the table. Frankie picked it up. Pushed it close to his face. His breath sizzled on his tongue when he realised what he was looking at. Jade. Amber. Ruby. Decked out in their best clobber in the room where they'd filled bags with his merchandise. His mind whizzed back, trying to remember when he'd seen them in all that get-up. Ping. It hit him. Early on New Year's Day ten years ago.

'Where did you find this?' he asked, his eyes still glued to the photo.

'I had to go over to a club today in Wapping and sort out one of my girls, and what should I find in the drawer of the owner's desk but this.'

'Who's the owner?' Frankie's gaze finally lifted to Finlay.

'Some tranny glamour queen called Misty McKenzie.'

'Never heard of him. Alright, so he's got a snap of our number-one bitches, that don't mean dick.'

'I can't be sure, but I found the club's ownership papers. Get this – the other owners of the club have got names that start with the same letters as our runaway bitches. How fucking stupid can you get? One of them is called Anna Crane, which sounds a bit too much like

Amber Craig to me. Roxy Malone, Ruby Munro. And this Jackie Jarvis has got the biggest green eyes you ever saw.'

Frankie swore as he threw the photo onto the table. 'Alright, say it is them. So fucking what? My goolies are on the chopping block and if I do anything to these women I'm gonna be fucked.'

'Frankie, I thought you were the brains of the outfit, bro'. Can't you see it?'

'See what?'

'The best birthday present you ever had.' Finlay leaned over the table. 'Thought you needed someone to do a job. Outsiders.'

'Job?' He stopped speaking when he realised what Finlay was suggesting. 'No way . . .'

'Think about it,' Finlay interrupted. 'They're ideal. Park their double-cross aside for a minute and see the potential. They've worked for us before. Alright, I know it was back in the day, but once a criminal, always a criminal. And they can't go to the Bill because they'll have to confess to what they did ten years ago. They can't put you in the frame without putting themselves in the picture. They must've used the dosh they got from the diamonds to buy that club. No way are they gonna swap the high life for the four walls of Holloway prison.'

'We can't be sure this is them.'

'No one can be a hundred per cent sure of anything in this life.' Finlay's voice dipped low. 'But I tell you how you can find out . . .'

Later that evening Jackie smiled with a mother's pride as her seven-year-old son took a bow with the other children onstage. She stood between Misty and Schoolboy, clapping with delight along with the other parents. In the middle of the children stood the two pint-sized young male acting tutors who ran the drama school – William Hart and Morris Jones, who together as a double act called themselves Whacky and Mojo. They were the only ones who realised that Jackie kept the school financially afloat. The day she learned that the council were planning to demolish the disused community centre next to Ryan's school, she'd secretly put forward a proposal to turn it into a place the kids from the estate she lived on could go to learn drama and dance. Better than hanging out getting up to all kind of naughties on the street, she'd told them.

She turned to Misty. 'I can't believe it. My little lad's a star.'

Misty grinned mischievously back, saying, 'He must get all those amateur dramatics from me.'

They left their seats, jostling with the other parents as they moved towards the main reception hall to collect their children. Half an hour later Ryan appeared through the crowd, with Whacky and Mojo behind him. Jackie held out her arms and he rushed into them. She swung him high, saying, "You were blindin." '

Whacky and Mojo smiled as Jackie gently placed Ryan back on the floor. Both the men were well into their twenties, but their size and smooth faces made them look like teenagers. Both were local lads who came from well-known rough-and-tumble families. That was why Jackie had chosen them to run the school, because they understood what she was trying to do.

'I can't thank you two enough for all you've done,' she said, beaming at them as she ruffled Ryan's hair.

'He's a cracking student,' Whacky said. 'He's a real asset to the group. And he's going to come over soon to help us tidy up to get things ready for the new term in September.'

'What about you two? Any luck finding work this summer?'

Although they ran the school they were still jobbing actors, taking work when they could find it.

'Not a sausage. We did some work on this kid's mystery drama about some girl who's got magical powers. But nothing since then.'

'Well, you can always come and do some casual work for us at the club. We always need an extra pair of hands during the summer.'

'Thanks, Jackie. We might take you up on that.'

Jackie took Ryan's left hand and Schoolboy took his right and then they pushed their way through the crowd towards the exit with Misty trailing behind them. Jackie's eyes darted nervously between Misty and Schoolboy when they got outside. Why oh why couldn't they just get on with each other? Here they were, her three favourite guys in the world, and two of them couldn't stand the sight of each other. Well, it was about time they learnt that soon they were going to become one big happy family.

Jackie tugged Ryan close to her as she said in a light, frothy voice, 'Right, we're off to bring the motor around. Why don't you two,' she pointed at Misty and Schoolboy, 'have a chat until we get back.'

Then she was gone. *Chat.* The word hung like poisonous smoke in the air. If there was one thing Schoolboy and Misty never did it was chat. Neither looked at the other. Or spoke. Misty pursed her lips. Schoolboy shoved his hands into the side pocket of his low-riding jeans. Since they'd been introduced neither had made any bones about the fact that they hadn't taken to each other. Misty didn't approve of her little girl bedding down for the rest of her days with a former drug dealer and Schoolboy thought Misty should keep her powdered snout out of his and Jackie's business. Tension began to tighten in the air. Misty pulled out a fag and lit up.

Finally Schoolboy balled his hands into fists, making his pockets bulge as he said, 'You got used to the idea of me and Jackie doing a his-and-her routine yet?'

Misty ran her eyes over Schoolboy insolently. 'Jackie's her own woman and knows what she's doing.'

'So how come you still eyeball me as if I'm something on the bottom of your high heel?'

'She ain't had the easiest of lives and all I wanna do is make sure that the arms she sleeps in at night know how to treat her right.'

'And you don't think a brother knows how to do that?'

'This ain't about the colour of your skin, matey, it's about the colour of the life you used to live.'

Anger crept into Schoolboy's reply. 'I don't have to prove myself to you or nobody.'

'Not even Jackie?'

Misty drew hard on her fag, casting her eyes across the street. She stopped mid-puff when she saw a figure standing by a car. A large silver Mercedes. The figure was staring at Jackie and Ryan's disappearing figures. No way, Misty thought, it can't be. The denial hit her mind at ninety miles an hour as she took a step forward. Then another. The person across the road must've known that someone was watching them because they quickly hustled back into the car. The engine kicked into life and the car drove away.

'Who's that?' Schoolboy asked. 'Wouldn't have thought they were your type.'

Startled by the nearness of Schoolboy's voice, Misty turned. 'Keep that tongue of yours outta my life, young man.'

'Now you know what I feel like every time me and you are in the same room.'

'Over here,' a voice shouted ahead of them. They turned to find Jackie's face at the half-opened driver's window of her convertible red Beetle. Schoolboy walked towards the car. Misty didn't move. Just stared into the night where the silver Mercedes had driven off. Shit, she must be more tired than she thought, thinking she'd seen . . . She shook the thought off and got into Jackie's car.

'Do you, Elijah Campbell, take this woman, Jackie Jarvis, to be your lawfully wedded wife?'

'I do.'

'Do you, Jackie Jarvis, take this man, Elijah Campbell, to be your lawfully wedded husband?'

'She does,' a chorus of female voices yelled behind Jackie.

She swung around and looked at the three women standing behind her. Anna, Roxy and Ollie. Her maids of honour, but they were behaving more like maids of humour. Except they weren't funny. They all stood in the midday Tuesday light piercing through the large stained-glass windows of St Matilda's Catholic church in Poplar. It was the church that Nikki had taken Jackie to when she was a kid. They'd always sat in the third pew from the back, tucked into a corner, yellow hymn books in their hands. Coming back here to get married made Jackie almost feel like her mum was there with her.

'Knock it off, you lot,' Misty, who stood on Jackie's right side, said sternly, twisting around to face the three women.

'Sorry about that, Father,' Jackie apologised. 'They don't get out of their cages very often.'

She turned back to Schoolboy. Gave him a shy smile. Clasped his hand. Nodded back at the priest. The rehearsal continued until Father Tom finally, joyfully, proclaimed, 'You may now kiss the bride.'

Schoolboy took Jackie's face in his hand. Leaned forward. A hand grasped his shoulder just before he met her lips.

'Oi, there'll be none of that until next Saturday,' Misty said in a mock-serious voice.

The group laughed, their joy echoing around the church. Father Tom made them sit in the front row as he did a final run-through of the service. He stopped speaking when he caught sight of a figure moving towards the confessionals situated along the right-hand side wall. He checked the time on his watch.

'I hadn't realised how time has moved on. Time to hear confession. Another sinner.' He passed a sweet smile over them as he let out a little tickle of a laugh. 'Don't forget, kids, any problems before the big day, give me a call.'

He inhaled a small breath, straightened his shoulders and moved towards the man who sat at the end of the pew near the confessional, head bent, hands clasped together.

'I've got to shoot as well,' Schoolboy said, jumping to his feet. 'Or I'm gonna miss my train back to Devon.'

'Leaving your bride so soon,' Misty said with an arched eyebrow. Her tone made it clear that she hoped that Schoolboy wasn't coming back.

Schoolboy gave her a mock-sweet smile. 'I'll be back,' he said in an Arnie-Terminator imitation. 'See you on Friday, babe.' He leaned over and gave Jackie a big smacker on her lips.

Once he was gone Jackie shot to her feet and stared hard at Misty. 'Why do you have to talk to him like that?'

Misty stood up. 'Just getting into the swing of the whole mother-in-law routine. How can you marry someone who was a drug dealer . . . ?'

'He's been outta that world for years and you know it,' Jackie cut in. 'Him and his mate from Devon have finally found some-where to open their restaurant in London. That will make three restaurants that they own. Since he won that chefs' competition on the telly, my Schoolboy is hot property.' Her voice softened. 'I know he ain't what you dreamed about, but he's all that I could've ever wished for.'

Anna waded in. 'Take no notice of Misty, she's just jealous.'

Roxy backed her up. 'Doesn't want to let her little girl to go,'

'A woman has to know when to step back,' Ollie added.

'And where did you get that one from?' Misty shot back at Ollie, hands firmly planted on hips. 'Inside the fortune cookie that came with your Chinese last night? I repeat, loud enough for the Lord to hear, I am not jealous.' She swept her gaze over all of them at the same time as the sinner came out of the confessional. The man knelt to do his penance as Misty continued to speak in a quiet tone. 'I've never told any of you this and anyone who laughs is gonna feel the back of my hand. About six months after you'd been with me I went and bought one of them "how to be a stonking good parent" books.' She ignored the expression of astonishment on their faces. 'I used to read it when you lot were all tucked up in bed. Do you know what it said? "Every child deserves a slice of happiness."' She held her hands out to Jackie. 'That's all I'm doing, sweetheart, making sure you get your cut. And I ain't got nothing against Schoolboy, but I ain't sure he knows what happiness is. I should know, I grew up as a member of one of London's toughest families.'

'Come on, Misty, you know Schoolboy's been as straight as an arrow for years.'

Misty let out a sigh. 'I just always imagined my girl getting hitched to a Quentin or a Nigel in some stately home somewhere. I'd be sitting next to his mommy and we'd be dabbing our eyes together.' Seeing the astonished look on Jackie's face, Misty waved her hands. 'I know, I know, Dreamsville. Look, I've got to run. Gonna be a bitch of a night with two stag parties to do. Anna and Jackie, don't be too long.'

As she left Anna, Roxy and Ollie got to their feet. They all stared at each other.

'Still can't believe that you're taking the plunge,' Anna said.

'Well, I am, and it's gonna be the biggest splash this side of London has ever seen.'

Without telling them what she was doing Jackie began to move towards the row of devotional candles set on high brass sticks underneath a statue of the Virgin Mary. A few of the candles were already lit. The others followed her. She hadn't done this in years. The last time had been at Ryan's christening. She picked up a long taper that sat on a low table. Moved it into a flame. Lit a candle. She could feel the others gathered around her, just like they had been that first time she'd lit her Holy Communion candle for her mum at St Nicholas.

'This one's for us, girls,' she said softly. 'We've come a long way.'

They stood there for a minute, locked in their own thoughts. Jackie finally broke the spell as she turned away. They moved down the aisle chatting excitedly as the man on his knees doing penance unclasped his hands. Slowly he raised his head. Spoke out loud, and it wasn't a prayer.

'Told you I'd always look out for you.'

Startled by the voice directed at them, the four women stopped moving. Looked at the man. Looked straight into a pair of blazing blue eyes.

twenty-nine

Jackie pulled in a stunned, trembling gasp. Frankie. No, it couldn't be. She snapped her eyes shut. Did a rapid three-count. Reopened them. But he was still sitting there, Satan in God's house. Hell's bells, her heartbeat was so bad she thought she was going to tip right over. She felt the others move towards her, just like they used to at St Nicholas, three frightened girls seeking her protection.

'What's the best hymn you've ever heard at a funeral?' Frankie asked, not taking his eyes off them as he pulled himself up to sit on the pew. '"Abide with Me?" "Amazing Grace"? "Rock of Ages"?'

None of the women answered, as a collective shock spread through them.

'You'll beg my pardon, ladies, if I don't get up, but you see I have a bit of problem with my right leg. It's never been the same since someone put two caps in it ten years ago.'

They still said nothing. Ollie stared him out without a flicker of emotion in her eyes.

'What's it they say, girls, nothing like weddings and funerals to bring people together?'

Jackie's hands tightened by her sides as she said with complete innocence, 'Excuse me, are you talking to us?'

'That depends on who us is. Is it Jackie, Anna, Roxy and Ollie? Or is it Jade, Amber, Ruby and the gun-toting refugee?'

'I think you must have us mixed up with someone else, mate. If you wait I'm sure that Father Tom can sort you out.'

'Still playing leader of the pack? Still five foot nothing and think you've got the biggest balls in town?'

'Come on, we're outta here,' Jackie growled, taking a step forward.

But she stopped when she heard Roxy's sobs behind her. Quickly she turned to her weeping friend and said between gritted teeth, 'Shut it.'

'Still the crybaby of the bunch?' Frankie taunted Roxy. 'I'll never forget that first time you were blubbing and we had to hang you out of the window to get you to zip it. Remember that, Ruby? Remember what fear felt like rushing all over you? Wonder what it would feel like if I came up to your house and did it there? Still think the fear would feel the same?'

'Leave us fucking alone,' Jackie stormed as she swung to face him.

'Tut, tut. What would Nikki say if she could hear her little girl cussing like some crack whore inside the four walls of the house of the Lord?'

'Like I said, mister, we don't know ya. Come on.'

The others followed her as she started to rush towards the exit. But Frankie's words stopped her.

'Take one step through that doorway into the afternoon light and the next time you're in here it will be burning candles for the soul of your son.'

The skin on Jackie's face turned a hot, blazing red. She rushed towards him. Anna lunged after her, catching her arm. Held her back. 'You leave my boy alone.'

Frankie eased up. Walked out of the pew. Took easy steps down the aisle. Roxy tightened her body into Ollie's as he reached them. He looked them up and down. Roxy and Ollie. Anna and Jackie. The corner of his lips tilted into a lazy grin as he screwed his gaze deep into Jackie. 'I like the weight loss. It suits you. It shouldn't be too hard to find a funeral outfit.'

'What do you want?' Ollie's calm voice echoed in the church.

'Finally, someone who's reading the writing on the wall. Meet me tonight at eight.'

Without waiting for a reply he turned his back on them. Walked away. As he reached the small font near the exit the turned back to them. His lips were fixed into a big grin. 'Oh yeah, nearly forgot to say, congratulations. You're going to make a striking bride. Shame your old girl can't be here.'

Then he stuck his finger into the holy water. Made a sign of the cross. Genuflected and was gone.

They stood in a trance long after he'd left. Finally Roxy broke the spell. Tears still slicing down her face, she moved, walking in a daze, handbag flapping against her side, towards the exit.

'Where the heck are you going?' Jackie shot out, shaking out of Anna's hold.

'I've got to get home to make Martin's tea.' Roxy's tone was flustered. Hesitant.

'Are you off your nut?' Anna jumped in. 'We've just had a visit from the Devil himself and you wanna go home and play the happy housewife.'

She didn't answer. Instead the intensity of her sobs began to rack her shaking body. Jackie rushed over to her. Enfolded her in her arms, softly crooning, 'It's alright, it's alright.'

'He's going to kill us, isn't he?'

'No, he ain't. If he'd wanted to do that no way would he have shown himself.'

'That's it. I'm going to meet him on my own,' Ollie suddenly said, moving towards the exit.

'No you ain't,' Jackie said, shaking her head, letting go of Roxy.

'I'm the one who shot him. He wants me.'

'He wants all of us,' Jackie countered in a defeated tone. 'You're forgetting that we all nicked his gear ten years ago.'

'I should've known as soon as you said you saw him . . .' Anna began.

'You saw him?' Ollie interrupted, fire lighting both her voice and her eyes.

'Why didn't you tell us?' Roxy gazed accusingly at Jackie.

'Hold your horses. I saw him on the box on Saturday night. He's in mega-shit. It turns out that the Old Bill are looking to put him down for good.'

'So why does he want to see us?' Roxy screeched.

'Dunno.' Jackie shook her head. 'But I do know we've got no alternative. If we don't turn up, he's gonna track our arses down and I bet you a fiver none of us will live long enough to tell the tale about what happened.'

'But he didn't say where we had to meet him.' Puzzlement swept over Anna's face as she spoke.

Jackie folded her arms around her middle as if a chill had filled the church. 'He didn't have to. Use your head, girls. Where's the last place you'd ever wanna be cooped up with Frankie Sullivan ever again?'

19.55.

The four women sat wired and tense inside Jackie's motor outside the one place only Frankie Sullivan had the power to drag them to – St Nicholas care home. But it wasn't a care home any more. Once Mr Miller had been arrested ten years earlier its cards were marked. Now St Nicholas was disused, its front windows boarded up, moss and bad weather providing the newest colours on its brickwork and its driveway a rubbish dump for fly-tippers.

Jackie didn't realise it but she'd cut the engine of her car in exactly the same spot Frankie had parked the first time he'd brought her here all those years ago. She felt scared, confused, just as she had as a fifteen-year-old. She took in a long breath through her nose. Flicked her head to the rear-view mirror. Gazed at Ollie and Roxy's reflection as they sat in the back. Roxy's face was strained and bloodless, her eyes large with dread and fright. Ollie's features were solemn and still, not a hint of what she was feeling on her face. Jackie dipped her head back down. Shifted her head to the side. Gazed at Anna next to her in the passenger seat. Anna's eyes were half closed, her leather-gloved hands painfully wrapped together in her lap like she was reciting the last prayer she would ever utter.

'Alright,' Jackie finally pushed out. Her tone was quiet and husky with determination. 'If you don't wanna do this, now's the time to open the door and walk away.'

She turned and stared hard through the windscreen and the gathering night. Waited for the sound of an opening car door. After leaving the church they'd bolted for the Shim-Sham-Shimmy to discuss what they should do. They'd fought, argued, even thrown around some tears, but by the end they knew they had no choice but to meet the one man they'd hoped never to clap eyes on again. Jackie's breathing relaxed when she didn't hear anyone get out of the car.

'What if he brought us all the way out here to murder us?' Roxy asked.

The same question had run through Jackie's mind so many times she'd lost count. Bang. Bang. Bang. Bang. One straight to each of their heads, that was all Frankie needed to do to take them out of this life pronto.

'Nah, he ain't looking to put us down. With the amount of publicity he's getting at the moment he can't afford to take us out . . .'

'Then why has he asked us here?' Anna's jumpy voice butted in.

'Only one way to find out.' Jackie reached for the door. Eased out of the car.

The four women stood outside, gazing up at a building that held only bad memories.

'You sure he's here?' Anna asked. 'It looks bloody deserted to me.'

Jackie shivered as she continued to stare at the building. 'He's here alright. And you don't need to tell me where he is. Remember what we agreed, I do all the talking. And if he gives us anything, Anna's the only one to take it.'

They all peered at the motorbike gloves Anna wore. Their shoes crunched through the gravel as they made their way to the back stairs. The gate to the garden was already open. Jackie went through first. A shiver shot through her as she saw the building at the bottom of the garden. Remembered the terrible sight she'd witnessed inside. They reached the iron stairs that led to the fourth floor. Jackie gulped as her eyes ran up to the top. Shit, she wasn't sure she could do this.

'I can't do this.' But it wasn't her voice. It was Roxy.

Jackie twisted around and lunged towards Roxy. She grabbed her arm. Roxy winced as Jackie got up close, in Roxy's face. 'You get your cosy, Harvey Nichols-lovin' arse up those stairs, you hear me?'

She shook Roxy. 'You think *I* wanna do this? The *others* wanna do this? No, we don't. We ain't got no choice. And don't think we can run away and disappear because we'll only spend the rest of lives looking over our shoulders waiting for him to come and get us.' Slowly she let Roxy go. Roxy staggered back.

Without saying another word, Jackie swung back around. Took the first stair. And the next. And another. Until she stood at the top.

'Everyone alright?' she quietly asked the others.

After they nodded she reached for the door handle. Pressed down. The heavy door eased back with a groan. Holding her breath, she stepped inside. The corridor was empty and semi-dark.

Sweat bubbled around her hairline. She thrust her fingers through her hair, lifting the strands off her forehead. She paused as she reached the closed door that had once led to their bedroom. Moved forward. Towards the one room she hoped never to see again in her life. Finally she came to a halt outside it. The others stopped behind her. She listened. Heard voices coming from the other side of the door. A drop of sweat burned into her eyes. She quickly swiped her hand over it. Forced her hand down. Reached for the handle. Grasped it. Hesitated. Finally pushed down. Eased the door forward. The light from inside flooded over her.

Her breath flipped inside her chest when she saw the three figures in the room. Frankie sat at the head of the table they had once packed drugs at. Standing on his left stood Finlay. On his right stood Jason. Behind them, through the windows, London's skyline darkened.

'Welcome home,' Frankie said.

Jackie pushed her chin out. Shoved her shoulders back. Moved cautiously into the room. The others followed her.

'Search her.' Frankie stabbed a finger towards Ollie.

Jason moved quickly, but Jackie pushed herself in front of Ollie. 'You ain't putting your hand on any of us.'

Jason gave Jackie a dangerous look and snarled 'That bitch don't get a second chance to pump another slug into Frankie.'

'Who do you think we are? Ma fucking Baker?'

Jason and Jackie glared at each other until Frankie broke the silence. 'It's alright, Jace.'

The big man stepped back. Frankie tilted his head, making a few strands of hair flop boyishly onto his forehead. 'The place is in a right state, ain't it? No one gives a monkey's about it any more. A bit like how I felt when you lot cut out on me. I looked out for you, gave you money, and what do you do? Mugged me over and scarpered with my gear. That ain't the way to treat a mate.'

'We ain't stopping, so what do you want?' Jackie felt the sickness roll in her stomach as she spoke.

'Four and a half mill.'

'You what?'

'That's how much you lot owe me. Finlay, tell them what the damage is.'

Finlay stared hard at the women as he spoke. 'Four unique diamonds. With inflation and interest that's a grand total of four and a half million quid.'

'Don't forget to include the bags,' Frankie chucked in.

'Four rucksacks at a tenner each. Mind you, the economy ain't bad at the mo so they're worth a fiver now. That's twenty nicker on top.' He muttered dramatically to himself as he pretended to do the sums. 'Making a grand total of four and a half mill and twenty quid.'

Frankie leaned back in his chair as he folded his arms and winced. 'See, that really hurts. Not in my pocket but here.' He tapped his heart. 'I trusted you. And how did you repay me? You try to whack me . . .'

'If I'd wanted to kill you,' Ollie interrupted, 'you wouldn't be here now blowing words out of that hole in your rear end.'

Jason swore viciously as he made a swift move around the table. But Frankie quickly grabbed his wrist. Held him back.

'I see your English has improved.' Frankie gave Ollie a lopsided grin and a small nod. 'Whatever way you look at it, ladies, you owe me. You're in my debt. . . .'

'You fucking murdered our mums,' Jackie shot out with fury. 'And you think we owe you. Fuck. You.' She swung around to her friends. 'Come on, we're outta here.'

'You ain't going nowhere.'

Jackie heard the scrape of the legs of a chair. A click. Without looking around she knew there was a gun pointed at her back. She turned slowly as her heart hiccupped inside her chest. Frankie was on his feet. Beside him Finlay held a revolver in his hand. Finger on the trigger. Ready to rock 'n' roll.

'Jason, I think our ladies have forgotten all the fun and games we used to have in here.' Frankie turned his gaze on Roxy. 'Come. Here.'

'What are you . . . ?' Jackie started.

'Shut it, bitch,' Frankie belted out. 'Or the next time anyone sees that annoying mouth of yours it will be the newest pattern splattered on the wall, you get me?'

His words reverberated around the room. Jackie tightened her lips. Frankie stretched out his hand towards Roxy with the ease of a gentleman helping his sweetheart cross the road. 'Come on, Ruby,' he coaxed. 'It's only good ol' Frankie.'

She swivelled her head around. Looked through nervous blinking eyes at the others. Her chin bobbed as she took a heaving swallow. Slowly she turned towards their foe. Gazed at his hand, still in the air. Then she moved, picking her feet up like she was wading through mud. Seven steps, that was how many it took for her to reach him. She shook as she bowed her head and stared at the floor.

'Now that wasn't so hard, was it, Ruby, babe?' His voice was gentle. He placed a fingertip under her chin. Tilted it up. He smiled but the blue of his eyes was like stone. He moved his head a fraction. Towards Jason. Jason understood the signal and began to move. In deep, long strides towards the centre window.

'Like I said, ladies, you need an action replay of what life could be like if you keep giving me bovver.'

By the time he had finished speaking Jason had opened the window. The cool night air dived wildly inside. Jackie's face grew pale as she finally realised what was going to happen. Finlay moved so quickly from the other side of the room none of them saw it coming. He reached Ollie. Hooked a foot around one of the legs of her chair. Ollie flipped into the air and tumbled onto the floor. He pushed his hard-heeled shoe across her throat. Aimed the gun dead centre at her head. Jackie jumped up, but a heavy hand snapped around her forearm and jerked her back. She turned to find Frankie glowering at her. He slammed her back into her seat. 'Stay down,' he ordered.

Roxy screamed, 'No,' at the same time as Jason began to move again. Straight towards her. He reached her. That was when Roxy understood what was going to happen to her for the second time in her life. She lifted her leg, ready to run, but it was too late. Jason lunged and caught her. Twisted his arms like flesh-covered ropes around her waist. Heaved her up and moved in great, long steps towards the window. Roxy pleaded, 'Help. Please help me,' her arms and legs kicking in the air.

Roxy flung herself to the right when Jason reached the window, her hands flailing against the wall. Jason grunted. Heaved her to the left. Her nails scraped along the wall as he moved her. He wriggled his arms from her waist to the tops of her thighs. Her upper body flopped over at the same time as he stepped forward. Towards the wide-open window.

'Hope you ain't put on too much weight. Wouldn't wanna drop you,' Jason ground out.

He pitched her out.

She screamed.

thirty

Jackie watched Roxy's legs kick in the air as Jason held onto her tight. Frankie rounded on the three women.

'OK, ladies, it's decision time. Your mate's life is hanging in the balance. Now you have to decide whether you're gonna listen to me and do what I say and save her. Or carry on pissing me off and watch . . . well, I don't think I gotta say what this evening's feature is gonna look like.'

Suddenly Jason stepped back, drawing Roxy's whole body back into the room. Her wild animalistic cries filled the room. Her chin bounced against her chest.

'OK, OK,' Jackie shouted. 'We'll do what you say. Anything, just let Roxy go.'

'Good girl. This is the deal . . .' Abruptly his words stopped.

As if this was a signal Jason shoved Roxy back out of the window. This time his hands slid down her thighs, stopping at her knees. He gulped in a huge wave of oxygen and grunted. Pushed her outside. Then slid his hands down her legs until he held her by the ankles. Roxy screamed as she slammed into the wall.

A disbelieving Jackie shot out of her chair, yelling frantically, 'You said you'd let her go.'

'So we've got a deal, then?'

'What do you want us to do, you fucking bastard?' Jackie shouted, her eyes darting between Jason and Frankie. Frankie and Jason.

'As you know I've got a real thing for kids. I love 'em. Think they're the best thing about this life. But here's the thing, there's this one kid, I just can't get him outta my head. Lovely boy. Obedient. Hard working. Loves his mum. You know, all the things you lot used to be. All you lot have gotta do is sorta pick him up and look after him for a couple of days.'

'You what?' Jackie said incredulously. 'You want us to kidnap a little boy?'

'Well, he ain't that little. No fifteen-year-old is by today's standards. Kidnapping's such a nasty word. Think of it more like you lot pretending to be his old dear for a couple of days. So what do you say?'

'We ain't putting our name to nothing until your gorilla gets his mitts off Roxy and brings her back inside.'

Frankie nodded at Finlay and said, 'Help him bring her in.'

Finlay removed his foot from Ollie's throat. Stepped back. Quickly he shoved the gun into his pocket and then obeyed Frankie's command. He helped Jason drag an hysterical Roxy back into the room. Her cheek was bruised and bleeding from where she'd slammed into the wall. They let her go. She collapsed onto the floor, filling the room with the sound of her ragged breathing. The other girls immediately rushed to help her. Roxy pulled out her inhaler with shaking fingers.

'Bring her to the table.' Frankie's voice was dispassionate as Roxy sucked hard on her inhaler. 'Make yourselves nice and comfy because now the real talking starts.'

'His name's Daniel Gray-Hammond.'

Frankie threw the name and a manila document folder at the women, who were sitting on the other side of the table. Jackie and the others huddled together. They were literally on the edge of their seats. Ollie's arm lay gently around a still-traumatised and shaking Roxy. Anna's throat bobbed as she continually swallowed. Only Jackie sat with her back straight, giving Frankie the evil eye.

The folder spun. Stopped a few inches from the women. They eyed it up as if it were a deadly disease. Suddenly Anna's gloved hand reached across. She picked it up. Opened it. On the top was a photo of a boy with close-cropped brown hair, a long face that ended with a dimple in his chin and adventurous brown eyes. Not a heartbreaker, but he might give a few women's hearts a flutter later on in life. She positioned the photo on the table so that the others could see. Anna started to take out the remaining papers inside the folder, but Frankie's voice stopped her.

'Inside is all you need to know about Danny boy. Take it away and make it your bedtime reading. Come next week Wednesday night I want you to have him tucked away somewhere nice and safe.'

'Who is he?' Jackie asked.

Frankie leaned forward. 'Keep that,' he tapped his nose, 'outta it. Just keep your snout on what I've told you to do.'

Jackie shook her head. 'But this is fucking bonkers. We can't just nab some kid.'

Suddenly he leaned forward and tweaked Jackie's nose, just as he had all those years earlier. Instead of slapping his hand away Jackie blushed furiously. She flicked her eyes up to Frankie's. Caught the smoky light blazing in his eyes. For a few seconds it was as if there were just the two of them in the room. Frankie ran his a finger down her hot cheek. Then his hand fell away.

In a soft voice he said, 'Remember what I taught you years ago? Distraction and deception. That's all you need to pull this one off.'

Feeling like a complete fool at her reaction to his hand on her skin, Jackie sent him a furious look. 'And how the f'ing hell are we meant to get him?' She finally asked.

'Like I said, digest the info and I'm sure you'll work it out.'

'And how are you gonna know when the deed's been done?'

'I'll know, just like I knew where to find you lot after all these years.'

Frankie shoved himself out of his chair. He walked slowly around the table. Around the women. Stopped when he stood behind Ollie. 'And don't try nothing stupid because I'm gonna know what you're doing every minute of every day. When you take a piss. When you have a shag. Just focus your little bimbo brains on how you're gonna get the kid by next Wednesday. You do this for me and you won't see my ugly mug ever again.'

Suddenly he bent down to Ollie. The sound of Ollie's sucked-in breath skated across the room. Frankie ran two fingers over her cheek.

He brought his fingers to his nose. Inhaled dramatically. On exhaling he lowered his head to Ollie's ear and said in a stage whisper, 'Remember how that petrol stank and felt on your black skin all those years ago? If any of you fuck up this time, I'm gonna get each of you and douse you from head to toe, light a match and torch you to death very, very slowly. And I won't need to wait for Bonfire Night to do it.'

Frankie watched from the window as the women scurried away in the dark. Without turning around he said, 'I want that Jackie watched twenty-four-seven.'

'I say we go to the cops,' Anna said as she threw the manila folder onto the table. They all sat around Anna's desk in the Shim-Sham-Shimmy club. Each one of them had been silent on the ride back from St Nicholas, each too shell-shocked to speak. Jackie still couldn't believe that Frankie Sullivan was back in their lives. Maybe they should've done what Misty had advised them to do years ago – take their money and hightail it outta London. If they had they wouldn't be here now. Wouldn't be faced with the worst decision of their lives. Mind you, if she'd done that she'd never have meet the one-and-only Schoolboy.

All thoughts of what ifs rushed out of Jackie's mind as she saw Anna's hand reach for the phone on her desk. Jackie lurched across the table. Slammed her hand over Anna's.

'No.' The word shot out of her mouth as she looked her friend straight in the eye. The expression in Anna's amber eyes wavered between defiance and fear. Jackie slowly released her hand as fear won the battle. Anna's hand dropped back as she leaned back in her seat with a dejected sigh. 'I don't want that scumbag back in my life,' she threw at the others.

'None of us do,' Jackie replied softly as she retook her seat. 'But we've got to talk this one through properly.'

'What's there to talk through?' Anna stormed. 'He wants to turn our world upside down again and we ain't gonna let him do it. End of story.'

'And what do you suggest we do instead?' Jackie threw back. 'Hold hands and start singing "We Shall Overcome"?'

Their verbal battle sizzled in the air. No one spoke.

A sharp sigh punched out of Jackie's mouth as she shifted to the edge of her chair. 'Going to the Bill is too risky,' she started, shaking her head. 'They're gonna wanna investigate our connection to Frankie and you know what they'll find out, that we nicked those diamonds off him. Then they'll put two and two together and find out how we financed the club. Find out the things we used to do for Frankie when we were young. I don't fancy celebrating my son's next birthday from the top bunk inside some damp cell in Holloway.'

'And if we go to the police we'll also be implicating Misty,' Ollie added.

'So what you're saying is we have to do this?' Disbelief coated every one of Anna's words.

'I'm saying we have to decide, *together*, whether we're gonna do this,' Jackie responded as she folded her arms across the table.

'I don't want to go back to being Ruby.' Roxy spoke for the first time, her hand moving over the plaster on her cheek.

'None of us wanna be those girls again,' Ollie agreed. 'But Jackie's right, if we go to the police we might as well put the handcuffs on ourselves.'

A loud *shit* exploded in the air. They all looked at Anna. Her unhappy face contorted with anger and anxiety.

'I suggest that we start by finding out what's inside that folder,' Ollie continued. They pinned their eyes to the folder on the table. Jackie reached across to pick it up, but Anna's voice stopped her. 'Remember what we said? Only me and my gloves touch it.'

Jackie's hands retreated as Anna leaned over and opened the folder. She pulled out the photograph and laid it on the table. Then pulled out a single piece of paper with writing on it. She picked it up, letting her gaze sweep from top to bottom.

'This looks like info about this Daniel.' Then she read aloud. 'He's fifteen years old. Goes to a boarding school in Richmond called Markhouse Manor. Likes to play cricket and the guitar. Brilliant swimmer.' She flicked her eyes up at the others. 'That's it. It says shit-all else.'

'What about his parents?' Jackie asked.

Anna shrugged her shoulders. 'Nothing.'

'OK,' Ollie said. 'So the next thing we've got to do is find out what his connection to Frankie is.'

'And how the heck are we gonna do that?' Anna asked.

'The Internet,' Roxy said. 'If we try and find out as much as we can about Frankie eventually we'll find the connection. We already know that the powers that be are trying to break his piggy bank, so whatever the link is has to be connected to that.' Five minutes later they were all gathered around Anna's computer. As Roxy was the IT expert they let her take control. She typed in Frankie's name. A total of fifty-six hits came up.

'How are we gonna know which one to start with?' Jackie asked.

'We'll refine the search,' Roxy replied, her fingers already moving across the keyboard. 'Let's see if we can find any newspaper articles about him. We'll try one of the tabloids.'

The screen changed.

'Here we go. Three articles from this year.'

She activated the first link. The article hit the screen.

'The many and varied attempts by the authorities to get at the assets of career criminals take a new turn next week when a case is heard in the courtroom of Judge Cynthia Gray-Hammond. If found guilty of tax evasion charges Mr Sullivan may then also be facing an investigation to decide whether his considerable fortune is the result of criminal activities and is forfeit on those grounds. Mr Sullivan has always denied any involvement in the underworld and has threatened to appeal to Strasbourg if he's found liable . . .'

'Bingo,' Ollie said, pointing at the screen. 'There it is.'

'I can't see nothin,'' Jackie responded as her eyes ran desperately over the words on the screen.

Ollie's finger touched the screen. 'Look at the name of the judge hearing the case.' *Cynthia Gray-Hammond.*

'No way,' Jackie said, swinging her eyes desperately to check the reaction of the others. They all looked as dumbfounded as she felt.

'The son of a judge.' Roxy's dazed voice said what they were all thinking.

'No fucking way are we doing this.' The words rushed out of Anna's mouth at high speed. 'If we did and got caught, we'd be banged up for life.'

As Jackie opened her mouth to calm things down the door swung open.

Misty stood in the doorway. She fixed the girls with her sharp, grey eyes.

'What's going on, girls? I didn't know you were here.' Her gaze skated over each one of them. She sniffed the air. 'Something smells fishy in here.'

'Just sorting out the entertainment for my hen night,' Jackie said quickly as Roxy flicked the computer off. If there was one thing she knew, it was that Misty was no fool. She gave Misty one of her instant smiles. 'Just cruising the Net for some top-class strippers.'

'Thought you didn't want no hanky-panky at your hen night?' Misty squinted at her.

'I might do, I might not.' Jackie lifted her shoulders in a carefree shrug. 'Just wanna make sure that I have a night to remember. It ain't like I'm planning to do it again in my life.'

Misty gave her a searching look. Then switched her gaze to Anna, who was busy shoving the papers and photograph in the folder. 'I could do with some help on the floor. Jackie, we're one short at the bar tonight, so you need to get that sorted. Ollie and Roxy, fancy a goodnight tipple?'

'I've got to go home,' Roxy said, reaching for her bag. 'Martin doesn't like me to stay out too late. He gets worried.'

'From the look of that plaster on your face,' Misty started, 'the only thing Martin looks like he wants to do is get his hands on you again.'

Roxy self-consciously touched the plaster as her eyes darted towards the others.

Ollie stood up, breaking the silence. 'I've got to be up bright and early to help out with a new family at work.'

'Why don't we all meet tomorrow for lunch at mine?' Jackie said as she too got up.

'So we can plan the rest of the . . .' She looked at the others meaningfully. 'Hen night.'

They headed for the door, with Misty still giving them the once-over.

'Oops,' Misty said. 'Nearly forgot why I came up. I just wanna run my eyes over the accounts. I'll be as quick as a flash and down in a jiffy.'

As soon as Misty closed the door she headed for the computer. She'd seen Roxy's nervous move as she quickly closed the screen on the computer. As soon as she'd entered the room she'd caught the tension heaving inside. If there was one thing she knew about her girls it was when they were telling a big, fat porkie. Hen night, my fat arse, she thought, they were up to something. She quickly parked herself at the desk in front of the computer. Reactivated the Net. Hit the history button. Drew a sharp breath as she realised that today's searches were all about one person – Frank Sullivan. Why would the girls be checking him out after all these years?

The ring of the phone on the desk pulled her away from her disturbing thoughts. She reached for it.

'I'm sleeping,' she said sharply. 'Call back later.'

'It's an urgent call for you.' The voice on the other end was Gio's.

'Who the bleedin' heck is it?'

'Don't know. Just said you would take their call.'

Misty let out a ragged rush of air. 'Alright.'

The phone clicked.

'Yeah?'

The reply made the blood drain from Misty's face.

The first thing Jackie did when she got home was look in on her son. One of her neighbour's teenage daughters usually stayed with him when Jackie was out in the evening. She tiptoed into the moonlit room. Ryan was tucked up under his West Ham Utd duvet. Jackie loved taking him to see the Hammers play, just like Nikki used to take her. She knelt by his bed. Smoothed her hand with the fragility of a feather across his red hair. He gave a soft sigh in his sleep. If anyone ever tried to take him away from her she'd kill them within the blink of an eye. And now she was going to do the same to some other mum. Take her little boy away from her. Her chest heaved as the tears came. But what alternative did she have? What the fuck was she going to do? What the fuck was she going to do? *Jesus, Mary and all the saints in heaven, I can't do this.*

thirty-one

'I can't do this.'

Jackie's decision hit the other three women, who were sitting around her kitchen table the following afternoon, like a thunderbolt. She stood, leaning back against the door of the automatic washing machine. Arms hugged her tense stomach. She'd thrown up that morning, which she put down to seeing Frankie again.

She carried on in a low, intense tone. 'I got home last night and do you know what I realised? If I do this, how the fuck do I have the right to look my little boy in the eyes again? I ain't doing this. I ain't letting that bastard take over my life again.'

'Are you fucking for real?' Anna stormed. 'Yesterday I,' she stabbed her finger in her chest, 'was the one saying we couldn't do it. And you,' she pointed her finger at Jackie, 'told me we had to, so I've only spent half the night going up and down in my mind, like some madwoman, deciding what to do. And that's when I realised that there's only one thing we can do, we've gotta do it. Now you're telling me *you* don't wanna do it.' Anna kissed her teeth in anger.

'That was yesterday when we were running shit scared,' Jackie explained, as she pulled her body off the washing machine. 'How the heck am I . . . are we . . . gonna live with ourselves when we do to some mum what he did to ours?'

'You know what's gonna happen if we don't do this, girl?' Anna fired back. 'You won't have a chance to look in Ryan's eyes again because you'll be dead meat along with the rest of us. Besides, Frankie said if we do this we won't ever see him again.'

'Do you know what you see when you're dangling out of a window?' Roxy joined in, looking squarely at Jackie. 'Death written in blood on the ground underneath. When Frankie catches up with you, he's going to make you watch as they hang Ryan out of the window . . .'

'Shut it,' Jackie growled, taking a step towards Roxy.

'Roxy's right.' Ollie's voice was as calm as ever. 'That's the reality. Are you willing to risk us, including Ryan, disappearing like a puff of smoke in the wind?'

The silence and the hum of the fridge rumbled in the kitchen.

'I feel exactly as you do,' Ollie carried on softly. 'God knows I've enough nightmares in my life without adding any new ones. And you're right, this is wrong. But what's right or wrong when you've got a gun pointed at your head? When the rebel soldiers came to my village they killed all of the adults and then gave us children a choice. Death or join them. Most of us decided to join them because at least we'd be together looking out for one another. If we don't take this boy do you think it will stop Frankie from finding another way of kidnapping him? The choice we have today is not whether we should do this but if we should let Daniel fall into the hands of psychotic killers like Finlay and Jason or hold him ourselves in which case we can make sure he is well looked after. And maybe, when we have him, we can start figuring a way to get ourselves out of this.'

Jackie let out a long sigh, saying nothing. Suddenly Anna slowly eased herself to her feet. Walked towards Jackie. Pulled Jackie's hands into her own. Squeezed them.

'I know exactly how you're feeling because, fuck me, I felt the same way yesterday.' A small smile flickered across her lips. 'Do you remember what you told us all those years ago at St Nicholas?' Jackie didn't move. 'That we're family. We're in this together. We've always looked out for each other and we're gonna continue doing that now.'

Anna slowly drew Jackie towards the spare chair at the table. Sighing, Jackie took the seat. 'OK,' she said. 'So how are we gonna do this?'

Surprisingly it was Roxy who answered. 'I've got a top-five tips on kidnapping someone.'

'Where the heck did you get that from?' Jackie asked as she leaned her chin on the palm of her hand.

'The Internet, of course. The Net is really hard to regulate so it's easy for anyone to set up a website on anything they like. After I got in yesterday I did a search and found a website called Snatcher.'

'So what's this Snatcher say we gotta do?' Anna said.

'Number one: identify your subject . . .'

'Who is Daniel . . .' Anna hunted in her bag for her gloves. Pulled them out. Put them on. She reached into her bag once more and pulled out the folder. She placed it on the table, next to the West Ham Utd table mats. She whipped the photo onto the table. Glided her gaze on to the paper with the writing on it. '. . . Gray-Hammond.'

'Number two: find out as much as you can about your subject's daily routine. Where they go, who their friends are, what they like to do, where they go on a Saturday night.'

Once again Anna skimmed the information in front of her. 'We know that he likes cricket and strumming the old guitar. And he's a blindin' swimmer. He boards at Markhouse Manor School in Richmond . . .'

'Which means he's at school most of the time,' Ollie cut in. 'Which means the only way we're likely to find out about what he does is to spy on his movements at school.'

'And how the hell are we gonna do that?' Jackie asked.

'They can't stay in school twenty-four-seven. They must come out for a breather some time. Two of us are going to have to do surveillance outside the school and just hope he appears. We take pictures and we follow him. The other alternative is one of us manages to get inside the school for a decent period of time.'

'Number three,' Roxy pressed on. 'Identify a safe and secure place to keep subject. Make sure it's isolated and a place that other people do not come to.'

'How about the club?' Ollie suggested.

'No can do,' Anna said, shaking her head. 'It's not isolated and most of London steps in and out of it.'

'One of our homes?'

The others all looked horrified at Roxy's suggestion.

'Bingo.' They all looked at Anna. 'Got it. *Miss Josephine.*'

'Come on,' she urged them, watching the expressions of disbelief hit their faces. 'It worked for us all those years ago. We lived on that boat for a whole year and no one found us. It's isolated. Misty rarely uses it any more. It's bloody ideal.'

'I know it is,' Jackie said as she shoved her hand through her hair. 'It's just I don't want Misty mixed up in this. If this all goes tits up I couldn't sleep at night if Frankie or the Bill came knocking at Misty's door.'

'They won't,' Anna assured her. 'Once we get the boy this is gonna all be over in a couple of nights. We let Frankie know we've got him and Frankie takes him away.

'What's number four, Roxy?'

'Identify the best place to snatch the subject. Make sure it's not a public place that is likely to have cameras.'

'So we definitely need to get into that school to check him out or follow him,' Jackie said.

'Number five . . .'

The bang of the knocker on the front door made them all freeze.

'Shit,' Anna said as she quickly put on her gloves, rustled the papers and photo together. Picked up the folder. Shoved the incriminating evidence inside it. Slammed it into her bag.

Jackie stood up. Took a deep breath. Headed for the door. The warm summer breeze sneaking in from under the gap at the bottom of the door flicked up her legs as she opened the door. Outside stood her son. But he wasn't alone. Two men stood behind him.

'Mum,' Ryan screeched.

He hurled himself into his mum's arms.

With a huge burst of relief Jackie caught him. As she hugged him tight she gazed at the two men standing outside – Whacky and Mojo. She'd completely forgotten that the two actors had said they would bring him back at two when they'd finished clearing up the drama school.

266 DREDA SAY MITCHELL

'Come on in,' she said as she placed Ryan on the carpet.

'You got time for a quick chat?' Whacky asked as he stepped inside.

'Sure. Ryan, why don't you go and get cleaned up.'

As her son skipped to his bedroom she drew the two men into the kitchen.

'Sorry, Jackie, we didn't know you had company,' Mojo said when he saw the women sitting at the table.

'This is Whacky and Mojo, everyone. They teach Ryan drama. They're fantastic. You should've seen them playing these two naughty kids in the play.'

'Jackie, we won't keep you,' Whacky started. 'We were wondering if that offer of work at the club this summer is still open?'

'Sure,' Anna said. 'I'm Anna. I do all the hiring. And the firing.' Everyone had a little chuckle at that. 'Come on over tomorrow, lads, and I'll sort you out.'

After expressing their gratitude the men were soon gone.

'Roxy, tell us what number five is before Ryan comes in,' Ollie said.

As Roxy spoke Jackie's eyes remained fixed on the doorway.

'Jackie, are you bloody listening?' Anna asked.

Suddenly Jackie's gaze snapped away from the doorway. She looked at her friends.

'Roxy, you don't need to tell anyone what number five is.'

The others all looked at her as if she'd gone stark raving mad.

'Distraction and deception, that's what the almighty Frankie says we've gotta use. So I'll tell you what number five's gonna be . . .'

Finlay sat in the front seat of a banged-up motor with a baseball cap pulled low over his face. He pushed his shades closer to his eyes. Picked up the tabloid newspaper on the seat beside him. Held it in front of his face. But he wasn't reading. He was watching the four women who had just entered the forecourt of Ernest Bevin House. The women walked huddled together, heads nodding, lips moving, whispering secrets only they were meant to know. They moved through the muted sunshine until they reached a car. Standard four-door runaround female issue. Then they talked in a rush for about thirty seconds. He watched Anna and Jackie leave the other two by the car and power-walk away. They stopped by a large red-rooster-coloured motorbike. He threw the newspaper back on the seat. Reached inside his leather jacket. Flipped out his mobile.

'It's me, boss. They're back on the street. But they ain't together any more, they're playing Terry and June. Which two you want me to keep an eye on?'

He nodded at the answer. Cut the call. Chucked the mobile on the passenger seat. Twisted the ignition key as he watched the two women climb onto the motorbike.

Frankie cut the call with Finlay as he shivered in the cemetery. The blanket of blue sky above should have been warmer but it wasn't. He stared at the headstone in front of him. Onyx marble. Gold writing.

Millicent 'Millie' Sullivan.

His mother

Born a bitch.

Died a bitch.

That was what he should have carved on her headstone. That was the type of person she really was. They'd found her dead, her liver packed up, in a diseased hovel in Whitechapel. Instead of turning his back on her, he'd decided to pay for the funeral, just like she had that belt she used to beat him with still tied around his neck, controlling his every move. Back in those days he hadn't had the readies to pay for a decent send-off, so he'd done four runs between Dover and Amsterdam, blocks of dope strapped to his body, to pay for it. Now every year he came to stand in the August air on the anniversary of her death. He told himself he came to gloat but he knew he was really seeking her approval that he was a top geezer. Except this visit was different. He could almost hear her laughing at him at the total mess he'd made of his life. His lips tightened as he bent down. Picked up the jug with water and the cloth. Tipped some water onto the cloth. He leaned over and gently wiped the dirt from the top of the headstone. He straightened. Read the inscription again. No, he wasn't going to end up like Millie Sullivan. He wasn't going to end up like that kid screaming for nine years in a corner until someone finally heard. He'd made it and only God could protect those who were brave enough to take it away from him.

'Do you like the flowers, Dad?'

Frankie looked sideways at his fifteen-year-old daughter. Daisy. The pride and complete joy of his life. She was already tall for her age, with hair as thick and as black as night and a reed-thin body as awkward as a teenage boy's. He'd only found out about her when she was four years old. Hadn't wanted to get attached, but as soon as he'd seen his blue eyes – Millie's eyes – staring back at him from her beautiful face he knew she was coming home with him. Now, if he got convicted, he might lose her. If that happened he had to make sure that she didn't end up in the care system. Not like him. Not like those four bitches who'd better get this job done or this time he wouldn't hesitate – he'd kill them.

Anna's motorbike dipped and weaved through the London traffic. Her faithful Harley was the first thing she'd bought with her cut of the loot from the diamonds. Jackie smiled. Held on tight. Closed her eyes. Felt the intense rush of London blast all over her. If they weren't in such shit she'd be tempted to yell out, 'Yihaaaa!' But they were in deep doo-doo and they were on their way to find a van to use in the kidnapping Frankie had ordered them to do. The smile shivered off her face. She peeled open her eyes. Suddenly London's intense pull felt like it was taking her places she didn't want to go.

Twenty minutes later the motorbike hit the back streets of Bethnal Green in East London. The motorbike trembled as they passed a boys' boxing gym and slowed as it took a smooth left into Vallance Road, where the Kray Twins' family home once was, and then a tight right into a narrower street. A street that everyone just called The Arches because of the row of garages and lock-ups that nestled underneath the railway track above. The bike hummed and bumped along the Victorian cobblestones. Finally stopped near a street light with a mustard-coloured poster advertising a boxing match between Jimmy 'Nose Crusher' Banks and Jack 'The Killer' Robinson. They jumped off the bike. Took their helmets off and looked up at the building in front of them. Mickey's Steam Cleaning Service.

The noise and sight of jets of steam came puffing out of the entrance. The women walked forward. Stepped inside. It was littered with vehicles and their parts. One man's legs shot out from under a black cab. The steam cleaner hissed in the air as two men worked on cleaning a very smart-looking car. The smell of oil and industrial fluids was so intense Jackie thought she was going to chuck up for the second time that day.

She took two steady breaths as someone called out, 'Can I help you ladies?'

Anna and Jackie twisted around to find a young man holding an Arsenal mug of steaming coffee beside them.

'Yeah,' Anna answered. 'We're looking for Mickey.'

'Well, ain't Mickey the lucky one,' the man said as he looked Anna up and down. He walked off towards the car with the man's legs sticking out from underneath it. He bent down and tapped the man's leg. The man crawled out from under the car. He stood up and gazed in Anna and Jackie's direction. Smiled as he walked over.

Mickey Preston was forty-one, sported a bald head he got professionally shaved once a month and had a compact body pumped up with bulging muscle and a smile full of gold teeth. He pushed the oil rag into his pocket as he said in a gruff cockney voice, 'If I weren't all dirty I'd give the two of you a bloody big hug.'

They stood there for a moment remembering the connection between them. Katie. His sister. A one-time employee at the club. A crackhead, now selling what was left of herself along Commercial Street. They followed him to a perspex office situated in a corner near the front of the garage. The room was definitely a working room, with a four-drawer steel cabinet in one corner and a desk teeming with a jumble of papers, account books and receipts. Above the desk was a framed photograph of Princess Diana wearing a tiara, her smile bright and wide, still enjoying the youthful days of her marriage.

The women pulled up a chair each as Mickey planted himself in the wooden chair behind the desk.

'I don't think you've come all the way to tell me what a good-looking bloke I am, so what can I do you for?' Straight talking, no bullshit, that was Mickey, and that was what they liked about him.

'You're a no-questions-asked kind of bloke?' Jackie asked.

'First rule of the school I went to was don't ask the teachers any questions and I've held onto that one all my life.'

'We need a van. Small. Tinted windows. Impersonal. Something that won't catch the eye.'

'There's always stuff like that coming through the midnight run.'

The midnight run was what some people called the illegal trade in stolen motors. A hush-hush cash-in-hand business that was carried on in garages, under the archways of railway lines, down grainy lanes or on remote industrial estates.

'When do you need it?'

'Like now,' Jackie answered.

'Shouldn't be a problem. I ain't got anything like that through at the mo but I am expecting a delivery soon.'

'What's the damage?'

'For you ladies, nothing. You did me a good turn once and . . .' He broke off and swallowed. Hard. 'I saw her last night, you know.'

Neither of the women spoke. Just let him tell his tale.

'You should've seen her, a bag of bones touting for business outside that white church on Commercial Street. So I drive up. Just wanted to talk. Know what happens? She wanders over to my car and without looking at me starts telling me what she can do for me for a tenner, a twenty. Fucking hell, she's selling her body for ten quid. Then she finally looks at me and clocks who I am. Runs off like a stray cat. I didn't go after her. Just drove off . . .'

'Mickey . . .' Jackie said softly with sorrow in her voice.

'You ever lost someone, knowing exactly where they were but just not able to reach 'em?'

Jackie gave him a tight nod. Yeah, she knew exactly what he meant. Hadn't she felt the same way about her mum stuck in prison somewhere? Except in her case someone had made her think she could reach Nikki. That Nikki was coming home one day soon. And that person had been Frankie. Bastard.

'You know what I'm gonna do?' Mickey's words dragged Jackie back from her own misery. 'I'm going back tonight and this time I'm taking her home.'

'You're a good brother, just like you're a good mate.'

He tilted his head to the side, gazing at both of them. Gave it a slight shake.

'I'll give you a tinkle when a van comes through.'

Anna threw the spare helmet at Jackie as they stood beside the motorbike outside Mickey's.

'You were thinking of your mum in there, weren't you?' Anna asked.

'No, I was thinking what a complete murdering arsehole Frankie is.'

'Patience, my girl, patience.'

They smiled at each other like they were sharing a secret.

'So that's the wheels sorted. What should we do next?' Jackie asked as she stared into the distance over the top of the banged-up motor parked at the end of the street.

'We need to find out where *Miss Josephine* is. And the only person who can tell us is Misty.'

thirty-two

A wind-up. That was what it was, Misty told herself, as she thought back to the phone call earlier that day. She'd told the caller to sod off and not call back again. The brass nerve of someone to call and say that. But still, it had shaken her up.

She shuddered as the peered down at the club's workers moving around the empty main room. Her eyes snapped around. No Anna. No Jackie. They were always here like clockwork, six days a week. And now it was minutes after three. So she was right, they were up to something.

'My giddy aunt,' she muttered as she turned around inside her office. Since finding out what the girls had been looking at on the Internet, the very thought that Frankie Sullivan might be trying to get his murdering mitts on her girls again was giving her kittens.

She moved towards the large framed photograph of David Bowie and Mick Ronson. She grabbed the left side of the picture and pulled it back. Inside was a camera and a tape machine. No one knew about the surveillance equipment she kept in her office. Not even Anna. She'd put a new tape in yesterday, just before Stacey's manager had arrived. She pressed 'eject'. The machine wheezed as it coughed the tape out. She slid it into the VCR under the flat screen on the wall. Moved to her desk. Sat down. Kicked the heels off her feet. Reached for the remote. Wiggled her turquoise-painted toes as she pressed 'play'.

Misty kept one eye on the screen as the anger began to heat her face. She was pissed with the girls. Pissed that they hadn't come to her if there was a problem. The idea that they might be holding out on her hurt. She was hurt that they might not need her any more. She was . . . Her thoughts skidded to a halt as she caught the action on the screen. Stacey's manager was standing by her desk.

'What the f . . .' she muttered, stunned, as she watched Finlay pull open her drawer. Take something out.

'Bloody tea leaf,' Misty said, her toes jack-knifing against the floor as she leaned over the desk and peered closer. It looked like a wad of paper and something else. Maybe it was Stacey's contract. No, she remembered they hadn't found it in the drawer. She got up and approached the screen at the same time as the grainy image showed Finlay walking over to the photocopier. Misty watched as he copied what he held in his hand. As he turned back towards the desk, the camera caught a clear view of one of the things he held. The photograph of Jackie, Anna and Roxy when they were fifteen years old. Misty's heart hammered in her chest as she watched Finlay place the picture and the wad of paper back in the drawer. What the heck was going on? Why would Stacey's manager be interested in that old photo?

Misty rushed back over to the desk. Opened the drawer. As soon as she saw the contents she knew something was wrong. The photograph sat on the top underneath the ownership documents of the club. She never put it there, always made sure to bury it deep so that no one else saw it. Not even the girls. She picked it up gently, as if it were the most precious thing in the world. She swung back around to the screen. Her palm covered her mouth as she watched what was happening. It showed Finlay with his hands around Stacey's neck as he pulled her off the floor. Suddenly the name Finlay swam in her head. Finlay? It couldn't be the same Finlay who'd . . . ?

The door to the office swung open. The photograph tumbled from Misty's hand.

Anna stood in the doorway. Misty rushed towards her desk, kicking the photo along the floor in the process. Grabbed the remote control. Pointed it at the screen.

'What you doing?' Anna asked as she stepped inside just as Misty pressed 'stop'. 'Watching something saucy?'

'See this.' Misty waved her clenched fist. 'You're supposed to use it to knock.'

Anna threw herself into the seat on the opposite side of the desk. Crossed one booted foot over her leg.

'Sorry I've been out so long, we just went off for a long lunch. We really want Jackie to have the hen night of all hen nights.'

Misty watched her through squinting eyes as she retook her seat. As she settled back she caught sight of the photograph, still on the floor. Damn. Keeping her eye on Anna, she slowly twisted the chair and extended her leg under the desk.

'So where did you go?'

As Anna babbled an answer Misty pushed her bare foot out until it reached the photo. Dug her toes into the surface. Slowly revolved the chair back to its normal position, using the movement to drag the photo towards her.

'Misty, you've got a piece of paper under your foot. Let me bin it.'

As Anna half rose Misty yelled, 'No.' She caught the startled expression on Anna's face and realised that she'd almost bitten the other woman's head off. She swallowed. Summoned the right tone into her voice and added, 'No. It's alright, sweetheart. It's just a love letter from an admirer. Said he gets all gooey-eyed over my feet. So I'm gonna post it back to him with the imprint of my devotion all over it.'

'Yucky.' Anna curled her lip as she plonked herself back down.

'Don't diss it until you've tried it.'

Anna unlocked her legs. Leaned across the desk.

'Talking about love and devotion, I've got a couple of mates who want to spend a week of lovin' on a houseboat, so I was thinking that maybe they could use *Miss Josephine*.'

'My Josie?' Misty's gaze roamed over Anna's face. Anna did a rapid eye-blink. Lowered her eyes. Squirmed as if she'd just placed her backside on the warm seat someone else had just vacated on a bus.

Definitely lying, Misty decided. 'Who are these friends of yours?'

'Oh, no one you've ever heard of.'

'No problem. Just tell them to come and get the keys off me when they're ready.'

'If it's alright with you I'll take the keys and hand them over.'

'When do they want to start their love-in?'

'Friday. But I wanna show it to them before.'

Now Misty was itching to ask what was going on.

'So where's *Miss Josephine* moored?' Anna asked.

'On the River Lea, between Springfield Park and Ferry Lane.' Misty opened the middle left-hand drawer of her desk and took out a set of keys. Chucked them at Anna. They landed, with a jingle-jangle, in her lap.

'Did you meet Stacey's manager when he was here?' Misty kept her voice light and offhand.

Anna shook her head as she played catch with the keys.

'Nice bloke. Quite a looker, especially if you like it homeboy style in the sack after midnight.' She allowed a dramatic pause. Caught Anna's shining brown eyes as she threw the keys in the air again. 'His name's Finlay Powell.'

Anna gasped. The keys divebombed onto the desk, knocking over a pen pot. Misty pushed herself urgently out of the chair. 'You alright?'

'Yeah. Cool,' Anna mumbled as she looked at her with a dazed expression. She pushed herself out of her chair. 'Gotta run. Got things to do. Thanks for these.' She grabbed the keys, waved them at Misty and exited the room.

Misty wearily retook her seat. So, as she'd suspected, Finlay was the same Finlay who'd poured petrol over a fifteen-year-old Ollie. She shook her head, berating herself for not figuring it out at the time. What a complete and utter dickhead. What did Frankie Sullivan have to do with her houseboat? She dipped her head. Stared hard at the photo on the floor. As she stared at her girls' smiling faces she knew that whatever the answer was she was the one who had led Frankie straight to them.

Misty knew she had no alternative now but to find out more about Frankie Sullivan. In her situation most people would go to the

Internet to fill in the blanks. Not her. There was only one place that was going to be able to help her. The one she hadn't been part of since she'd changed her name from Michael to Misty. London's underworld.

Anna found Jackie chatting to Gio at the bar. She quickly drew her aside.

'What did Misty say about *Miss Josephine*?'

Anna wet her lips and gave Jackie an uncomfortable look. Finally she spoke. 'Finlay was here.'

'You what?' Jackie gasped as she took a step closer to her friend.

Anna quickly explained what Misty had told her.

'Do you think that's how Frankie tracked us down?' Anna finished.

'Don't matter how Frankie found us, what matters is that he did. So are we on for *Miss Josephine*?'

Anna nodded. Jackie dug into her pocket. Whipped out her mobile.

'Ollie, it's me. We've got the boat. Meet us at Springfield Park at eight. And bring the stuff with you.'

Frankie grunted as he was expertly slammed to the floor.

He stared up at his daughter Daisy, who stood over him.

'Well done, babe,' he congratulated her. 'You're getting really good at this.'

They stood in the gym in Frankie's eight-bedroom house. He lived with Daisy in a sprawling hacienda-style mansion in the depths of Essex. His drum used to be in London's Docklands, but as soon as Daisy came into his life he'd changed all that. No way was a kid of his being brought up in the filth of the city. The house had the works – indoor swimming pool and Jacuzzi, games room, TV room down-stairs and three bathrooms (although he'd never figured out why people needed more than one place to piss in). He knew the house was all a bit *Dallas* – red brick, a beige tiled roof and with two large cartwheels attached to the outside walls – but his daughter had loved it.

Daisy grinned at her dad as she held out her hand and helped him up. They had just completed a vigorous kick-boxing mixed with kung fu exercise routine. Although Daisy knew nothing about his world he wanted to make sure that if she ever needed it in the future she would know how to fight. So since she was twelve he'd employed private tutors to instruct her in martial arts and boxing. Training her how to use a gun he did himself.

He ruffled her hair. 'You done good.'

'Mr Sullivan?'

Frankie twisted his head to find his housekeeper standing in the doorway.

'Ms Dream is here.'

'Make her comfy in my office.'

'Oh, Dad,' Daisy said in a disappointed voice. 'We haven't done the punchbag yet.'

'Sorry, babe. Gotta go.' He kissed her on the forehead and was gone.

As soon as he reached his office, the good-natured feeling he'd enjoyed with his daughter disappeared. He stepped inside. He found Bell Dream on her feet, her briefcase on the ground, staring at his huge collection of books.

She turned to him, surprise covering her face when she saw the sweaty tracksuit that he wore. 'So you're a lover of Graham Greene.'

'Nah. They're just there so that people don't take me for an uneducated prick.'

Bell gave a small laugh as he waved for her to take a seat.

'So what kind of odds are we playing for now?' he said as he settled himself into the leather chair behind the desk.

'I'd say we were still around the fifty-fifty mark. In your favour you've only ever been incarcerated once, many years ago, you're a devoted father and have given generous donations to the community. We aren't disputing the fact that you may have had a rocky youth, but you've learned your lesson and moved on. Our biggest defence is going to be that you were the innocent party. A genuine businessman who got played for a fool by his accountant, who has long since disappeared. As there's no jury it all rests on Judge Cynthia Gray-Hammond's decision.'

'You got any kids?'

A guarded expression came over Bell's face. She nodded. 'A daughter. Twenty years old.'

Frankie pointed at the heart-shaped framed photo on the desk. The lines around his eyes crinkled as he gave a lopsided smile. 'That's my girl. Daisy. Fifteen years old. On her way to becoming a woman. But she'll always be my little girl. She's the reason I wanted you to come here today.'

'What do you mean?'

'What's gonna happen to her if I get done or die?'

Bell's expression portrayed no surprise at his question. 'I take it Daisy's mother is out of the picture?'

'She might as well be six feet under as far as I'm concerned. She's well and truly outta Daisy's life. I ain't got no family, so what'll happen to her?'

'She'll most likely be put into foster care . . .'

'No way is a kid of mine ending up in any kinda state fucking care.'

As he drew in deep shots of air loaded with anger he saw her face and realised he'd been shouting. But he wasn't about to say sorry because that was how he felt.

'I just need you to tell me if I can make someone her legal guardian.'

'Of course you can. All you have to do is draw up a legal document.'

'OK. I want you to write down this name and get the paperwork done and dusted for me.'

He told her the name. Bell didn't betray the astonishment she felt at the name he gave her.

Have a shag.

Paint your toenails.

Yell out 'full house' at bingo.

Jackie thought about three of the million and one other things she'd rather be doing on a Wednesday night than treading the footpath beside the River Lea. The part of the river where London flowed from east to north-east. From Hackney to Haringey. She walked with the others in let's-get-this-over-with steps as they searched for Misty's boat. The path was only wide enough for them to move in a formation of two. Two at the front, two at the back. Jackie and Anna. Ollie and Roxy. Ollie held a small black holdall in her hand.

Jackie shoved a half-smoked cigarette to her lips. Snapped in some smoke. That's it, deep breath, girl. Stillness and peace, that was what Misty had told them years ago was the beauty of the rivers and canals around England. But tonight she couldn't feel it. Instead the distant repetitive strain of a here-today-gone-tomorrow pop tune playing inside one of the flats in the block on the right beat inside her. The lights shining from the windows of the boats they passed stared at her with the curiosity of featureless faces. The breeze whispering in the grass and weeds on the footpath's edge brushed against her every move.

'Can you see *Miss Josephine* yet?' Ollie called directly behind Jackie.

Jackie took in her last lug of smoke before she answered, 'Not a dicky-bird.' She flicked the butt into the air.

They shuffled on until they saw the shape of a quiet figure sitting on the tufts of grass that lay at the edge of the path. Jackie heard Ollie and Roxy stop. She twisted around. 'What you stopping for?'

'Who's that?' Roxy asked, her hand clutching her shoulder bag.

'How the fuck do I know? I ain't a mind reader.'

'Say it's a . . .'

'A what? A ghost? Come on, we've got things to do.'

They moved on. Reached the figure. A ragged homeless man with a can of brew in his hand. He looked up at them with bleary eyes. Held the can out towards them and slurred, 'Fancy a drop of the Holy Spirit?'

Anna kissed her teeth at him and moved on. The others followed. They kept moving. As they reached a rusty gate across the path they heard footsteps crunching behind them. They all turned at the same time to find a man wearing three-quarter-length summer shorts and a hoody shielding his face moving towards them. He propelled his body in urgent, swift steps. Held a mobile phone to his ear, nodding his head, saying, 'Uh, yeah.' Pause. 'Uh, yeah.' Pause. He didn't stop moving his legs or his mouth as he reached them. They stepped aside to let him pass, except Jackie, who wasn't quick enough. The man knocked into her shoulder. He kissed his teeth and muttered, 'Watch it.'

'Oi, didn't your mum bring you up with any manners?' Jackie demanded, taking a step forward.

But he didn't answer her. Just carried on walking, his patter disappearing into the distance. Suddenly Jackie started wobbling as the world spun around her. Anna rushed over to her to steady her. Jackie bent over and threw up in the grass.

'You alright?' an anxious Roxy asked.

'Yeah, yeah,' Jackie mumbled as she straightened up. But she wasn't OK. She felt like shit. Had for days.

'You ain't got a certain something in the oven, have you?' Anna asked quietly. Pregnant? Jackie thought, stunned. But before she could answer Ollie called out, 'There she is. *Miss Josephine* herself.'

The man with the hoody watched the women board the boat. He pressed his mobile on.

'It's Fin. They're on one of them longboats on the river just after Upper Clapton. Want me to wait?'

He nodded at the answer. Cut the call. Pressed the mobile to silent. He leaned back into the shadows of the overgrown bushes and the night.

thirty-three

Miss Josephine had what most men dreamed of in a woman – she was long, beautifully made up and did what she was told. They stood inside the doorway, each one of them remembering that terrible night they had arrived here ten years ago.

'Misty must've given her a makeover,' Jackie commented as her eyes ran over the renovated beauty of the main room of the boat. The furniture hadn't changed – the same portable telly, shelves of books and music, chairs and Misty's Aunt Glad's second-hand table. Even the pot plants were the same. The one difference was a wireless laptop sitting in a corner.

Jackie was the first to step forward, naturally moving to the tan-coloured rocking chair. The chair had been her favourite place on the boat because it moved with the motion of the water, soothing, calm, all the things her life had lacked at that time. She sat down. Ran her hands over its smooth arms. Kicked her legs off the ground, starting to rock. The other women followed what she had done, going to their own favourite spots. Ollie to the cushioned chair next to the kitchen. Anna cross-legged on the Peruvian rug. Roxy on the lazy chair by the drinks cabinet.

'So do you reckon *Miss Josephine* is the place for the job?' Jackie began the discussion.

'It's secluded. Off the beaten track. Seems pretty ideal,' Anna answered.

'So we're agreed this is the place to do it?' Ollie swung her gaze around to each of them as she popped the question.

'Don't feel right, though.' Roxy's voice was small. 'This is our place. Ours and Misty's. It's like we're walking arm in arm with Frankie and bringing him through the door.'

Anna hiked her legs up to her chest and rested her chin on her knees. '*Miss Josephine* helped us out in the past and I'm sure she wouldn't mind giving us a helping hand again.'

Jackie looked over at the bag next to Ollie. 'We ain't gonna be able to do this if we haven't got the necessary gear, so Ollie, show us what you've got.'

Ollie pulled the bag into her lap. Unzipped it. Then, one by one, she began to show the items inside to the others: metres of thick rope; metallic gold duct tape; white pillowcases.

'Right, we keep that lot in the kitchen,' Jackie ordered.

After Ollie got back, Jackie tilted her head as she pushed out a tiny sigh. 'Do you remember when we used to sit on top of the roof in the sun?'

The others nodded. Jackie uncurled her legs. Jumped to her feet.

'I fancy feeling like fifteen all over again.' She didn't miss a step as she kept moving towards the doorway. She moved along the deck until she found the small five-rung rope ladder that led to the roof. Climbed up. Dropped to her knees, making the boat rock as she cautiously crawled to the other end of the roof. She reached the last lifebelt, one of four. Placed her bottom inside it and crossed her legs, just as she'd done when she was young. The others joined her on the roof. They each sat on the same lifebelts they would sit on when they were young. She was number one, Anna number two, Roxy number three and Ollie number four. All they were now missing were the sunhats they used to wear.

'Roxy, pass that bottle around,' Anna called out.

'I beg your pardon?'

'The bottle hiding out in your bag. Come on, we know it ain't spring water.'

Roxy reluctantly did what she was told. Opened it up and took a healthy swig before passing it on to Ollie. The bottle went down the line. Jackie sucked in her breath as the heat of the vodka burned towards her tummy.

'Do you remember Vicky Park?' she asked.

Only the silence of the night and their memories answered. Jackie smiled as her mind drew her back to those gorgeous days in Victoria Park in East London. Funny, of all the places Misty had taken them all over the country the one place they were drawn back to was East London. Mind you, didn't they say once an East End girl, always an East End girl? And Victoria Park had become their favourite mooring spot. They'd lie on the roof, decked out in sunhats and summer joy, catching any shade cast by the neighbouring housing estates and the huge trees, watching the families, couples and friends in the park. And life at St Nicholas became someone else's nightmare. The bottle was back in Jackie's hand. This time she took a deep, long drag.

'Do you ever think we should have done the right thing and gone to the police?' The unexpected question came from Roxy.

Jackie knew that she wasn't talking about now but ten years ago. 'What's right when you're fifteen years old, scared and you don't know who to trust?' she answered.

'If we had gone to the police you know what would have happened to us,' Ollie continued Jackie's argument. 'They would have put us in another home and God knows what would have happened to us then. I read this report recently that said half of all prisoners under the age of twenty-five have been through the care system, a third of the homeless are people who were brought up in state care, only sixty out of six thousand young people leaving care each year go to university. "Boys do crime and girls do sex", that's what the big tagline for the state care system in this country is.'

'What do we do next?' Anna asked.

'Find out about Daniel's movements,' Ollie said in a rush.

'How we gonna pull that one off?' Anna continued.

Jackie thrust the bottle to her lips. Took a slug and said, 'One of us has to get their foot inside his school.'

Markhouse Manor School was situated in the London borough of Richmond upon Thames with a stunning view of the river. The large, red-brick nineteenth-century building was located high on a hill, proclaiming to the world the type of elevated education it provided inside.

'How much do you reckon it costs?' Jackie asked as she peered through the windscreen of her car the following morning.

The car was parked under a tree on the opposite side of the road from the school.

'What?' Anna continued to get her disguise ready. Diana Ross-style fluffed-out hair, Jackie O sunglasses and lipstick so red it made a cocktail cherry look anaemic.

'To get your kid inside those fine gates.'

'You've got the dosh just like the rest of us, so there's nothing stopping you from getting Ryan in.' Anna did a final circuit of her bottom lip with the lipstick as she checked herself over in the passenger mirror.

'Yeah, but it just don't seem right that just because you've got a bigger bit of poke in your pocket than the general population your kid gets a better education. Every kid should have a right to go to a place like that.'

Anna folded her lips over, cementing the lip colour. As she shoved the lipstick back into her tiger-print Prada bag she countered, 'Are you for real? Are we really having a chat about right and wrong as we sit here trying to figure out the best way of following some kid?'

Jackie twisted her head around to stare at her friend so intensely it was as if they were involved in a parliamentary debate. 'Yeah, but that's what I'm talking about. If me and you had been educated in an outfit like that we wouldn't be sitting here now.'

'But we are. So do I look the part?'

Jackie checked out Anna's disguise.

'You'll do.'

Anna reached around into the back seat where a large, tan fur coat lay. As she pulled it on, she asked, 'You think the coat is overdoing it a bit?'

'Nah, these people like to see money upfront. If they don't they'll sniff out the working woman in you straight away. . .'

Jackie's words were stopped by the ring of her mobile. She flipped it out of her pocket. The call was quick. She flicked her gaze at Anna once it was over.

'That was Mickey. He's got a van coming through. He'll give us a bell once it's in his hands.'

Three minutes later Anna was strolling through the breaking sunshine in the guise of Mrs Marianna Marsden. She got the jitters as soon as she walked into the reception area. She hated schools. Always had, always would. She learned dick at the East London comp she'd attended. Hanging out with the 'in' group who did everything that the school rules said were 'out'. She kept her head down, looking furtively for any cameras. She spotted one. Walked with her body at an angle to it so her face wasn't visible. She approached the main reception desk, where a woman with neat pulled-back, blonde hair and carefully applied make-up stood.

The woman gave Anna a lukewarm smile. 'May I help you?'

Anna leaned her hands deliberately on the counter, showing off the Rolex and the diamond ring she wore.

'My name is Mrs Marianna Marsden,' Anna said with a flourish in her best mock-posh voice. 'And I would like to find out more about your establishment as I'm thinking of sending my little Robbie here.'

The woman's smile became a full-stretch beam as she eyed up Anna's jewellery.

'May I offer you something to drink? Tea?'

'No thank you.'

'Well,' the woman carried on in a flustered tone, her hand reaching out to the right side of the counter, where a bundle of school prospectuses were displayed. She grabbed one and gave it to Anna. 'This is our school brochure. Why don't you take it away and then give us a call to make an appointment to meet with the admissions tutor.'

'Yes, I might do that. But as I'm here maybe you can answer some questions for me. Give me a run-down of the school day.'

The woman behind the desk obliged. Time for morning bell. Morning lessons – English, maths. Lunch. Anna jumped in on lunch. 'So do the boys stay for lunch or are they permitted outside?'

'We provide a very nutritious meal that upholds our healthy-eating school policy. So the boys all stay inside most of the time. On a Friday we let Beta and Alpha classes go outside. We believe that it's very important for them to develop their independence. Of course, we discourage the boys from eating in the streets. It wouldn't do for the local community to associate us with bags of chips.'

'And how old are the Beta and Alpha boys?'

The woman told her. So Danny was a Beta boy. Which meant he might leave school at lunchtime. The woman carried on talking about the afternoon programme.

'I've had it,' a voice yelled.

Anna swung around. A bulldog of a woman with a coat half on, half off moved as if there was fire under her feet towards the reception desk. 'I'm not prepared to work here one minute longer.'

The woman swept past the reception desk.

'Excuse me,' the receptionist called, leaning frantically over the desk, 'you can't just leave.'

The woman stopped. Screwed her furious eyes into the receptionist. 'Look, love, I told ya that if that bunch of animals did one more thing to me while I was serving 'em lunch I'd be outta here.'

'But what happened?'

'That Jerome looks at my breasts and asks me if I've got any plum pudding. Then he leans over and tries to touch 'em. And that's when that little gang of his, Danny and Thomas, start laughing. Well, you know what, love, I might need the cash but the agency never told me nothin' about working in no bloody zoo. And don't bother getting on the blower to the agency because I was the last mug willing to come here. Posh education my big fat arse . . .'

An idea sprang to Anna's mind as she watched the departing figure. She immediately began to follow her.

'Where are you going?' the receptionist called after her.

Anna swung around, her hair and coat flapping in the air. 'I'm so sorry but I can't possibly send my precious Robbie to an establishment that terrorises women, even though they might be working-class. Good day to you.'

With that Anna followed the harassed former employee. Through the school exit. Down towards Richmond Green. Past Jackie's car. A bewildered Jackie mouthed, 'Where you going?' as she wound down the window. Anna gave her the thumbs-up sign but carried on walking. A few minutes later the woman stopped outside a shopfront. Martha's Agency was printed in large orange letters above the door. The woman pushed inside with the force of a hurricane.

'What the hell was all that about?' Jackie asked ten minutes later as Anna flung herself into the car.

    'Seems that Danny and his mates are the school's local hard men.'

    'But did you find a way for us to follow him?'

    'Yeah and no.'

    'What the heck are you on about?'

    'All depends on you, Jack.'

    'Spill.'

    Anna looked her up and down, making Jackie squirm in her seat.

    'Yes, I can just see it now in neon lights,' Anna said dramatically. 'Jackie Jarvis. Dinner lady of the year . . .'

thirty-four

The next day Jackie decided that school dinners hadn't changed much over the years. She wrinkled her nose as she stared down at the food on the hotplates in front of her. Offensive seemed too mild a word for it. It put the perils associated with BSE to shame, she thought. As she lifted her hand to administer another slop of something onto a plate, her gaze bounced around the hall. What a complete letdown. She'd always had an image of how the other half lived. Before she'd arrived she'd imagined it was going to be all Goodbye, Mister Chipsville. Tomorrow's potential prime ministers all neatly turned out, sitting stiff-backed at a long table, looking at a steel-haired and-eyed gowned master as he reminded them of their duty to patronise working-class people for the rest of their lives. No, Markhouse Manor dining hall was like any other school – dish it out, eat it up and get 'em out as soon as possible. She wondered if parents knew what they were getting for their thirteen grand a year. She sighed. Not her problem.

Her problem was to keep her fingers crossed that Daniel came into the dining hall. Instead of driving home the previous day, Jackie had gone to Martha's Agency, hoping that the job of dinner lady was still vacant. The agency had been a rollover, looking at her like gold dust when she'd arrived to register with them. As predicted, the job they had handed over was casual kitchen assistant at Markhouse Manor.

So here she stood, with a catering hat, overalls and size-three soft black shoes encasing her feet, numb from standing in the kitchen cutting, peeling, mixing and washing all morning. She'd been doling out this muck for fifteen minutes and still no sign of their target. She was raising her spoon for the umpteenth time when she heard the voices. Boys, loud and boisterous. Verbal, verbal, verbal. Stomp, stomp, stomp. And from the chatter and pseudo-tasty London-geezer swaggers they were adopting she realised they were posh boys playing street. She grimaced. A bunch of baby mockney-cockneys in her midst. Three of them, although there was a fourth who appeared to be the quiet tail. All the other kids looked with adoration in their eyes as the group sauntered over to the line. And her target, thank God, was one of them. Daniel Gray-Hammond in the flesh, looking anything other than the innocent smiling teenager she'd seen in the photograph. His hair was messy, his tie loose and he had a rebellious gleam in his eyes.

The gang finally reached her part of today's yuck-fest. The first one, who she immediately christened Ronnie Kray, looked her up and down. Settled his brazen brown eyes on her chest and declared in a voice loud enough for all to hear, 'Well, well, well. Looks as if we've got a new tart with a heart.'

Tart with a very heavy spoon, Jackie said in her head, but she kept her lips buttoned tight.

'She ain't got a lot up top,' the second one, who she name-tagged Reggie, scoffed.

Daniel high-fived 'Reggie' and giggled.

'So what we got in the joint today?' 'Ronnie' carried on, looking at her like she was Doris behind the bar at the Dog and Truck.

'Gaff,' she corrected him, slopping some baked beans onto his plate.

'I beg your pardon . . .' he started, confused at her comeback. Then he remembered the part he was playing, puffed his chest out and corrected himself with a swaggering 'You what?'

'It's gaff. Joint's more American. Gaff's what you would say if you were living it hard on the streets of East London.'

'What?' He leaned over the instant mash and whispered, 'You're a real cockney?'

'You better Adam and Eve it, my young cockle,' she hammed it up. Next he'd be asking her to do 'The Lambeth Walk . . . oi'. He turned quickly to 'Reggie' and Daniel and began to whisper. He twisted back to her, once again leaned over the hotplate and said, 'Do you know loads of rhyming slang?'

At first she was confused by his question. Then, when she saw the gleam in his eye, she realised what was going on. Ping. She had something they wanted. A knowledge that would raise their status in the school. A knowledge she might be able to use to worm her way into their lives and find out what Daniel got up to. She smiled. Tucked a few undercooked fish fingers onto his plate and said, 'Yeah.'

'Can you teach us some rhyming slang on Tuesday? We can't do Monday because we've all got rugby practice.'

'Alright. On one condition.'

He looked expectantly at her.

'You don't ever call me a bird.'

Lesson one started on Tuesday, five days before Jackie's wedding, twenty minutes after all the kids cleared out of the lunch hall. She hoped that lesson one was all that was needed to find out the information she was after. She'd put herself forward for table-cleaning duty, so she had time to talk to the boys. They sat at a table that she had just wiped clean. Jackie sat down at the table, the smell of disinfectant between her and the boys. The only other person in the hall was one of the female teachers, who kept looking over, gobsmacked that they were finally behaving themselves. The fourth boy in the group, the quiet one, held a notepad and pen ready to take notes. The ones she'd called Ronnie and Reggie were Jerome and Ben.

'See my old man,' Jackie started. The quiet one quickly scribbled 'old man'. 'He was a bit of a geezer. Used to box with the Krays when he was a young 'un. Became a well-known face.' She leaned over the table towards Daniel and Jerome and whispered, 'No one knows this, but me and me sister use to sleep with a load of shooters under our bed. 'Course, when he got done after that last blag he did, the Old Bill found the lot. Got sent down for a fifteen stretch in the Scrubs.'

She carried on talking, throwing a barrage of other cockney slang in the air:

Tea leaf – thief.

Trouble and strife – wife.

Pete Tong – wrong.

She kept it up for ten minutes, then she turned the tables on them. 'What do your parents do?'

Jerome's father was the director of a City bank, Ben's was an ambassador. Danny confessed, with blushing embarrassment, to being a judge's son. Jackie saw the loneliness in his eyes and knew he missed his mum. Then they all looked at the quiet one with raised eyebrows, like there was a secret between them. Finally the boy said, in a quiet foreign accent, that his dad was a Russian businessman.

'Why would good boys like you wanna know about the street?'

'We're not that good,' Daniel responded, puffing out his chest.

Jerome's eyes darted to the others. 'Should we tell her?'

They gave her boyish grins and nodded. Daniel was the one to divulge their secret 'We sneak out every Wednesday night at nine . . .'

His words stopped as Jackie felt someone tap her on the shoulder. Standing next to her was young woman who worked in the kitchen. 'The cook wants you.'

Fuck, what timing.

Jackie stood up and said, 'Alright, next lesson tomorrow. Same place, same time.'

Jackie followed the other woman into the kitchen, which was teeming with heat, bodies and unwashed plates and pans. She moved towards the cook, who stood with her hands deep in water at the sink.

'We've found a permanent replacement, which means we won't be needing you again.'

Jackie's mouth fell open. 'But I've got to come back.'

The cook stared at her with no-can-do eyes.

'How the hell did you manage to get fired?' Anna blasted at Jackie.

Jackie sat with the others later that day in Anna's office in the club.

She threw the other woman a pissed expression. 'I did not get fired, I got laid off . . .'

'But what did you find out?' Ollie cut in.

'They sneak out every Wednesday night at nine.'

'Where do they go?' Anna's annoyance with Jackie was still in her tone.

'That I can't say because the cook told me to sling my hook.'

'Only two places teenagers bunk school for – the pub or a club,' Roxy chipped in as she dug into her bag for her travelling bottle of vodka. 'At least we've got a time they won't be in the school and we can follow them.' She refilled her glass with a liberal amount of booze.

'Which gives us a couple of days. What's happening with the van?' Ollie addressed her question to Jackie and Anna.

'Don't worry,' Anna answered. 'Mickey won't let us down. So when it comes through, Roxy, we're all agreed that we keep it at your garage.'

Roxy nodded. Drank heavily from her glass.

'I kind of felt sorry for them,' Jackie muttered. 'Don't get me wrong, that school ain't St Nicholas, but it ain't home either . . .'

'How can you feel sorry for them?' Anna let out in astonishment. 'Their parents have got money to burn.'

'I know that, dumbo. But you should've seen their eyes when they talked about their mums and dads.'

'I knew this would happen.' Anna slammed her hands onto the desk.

'What?'

'You can't stop playing mum. Can't stop wanting to dole out hugs all the time. You got to remember we can't afford to get attached. We've got our own problems going on here.'

'I tell you what was funny, though.' A frown etched itself into Jackie's forehead. 'They all got shifty when the quiet one was gonna say what his dad did. Maybe his dad's some type of mafia boss or something?' Jackie laughed. No one else did.

'Are we sure we shouldn't be going to the police?' Roxy asked as her hand shook around her glass.

'No.' Jackie shook her head. 'Our plan is the only way to sort this out once and for all.'

Pregnant.

Jackie stared, stunned, at the little blue line as she stood in the toilet cubicle. She was going to have another kid. No wonder she'd been feeling woozy and sick. Anna had been right, she had something in the oven alright. Why now of all times, with Frankie back in her life, did she have to be up the duff? She'd have to be careful or she might hurt her baby. Her baby. The words rang sweetly in her head. She smiled as her hand touched her still-flat tummy. School-boy was going to become a dad. He loved kids. Should she let him know today? No, she'd keep it as a big surprise until after the wedding. She let out a joyful laugh as she placed the pregnancy testing kit in her pocket. She turned around. Before she realised what was happening two hands shot out and grabbed her arms. Lifted her up. Slammed her against the toilet wall.

Frankie.

Instinctively, Jackie's hands tried to cover her stomach to protect her baby, but Frankie's hands squeezed and pinched the skin of her arms.

'Nice place you've got here.' Frankie spat the words into her face. 'Glad to see you and the others spent my readies well.'

'Get your filthy mitts off me.' She slashed her arms towards his face. Kicked her legs out at any part of his body she could connect with. But he just laughed. Slammed her harder into the wall. Winded, she stared at him with a dazed look in her eyes. How could a man look so beautiful and terrifying at the same time?

'Settle down.'

'I said get off me.' Her body remained still as she ground out the words.

'What you gonna do if I don't?' He pushed his face closer. 'Get your mum onto me?'

'Oops,' he carried on in mock reproach. 'Silly me, forgot your mum won't be coming back . . .' One of his hands dropped from her arm. Shot sideways towards the toilet. Found the chain and pulled. The sound of the swirling disappearing water crashed inside the cubicle. 'Ever.'

'At least I had a mum who gave a fuck about me,' she spat back at him.

His face flushed. Moved back an inch. Then he twisted the corner of his mouth into a cocky grin. 'Don't come over all stupid. I just thought we needed a one-to-one without the other hens clucking around. Frankie and Jackie. Sounds like a Broadway musical, don't it? We were almost best buddies once. I taught you so much. Still remember how to pick a pocket or two?'

Her glare intensified. But she said nothing.

'So give me an update on how our special project's going.'

'Let go of my arms and I might be able to help you.'

The grin fell from his face as he eyed her up, deciding what to do. Then, one finger at a time, he removed his hands. As he took a step back she made her move. She leapt at him, fists flying. Surprised, he staggered back against the cubicle door. She caught him on the shoulder. On his chest. Then his street-fighter instincts kicked in. He righted the balance of his body. Held his palms up to ward off her blows. His hands reached out like claws, trying to catch her arms. But her arms dropped, her hands touching the side pockets of his jacket. One of her hands quickly shifted behind her. He followed her movement, finally capturing one arm. His fingers dug into the flesh above her elbow. Twisted. She cried out in pain. Seeing his opportunity, he easily caught her other arm. His hands circled her flesh like bands of steel. He jerked her towards him. Her hands shot protectively over her tummy. He lifted her. Swung her around. Slammed her with incredible force into the wall. She cried out as a sharp pain shot through her back. Please God, she pleaded, don't let him have hurt my baby. He raised his hand. She cringed into the wall. He cocked two fingers together, forming his hand into the shape of an imaginary gun. Pushed it into her forehead, dead centre. Matched her shocked gaze with a look that was dead cold.

'Bang, bang, baby,' he whispered. 'That's all it takes to flush you away with all the other shit in this city. That's what my mum tried to do to me for years. Push my head down the toilet and pull the chain. She couldn't flush me away, nor can you, so stop playing the cunt or I'm gonna hurt you real bad, alright?' The fury of his words smashed into her face.

She gave a shaky nod. His hand fell from her forehead. He widened his stance. Bent his knees. Braced his hands on the wall on either side of her head. The cubicle filled with his breathing. Her breathing. The ragged gurgle from the tank.

'Now we've established you ain't Wonder Woman, maybe we can get back to what you do best in this life, which is following what I fucking tell you to do. So what's happening with the kid?'

Her hands pressed into her stomach. 'We've identified who he is and know what he gets up to. So we're gonna pick him up tomorrow. Him and his mates sneak out of school every Wednesday night.'

'Where does he go?'

'Dunno. I couldn't find out that piece of info . . .'

'Don't fuck me around, babe . . .'

'I ain't. I'm telling you the God's honest truth. We're gonna tail him and find out where he hangs out. If you want us to nab him properly, you need to give us time to check out where he goes. Then we'll be able to . . .'

'Tomorrow's Wednesday so you do it tomorrow,' Frankie cut in. 'And when you do you'd better make sure you do the business, because I can see you, but you can't see me. I'm like a fly on shit on your every move. At the boat. At the arches. Playing fancy dress as a dinner lady. Playing mummy dearest dropping her beloved boy off at school . . .'

'You leave my boy outta this . . .'

'That's up to you. One false move and who knows who might be holding Ryan's hand the next time I see him.'

Jackie bit her lip as his words hit her full in the face.

'I sometimes think,' Frankie continued in a soft tone, as his head dipped closer to hers, 'if we'd met years later, we could've been a stand-out couple.' His face moved closer. He trailed a single finger slowly across her cheek. Down her throat. Across Nikki's necklace. 'Stepping out together. Setting up home. Having a couple of young 'uns.' His lips hovered over hers. 'His-and-hers pillows. You used to remind me of the kind of woman I wanted my little girl to grow up to be.'

His lips touched hers. The touch deepened into a long, lingering kiss. Gobsmacked by his action, Jackie remained still. Then a trembling feeling washed over her. Shit, his lips felt like heaven. She began to slowly move her mouth with his. He caught her face, deepening the kiss. His hand found her breast. Trailed down to caress her stomach. That was when her heartbeat nearly stopped. Frankie's murdering hands were over her baby.

With a cry, Jackie ripped her lips away. She didn't even think. Just did it. She tipped her head defiantly up. Opened her mouth. Spat into his face. He flinched as her spittle lay thick against the deepening colour of his cheek. She didn't see his fist move, but she felt it coming. He punched her in her belly. She groaned. The pain pushed her down the wall. She gasped as the pain radiated inside her. She raised her head at the same time as he crouched down beside her. His hands shot out. His fingers found her nipples. Squeezed. She let out a harsh gasp. He tugged her nipples out, stretching them. Twisted.

His blue eyes were hot and hostile as he said, 'That's always been our problem, ain't it, babe?' The pain in her belly and nipples rushed up into her eyes. 'We can never decide whether to fuck or fight. You've so grown into the kind of woman my dick wakes up in the morning for.'

He let go of her nipples. She inhaled sharply as the blood rushed back into them. He wiped the spit from his skin. Jackie drew her knees protectively to her chest. He laughed without any merriment dancing in his eyes. 'When the clock strikes midnight on Wednesday I'll be waiting for your call. Don't disappoint me.' He tweaked her nose. Stood up. Moved leisurely towards the door. As he reached it he turned. 'Don't disappoint Ryan.'

He left her lying on the cold floor. She relaxed her head against the wall as the air whooshed out of her body. Finally she staggered to her feet and moved towards the toilet. She pushed the toilet seat down. Sat. She moved her hand to her back pocket. Pulled out what she'd hidden inside it. Frankie's wallet. Soft tan leather. Distraction, that was what he'd taught her. The best way to pick anyone's pocket. In the midst of their tussle her fingers had gone for his pocket. She'd only ever picked a pocket once before in her life. Ryan's long-gone dad. When she realised he was going to dump her she'd done it for Ryan. She had more than enough money to bring up her son, but she wanted to make sure that his dad paid his dues as well. She'd found £157 and put it in a high-interest account for her little man when he reached eighteen. Now she'd done it again. To Frankie. She placed the wallet in her lap. Stared at it and contemptuously growled, 'Tosser.'

As she began to open the wallet her mobile vibrated in her pocket, stilling her fingers. She snapped the wallet shut. Stood up and groped for her phone. She gazed at the screen. Text message.

The midnight run has come thru
M

Mickey. The van was ready for collection. She dialled the number of the bar upstairs.

'It's Jackie. Get me Anna.'

Anna came on the line a minute later.

'Have your wheels ready in ten minutes. The van's ready.'

The line went dead. Jackie looked down at her belly. Touched it and softly said, 'Don't worry, little one. Frankie's gonna get what's coming to him one of these days. Very soon.'

thirty-five

The van was just what they hoped for. Black. Tinted windows. A rear big enough to throw a person inside quickly.

'This what you had in mind, ladies?' Mickey asked, rubbing his oil-coated hands down his overalls.

Jackie and Anna didn't answer him because they were too busy giving the van the once-over. Jackie was the first to look away from the vehicle. Anna sensed her movement. Lifted her head. Jackie caught Anna's gaze. Finally she nodded, half her mouth trembling in a crooked smile. The ground beneath her feet shook as a train thundered overhead. Anna grinned back. She moved in her long-legged leather-clad sexy walk towards Mickey. Her curtain of black hair gave a joyous swing behind her shoulder line as she threw her arms around his neck. She cupped her fine fingers under his chin. 'You, my man . . .' She planted a theatrical kiss onto his midnight-shadowed cheek. Lifted her head and smiled into his startled eyes. '. . . are a megastar.' She pressed her lips to the other cheek.

Mickey blushed as she let him go.

'I ain't asking what you need it for but the plates are bogus.' Mickey pulled out the keys. Lobbed them to Jackie. She caught them and winced from the pain in her back, reminding her of her earlier tussle with Frankie.

'You alright?' Anna asked, seeing the pinched pain on her face.

Jackie swiftly nodded, not wanting Anna or anyone to know that Frankie had paid her a visit. 'Let's load your bike up.'

After Mickey had helped them load Anna's bike into the back of the van they jumped in the front. Neither of them spoke. Just stared straight ahead.

'You still sure we're doing the right thing?' Anna finally broke the silence.

'When I was young I used to think I knew what right and wrong were. Now I realise that life ain't that cut and dried. So let's get this over to Roxy's.'

Mickey watched the van drive away. As soon as it was out of sight he went back to his office. Shut the door. Picked up the phone.

'It's Mickey. I think there's something you need to know . . .'

An hour later, Jackie and Anna pulled up outside Roxy's place. Anna cut the engine as the final chords of Aretha Franklin's 'Respect' died inside the van.

'I've got a call to make, so I'll see you back here,' Anna said as she pulled her hands off the steering wheel.

Jackie nodded. Jumped out. Took the few steps it took her to reach Roxy's door. She pressed the bell with one hand, shoving the other through her short strands of hair. She heard footsteps. Heavy. Hesitant. Then she caught the outline of a person through the frosted-glass panel.

'Who is it?' Roxy's voice. Strained and small.

'It's Jackie. Come on, open up.'

'This isn't a good time. I'm busy.'

'It's never a good time. Come on, my fanny's getting friggin' frozen standing out here.'

The next five seconds filled with silence as Roxy apparently made up her mind. Then the door slowly began to open. When Jackie saw her face she understood why she hadn't wanted to open the door. The right side of Roxy's face was swollen and bruised, her eye sporting the trademark of a classic black eye.

'I'm gonna fucking slaughter him,' Jackie stormed as she pushed past Roxy into the house.

A quiet click sounded as Roxy closed the door. She folded her arms, the fingers of her right hand running nervously over the skin of her left arm.

'Shit,' Jackie let out in a harsh whispered breath as she reached her hand across to her friend's face. Roxy flinched, taking rapid shallow breaths.

'How it's going, Jackie?' a confident male voice asked.

Jackie angrily turned to find Roxy's husband, Martin, standing in the lounge doorway. He stood there, neat and tidy, everything about him in the right place. She trailed her gaze down to his hands, which he held by his side. They were long, thin, but with a slight curved tenseness, like they were ready to spring into life. Rage tightened her own hands as she moved her head up to stare straight into his dishwater-coloured eyes.

'Look, scum . . .' Jackie shouted, but Roxy's fingers dug into the top of her arm, stopping her words.

'Jackie,' Roxy's plea wobbled thin and long behind her.

The breathing of each person beat in the air. Roxy by the door, Martin by the lounge. And Jackie in the middle.

'What did you want to see me about?' Roxy broke the silence as her hand fell from Jackie's arm.

Jackie turned back to her. 'Remember we talked about using your garage for a bit.'

'Oh yes. I'll get the key.'

Roxy moved, head bowed, with quick steps. Past Jackie. Shrinking past her husband. Jackie pivoted back to Martin. She stared hard at him with eyes that shone with 'it's just you and me, scumbag'. The atmosphere in the hallway became still and strained. Jackie crossed her arms as she angrily stared at the man her friend had declared to the world she would honour and obey five years ago. His eyes shifted, looking over her head.

'Not making you uncomfortable, am I?' Jackie jeered. 'It's just that I thought you enjoyed having a woman all to yourself.'

His eyes flicked down to her face. His tongue ran over his bottom lip, as if he was debating whether to stay or go. He decided to go, turning back towards the lounge. Her words stopped him.

'You know what the nuns used to tell us at school? If your right hand causes you to sin you should do the world a favour and cut it off. It got me thinking that there are other things you can cut off to get the point across. So I'm giving you notice now that if I *ever* see one more mark on Roxy's skin I'm just the right height to rip your prick off.'

Martin flinched, remaining immobile, while her warning hung over him. Then he went into the lounge.

Still shaking with anger, Jackie made her way to the garage. It was rectangular, its walls a patchwork of large grey blocks. Apart from a few boxes in one corner it was bare, the ideal place to hide a hot van.

'As soon as we discussed it the other day I got it ready,' Roxy babbled in a high, rapid tone. She moved into the middle, her arms waving around. 'We made it nice and clean. Me and Martin. Of course, I never told him why. He helped me carry stuff out. He's a real sweetie. A doll. Gets me roses every Friday night. And . . . And . . .' Her voice shattered into huge sobs that rocked her body. Jackie rushed over and embraced her.

'Sometimes,' Roxy shook as she clung onto Jackie, 'when he hits me, my mind cuts off and starts dreaming. Dreaming that when my mum got up that morning ten years ago she took me to school. Walked with me arm in arm. Kissed me at the gates. Then later on she collected me. Told me that she'd cooked my favourite meal. Then all of a sudden the pain of his belt or fists comes back and reminds me that my mum rarely came to meet me at school, never cooked me my favourite meal. All she did was drink her life away. That's why I hate what he does to me because it reminds me what my mum really was.'

Jackie felt her lip tremble. Her eyes watered. But she hadn't come across the river to bawl her eyes out. She shook the tears back as she gently eased Roxy away from her, but still held onto her arms. 'You listen to me and listen good. Your mum might not have been Mother Teresa, but she was a good woman. Just like all our mums were. All they were trying to do was make a quick dollar to put bread on the table. Let me tell you why it hurts when that pig hits you – because he's a brute, a thug. Alright?'

Roxy simply hung her head. Jackie let go of her arms. 'You need to dry those tears because we've got work to do. I'll tell Anna to bring the van around.'

Jackie walked briskly to the exit. She stopped but didn't turn around as she said, 'When all this stuff with Frankie is over, don't think I'm gonna let you bury your head because I'm not. One way or the other this business with Martin is gonna get sorted out.'

Jackie's Juicy Lucy vibrator massaged her bruised back. She sat in the dark of her front room. The window was open with the breeze from the canal circulating chilled currents inside the space around her. The mewling of a baby and Connie Francis's 'Who's Sorry Now?' coming from a neighbouring flat kept her company. Not that she needed any. Frankie had left her with all the company she needed – his brutality and his wallet. Her back stiffened as Juicy Lucy hit the right spot. She sucked in some air. Sighed. Oh yeah, that felt sooo gooood. She rotated the vibrating head deeper into her skin. She stayed like that, at peace, for five minutes, until the ache had eased. She turned the vibrator off. Placed it on her lap next to Frankie's wallet.

She reached for it. Opened it. Peeped inside. It looked pretty empty. Carefully she took out each item and placed it on her lap.

Cash – five tenners, six twenties.

Photo – Frankie smiling, with love in his eyes, as he held a grinning young girl. A young girl who had his piercing blue eyes. It had to be his daughter. Funny, but she'd never imagined him with kids. She turned it over and found some writing on the back. *Daisy and Dad at Southend.* She tried to picture Frankie building sandcastles, walking ankle deep in the sea, holding the little girl's hand while they licked ice creams, strolling along the beach. The images disturbed her because it made him human, not the monster she'd always pictured him to be. She turned the photo back over and this time stared at the girl. Bob-cut brown hair, a missing front tooth adding a sweet edge to her grin and dimples on both cheeks. What a cutie. Reminded Jackie of her Ryan when he was that age. Ryan. She remembered the threats Frankie had made to her son. Jackie's heart began to harden again. No, Frankie wasn't human, he was a wrecker of lives, a dickhead. A murdering monster. She dropped the picture onto her lap as if her fingers were burnt.

She picked up the final item. A business card.

Bell Dream
Solicitor

Where had she heard that name before? The name did a couple of circuits of her brain. She tapped the card on her knee, trying to remember. Shit, it wasn't coming to her. She'd bring the card with her tomorrow and show it to the others. Mind you, she hadn't a clue what they would do with the information.

She gathered Frankie's belongings and Juicy Lucy into her hands as she stood up. She marched into the kitchen. Moved towards her West Ham Utd lunchbox, which sat on the side next to the fridge. She'd kept it for all these years because it was one of her last connections to her life as Jade Flynn. She opened it. She stared at the two items that were reminders of Nikki – the Soft Cell cassette and the remnants of the candle that she'd lit for her mum all those years ago. Throughout the years she'd never felt the need to light the candle again. Until now. She could do with a prayer to guide her through the next days. But she didn't light it. Instead she placed Frankie's wallet inside, nice and safe, next to the photograph of Daniel Gray-Hammond.

'What's the full SP on Frankie Sullivan?'

The man who spoke was kitted out in a sharp Armani suit, his hair pulled back in a ponytail and two gold studs shining in his ears.

He popped the question at the man who sat opposite him. The man who was the head of one of London's most feared families. The man who was also his older brother Charlie. The rousing drama of the Kinks' 'Lola' stomping around the boozer they sat in, which was on the housing estate they'd grown up on as kids – the Ashbury Estate, or Trash City, as most people called it.

Charlie pulled his pint to his lips. Then answered. 'Depends on who you're jarring with. Some say he's the most feared face London has ever seen. Others say he's a fucking psycho who's gonna get what's coming to him when that judge bangs her gavel next Friday.'

'What do you say?'

Charlie took another slug from his glass. 'The fucker's a bit too pretty for my liking.' Both men roared with laughter at Charlie's statement. 'A hard man should have more scars . . .'

'So you ain't emotionally attached to him?'

'First thing I ever taught you as a nipper was never get emotionally attached to no one unless they're family.' Charlie drained the dregs from his glass. 'So, little brother, what do you need doing?'

'If I wanted him to disappear, you could arrange it?'

'It's a bit risky. If he don't turn up for that court case it could go either way with the Bill. They'll either tear this town apart looking for him or say good riddance to old rubbish. He won't be an easy man to take down, but I can sort it out.'

'If I give you the nod I want you to set it up, but I'm gonna be the one to take him down . . .'

'Hang on a minute . . .' Charlie cut in, rearing straight in his chair.

'This is personal, Charlie. It's about family.'

He stood up and left. A few minutes later he was inside his Mini. Flipped the light on. Pulled down the rear-view mirror. Pulled his hair free of the elastic band. Finger-combed it out. Popped the lipstick from his pocket. Changed the colour of his lips from pale pink to ruby red. Michael McKenzie stared at his reflection as he turned back into Miss Misty McKenzie.

After getting Mickey's phone call earlier that day telling him about the girls and the van, Misty knew that she couldn't ignore the fact that Frankie Sullivan might have the girls in his web again. But other things were telling him that the girls were involved – the whispers; the way Jackie and Anna were there one minute and then gone the next; Anna's eagerness to take *Miss Josephine* off her hands; a terrified Stacey's confession about why her manager, Finlay Powell, had slapped her about.

It wasn't like she hadn't asked the girls what was going on. But their lips weren't moving. So Misty didn't have an alternative. If Frankie Sullivan tried dragging her girls back into his world, Misty would be waiting for him.

thirty-six

Jackie met the others bang on midday on Wednesday, two days before Frankie's trial, three days before her wedding. A day that Frankie expected to end with the kidnapping of a judge's son. She met the others in a café on Commercial Street. Like Jackie, the area of Spitalfields had changed in the last ten years. It had taken itself from well-known prostitute-pimp dive to trendy café culture, with a refurbished Hawksmoor church for those looking for salvation and plushed-up Georgian houses for those with a cool million-plus in their pocket.

They sat at the table in a corner with four cups of strong coffee. Away from prying eyes. Away from the noise of the snarling tail-to-tail traffic outside.

'We need to make this snappy,' Jackie started. 'Frankie paid me a visit at the club yesterday . . .'

Roxy choked as the liquid in her mouth went down the wrong way, upsetting the large sunglasses she wore.

'Why didn't you say anything yesterday?' Anna said as she eyeballed Jackie.

'Did he touch you?' Ollie's perceptive eyes ran over Jackie.

She decided against the truth. 'No.'

The doorbell tinkled as another customer entered the café, but none of them paid any attention. The music in the background changed to Amy Winehouse's sassy 'You Know I'm No Good'.

Jackie leaned forward. 'Alright, let's go over the plan . . .'

'Looks like I've arrived just in time.'

Startled, the women looked up. Frankie brazenly stood grinning down at them. He wore designer shades, a blue-and-white-striped polo shirt and three-quarter denim shorts, and the look of a man who was enjoying the best day of his life. Two women sitting at a nearby table gazed at him with dreamy eyes, their mouths half opened. He pulled a chair from a neighbouring table. He straddled it, legs braced wide, arms lounging and his chin resting on the back. A strong ray of sunshine darted through the window. Settled onto him. Gave him that haloed-angel look Jackie remembered he had had the first time she'd clocked eyes on him ten years ago. He shot his bright, white smile around the table. 'Don't stop on my behalf, Jackie, girl. Carry on.'

Jackie swallowed as she looked back at him.

'I thought you were staying in the background. I mean, you wouldn't wanna be seen with us lot,' she managed.

'I just couldn't help checking up on my favourite girls.'

She wanted to tell him to take a hike. But didn't. 'If we're gonna do this proper-like we need to have a chinwag without you around, so why don't you come back in ten minutes.'

He tilted his head as if basking in the warmth of the sunshine. 'Why waste time? I mean, we're almost family, ain't we?' Suddenly his hand whipped out. Picked up the closest cup to him. Ollie's. He took a deep slug. Twisted his mouth as he set the cup back down. 'Tastes like piss. I remember the days when this area might've been an all-time number-one dump but at least you could get a decent lick of coffee. That's what happens when money moves in, standards move out. Don't make me start knocking some heads on the wall. . . .'

Jackie took a deep breath. 'As I've already told you, we're ready to nab the kid tonight.'

'So how you gonna do that?'

'Like I told you yesterday, the kid bunks school every Wednesday night with his mates. We don't know where they go but boys out for a midweek rave ain't getting ready to go to midnight mass They're gonna hit a nightclub or boozer. We figure this place ain't too far from the school. Anna and Roxy are gonna follow him on foot because he already knows what my mug looks like. Me and Ollie stay in the van.' Suddenly she stopped talking as she dug her hand into her bag. She pulled out three mobile phones. Threw them onto the table. 'We keep in contact by mobile. These are throwaway, so when the job's done, that's exactly what we do, we get rid of 'em. Once Roxy and Anna are in the boozer or club we're gonna have him.'

'And how the heck are you planning to nab him in a room full of people? Plus his mates are bound to come out with him as well.'

'We've never met a man yet who could pass up a bit of pussy, so Anna's gonna lure him away from his friends with the promise of a night he's never gonna forget.'

Frankie pinned Anna with his eyes and started laughing so hard that the gazes of the women at the nearby table were on him again. 'Thought dykes kept their pussies under lock and key from the male population.'

A stunned silence hit the table. A defiant expression hit Anna's face.

'You really surprise me, Anna, babe. I thought all shagpile-munchers looked like beefy boys.'

Angry at the insults he was throwing her mate's way, Jackie half rose out of her chair.

'If you're finished with us we'll be on our way.'

'Drop your fanny back in that seat.'

Jackie eased back down.

'So how are you planning to get him to the boat?'

Jackie's hands clenched tight under the table. She uncurled them as she spoke. 'We get the van into position. Anna and Roxy lure Danny outside. Wham-bam, before he knows it he's in the back of the van taking a trip to the other side of town.'

Frankie eased his chin off the chair. 'As soon as you have him on that boat you give me a bell. And don't try any shit moves because I'm watching you every mini-step of the way.' Suddenly Frankie gave Jackie a direct hit with his eyes. 'Since our little chinwag yesterday, my wallet seems to have gone for a little walkabout . . .'

Jackie cut in, eyes flashing. 'Sounds like you didn't only lose your head yesterday.'

'If I thought that you took . . .'

'Get real. You think I had time to rip you off while you were trying to rip my raspberry ripples off my breasts? It must've fallen outta of your pocket. No telling who's got it now.'

Frankie stood up. Plastered a smile back on his chops for the benefit of the women ogling him from the other table. 'Tonight, ladies.' Then he was gone as the sunshine slipped away.

As soon as Frankie was gone Jackie picked up a serviette from the table. Shoved it into her bag. Pulled something out. Slapped what was in her hand onto the table. Frankie's wallet.

'Is that what I think it is?' Ollie asked.

'Yeah. While he was giving me the once-over yesterday my hand sneaked in and swiped it.' Jackie opened it. 'This . . .' She placed the photograph of Frankie and the little girl on the table. 'I think it's his daughter. Her name's Daisy. Now this . . .' She dragged the solicitor's card onto the table. 'I think it's his brief. Bell Dream. I know I've heard that name before. . . .' She stopped when she saw the shocked look on Anna's face.

'You alright, girl?'

'Yeah.' Anna's voice was shaky. She shoved a disjointed smile onto her face. 'Just a bit worried that Misty might be going ballistic if me and you don't get back soon.'

'Anyone heard of her?' Jackie swung her gaze around the table.

Ollie answered. 'She was the lawyer who helped Misty buy the club.'

'Of course. I remember now. She comes into the club quite a bit. She chats to you quite a lot, don't she, Anna?'

'Not any more than I chat to anyone else.'

'Shame,' Jackie said. 'You might've been able to get some info outta her.'

'What happens if it all goes wrong tonight?' Roxy asked.

Jackie gave her a hot look. 'Just follow the script and everything will be cool and dandy.' She swung her gaze over each of her friends. 'This is it, girls. Are we ready?' They nodded at each other.

*   *   *

Anna felt shocked as they left the café. Shocked that her lover, Bell Dream, was representing that scumbag Frankie.

'Shame. You might've been able to get some info outta her.' Jackie's words whizzed around her head as she jumped on her motorbike. No way, she told herself. She could never do that to Bell. Never betray her. Then why couldn't she get the image of the briefcase Bell took everywhere with her out of her mind?

Wednesday night at the Shim-Sham-Shimmy was more hectic than usual. There was a hen night in the rooms upstairs and a stag night in the converted basement. Punters spilled out of every corner, making Jackie think there was no way her and Anna were going to make it to Richmond on time. She rubbed her tummy, trying to ease the sick feeling inside.

'Be a good baby for Mummy,' she whispered.

She strained her neck, desperately seeking Anna across the crowded dance floor. Frustration bit into her when she couldn't find her. Shit, shit, shit, she cursed in her head. She moved towards the bar. The area was crowded. The whole of London was thirsty tonight. She battled her way through a gap between a man and woman trying to catch the barman's eye.

'Oi, Gio,' she called. He turned to her. 'You seen Anna?' His eyes moved behind her at the same time as she felt a tap on her back. Jackie twisted around to find Anna standing behind her.

'I've been looking for you everywhere.'

'Sorry, got caught up,' Anna replied breathlessly. 'The place is heaving. We need to get outta here now.'

Jackie followed her as they made their way out of the room. Into the cool corridor. Up the staircase to Anna's office.

'Where are you two lovebirds flying off to?' a voice called behind them.

Misty stood at the bottom of the stairs. Her arms were crossed over her knee-length lilac dress.

'I ain't moving, girls, until I get an answer.'

Think, think, think, Jackie told herself. She found the lie she was looking for.

'We were just gonna run over to *Miss Josephine* to make sure every thing was sorted for Anna's mates who are gonna be staying there from tomorrow.'

Misty gave them both the eye.

'I don't know if you two have noticed but it's like Piccadilly Circus in here tonight. I need you both here.' She folded her arms again.

Think, think, think. This time Anna supplied the line. 'I didn't wanna say nothin' to you before, but my mates have had a real rough ride lately. So we just wanted to make sure everything was nice and cosy for them.'

'If you two sod off it ain't gonna be nice and cosy for me here.' Misty searched both their faces. 'What are you two really up to? You've been sneaking off a lot lately. If you were in trouble you'd come and tell ol' Misty, wouldn't you?'

'Must be your age, Misty, because you're getting proper paranoid. All we're doing is sorting some mates out, ain't that right, Anna?'

'Yeah,' Anna agreed.

'I thought you said you had a couple of lads, actors, who could help out this summer?' Misty asked.

Jackie and Anna shot each other a look.

Jackie answered. 'They found some work. I think in some musical up West.'

Misty opened her mouth a few times, like she was going to say more, but then closed it. Turned around and left.

'Do you think she knows?' Anna asked after Misty was gone.

'How could she? She ain't psychic. I'm just worried she might do something when we don't come back.'

'I'll send her a text saying you got ill and I had to take you home.'

'Let's hope she don't smell a rat. The one person we can't afford to get mixed up in all this shit is Misty.'

'What's the time?' Anna asked

Jackie checked her watch. 'Seven twenty.'

'Shit, this is gonna be tight. We need to be in position outside the school in Richmond by eight thirty.'

* * *

Misty knew she had no alternative. She had to make the call to Charlie, her brother. Her gut told her that whatever the girls were up to with Frankie Sullivan it was going down tonight. She pulled out her mobile as she stepped out into the alleyway, around the back of the club.

As she raised the phone to her face, a hand clamped over her mouth from behind. The shock held her still as the hand tightened on her mouth. Fear tickled her spine. Then she felt hot breath skating against her neck.

A voice whispered in her ear. 'Sh! When I take my hand away I want you to turn around.'

The hand fell way. Misty took a deep breath. Slowly she turned around. What she saw made her clamp both her own hands tight over her mouth in complete shock.

21.30.

They'd been waiting in the van for an hour with no sign of Daniel Gray-Hammond or his mates. Jackie and Ollie sat in the front while Anna and Roxy were in the back. Both Anna and Roxy were tarted up like it was Saturday night. Miniskirts, flimsy tops and enough make-up to keep the cosmetics counters at Selfridges going for a month.

'You sure he said they left at nine?' Anna said as she wriggled, pulling her skirt down.

'That's what they told me.' Jackie swung her head to gaze at Anna in the dark. She threw her a cigarette, even though the other woman didn't smoke. Anna popped it inside her cleavage.

'Their school sounds like the prison cell I shared with Nik . . .' Ollie's voice trailed off.

Jackie twisted back around to look at her with curious eyes. 'You never said you'd been a jailbird.'

Ollie let out a puffed breath. Avoided Jackie's eyes. Jackie's curiosity deepened, because it had been a long time since she'd seen her friend that flustered. 'I bribed a guard with diamonds to help me escape,' Ollie answered, head slowly rising. 'That's how I made it to England.'

'Shame our mums never did the same when they were banged up in Sankura . . .'

'Look.' Ollie pointed at the windscreen, her voice breathless. 'Do you think that's them?'

Jackie squinted as she leaned forward and followed the direction of Ollie's finger. Two males, head down, scurrying away from the back entrance of the school. 'There's only two of them. I can't see their faces. What if one of them ain't Danny?' She shuffled farther forward until her face was almost pressed against the windscreen. Still she couldn't make them out. 'Shit. They're coming this way.'

Instantly the woman all slid down in their seats. Their collective ragged breathing pooled in the air. The male chatter got louder as the boys neared the van. They reached it.

'Danny . . .' one said excitedly to the other. The voices drifted away.

The women sat back up straight. Jackie looked at Anna and Roxy. 'That's our target. We're on.'

Heads down, eyes up, Anna and Roxy hit the nightlife of Richmond Green. They kept their gazes squarely on the boys ahead of them.

thirty-seven

'Fucking amateurs. If they walk any closer the boys will spot them.'

Frankie watched the goings-on from a rust-bucket across the road. He sat in the passenger seat with Finlay at the wheel beside him. Their faces were hidden under hoody tops and camouflaged by the street's shadows. They watched as two of the women walked behind the two boys. He knew he shouldn't be anywhere near the actual kidnapping, but he still didn't trust those bitches.

'Let's slow-roll behind them,' Frankie instructed Finlay.

Finlay juiced the engine.

The boys were decked out in low-riding jeans, baggy shirts and the bounce and bravado of typical teenagers looking for a night to remember. Anna and Roxy maintained a steady pace as they moved behind them. Through the dark. Across the shifting lights coming from the restaurants, pubs and theatre that lined Richmond Green. Weaving between the laughter and movement of people out on the razzle on a Wednesday night.

Roxy flicked her head up, caught by an item displayed in a shop window. Anna swore and said, 'Keep your bloody head down. We don't wanna get caught on CCTV.'

Roxy quickly followed Anna's instruction. But she flushed at the way the taller woman had talked to her. Like she was a kid who needed Mummy to hold her hand every time she wanted to go to the toilet. Well, fuck Anna, she thought.

'Don't talk to me like that. I am not stupid.' She said the last four words slowly through clenched teeth.

'If you're so smart, why do you let your old man drop one on you anytime he feels like it?'

Roxy's feet faltered at the audacity of Anna's remark. Was that what everyone thought of her? A punchbag lost in the swinging breeze, up for anyone to hit? The fury bubbled from her feet to her brain.

'Look.' Anna grabbed Roxy's arm. 'They're turning.'

They watched as the boys turned right at a main set of traffic lights at a corner with a Thai restaurant. The women picked up pace. Hustled forward. They reached the corner. Looked down the street. No sign of the boys. Anna looked wildly around. 'Where the hell have they gone?'

They rushed down the street, urgently checking each building, many of them shops shut for the night. 'Shit, shit, shit,' Anna growled as she swung her head back and forth.

'What are we going to do?' Roxy asked as they stood outside a boutique.

'No alternative,' Anna puffed out. 'We'll have to let Jackie know we lost him.' She pulled her mobile out from her bag. Shoved it up to her face.

'Sh,' Roxy suddenly commanded as she pushed her head forward.

'What the fuck are you doing?'

'Listen.'

The silence settled between them as they both listened.

'I can't hear a thing.'

'Can't you hear it?'

'What?'

'Music.'

Anna strained her ear against the night. Then she heard it. A distant thumping noise. A noise that she had become impervious to in her adult life – the beat of music.

'Wherever that music's coming from, that's where they are,' Roxy said.

'But there's no clubs along here.'

Roxy began a slow walk along the street, looking up. Gazing down. She reached a café. Looked up. Gazed down. She caught the movement of a flashing light. She rushed towards the iron rail that led to a staircase. Leaned over. 'I've found it. It doesn't look like I'm that stupid after all.'

Anna scooted over. Leaned over the rail, saw what Roxy saw. A basement club.

Above the door was the name of the club, flashing in bold, silver and red neon lights.

EXCESS

The party club for party people

In front of the door two burly bouncers were stationed. They watched as Danny showed what was undoubtedly a fake ID to one of the bouncers. He motioned for Danny to step inside.

'OK, here we go. Any problems with the big boys on the door you let me do all the sweet-talking,' Anna whispered.

They moved down the stairs.

'Hiya, boys,' Anna called out. She fixed her body in a loose, sexy pose. And smiled.

'Ladies,' one of them replied, running his appreciative eyes over her.

'As you can see, boys, we're all grown up, so I'm sure you don't need to see our IDs.' Both men laughed and stepped back, letting them through. As soon as Anna made it through the metal detector the mock merriment fell from her face. Her hand dipped inside her bag. Pulled out her mobile. Pressed it to her mouth.

'We're in. It's a club called Excess . . .'

'Do you want me to go in and check out what's going on?' Finlay asked Frankie as they waited in the car on the opposite side of the road to the club.

'No. Too risky. We wait here. See what happens.'

*　　　*　　　*

Twenty minutes later, Anna and Roxy watched as the laughing boys weaved through the midweek crowd, leaving the dance floor.

'They're on the move,' Anna said to Roxy. 'This is it. Are you ready?'

The other woman gave a swift nod.

They followed the boys. Through the crowd. Out the door. Down the dimly lit red stairwell that led to the toilets. They reached the tight corridor at the bottom. Saw the Gents' door swing shut as the boys disappeared inside.

Anna turned to Roxy. 'Let's do it.'

Quickly they propped themselves against the wall opposite the Gents. Anna wiggled her top down a bit more, exposing more cleavage. Hiked her shirt higher.

'Relax,' she whispered at a nervous-looking Roxy as she took the cigarette that she'd accepted from Jackie earlier. She popped it to her lips. And waited.

'Twenty grand . . .' The words burst into the corridor as the Gents' door opened three minutes later.

The women watched the boys stop dead when they saw them.

'You alright, boys?' Anna said seductively as she tilted her head. And smiled.

The boys looked at her. The one who she knew was Danny blushed as his eyes caught the tops of her breasts.

'We come down here to have a smoke, but I ain't got a light.' Anna eased herself off the wall. Walked over to Danny. His throat bobbed as he swallowed. 'You boys ain't got one?'

Danny swallowed hard. Then spoke. 'I don't think you're allowed to smoke in the club . . .'

'What a shame,' Anna cut in quickly. 'I'll have to go outside.' She ran her tongue, slowly, from right to left, over her top lip. Her bottom lip. Leaned forward. 'Don't suppose you boys fancy a stroll in the night air?'

Danny gulped. Pushed his chest out. 'Of course we do.' His gaze shot towards his friend. 'Don't we?'

The other boy nodded.

Anna swung her hair back. And laughed. 'I knew you were the type of men who liked to have a good time. Come on.'

The four turned and headed for the stairs.

Anna kept up a steady stream of chatter as they walked across the foyer towards the exit. They went through the metal detector. Hit the main door. The bouncer who'd spoken to Anna earlier smiled as she came by. She winked at him.

Once she got the boys and Roxy to street level Anna said, 'Let's see if we can find somewhere to have a puff and a bit of fun.'

The boys eagerly followed both women down the next street, a side street, which was dark and narrow.

'They're out,' Finlay whispered.

Frankie said nothing. Instead he continued to watch the goings-on on the other side of the street.

Silence is golden? What a laugh, Jackie thought, as she waited in the van. The silence was killing her. It had been at least half an hour since she'd heard from Anna with directions to the club. The small, orange digital figures on the van's dashboard seemed to show the minutes passing more and more slowly, as if the clock was as fed up with the waiting as she was.

The dense night pressed against the windscreen as Jackie's hands tightened around the steering wheel. Her shoulder blades were jacked forward. Her face set in serious lines. 'What's the time?' she asked.

'The same as when you asked last, plus four minutes and eleven seconds.'

Jackie had no idea how Ollie managed to stay so calm. That was what she loved about the other woman – her calmness. Her mind whizzed back ten years to Ollie standing over Frankie with a gun. Even then she'd been calm. Jackie inhaled a few deep breaths but her heart raced up instead of speeding down. She pulled out a ciggie. Then she remembered her baby. She crammed the fag back into the packet.

'Take it easy. Give them time. Everything is going to be alright,' Ollie reassured her. 'They've been gone too long. Right, we're gonna go and get them.' She twisted the key in the ignition.

'Stop.' Ollie's voice was firm as she leaned over and placed her palm over Jackie's hand. She pulled Jackie's hand away from the ignition key. Moved her hand to Jackie's face and gently pulled her head around.

'What am I gonna do if we get caught? Who's gonna look after Ryan? Say the social gets him?'

'Jackie, calm down.'

'This ain't what Nikki would've wanted me to be doing.'

'Nikki above all people would understand.'

'I know she'd think I'd let her down.'

'No she would not. When she held me in her arms . . .'

Jackie jerked her head out of Ollie's hand. 'What did you just say?'

'Nothing.'

'You said that my mum held you in her arms. Don't bullshit me. When?'

'This is not the time . . .'

'When?' Jackie's tone was deadly soft.

'I shared a cell with Nikki ten years ago in Sankura.'

Roxy stepped away from Anna and the boys in the dark side street. She turned her back on them. Pulled out the mobile Anna had given her. Began to dial the number of Jackie's mobile.

'You're shitting me, ain't you?' Jackie's voice came out in painful gasps as she tried to deal with the devastating news Ollie had just given her. They stood outside, face to face, in the open, by the side of the van, with London's erratic wind whipping over them.

'I mean, you've gotta be. You're my mate. You would've told me if you'd met my mum.'

Ollie stretched her hand out to touch Jackie's arm, but Jackie shook her head and moved out of her reach. Ollie's hands fell flat as she said, 'We can talk about this later. Now we need . . .'

'No, this is about what I need,' Jackie shouted, stabbing a finger into her chest. 'Why did you never tell me . . .'

'We need to listen for the phone . . .'

'Fuck the phone. Tell me about Nikki.'

'OK. I was part of a band of rebels that got captured by the army. Most of us were killed but for once in my life I got lucky. I managed to bribe one of the guards, but then one of those bastards decided he was going to rape me.' Ollie stopped when she saw the look of horror on Jackie's face. 'That's how I met your mother. She saved my life. That's why I've always been a shadow behind you, Jackie, because I owed your mother. That first night she held me in her arms and soothed all the pain away . . .'

'Why didn't you tell me? How could you have hung onto this for ten years?' Jackie's voice shook.

'Sankura was a dictatorship and you soon learn not to volunteer any information unless someone asks you. I'd lived such a long time by that belief it was hard for me to change how I behaved when I got to England. And what would have been the point in telling you? You would've just got upset, like you are now. And going back makes me remember all the nameless people I killed . . .'

'Did they hurt her? Did she . . . ?'

'Jackie.'

'Did she . . . ?'

'Jackie.' Ollie grabbed her. Shook her hard. Jackie stopped talking. 'Listen.'

The ring of the phone, which was still inside the van, filled the air. 'That's the phone. That's them. Where is it?'

'I left it on the seat.'

Ollie swore as she pounced on the van door. She lunged forward. Grabbed the still-ringing phone. As she placed it to her face it stopped ringing.

'Shit, we missed their call.'

Roxy looked dumbstruck as she stared at the mobile in her hand in the dark side street. She looked deeper into the street, where Anna stood with the boys. Anna kept them chatting away so that their attention was diverted from Roxy. This shouldn't be happening. Where the hell were Jackie and Ollie? She pressed redial. Her heartbeat raced as the connection was made. Her body sagged when she heard Ollie's voice.

'Where the fuck were you?' Suddenly she shook her head, deciding there was no time to listen to Ollie's explanation. 'We're ready to make our move. Bring the van around . . .'

She cut the call. She caught Anna's eye and nodded her head. She approached Danny's friend, looped her arm into his and drew him deeper into the street. As she did this, Anna made her way to the judge's son.

She smiled at him seductively and said, 'While my mate takes care of your friend, I'm gonna be taking care of you.' She leaned towards him. Her mouth found his ear and she began to whisper to him.

'We're on,' Ollie told Jackie as she flung the phone on the seat. 'They've got the boys in position.'

Jackie twisted the ignition key. Revved up the engine. Pushed her foot down on the accelerator.

Frankie watched the van swing into the street. It blocked his view of the dark side street, where the two women stood with the boys. One of the women inside the van jumped out. Jackie. She ran towards the back of the van. Flung the doors open. The door nearest to him blocked Frankie's view. He stretched up but couldn't see what was happening on the other side of the door. Suddenly he heard a cry. Running footsteps. He saw a number of legs under the door. Then they disappeared inside the van. Suddenly Jackie rushed out of the dark. Banged the doors shut. Ran back towards the front of the van. Jumped in as the engine blasted on. The van skidded and swerved down the street like a drunken man, leaving Frankie with a view of an empty side street. He turned to Finlay. Smiled.

'It's done. Let's get outta here.'

*   *   *

Frankie's mobile rang dead on midnight as he sat in the back room of the Dirty Dick boozer. He picked it up. A large grin spread across his face as he put it to his ear. He leaned back in the chair, waiting to hear Jackie's voice. Her voice came, but they weren't the words he was expecting to hear.

'We've got a problem. A big problem.'

thirty-eight

'What do you mean, we've got a problem?'

Frankie shot to his feet, furious.

'You need to get over here pronto.'

'What do you think I am, stupid?'

'This ain't a set-up. You need to get here right now.'

'So tell me what the problem is.'

'Can't do it over the blower. It's too dangerous.'

'If there's a problem you get it sorted out. I told you from the word go that I was never gonna be seen anywhere near this.'

'And I'm telling you that if you don't get your carcass down here, right now, you're gonna be lucky to be alive this time tomorrow night.'

'Get in here now.'

Frankie shot his words at Finlay and Jason, who were playing cards at a small table in the dimly lit corridor of the pub.

They obeyed his furious command.

'What's up, bro?' A frown wrinkled Finlay's forehead.

Frankie was back behind the desk. 'A little bird has just told me that we've got a problem.' He pulled a drawer out.

'Whatcha chatting about?'

He slid both hands inside the drawer. 'I'll give you the full SP on our way there.'

His hands came out of the drawer full. 'We're all gonna need to be packing one of these.'

He placed three handguns on the desk.

The three men walked cautiously along the bank of the River Lea. The blanket darkness of the sky blended with the murky waters of the water below. The thumping beat of James Brown's 'Sex Machine' boomed from a house party in one of the blocks near by. Frankie took the lead, with Finlay and Jason walking together behind. All three had their hands near their guns, ready to spring into action if they needed to. 'This could be a set-up,' Finlay said.

'Nah.' Frankie shook his head. 'Jackie sounded piss-yourself scared.'

'I hope for your sake it's kosher.'

'There it is,' Jason said, pointing towards *Miss Josephine*.

Frankie halted and held his hand up, signalling for the others to stop. His eyes darted around, casing the scene for clues that that this might be a double-cross. But the only movement he found was the silent breeze skating on the water and grazing in the bushes. He began to move again. Confidently. Until he reached the boat. His palm tightened around the gun. He jumped down onto the deck. Finlay and Jason followed him. They stood still for a few seconds as the boat rocked with their weight. Then Frankie lifted his feet in long, quiet strides towards the main door. Without warning the main door shot open. In one fluid move, Frankie pulled the gun out of his pocket. Held it steady with both hands as he aimed it at the person who stood in the open doorway.

Jackie.

'Frankie?' Jackie asked, her tone unsteady as her gaze caught the gun in his hand.

'What you doing with that?'

'Inside.' Frankie waved the gun at her.

Jackie immediately moved back. He followed, not moving his aim away from her. He stepped over the threshold into the light of the room. His eyes swung from side to side, quickly identifying the other occupants. Anna, Roxy and Ollie, all standing nervously together near the entrance to the kitchen. When they saw the gun in his hand they huddled together, reminding him of ten years ago. Jason and Finlay moved into the room behind him. Finlay slammed the door. Frankie switched his gaze to Jackie.

'OK, I'm here. And the only problem I can see is that Danny boy don't appear to be in residence.' He shifted the gun so that it was aimed dead centre at her heart.

'We ain't talking until you put that thing away,' Jackie said as she took a step towards him.

'If you don't tell me what's going on, this shooter's the only thing that's gonna be exercising its mouth, get it?'

He watched Jackie swallow. Her hands rubbed nervously together as she began to speak. 'We've got him.'

'Show me.'

Jackie nodded her head in the direction of the other women. Anna and Roxy turned and stepped into the kitchen. Suddenly muffled noises filled the air. The women came back into the room, each holding the arm of a struggling young male. A white pillowcase was over his head. Anna pulled it off. His eyes and mouth were bound with gold duct tape. Dirty dry water marks streaked his face, making it appear that he'd been crying. His arms were secured behind his back with rope. He tried to talk but the tape held down the sounds.

'Meet Danny,' Jackie said.

She signalled again with her head. The women holding him forced him to sit on the two-seater sofa. Anna placed her hands securely on his shoulders and whispered, 'Stop moving.' He stopped.

Frankie finally lowered his weapon. 'So if that's the mark, what's the problem?'

Jackie avoided looking in Frankie's eye as her teeth bit into her bottom lip. Finally she raised her head. Nodded, but this time in Ollie's direction. Ollie turned. Disappeared into the kitchen. Ten seconds later she was back, but not on her own this time.

'What the fuck . . . ?' blew out of Frankie's mouth as he watched her march another hooded youth into the room.

*   *   *

Frankie turned so swiftly that Jackie never saw it coming. He back handed her across the face, splitting her lip. Her cry of pain mingled with the gasps of the other women. As her head came up he grabbed her arms. Pushed her forward. Slammed her into the wall. Terror widened her eyes. He pushed the gun into the middle of her forehead. Over his shoulder she saw Ollie begin to steam towards them. But Finlay quickly moved from the door. Aimed his gun at her and growled, 'Back up, bitch.'

Ollie stopped in her tracks, anger radiating off her face.

Jackie flicked her gaze back to Frankie. An intense red stained his face. His blue eyes brimmed with anger. Through gritted teeth he demanded, 'You've got ten seconds to explain who the fuck that is.'

The explanation flew out of Jackie's bleeding mouth. 'We did everything that you asked. But Daniel didn't come out on his own. He had a mate with him. Roxy tried to lose his mate by taking him down another street. When she got his trousers around his ankles, she legged it. Just as we're loading Daniel in the van his mate pops out of nowhere again. He starts making a right racket and fighting, trying to get Daniel away from us. So we didn't have no choice, we had to bring him along.'

Frankie pressed the gun deeper into Jackie's skin. She cringed back against the wall.

'You stupid soddin' sow. Why didn't you just dump him?'

'Use your head. If we'd done that he'd have gone straight to the Bill and blabbed. And who would you've blamed? Us. Ain't just your life on the line here . . .'

'Shut it.' His finger curved around the trigger.

Sharp puffs of air jumped out of her mouth. Jesus, Mary and all the saints, she knew she was brown bread. Regret gripped her. Regret that she hadn't hugged and kissed her beautiful son one last time. She squeezed her eyes tight. Entered a dark world where it was just her and the devastating hard metal of the barrel of a gun. She waited and prayed. Prayed and waited. Finally she felt the heat from the man who held her life in his hands diminish. The gun eased from her skin, where it had been pressed so deep the mark of the barrel was indented in her forehead. Apprehensively, she opened her eyes to find Frankie moving away from her. She collapsed, shaking, against the wall, wiping the blood from her burning mouth. Then her hand lightly touched her tummy.

'Sit him down next to the other one,' Frankie yelled at Ollie. She immediately followed his instruction.

'You,' he crooked his finger at Jackie, 'over here.' He stabbed his finger at the spot in front of him. Jackie pushed herself off the wall, desperately trying to get the normal rhythm of her breathing back. She kept her gaze on Frankie as she moved towards him. Reached the spot.

'OK, numbskulls, since you all appear to have been munching stupid flakes for brekkie before I saw you in the caff this morning, let me tell you slowly and clearly what's gonna happen next.' He left a dramatic pause as he insolently swung his head towards the other women. He jammed his gaze back on Jackie. 'Now we've got this other boy we can't let him go, so we've got no alternative but to hang on to him as well. When I get you to contact the judge . . .'

'Who?' Jackie gave him her best mock-surprise look.

'Don't play me for a mug, girl. I know you lot are likely to have looked me up on the Net and found out that I'm deep in the heart of Bookie Street. So don't give me the innocent one about Judge Gray-Hammond. You tell the judge to ring the school and tell them that both boys are staying with her for a few days. Big problem sorted.'

'No.' Jackie shook her head. 'Big problem just begun.' She stopped talking, so that her tongue could do a quick circuit of her dry lips. 'The other boy's not the problem.'

'What are you chatting about?' Frankie snarled.

'Like I said, the boy ain't the problem.' She stared directly into Frankie's eyes. 'It's his dad.'

'What the hell has his dad got to do with this?'

'He claims that his old man is Fonrims Akdov.'

'Who?'

'One of Russia's top gangsters.'

Jackie watched the blood drain from Frankie's face, making his eyes stand out like thawing blue ice. Then Jason's voice called out behind them, 'Don't believe her, Frankie. She's trying to make you out to be a top-notch tit. Fonrims? That ain't no fucking Russian name. I should know, I get most of my girls from 'em. They're all called Yuri or Ivan or some other unpronounceable shit.'

Jackie saw Frankie begin to raise his gun again. 'He's wrong,' Jackie yelled. 'That's exactly what I thought when the kid said his dad's name. But he says that it's some kind of traditional name from the part of Russia they hail from, Mugistan or something. Also, when I met Daniel and his mates at the school they all started to tell me about their parents, except one of them. He didn't say what his dad did at first, then he says his old man's a Russian businessman. We didn't believe him at first so he tells us to check his dad out on the Net. So we did. I tell you this much, Frankie, after we finished reading we were almost wetting ourselves. If you don't believe us, look him up yourself.' She nodded towards the wireless laptop in the corner.

Frankie quickly moved towards the computer. Leaned down. Tapped the space bar. The page from the last Internet search was still on the screen.

It was from a pop crime website. There was a list of the world's top twenty criminals: 'The Badd-est Boys On The Block! Don't Dent Their Cars!' There at number nine, just above a Latin American narco-terrorist and just below an Afghan opium warlord, was Mr Akdov:

Son of a miner from the Donets Basin, he was conscripted into the Russian army at 18 and rose to be an officer in their special forces. Went into security work in Moscow's Wild West protecting cowboy billionaires from other cowboy billionaires. Became a cowboy billionaire himself after doing some completely legitimate business deals and benefiting from dozens of assassinations that were absolutely nothing to do with him (cross our heart!)

Net worth: Ask the Russian taxman.

Trivia: It's rumoured that his son is at one of England's top public schools. Nice to know there'll be at least one gentleman in the family. Don't nick his dinner money, boys!'

Underneath was a square space for a photograph. But it was simply a black silhouette with a question mark inside it.

'Now do you believe me?' Jackie called out.

Frankie straightened up and looked not at her, but at the two boys. He moved towards them, raising his gun.

He pointed the nozzle at Daniel. Then at the other boy. 'Put them back in the other room.' All the women began to move at once, but he swung around and faced Jackie, stopping her. 'Not you.'

'Shit, what we gonna do, man?' Finlay asked, rubbing his hand over his forehead.

'Sweet FA, that's what we gonna do. It's not as if this Fonrims Akdov knows we've got his kid . . .'

'He don't now,' Jackie butted in. 'But he might know soon.'

'How do you figure that one out?'

'The boy – Boris, that's his name – said that his dad is arriving tonight and coming to see him at the school tomorrow. When he realises that his son ain't there he's gonna twig that something's up. And that's when he's gonna create some mad shit tearing this town apart looking for his boy.'

'Those Russians are mad fuckers,' Jason added.

Frankie swore. Began to pace. Finally, he stopped and gazed back at Jackie as he shoved his gun into his pocket. 'Since you created this shit you're gonna get it all sorted. You go in there.' He pointed at the kitchen. 'Get the boy to ring his old man and tell him that he can't come tomorrow because he's staying at his mate Danny's for a bit. That way Dad stays off the scent.'

Jackie rushed towards the kitchen, but Frankie's voice stopped her. 'And don't try anything dodgy because I'm gonna be standing right in the doorway watching your every move.'

She started walking again. Entered the kitchen. Approached Boris, who sat huddled, knees bent, in a corner. She bent down beside him, pulled off the pillowcase and said, 'I'm gonna take the tape off your mouth. Don't make a sound because you don't wanna find out what's gonna happen to you if you do.'

The boy briskly nodded his head. She peeled the tape from his mouth. His ragged breathing filled the room as he pulled in strong gulps of air.

'This is what I want you to do,' Jackie explained as she raised the phone. 'First I need your dad's number.' He told her, his voice croaking. She tapped the digits into the mobile. 'I want you to tell your dad that he can't visit you tomorrow because you're stopping at your mate Danny's for a bit. Tell him that when you get back to school you're gonna give him a bell. Alright?' He nodded. She pressed the green dial button. Held the phone to his mouth. Then the boy started speaking rapidly in another language. His words stopped as if he was listening to his father talk.

Frankie leapt forward. Grabbed the phone from Jackie's hand. Shoved his face into the boy's space. 'That weren't smart, kid. What did you say to your dad?'

'My father says that he's coming to kill you,' Boris snarled back. 'But if you let me go I'll tell him to stop hunting you.'

'Shut the fuck up,' Frankie screamed.

'We can do without this shit,' Finlay said from the doorway. 'Let's dump the boy . . .'

'I can't risk it. Say he goes to the cops and tells them that we kidnapped them?'

'I won't say anything . . .'

'Like I said before, kid, shut the fuck up. Put him back in his hole.' Jackie quickly grabbed him and pushed him back down into the corner.

Frankie ran his hand through his hair as he moved back into the main room. Jackie quickly followed.

'We can't afford to have this Russian on our arse at a time like this,' Finlay said. Frankie ignored him. Looked at Jackie. 'Time to let the honourable Judge Cynthia Gray-Hammond in on the action . . .'

'But Frankie,' Jason interrupted, bewildered. 'What we gonna do about the Russian?'

Frankie shoved his hand in his pocket. Tightened his hand around the gun and said, 'London is my manor. If this Fonrims Akdov comes looking for us he's gonna find a few surprises, but in the meantime we stick to the plan.'

Suddenly Roxy yelled out, 'I've had enough of this. I need to get outta here.' She stormed towards the door.

'Roxy,' Jackie yelled as Finlay lunged for her. But Roxy evaded him. Reached the door. Frankie pulled his gun. Aimed at her back. 'Get your tush back here.' But Roxy ignored him, wildly jerking open the door. Jackie ran towards her, stepping in the line of fire of Frankie's gun. Roxy rushed onto the deck. Leaned over and began sobbing.

'Please,' Jackie pleaded. 'Let her be. She just needs to calm down. You can see she ain't going nowhere.'

Finlay ignored her pleas as he strode towards the door.

Jackie put her hand up to stop him. 'Please.' She turned swiftly to Anna. 'Go outside and stand with her. Get her to put a sock in it.'

With Roxy's cries echoing outside, every eye in the room turned to Frankie. Finally he nodded at Anna. She rushed outside. Jackie leaned heavily on the door, closing it. Her face flushed with heat and emotion she looked at Frankie and said, 'Let me make that call to the judge.'

Frankie called out the judge's phone number. Jackie punched out the digits.

'Speakerphone,' Frankie instructed.

She did what he asked. Pressed the dial button. Waited.

'Hello?' The voice was crisp, polished, low.

Jackie wet her lips. 'Do you remember what happened to your husband?'

'Who is this?'

'What you need to decide is whether you want the same happening to your lad.'

'Danny?' The voice was frantic.

'Nice kid. Mind you, he don't look so great all taped up.'

A gasp sounded.

'I've got Danny, you want him back. But the only way your gonna clap eyes on him again is if a certain court case on Friday swings a certain person's way. Now don't be thinking about giving the cops a bell because the next time you see Danny it will be like a mirror image of the last time you saw your husband – minus his head.'

'Please.' The word shook. 'Let me speak to him.'

Frankie signalled to one of the other women to bring Danny out.

'And make sure he doesn't do anything stupid like his mate,' Frankie warned.

As soon as the boy was kneeling next to Jackie, Frankie ripped the tape off his mouth. Jackie shoved the phone to his face.

'Mother . . .' he screamed. As he went to say more Jackie pulled the phone away from him.

'Please don't hurt him,' the voice at the other end pleaded.

'Please ain't gonna help you. Only one thing will. Whatever evidence is presented to you, make sure it swings Mr Sullivan's way and Danny will be back home by Friday teatime.'

Jackie cut the call. Looked anxiously over at Frankie. He sauntered across to her with a chilling smile.

'Good girl,' he said quietly.

The door opened. Everyone swung around. Roxy and Anna stepped back inside. Frankie looked at Roxy with scorn. 'You're turning into a right headache, just like your old girl used to be. The next time you have one of your hissy fits in my presence I'll shut you up permanently.' He looked over at Finlay and Jason. 'We're outta here. I'll be in touch tomorrow.'

As he stepped through the door Jackie yelled, 'But what if Boris's dad finds us?' Without looking back he said, 'That's your problem.'

thirty-nine

Jackie stood on tiptoe, peeping out of the window. The one that had the longest view of the canal's west path. Her eyes stayed on the disappearing figures of Frankie and his crew.

'They're gone,' she finally said with a tremendous breath as she twisted back into the room. 'Well done, ladies.' For the first time in hours her heart resumed its usual steady beat. But the shattered expression on her face reflected the exhaustion she felt. She staggered to her favourite chair and plonked herself down. The others, except Ollie, all followed her action, finding their own seats to rest in. Ollie came over to her. Looked at Jackie's mouth.

'Shall I clean it for you?'

Jackie gingerly touched the corner of her mouth with a fingertip. 'I'm alright. You won't even notice it's there tomorrow.'

Reluctantly, Ollie moved away from her. Found a seat. Roxy broke out a quarter-bottle of vodka. Titled it to her head and swallowed like it was the purest water she'd ever known.

'Hey,' Anna said. 'Pass it on, girl.'

Roxy handed the bottle to Anna. And that was what they did for the next five minutes – they didn't talk, just passed the bottle of vodka around. Even Jackie had a lug, despite the baby, knowing that she needed something at a time like this to calm her down.

'What about . . . ?' Ollie's voice trailed off as she pointed towards the kitchen.

'Let's give it a good ten minutes before we do anything else,' Jackie answered.

'So what happens next?' Anna asked, a drop of vodka glistening on her mouth like lipgloss.

'Those guns freaked me right out,' Roxy said.

'They wouldn't have if we had our own.'

A choked silence tightened in the room as one by one they looked at Ollie.

'You what?' Jackie shook her head like she couldn't believe what she'd heard.

'The only way to fight fire is with fire.'

'My name's Jackie Jarvis, not Jesse James.'

'No it's not. It's Jade Flynn.' Silence fell again, as it something forbidden had been said. 'And you can't allow yourself to forget that. That's who Frankie sees when he looks at you. Jade Flynn, fifteen years old, scared because she'll never see her mummy again. All I'm saying is we don't want to be in a situation where we can't protect ourselves if Frankie finally decides to pull the trigger.'

They all looked at Jackie. She stood up as if the pressure of their eyes was too much. She didn't want to consider what Ollie was saying. No way. Shooters were for crazy people like Frankie, not people like her. For fuck's sake, she hadn't even ever used one. But what if Ollie was right? What if Frankie did do the ol' bang-bang routine and took them out of this life. What was going to happen to her beloved boy then? Her hand touched her tummy. Her little one wouldn't even have been given a chance to breathe. She reached for the vodka on the table. Took a deep, swift lug. She gazed at Roxy and Anna as she put the bottle back on the table. This was their decision as much as hers.

'What do the rest of you think?' she finally asked.

'You're the head of the table, Jackie, it's up to you.' Anna's voice was quiet.

'Here,' she pointed at her heart, 'tells me that getting tooled up is wrong. But here,' she tapped her head, 'tells me I ain't ready to die. I've got a fucking long life to live. I've got a son I wanna watch grow into a man. A decent man. So I say we get some. Mind you, how the fuck are we gonna lay our hands on any? Ain't as if we know anyone in that line of business.'

'Yes we do.'

'What do you mean?' Jackie fired back at Ollie.

'Someone we met ten years ago . . .'

The boat dipped. Ollie's voice abruptly stopped. They all froze.

'What was that?' Jackie whispered as she half swung to face the door.

The boat rocked again. Footsteps. Light and even. The three seated women jumped up at the same time, staring fearfully at the door.

'Shit, they've come back.'

The door handle turned. The women all flinched. The door was thrust open, sending a blast of chilled air inside the cabin.

They stared at the figure in the doorway and knew they had been caught. By the one person they had tried to keep out of this mess. Misty.

Her gaze ran over each one of them. Ran over the cabin. She stepped inside. Slammed the door. 'Right, one of you better start yakking right now. And don't give me any bollocks bullshit. This time I want the truth.'

The three occupants of one of the most exclusive hotel rooms in Park Lane stared out of the bulletproof window. The penthouse suite gave them an exquisite panoramic view of London in its early morning glory. The three turned when they heard the sound of the suite's own private lift announcing someones arrival. They moved to seat themselves at the glass table in the middle of the room. A tall, well-built man stepped out of the lift.

'I have the information,' he said in a strongly accented voice.

He moved towards the table and placed an envelope in the middle. One of the people seated picked it up. Opened it. Took out three photographs and laid them side by side on the table.

'We start with this one.' Pointing at the photograph of Jason Nelson, his hand then skipped to the next photograph. 'Then him.' Finlay Powell. Finally arriving at the last picture. 'And then we close in on

Frankie Sullivan.' He looked up at the man still standing. 'We start now.'

'Kidnapping.'

Misty finally uttered the word that had been storming around her head since the girls had sat her down and told her what was going on. She sat in shock in the chair nearest to the kitchen. The girls sat around her in a semicircle.

'Did he fucking hit you?' Misty said, looking at the cut on Jackie's mouth. Without waiting to hear her reply she carried on, 'Right, that's it, we're dropping this one into the lap of the law . . .'

'You know we can't,' Jackie threw back at her. 'Tell the Old Bill now and they'll be in our lives like flies in a honeypot. And you know what'll happen then – they'll find out who we really are. How the club got financed.'

'And it will be Frankie having the last laugh and you know you don't want that,' Anna quickly chipped in.

'But why didn't you come to me?' Misty said in a hurt voice. 'Each one of you is like my own flesh and blood.'

Jackie scooted to her knees in front of her. Grabbed her hands. 'That's exactly why we never came you because you're the one person we look up to. We care about. I didn't wanna see the disappointment I have to look at now in your eyes.'

'Disappointment?' Misty cried. 'It ain't disappointment you see in my eyes but fear. It don't matter how big you lot get, you'll always be those tough but shaking fifteen-year-olds to me. I decided to look after you lot not because I had to but because I wanted to. I know what it's like being young, discarded, shitting-yourself scared. I was twenty-three the first time I went public in a frock. I walked outside, and you know what happened? This lady grabbed her kid and rushed to the other side of the road like I was a disease or something. I thought "two fingers to you, love," but instead of carrying on I bolted back home. My heart was beating like the clappers. That's how my heart's going right now. So it ain't disappointment you see in my eyes, but fear. I'm frightened that my little girls . . .'

'Nothing's gonna happen to us,' Jackie reassured her, fingers tightening around hers.

'What the f'ing hell am I gonna tell . . . ?' Suddenly Misty's words froze.

'Tell who?' Jackie asked curiously, seeing the look of alarm on Misty's face.

'No one.' Misty waved her hands dismissively. 'If Frankie Sullivan thinks he's gonna take my darlings away from me he's got another thing coming. He's gonna have to come through me first.'

'What do you mean?' Jackie reared up on her knees.

Misty straightened her back. Tilted her chin. Kicked off her shoes. 'We're in this together and we'll get out of it together. So give me chapter and verse about what's gonna happen next.'

Jackie and Ollie looked at each other. Their eyes both held the same question – should they tell Misty about their decision to get tooled up? Ollie gave a single shake of her head. Jackie nodded back in agreement. Misty would only go ballistic if she found out.

'This is what we're gonna do next,' Jackie announced as she stood up.

She moved towards the kitchen.

Four-twenty in the morning.

It had taken the SUV, with the bogus number plates, just over an hour to transport the four occupants of the penthouse suite in Park Lane to their destination – the disused building that had once been the St Nicholas residential home.

The passengers jumped out, all wearing black ski masks. One of them carried an Uzi. Another a black holdall. They stared at their target As they had expected there were no sounds coming from inside. They moved in quick, long strides towards the back of the building. Found the iron steps. Began to climb. They reached the top and pushed inside. The rhythm of their footsteps quickened as they moved along the corridor. They stopped when they found the room they were after. Listened. Heard no sound. They moved smoothly inside. Looked around the room. The person with the gun looked at the others. They nodded their heads, giving the signal. The gun was raised. Aimed. The trigger pressed. The continuous sound of automatic fire peppered the air as bullets sprayed all over the room. Against the walls. Onto the table. Through the portable television. Shattering the glass on the window that overlooked the garden. The firing stopped.

Silence.

The person with the holdall moved away from the door. Crouched down. Unzipped the bag. Pulled out a CD player. Pressed 'repeat play'. The haunting, lilting riff of the Specials' 'Ghost Town' shivered in the room. They returned to the bag. Pulled out a can of red spray paint. Moved to the bullet-ridden wall near the window. Aimed. Began to write. One minute later they stepped back so that the others could see. They all smiled, as they read the large writing that resembled letters dipped in blood.

Frankie Sullivan
RiP

forty

'It's all been tarted up,' Jackie said in wonder at lunchtime the next day, the day before Frankie's trial. Two days before the wedding.

She stood with Ollie in the part of London they hadn't been back to since they were fifteen years old. Peckham. A Peckham they hardly recognised. Regeneration, regeneration, regeneration. That was what shouted back at them everywhere they looked. New shops, new low-rise housing, new leisure centre, new state-of-the-art library. Even street art. But the yellow police incident board they stood beside, appealing for witnesses to come forward about the latest fatal teenage stabbing, maybe said that under all that spanking new glass and gloss paint some things just hadn't changed.

'Except that.' Ollie pointed her finger across the road. Straight at Glen's Grill. The café stood out like a museum piece on the high street.

'This idea of yours is totally bonkers,' Jackie said, her fingertip rubbing the raised cut on her lip that had resulted from Frankie's slap. She still couldn't believe that she was in South London trying to purchase some shooters from a man they had met once ten years earlier. 'Frankie's showdown with the law is tomorrow, so he ain't got enough time to come gunning for us.'

Ollie swept her gaze away from the café and gave Jackie one of her intense stares. 'And what about after his court case? His hound dogs, Jason and Finlay, will still be loose. What if they come looking for us? Do you fancy having your death advertised on one of these street boards like all the other street art?'

This is still wrong, Jackie told herself, but she knew that a girl had gotta do what a girl had gotta do.

'Alright,' she said finally. 'But you do all the talking because I know fuck-all about shooters. Say Dave don't come here no more?'

Ollie gave her a cheeky half-grin. 'Bet you a fiver he still does.'

Jackie's first smile of the day propped up her cheeks. She held out her hand to Ollie.

They shook hands as they both announced in unison, 'Done.'

As Jackie's hand fell away she said, 'How we gonna play this?'

'We order the dish of the day. Wait a maximum of two hours and if he doesn't turn up we leave. And never come back.'

The sun dipped out of view as they reached the café. The strong aroma of chips, overdone burgers and singed oil greeted them as Jackie pushed the door. They moved over the threshold. Straight back into their past. Like magnets, without thinking, they moved to the table they had sat at all those years ago. A young waitress came and took their order.

Jackie locked her fingers together on the table. Looked at Ollie. She knew her statement was going to startle the other woman. 'Tell me about Nikki.'

A sudden pinched expression took hold of Ollie's face. Her eyes dipped to the table. 'Don't worry,' Jackie reassured her softly. 'I ain't gonna give you a load of earache. I wanna know what she looked liked the last time you saw her.'

The waitress arrived with toast and mugs of tea. The steam from the mugs rose between the two women. Neither of them spoke. Finally Ollie slowly lifted her composed, dark eyes. 'You sure you want me to talk about this?' Her tone was gentle, as if she was holding Jackie's hand. Jackie nodded.

'OK.' Ollie reached for her mug. Wrapped her fingers around its warmth. 'The first time I saw Nikki reminded me of something that hadn't touched me in years. True beauty. And her hair . . . I had never seen hair that colour before. Ripe like the setting sun . . .'

And that was how they went on for the next hour. Jackie questioning, Ollie answering. Voices soft, low, lost in their own world. Suddenly the breeze from the outside touched their table as the door opened, just as Ollie started to tell Jackie about the diamond she'd given her mum.

'The usual, Glen.'

The voice drove Jackie and Ollie back to the present. They both swung around towards the counter at the same time as the man who stood there turned. Dave. A man who now looked startlingly different from the man they had known all those years ago. He wore a neat tracksuit and had a face that was older but gleamed with the evidence of a recent holiday in the sun. He carried a newspaper and sat down at a table near the back.

'You owe me a fiver,' Ollie whispered.

They got up and approached Dave's table. His head was low as he flicked through the paper.

'It's Dave, isn't it?' Ollie asked.

Dave angled his head up and stared at them with suspicion. 'Who's asking?'

The women quickly shuffled down into the chairs opposite him.

'Names aren't important. All you need to know is that we've got friends in common and they told us that you're a geezer who we can do business with.'

'Oh yeah?' The suspicion in his face deepened. 'And what sorta business would that be?'

Ollie's voice dropped an octave. 'We're looking to purchase some small hand-held friends.'

Dave snorted. Turned his head back to his paper. 'Dunno what you're chatting about, ladies. Got the wrong bloke.'

'Shame. Our friends assured us that you are one of the best in the biz.' Ollie stood up. Jackie sent her friend a 'what the hell are you doing?' look as she anxiously dragged herself to her feet.

'No worries,' Ollie carried on calmly. 'Thanks for your time. We understand that there are plenty of other players around here who will be willing to lend a hand, especially as we are prepared to pay well over the odds.'

'Hold up a minute.' His head came up as he spoke. He gave them a hard look. Then leaned back in his chair. 'Why don't you ladies park yourselves back down again?'

They quickly followed his suggestion.

'What you after and when?'

'Four hand-held, ammo included, nothing glitzy. Something that knows how to do the job quick and easy.'

'When?'

'ASAP.'

'I need a bit of insurance that you ain't taking me for a dick.'

Ollie pulled out an envelope. Passed it across. He placed it in his lap. Peeped inside. Let his eyes run over the wad.

'Meet me at the London Eye at eight tonight. Bring the rest of the cash in a black rucksack.'

'So sorry I'm late, darling.' The words rushed out of Bell Dream as she stood smiling down at Anna in the packed Soho restaurant.

Anna smiled back and let her eyes sweep over her lover. Bell was still decked out in her business clothes – formal grey suit and white blouse. In her hand she held her briefcase. The smile dropped from Anna's face as her gaze stayed on the briefcase. The one she knew might contain information about Frankie.

'You alright?' Bell's tone was full of concern as she took her seat. 'You look like you've seen a ghost.'

Anna didn't even hear her because her eyes were locked on the briefcase that Bell placed on the floor by her chair.

'Anna?'

'Uh?' Anna finally lifted her head. 'Sorry, I'm miles away. I'm fine.' She stretched her hands across the table as she continued, 'You look tired.'

Bell entwined her fingers with Anna's. 'The usual. Just a bit worried about one of my clients, who's up in court tomorrow. The case could swing either way.'

Anna's hands went cold. 'You talking about Frankie Sullivan?'

'How do you know that?'

Realising her slip-up, Anna hastily tried to cover her tracks. 'You must've mentioned it to me.'

'Are you sure? It's not like me to talk about a client.'

Anna felt herself sink deeper into the hole she had created. She had to get out of this one in a hurry. Think, think, think, she desperately told herself. Suddenly she pushed herself over the table. Stretched her body across until her face was inches away from her lover's. She saw Bell's eyes widen because she knew what she was going to do. She lowered her mouth to the other woman's lips. Their first public kiss. Anna had always imagined this moment being one of celebration when they both gave the finger to those who didn't like it. But instead of elation Anna felt complete desperation. And instead of feeling her love for this woman all she was aware of was that briefcase. As Anna disengaged her lips she became aware of eyes and silence coming from the nearby tables. Fuck 'em, she thought. If they didn't like it they could find somewhere else to stuff their faces.

'Wow,' Bell said self-consciously as her face beamed at Anna. 'Maybe I should be late for all our dates if that's what happens.'

'You know I love you, don't you?' Anna ran a finger across Bell's cheek.

'Yes.'

'And whatever happens please promise me that you'll never forget that.'

'What's going on?'

'I just thought it was time that everyone knew that I've got the best girl in the world.'

Bell smiled. 'Maybe we should go back to my place and really celebrate.'

'Later,' Anna whispered. 'Right now I could eat a horse.'

Anna tried to banish the briefcase from her mind as they ate. How could she love this woman and then steal from her? You just didn't do that to the people you cared about, no matter what the situation. Besides, there was no telling what was in that case. Could be anything. But what if it was about Frankie? What if there was vital information that could help them all get out of this shit? What if . . . ? The fork stalled halfway to her mouth. I don't care what's in that case, Anna told herself as she shoved the food into her mouth, I ain't gonna do it. I ain't gonna do it. I. Ain't. Gonna. Do. It.

'I'm just heading off to the Ladies.' Bell's voice snapped Anna back to the restaurant.

Anna watched Bell as she moved away from the table, leaving her on her own. Her mouth tightened as she realised that she wasn't on her own. Now it was just her and the briefcase. Her eyes zoomed to the case. I ain't gonna do it. She squeezed her eyes closed. But what if . . . ? She reopened her eyes. Quickly placed the fork on her plate. Made her move. She leaned over, hand moving . . .

'Oops, I forgot that I . . .' The sound of Bell's voice made Anna bolt up straight. Startled, she gazed at the other woman, who was standing on the opposite side of the table.

'Just need something from my case,' Bell finished.

She leaned down and picked the case up. Smiled and retraced her steps to the toilet. Anna leaned back into her seat, deflated.

Bell Dream, knickers around her ankles, pulled hard on a cigarette as she sat on the loo. Her briefcase lay on its back just in front of her feet. Frankie Sullivan's case was turning into a real stinker. She knew she should have never taken it. She knew he was guilty as hell, but her reputation was built on getting people off and Frankie Sullivan was no different. She heard the creak of the main door opening as she pulled on the last dregs of the fag. Whoever had come in might report the smell of smoke to the establishment. Quickly she dropped the fag on the floor, ground her heel into it. Her hands did a mad wave in the air as she tried to dispel the smoke.

Suddenly two arms shot through the gap between the door and the floor. Grabbed her case. Before she could react the case was whipped out of the cubicle. She heaved herself up. Crashed forward as her feet tangled with her underwear. Quickly she used her hands to right herself. She heard the main door bang against the wall as she scrambled to pull up her underwear. Shit, they were getting away with her case. Frantically she reached for the lock. Thrust the door open. Ran towards the main door. She rushed out into the corridor. No one was there. Shit. She kept up a furious pace back to the dining room. She found her table, but no Anna. She marched towards the foyer, where a young woman was standing by the main desk and till.

'I need to see the manager right now,' she demanded. 'My brief-case has just been stolen.'

The young woman uttered a horrified noise, made a hasty apology and then scurried off to find the manager.

'Bell?' Hearing her name, she turned to find Anna standing behind her.

'You won't believe this, but someone has just nicked my brief-case.'

'You are joking,' Anna said, stepping forward to hug her.

'Where have you been?'

Anna moved her head to the side, so Bell couldn't see her eyes. 'I just remembered that I left these,' she held up her bike keys, 'in the ignition.'

The manager appeared. Bell quickly told him what had happened. 'I'll contact the police.'

'No, no, leave it,' Bell responded, raising her fingers to rub her temple. 'There's no point. I've got copies of everything at my office. The case was a present from my father when I was called to the bar. So please just tell your staff if they find it to let you know. Here's my card.'

The manager took the card, apologising profusely, and assuring them that their meal was on the house.

'I'm so sorry, babe,' Anna said as they walked towards Bell's car. 'This whole bloody town's full of tea leaves.'

'I'm going to have to go back to the office. Damn.'

Anna gave Bell a long, lingering kiss. As she raised her face she smoothed Bell's hair out of her eyes. 'I'll give you a tinkle later.'

Bell got into her car. As she turned the ignition key her lawyer's mind kicked in and she thought how strange it had been that Anna wasn't at the table. If there was one thing she knew it was when people were telling lies. And she knew Anna well enough to know that she'd been lying about where she said she'd been.

As soon as her lover's car disappeared, Anna let out a long breath of relief. She briskly walked towards the alleyway around the side of the restaurant. She approached the collection of bins up against the wall. She crouched down beside the central bin. Curved her arm around the back of it. Her hand grabbed the handle of Bell's briefcase and pulled it out. As she stood she pulled her mobile out of her jacket pocket.

'It's me. Are you on *Miss Josephine*? . . . Great. You won't guess what I stumbled across. Stay put, I'm coming over.'

She terminated the call and slowly lowered the phone. She hugged the case close to her as she began to walk. She convinced herself that she'd had no option but to do it. But that didn't stop her feeling like a Class A bitch.

Jason and Finlay were already waiting for Frankie when he pulled up outside St Nicholas. He was knackered after last night. Still couldn't believe that he now had some Russian lowlife on his tail as well as the law. But he had to put that on the back burner because tomorrow was the day of the trial. He'd checked with Jackie that morning that things were still cool on the boat. The stupid bitch had still sounded like she was shitting herself, which was good, he decided, because she'd be less likely to do something stupid.

'Not a peep on the street, bro,' Finlay said as Frankie jumped out of the car.

The previous night he'd instructed Jason and Finlay to find out if this Fonrims Akdov was making any noise in town.

'Good. It's gonna take him a while to locate us, which means we can concentrate on the judge and tomorrow. Everything's going according to plan. All we've got to do is sit tight and hope that the judge does her bit. Let's go upstairs for a bit of a chat.'

They made their way to the back entrance. Climbed the stairs to the fourth floor. As soon as they stepped inside Jason said, 'What's that?'

They jerked to a halt. Listened. Heard a distant beat, like music. Stepped back. Drew their guns. In long, silent strides they moved along the corridor. Past the room the girls used to sleep in. Towards the fourth floor's main room. His gun in a tight two-hand grip, Frankie stepped forward. Raised his foot. Kicked the door. The music came full blast in his face. The eerie, doomed rhythm of the Specials' 'Ghost Town' grated against his nerve ends.

'Shit' flew out of his mouth as his eyes swept the chaos in the room.

The bullet-ridden walls. The shattered windows. The smashed furniture. The only item left standing was the stereo.

'What the . . . ?' Finlay said behind him, but Frankie didn't hear the rest of his words because his gaze found the red writing on the wall.

Frankie Sullivan
RiP

Shock and anger steamed out of Frankie. Shock that the Russian had caught up with him so quickly. Anger that the bastard had the brass nerve to try and put the frighteners on him on his own turf. Puzzlement joined the other emotions on his face How had Fonrims Akdov known about St Nicholas? Only he, the four bitches and his men knew about this place. He felt Finlay and Jason move behind him, staring at the wall.

'Think this is that Russian?' hissed Jason.

Frankie stepped back as his gun hand fell to his side.

'What we gonna do, man?' Finlay whined.

Frankie finally turned to look at them. His eyes had taken on a deadly deep blue hue.

'If the trial weren't on the horizon, I'd hunt that motherfucker down, but I can't take the chance of being caught in any gunplay with the Bill on my tail.'

'You mean you gonna do jack about it?' Jason was furious.

'Easy. All we can do now is put the word out and watch our backs. He ain't gonna do nothin' stupid. We've still got his kid, that's why these four walls have caps in them, not us. He's just trying to warn us. Make us give his boy back.'

'And are we?'

Frankie said nothing. Instead he strolled over to the stereo. Raised his gun. Pointed it at the machine. 'Not now we ain't. Once this courtroom drama has been played out I'm gonna show that Russian who's the king of London town.'

He pulled the trigger. Blew the stereo apart with a single bullet.

forty-one

They left St Nicholas. Went their separate ways. Frankie jumped into his motor. As soon as he revved the engine his mobile started to ring.

'Yeah?' He wasn't in the mood for small talk.

'Daisy, Daisy, give me your answer do . . .' A male voice sang the words.

'Who the fuck is this?'

'I'm half crazy, all for the death of you . . .'

Shit, Daisy. The Russians were going after his daughter. The phone slid out of his hand. He pushed his foot down and sped towards home to save his little girl.

Jackie was doing a fry-up when Anna arrived at *Miss Josephine*. As Anna stepped inside Jackie immediately noticed the briefcase in her hand. It surprised her because while Anna might be a business-woman she was definitely not the briefcase type.

'What you got there?' Jackie said, stepping forward.

Anna moved to the table, which was set up for two to eat. She placed the case gently on top of it. 'I'm not sure but I think there might be stuff in here that's related to Frankie.'

Curiously Jackie moved to stand with Anna at the table. She looked down at the case.

'What you talking about?'

Anna opened the case. Inside was a single folder.

'Have a look yourself.'

Jackie took out the folder. Frankie Sullivan's name was written on the front. She eased herself down into a chair as she opened it. Stacks of paper. Each one gave details, including photos, of five substantial houses in London. She quickly flicked through the papers. As she came to the last one she realised that she might be looking at properties that belonged to Frankie.

Jackie looked up at Anna. 'What if this lot belongs to Frankie?' Jackie said. 'I bet he ain't declared none of this dosh as part of his earnings. What if the Bill and prosecution ain't seen this stuff? Where did you get it from?'

Anna's teeth caught her bottom lip as she dipped her head. 'Don't matter where I got it, what's important is that it's ours now and we can use it.'

Jackie jumped up and hugged her friend. 'You're a bloody angel, you are. You . . .' Her words dried up when she felt Anna shaking. She eased back from her, still holding on to her arms. She looked hard into Anna's face and saw a tear rolling down her cheek.

'What you booing about?'

Anna pulled herself away from Jackie. Shaking her head and sniffing, she said, 'Nothing. All this business is just making me a wreck.'

Jackie knew she was hiding something. 'Don't try shitting me. What the heck is going on?'

Anna remained silent.

Suddenly, Jackie's eyes grew large with incredulity. 'Flippin' hell, you never slept with Frankie and nicked it?'

'Of course I didn't, what do you take me for?'

'Then tell me where you got it.'

Anna's voice rose. 'I told you, it don't matter.'

'The only other person who could've had this info was his brief, what's her name? . . . Oh yeah, Bell Dream.' Anna turned her head away. 'That's where you got it from, ain't it? But how?'

Anna headed for the door. 'I'm off. I've got a club to run and your hen night to get sorted for tomorrow.'

'Anna.' Jackie grabbed her friend's arm, stopping her in her tracks. Gently turned her around. 'You remembered her from when she did the work for Misty, didn't you?' Anna slowly nodded. 'So you went to see her and you got . . .' Jackie stopped as the pieces started to fall in to place. 'Bell Dream is your lady.'

Anna wrapped her arms around herself. Then she nodded.

'Right,' Jackie said briskly. She turned and marched back towards the table. With scrabbling hands she picked up the papers and folder. Shoved them back into the case.

'What are you doing?'

Jackie snapped the lid shut without answering. Picked the case up and held it out to Anna.

'Take it back.'

'Have you lost your marbles?'

'I mean it.' Jackie took the other woman's hand and placed it on the handle of the case. 'You take this back, you hear me.'

'I don't get it.'

'You should. The only people we never crap on are our mates. No matter what it is. Or we're gonna end up just like Frankie, a user.'

Anna began to sob as she held on to the case. Jackie took her in her arms.

'I really love her, you know.'

'I know you do.'

'How am I gonna explain this to her?'

'You don't need to. Why don't you play the Good Samaritan and leave it at the nick with the Old Bill and pretend that you found it. Let them contact her.'

They held on to each other for a time. Then Anna stepped back. Wiped her eyes. 'How's everything else going?' she asked.

'A treat. I'm just making a bite for the lads.' Jackie nodded her head towards the closed kitchen door.

'You heard from Misty?'

'Yeah. Everything is sorted. You get outta here.'

Anna headed for the door. She opened it, but hesitated and quietly said, 'I'm glad we're family, Jackie.' She stepped outside and closed the door.

Jackie walked slowly towards the table. She couldn't believe what she'd just done. Let all that information about Frankie go waltzing out of the door. But she'd done the right thing. Nothing was more important than family. And in two days' time she and Schoolboy were going to create their own new family in front of an altar. Jackie's hand gently rubbed her tummy.

Frankie's motor screeched to a halt outside his house. He removed his gun. Forgot the keys swinging in the ignition. Flung the door open. Leapt outside. Twisting wind full of rain hit him straight in his face. He gave the house a quick once-over, trying to detect anything that was out of place. Nothing. If anyone had dared to touch his Daisy . . . He started running, helter-skelter, towards the front door. His shoes crushed the gravel. The rain lashed him in the face. The wind whined in his ear. His feet skidded to a halt when he finally realised what was wrong. The door was partially open. His heartbeat hit hyper-high alert.

He reached the door. Pushed it fully open. Jumped inside the hallway. Spun around, the gun pointing in the air. No one. Nothing. His breathing came erratically as he moved towards the main room. The door was closed. He reached out. Twisted the handle. Pushed. The door swung back as he entered the room. Once again he swung the gun from left to right. Right to left. The room was empty. He ran back into the hall and charged up the stairs, screaming, 'Daisy.' He found her bedroom. Moved inside. Everything looked in place. Her teddy bear's head peeping out of the duvet, nestled between the pillows. The books on the bookcase stacked neatly on the wall on the opposite side of the bed. He ran back onto the landing. Took two steps at a time as he bombed down the stairs. He kept yelling her name as he checked all the other rooms. The kitchen. His office. The games room. He found himself back in the main room. No sign of Daisy or the housekeeper. Despair hit him. His gun arm fell limply to his side. He spun around, screaming her name. Over and over.

'Dad?'

He jacked around to the doorway, his gun flipping up. Daisy and the housekeeper stood in the doorway peering anxiously at him. His daughter's eyes were round, teeming with horror as she stared at the gun in his hand, pointed at her. It dropped from his hand, banging to the floor. He tried to steady his breathing as he said, 'Come here, baby.'

Daisy hesitated. He knew she hated him treating her like a little kid. But when he stretched out his arms she flew into them. He hugged her. Inhaled her innocent sweetness. He looked at his housekeeper, whose eyes were riveted on the gun on the floor. 'You interested in earning one year's wages in two days?' he asked her.

The housekeeper said nothing as she moved her gaze from him to the gun, the gun to him.

'Yes or bloody no?' he yelled.

Daisy whimpered. The housekeeper nodded. 'I want you to pack her stuff. Enough for a week. I'm gonna give you the name of a hotel. Once you get there, don't answer the blower or the door to no one but me, get it?'

'What's wrong, Dad?'

His daughter's words made his mind storm back to another voice asking a similar question.

'What's wrong, Mum?'

It was his voice. Years ago, as he looked at his mum crumpled in an armchair in the sitting room. Three in the morning, her face criss-crossed with bruises and a black eye. And of course a bottle of whisky tipping out of her right hand. She hadn't answered him, just stared at him like she'd never seen him before. Then she'd smiled, and even all the damage that the fist she'd walked into that night couldn't hide the beauty she still had the chance to retain. The whisky bottle had fallen onto the bare floor. She'd leaned over and with her drinking hand had caressed his cheek. 'Why couldn't you just look like me?' she'd slurred.

Then she'd fallen asleep. He'd gone to her room and torn her blanket from her bed. Gone back to his mum and tucked the blanket around her. When he'd woken up in the morning she was gone. The next time he'd seen her was three days later, weaving through the front door, with a bottle in one hand and a bloke in the other.

'Dad?' Daisy's trembling voice pulled him back into the room.

He looked her right in the eye and gave her that special daddy smile. 'Don't ask me no questions but I'm gonna need to keep you tucked away in the background for a while . . .' He stopped when she opened her mouth to interrupt him. He laid his finger across her mouth. 'Like I said, no questions. If anyone you don't know comes to the hotel you take them out with every dirty trick I ever taught you. Got it?'

Without hesitation Daisy nodded. Twenty minutes later Frankie stood outside the house, watching the cab take his daughter away from him. As the car disappeared in the distance the name of his newest enemy grew in his mind. Fonrims Akdov. So the Cossack bastard meant business. Well, threatening Daisy was his biggest mistake, because Frankie still had his son.

He returned to the house, emptied drawers, his wardrobe, the safe containing his guns, and packed a bag. He stopped only when he came across the photographs. The ones he'd used to blackmail Mr Miller with. Three photographs. Mr Miller doing the dirty with three different underaged boys – him, Finlay and Jason. Frankie's gut and mouth twisted. That bastard had kept up his abuse for two solid years until one day Frankie had rebelled and beaten him to a pulp with the same belt Miller liked to bind Frankie's arms with. The boys had scarpered, ducking and diving on the streets for years until their moment had arrived. Making St Nicholas their base, in the early days, had been easy. Mr Miller just couldn't help keeping trophies of his activities with the boys. Frankie himself had committed the burglary of Mr Miller's office, to find the photos forever trapping that paedophile in his power.

He slipped the photos into the bag. Picked it up and briskly moved to the landing. He passed Daisy's room. Stopped. Turned back and peeped inside. Her teddy bear was still in the bed. He knew she couldn't sleep without it. He moved inside. Picked it up. Popped it inside his jacket pocket. Two minutes later he was back outside the house, bag over his shoulder, with a teddy bear in one pocket and a gun in the other. He moved quickly towards the space where he'd left his motor. And that was when he realised that his car was gone.

*   *   *

The man behind the wheel of Frankie's stolen motor crossed over into East London an hour and ten minutes after he'd taken it from outside Frankie's Essex home. Three minutes later it stopped outside its destination. A lock-up in a side road, one street up from where Jack the Ripper had topped his last victim. He pulled his mobile out.

'The car's sorted.'

Shirley Bassey's 'This Is My Life' belted out of the low-rise housing block as Frankie stormed along the riverbank towards *Miss Josephine*. His gun was in his waistband, his daughter's teddy bear peeping out of his pocket. Fury and revenge drove him as he jumped onto the boat. His lips twisted into a snarl as he reached the door. He leaned back. Raised his foot. Booted the cabin door. Bolted inside. Jackie leapt up from the table. Stunned surprise rippled across her face. Breathing hard, she looked at Frankie. He looked back at her. Then his gaze skidded to the two other occupants of the table. His heel flicked backwards, banging the door shut. Closing out the world. Silencing Shirley Bassey.

'What the heck is going on?' he ground out wildly, gazing at the two boys, who were sitting at the table. Their eyes were still blindfolded but their mouths were free. 'They're meant to be tied up, you stupid cow.'

Jackie reared back as his last two words slapped her in the face. Her reply flew out of her mouth with equal harshness. 'I'm just giving 'em a munch and a brew.'

'What do you think this is? The flamin' Ritz?' Frankie took a menacing step towards her.

No one spoke. Finally Frankie broke the silence. His voice was chilled and quiet.

'Put that one,' he said, pointing to the judge's son, 'back in the other room and make sure that he's tied up. And bring some of that rope when you come back.'

'What for?' Jackie swept her eyes anxiously over him.

'Just do it.'

Jackie quickly did what she was told. When she came back with the bundle of rope she saw that Frankie was screwing his silencer to his gun. She gulped as she watched him fix it with a slow, menacing movement.

'Frankie,' Jackie said, her tone shrill and frantic, 'what's going on?'

Frankie didn't reply. Instead he flicked his head up and ran his gaze over the upper walls and ceiling. He stopped when he found a beam attached to the ceiling. He pinned his gaze back onto Jackie.

'Give me the rope.' Once again Jackie did what he asked.

He turned his attention back to the beam. Swung the rope high towards it. It missed and tumbled back down. He tried again. And again. Finally the rope swung over the beam. 'Get me a chair.'

'Frankie, I don't like this.'

'This ain't about what you like. Just do it.'

She rushed over to one of the chairs at the table. Dragged it over to him. He snatched it out of her hand and moved it under the beam. He climbed on the chair. Reached up and tied the rope securely around the beam, leaving one end dangling. He jumped down. Stretched up to the rope and began to make a noose at the end of it. He turned around and looked squarely at Boris. Then he started to walk towards the boy. Jackie swooped around him with the quickness and agility that her small size allowed. Planted her body in front of him, blocking his path.

'Frankie, what the fuck is going on?'

He levelled the silencer straight at her. 'Get outta the way.'

'No. Not until you tell me why you're acting like Rambo on speed.'

He twisted his mouth. Then his hand moved quickly, straight towards her chest. He grabbed the front of her T-shirt and lifted her slightly in the air. Swung her around and deposited her at the side. It took three strides for him to reach Boris. The boy wriggled and groaned as he was marched towards the chair.

'Put him on the chair.'

Jackie quickly looked from the noose to the chair to Boris. The blood drained from her face as she finally realised what was going on.

forty-two

'I ain't doing it,' Jackie yelled.

He strode towards her. Pressed the gun between her eyes. 'This time I ain't gonna just leave you with a thick lip, believe me.'

Jackie slowly walked towards Boris. Gently took his arm.

'Boris . . .' Her voice trembled as she spoke. 'Everything's cool. Just do what I say. I'm gonna help you stand on a chair.'

She spoke to him quietly, instructing him to put one foot, then the other, on the chair. Finally he stood high, his hands fluttering by his sides.

'Get another chair,' Frankie continued his instructions. 'You know exactly what I want you to do.'

Ten seconds later she was standing on another chair next to Boris. Her hand reached for the noose. She hesitated.

'Do. It,' Frankie yelled as he levelled the gun straight at her.

Teeth gripping her bottom lip, she slipped the noose around Boris's neck.

'Tighten it.'

She moved the knot down until it touched the back of Boris's neck. The boy's hands began to flutter madly at his sides.

'Get off the chair and get your mobile.'

Jackie quickly scrambled down and pulled her phone out of her hipster pocket.

'Give me the number for your dad,' he yelled at the boy.

The boy shouted out the digits. Jackie's fingers shook as she punched the number into the phone.

Frankie looked at Jackie. 'Text this message – 'Don't fuck with me.'
She followed his instructions. 'Done it.'

'Send it.'

She did.

'Now come and stand in front of the chair and take a nice photo for his daddy's family album.'

Jackie positioned herself. Raised the phone.

'Ready?' Frankie asked.

She nodded. Frankie gave her one of his angelic smiles as he strode towards the chair Boris stood on. His foot moved, kicking the chair from under the boy. A horrified gasp flew out of Jackie's mouth as she watched Boris's body swing in the air. The boy's hands flew to his throat, trying to dig between his skin and the rope.

'Ohmygod,' Jackie screamed, the phone going into free fall from her hands.

'Shut up, you stupid bitch, and take the fucking shot,' Frankie yelled, pointing the gun furiously at her.

Jackie scrambled to her knees on the floor. Grabbed the phone. Quickly stood back up and repositioned herself. Angled the phone's camera towards a swinging Boris. Her trembling finger pressed. She took the shot.

'Now send it to his old man.'

Jackie quickly did what he asked. Then she dashed the phone to the floor as she rushed towards Boris. When she reached him she wrapped her arms around his legs.

'Get the chair,' she shouted at Frankie.

'I should let the fucker swing,' he replied.

'Please,' she pleaded.

Frankie shoved his silencer into his waistband. Bent down and pulled the chair back onto all fours. He rested it under the boy. Jackie eased the boy's legs back onto it. She clambered up beside him. Stretched up and pulled the rope from around his neck. She pulled him into her embrace and soothed him as the boy dragged massive amounts of air back into his lungs.

'Sling him with the other one and then get your arse back in here.'

*   *   *

A minute later Jackie leaned, shaking, against the kitchen door as she watched Frankie. He lounged back in her favourite chair as cool as you come. Bastard. If she had a shooter she would . . . Instead of her finishing her thought the contempt she felt burst out of her mouth. 'You know what you are, don't you? You're a . . .'

'Mega-cunt,' he finished for her. He laughed as he watched her mouth dangle open in surprise. 'Took you long enough to figure that one out. But then you were always a bit slow. Just like that dear dead mum of yours.' The blood turned cold in Jackie's face. Frankie smirked as he pushed himself to the edge of the chair. 'Wish we had time to chat about the good ole days but we don't. Get on the blower and contact the judge and find out if she's done what she's meant to do.'

Defiance held Jackie back for a few seconds. Then, sighing, she pulled herself off the door and found her mobile. Punched in the number.

'Speakerphone,' Frankie reminded her.

'Judge?' She asked as soon as the line connected.

A slight thumping sound could be heard in the background.

'You wh . . . ?' The voice fell silent. The thumping noise receded into the background.

'You haven't hurt my Danny.' The judge's voice now sounded desperate.

'That depends on whether you've blabbed to the boys in blue.'

'Of course I haven't. I just want my Danny back home with me.'

'Don't get all hysterical. He's fine and will continue to be well looked after as long as you do what you're told. So are we all sorted for tomorrow?'

'My summing up will go the way you want it to.'

'Good girl. Don't forget, after this has all played out there's no point going to the Bill with tales about Frankie because he ain't involved in this. Besides, if you do we'll only come back for Danny boy again. Now you wouldn't want that?'

The silence on the other end of the line was chilling.

'As soon as the case is finished tomorrow I'll contact you with details about where to find Danny.' Jackie clicked off.

'I knew I could rely on you,' Frankie said smugly as he got to his feet. 'That noise at the beginning sounded like the right honourable judge was in a disco.'

'What, you think the judge's gonna be raving while her kid's been nabbed?' Jackie said quickly. She took a deep breath as if she needed as much courage as possible to say what she had to next. 'You ain't gonna kill 'em, are you?'

'Once I'm walking free from that court tomorrow you'll find out what I'm gonna do. Just keep an eye on them and I'll be in contact tomorrow.'

Before she could guess what he was about to do he grabbed her face and kissed her hard on the mouth. The kiss was over before she could think of a way to respond. 'You fuck up . . .' He left his words hanging.

Jackie stared at his disappearing figure as he walked out and left her alone. A grim expression settled on her face. Only one more day to go, she told herself. She walked over to the kitchen. As she raised her fist to bang on the door her mobile started to ring. What fucking now? she screamed in her head. She leaned on the door. Pulled out her phone.

'Yeah,' she said wearily.

'We've got trouble.' Her body became taut at Misty's words. 'The Bill have got Roxy.'

For the first time in ten years Anna felt like popping an E. She'd never been a chicken and she wasn't going to start now, but a bit of chemical courage might give her some much-needed confidence. She stood outside the renovated warehouse overlooking the Regent's Canal in King's Cross where Bell lived. In her hand she held Bell's briefcase. Anna used her key to let herself into the warmth of the reception area. Nodded and smiled at the concierge. Walked up the four flights of stairs. Let herself into the penthouse. She loved Bell's place. Always made her feel calm with its pastel walls, its homely aromas and almost monastic use of space. She made her way through the soft lighting and Billie Holiday's voice, which beat in the background, towards the glass French door that led to the balcony.

She found Bell leaning on the silver rail, a brandy in her hand, as she gazed down at the canal. Anna stood nervously in the doorway.

'So you brought it back?' Bell suddenly said without turning around.

Anna let out a disbelieving gasp in the night air. 'How did you know?'

Bell finally turned around and looked at her. Looked at the briefcase in her hand.

'I could say I'm a lawyer and figured it out, but that's not quite true. You've been waking up in my bed for the last year, so I've got to know all those different expressions on your face. When you're passionate, angry . . .' Her voice dipped 'Avoiding the truth.'

Tears shimmered in Anna's eyes. 'Why didn't you say anything?'

'I needed to see if you were going to bring it back.' Anna hung her head in shame.

'Besides, if you hadn't brought it back I wouldn't have been able to ask you to move in with me.'

'What did you say?' Anna asked, shocked.

'I've been meaning to ask you for ages. I was hoping you would say yes so I've already been to some estate agents to get details of houses I was hoping to entice you to look at with me.' Bell pulled herself straight. 'So what's your connection to Frankie Sullivan?'

Anna thrust her head back up. 'My what?'

'As soon as you sat down at lunch you asked about him and then you run off with my case. I'm not a fool. If I was you wouldn't love me.'

'I do love you.'

'I know you do. So why don't we go inside, make ourselves homely, ease back with a drink and you can tell me all about Frankie Sullivan.'

Jackie and Misty rushed through the doors of the nick in south-east London. They didn't stop moving until they reached the reception desk, which was manned by a fresh-faced young uniformed policeman.

'Excuse me.' The words rushed out of Misty. The stress and anxiety she felt trembled in her voice.

The policeman gave them a sombre look. 'How can I help?'

He frowned as he realised that behind the make-up and clothes, Misty was a bloke. Misty lifted her 'you got something to say about it?' eyebrow. A tinge of pink erupted across the policeman's face.

'I understand that you've got a Roxy Malone in custody,' Misty started. 'We're not sure what the problem is but the Bill . . .' Misty gave a nervous cough at her wrong choice of words. 'I mean, one of your colleagues contacted me.'

The policeman flicked his eyes over a sheet of paper on the desk in front of him. Gave Misty a look that said he still couldn't believe what he was seeing in front of him.

'I'll get someone to see you. Please take a seat.'

They sat down at the same time as three policemen dragged in a rowdy crowd of pissheads, f'ing and blindin' for all they were worth.

Jackie turned to Misty. Whispered, 'You don't think she told . . . ?' Her sentence remained unfinished. She'd already asked her the same question on the way here. Her answer was the same. 'No bloody way. Roxy might be the world's biggest sob artist, but she ain't stupid. Besides, if she told them they wouldn't have asked me down the nick, they would be breaking down my door.'

'But what else can it be . . . ?'

'Fancy a dance, darlin'?' a voice said, stopping her words. She looked up to find one of the drunks' eyeing up Misty with lust brimming in his eyes.

'Well, if it isn't Fred Astaire,' Misty growled back. 'If I thought you might stay upright for more than five seconds I might be tempted to take a spin with you.'

The drunk wobbled. 'Hang on a minute, lady, I was only . . .'

'Miss Misty McKenzie?'

Both Jackie and Misty looked around in the direction of the voice. A uniformed policewoman stood next to them. They both shot to their feet. Misty nodded.

'Please come with me.'

They followed her through the security doors into a bright corridor, throwing nervous looks at each other as they went. They stopped outside a white door. Entered. Inside Roxy sat shaking on her own at a table, her shoulders hunched and her hair a chaotic mass.

'What's going on?' Jackie asked as they took the seats the policewoman signalled to.

'Late this afternoon we were called to a disturbance at Ms Malone's home. When we entered we found Ms Malone standing over her partner holding a knife.'

Both Misty and Jackie gasped.

'As you can see from the marks on Ms Malone's face, it would appear that she and her partner were involved in a domestic dispute. From what the neighbours say this is not the first time it has happened . . .'

'Did she knife the bastard?' Jackie interrupted.

'No. Although we found her with the knife her partner does not want to press charges . . .'

'Press charges?' Jackie shot out furiously. 'He's the one who should be in the dock.'

'Jackie,' Misty warned.

'As Ms Malone did not inflict any injuries we are happy to let her go, but due to her distressed state we felt that it was important not to let her leave the station on her own.'

Roxy started sobbing softly. Jackie crooned, 'It's alright. You don't have to go back there.'

'Thank you,' Misty said to the policewoman.

The policewoman nodded as they all stood up. She pushed her hand into her trouser pocket. Pulled out a card and passed it to Roxy. 'If there's ever any other problems in the future please do not hesitate to contact me.'

They gently led a distraught Roxy out of the station. The traffic was thick and fast on the neighbouring main road.

'You alright, babe?' Misty asked as she wiped the tears from Roxy's face.

'He just kept hitting me.' Her voice wobbled as if she was back in her home. 'And hitting me. And I just lost it. Picked up the first thing I could find . . .'

'Sh,' Misty soothed. 'You're bunking with me from now on. I don't care what you say this time, you ain't going back to that nutter.' Misty looked at Jackie. 'Come on, let's get outta here.'

'I'm gonna have to love and leave you both,' Jackie said as she checked her watch. 'I need to get back to *Miss Josephine* and then I'm meeting Ollie.'

'What you meeting her for?' Misty asked suspiciously.

Jackie avoided her eyes. 'You know, a bit of this, a bit of that.'

Jackie knew that if Misty found out that this and that meant a consignment of guns she would go totally ballistic.

What a fuck-off city, Jackie decided, as she stared at London's skyline. She stood in a pod of the London Eye, next to Ollie and Dave. The city spread itself, magical and dusky, filled with buildings jutting in and out in a wave of history and heritage. The way the reflected lights twinkled in the deep river below it wasn't hard to see why people once thought that this city was paved with gold.

Dave had been waiting for them since eight. Ollie carried their black rucksack with cash and Dave had his own bag, filled, they hoped, with the merchandise. As soon as they got on Dave instructed them to put their bag on the tan bench in the middle. Then he placed his bag next to theirs. Now they stood, in the transparent pod, high above London town.

'Our city's beautiful, ain't she?' Dave said.

Jackie and Ollie gave each other a sharp look, but remained silent.

'OK, this is the set-up,' Dave carried on. 'I've got four hand-held beauties including an Uzi. We go over to the bench. You take my bag and I take yours. We both inspect our goods and if we're both happy we just nod, get off the ride and you go one way and I go mine.'

Ollie gave Dave a single, curt nod. They made their way to the bench. Jackie and Ollie huddled together as they opened Dave's rucksack. Jackie sucked in her breath when she saw the guns lying against the startling white lining.

'Nice doing business with you ladies,' Dave said as he stood up, swinging the bag over his shoulder. Whistling, he moved back towards London's skyline.

As Ollie zipped up the bag, Jackie whispered, 'Where shall we keep them?'

'On *Miss Josephine*. After that, at the club. Then, if everything goes according to plan, we dump them.'

'You still know how to use one of these things?' Jackie asked.

Ollie threw Jackie a surprised look. 'Yes. Why?'

'Good, because I'm gonna need your trigger finger tonight . . .'

The smell of sex hung like an invisible stain in the air.

'Oh yeah,' Jason groaned as he shuddered on top of the naked girl sobbing underneath him.

He didn't know how old she was but she was young. Didn't know her name either. All he knew was that she was one of the new lot supplied from eastern Europe to the string of massage parlours he owned in North London. Life could have been so simple for her if she'd just played the game. Take the punters upstairs, give them a quick rub-down and then flash her jugs and ask them what they really wanted. Except she hadn't wanted to play. So he'd taught her a lesson. Slapped her and screwed her on the floor in the main room in front of all the other new girls, just in case they got any ideas. From the stunned look on her face he realised she now knew who was boss.

He stared hard into her wet, empty eyes and warned, 'The next time you decide to play silly buggers I'll get a wagon-load of blokes up here to gang-bang you.' His rough hand snaked out and grabbed her right breast. 'Got it?' He twisted her flesh to the rhythm of his words. She gritted her teeth as she moaned.

Jason belched as he rolled off the body and stared at the other terrified women who stood in the room.

'Right, get her outta here. Clean her up and have her arse downstairs ready for the punters in twenty minutes.'

Two of the women scurried over and helped the girl to stand up. Holding her arms, they led her out of the room, leaving Jason alone.

He stood up. Pulled up his jeans. He strutted towards the mirror that was mounted above the large cast-iron fireplace. Checked over his reflection. A love of hard liquor had altered the permanent colour of his face. He pulled a small transparent bag filled with charlie from his inside pocket. Tipped some out. Cut two lines. Rolled up a fifty note. Snorted. Once. Twice. Yeah, that felt fucking awesome.

He hitched his wrist up, checked his watch. He had a good hour to get to the meeting with a new contact who had some potential new flesh for him to inspect. It was late to meet but that didn't worry him because some preferred to do business outside of the light of day. He was meeting them at Frankie's office on the Isle of Dogs. Frankie would go nuts if he knew he was using his place for this, especially with the Bill crawling all over him. But what Frankie didn't know wouldn't hurt him.

Minutes to ten Jason pulled up in his Lexus outside the back entrance to Frankie's office. As he got out he heard footsteps. Swiftly he turned to find four people standing behind him. All wore baseball caps, which made it hard for Jason to see their faces. One appeared bulky with a six-foot-plus physique. The others appeared slightly smaller, keeping themselves well hidden in the shadows. Jason wasn't in the mood for any funny business, especially with the coke still rocking his head. He faced them off with his best hard-man pose.

'Jason Nelson?' the large man asked in a slightly accented voice.

'Who wants to know?' Jason replied cautiously.

'We are here to do business.'

'You never said you'd be bringing the family.'

The man stepped forward and laughed. 'Just a precaution as we are visitors to your country.'

Jason sniffed. Smiled. He turned his back on them as he rattled out, 'Let's go.'

They were the final words he said before he felt a huge force hit him from behind.

forty-three

'What was my mum like?'

Daisy's question came as no surprise to Frankie. He sat on the edge of her bed in the large hotel room off the King's Road in Fulham. The owner and Frankie went back years. Back to the days when she'd been selling herself in Brick Lane, that was until she hit the jackpot and married one of her clients, a millionaire three times her age. She'd been more than happy to offer Frankie a hideout with no questions asked. Frankie gazed at his daughter, her question still in the air. From the age of five to fourteen and a half Daisy had never shown a blind bit of interest in finding out about the mum she could barely remember. Then wham-bam, six months ago she couldn't stop firing questions at him. *How old was she? Did she have any family? Did she love me?* He couldn't tell her the truth. No kid deserved to know that about the woman who'd given birth to them. So he did what he always did – he lied.

'Let's just say your mum's in heaven.'

'Stop treating me like a kid, Dad. I'm fifteen now, old enough to know about my mum.'

'Believe me, Daisy, baby,' he stroked his finger under her chin, 'you'll never be old enough to know about your old girl.' He stood up. 'Now close those beautiful eyes of yours and get some shut-eye.'

He started to stand up, but his daughter's question stopped him halfway.

'Are they going to lock you up?'

Frankie shot back around. Shock pummelled his face. He'd done everything in his power to make sure that Daisy knew nothing about the court case. He didn't want her mixed up in that part of his life. He gazed down at her. Gave her one of his special dad smiles. 'No one's gonna take me away from you. I'll be straight with you, babes, I'm gonna have to go to court tomorrow. I just need to sort out a thing or two with a judge, then I'm on my way back home to you.' He pointed at her with a finger from both hands as if she were the star of the show.

'That's why I want to find out about my mum. Just in case they take you away from me.'

The one thing Frankie knew he would regret in this life was the pain he saw shooting from his daughter's eyes. He leaned over. Caressed her head.

'Daddy, one more question.'

'Alright.'

A mischievous light glowed in her face. 'Can I watch my DVD before I go to bed? Just for fifteen minutes.'

He sent her a mock-stern-daddy look, but he knew with his trial looming tomorrow he couldn't deny her anything. He got up. Put the DVD on. Lounged back in a soft-backed leather armchair. Soon Daisy was giggling her head off as her two favourite characters, the Al Capone-style wizards in a kid's mystery about a time-travelling teenage girl with magical powers, came onto the screen. Frankie soaked up the relaxing effect of her laughter. And he needed it because he was feeling as tense as a rent boy on the street for the first time.

'Dad, Dad, watch this bit,' she squealed.

He turned his head towards the telly. One of the wizards spoke with a strange foreign accent that reminded him a bit of Boris. The character even looked a bit like him. Frankie shook his head. He just couldn't get this business with the Russian out of his head. After seeing that photo he'd sent Boris's dad no father would have the balls to come after him. Would they? Shit, if someone sent him a picture of Daisy with a noose around her neck he'd tear the town apart looking for her. But Fonrims Akdov could do what the heck he liked, he wasn't going to find him. Maisie, the hotel owner, knew how to keep her mouth well and truly shut. Daisy let out another squeal at the same time as Frankie's mobile made its ping text message sound. He hesitated. What if . . . ? No, couldn't be. Only Jason and Finlay had the number for this mobile. He reached for it.

> Meet me at St N
> Got new info
> J

Finally, word on the Russian. Frankie got up and rapped on the connecting door to the next room, where his housekeeper was. As soon as she appeared he reached for his coat. And his shooter.

'How does it feel to have your balls swinging in the air?'

The question was distant. Hazy. But Jason heard it as he started to come to. He tried to open his eyes, but it hurt the back of his head. He cringed as he tried again. He felt chilled all over his body. What the fuck was going on? Then he remembered the blow to his head. His eyes sprang fully open. He felt dizzy, as if every blood cell he had was crammed inside his head. A massive shiver ran through his body as he tried to look around. He realised he was outside. But the world looked odd. Behind him were bricks. A wall? And there was a tiny patch of stony ground beneath him. Where the fuck was he? He tried to move. His legs. His arms. That was when he realised that his legs were being held at the ankles. His arms tied behind his back. Suddenly he realised where he was. Hanging upside down outside the window at St Nicholas.

The Animals' 'Misunderstood' pumped inside Frankie's motor as he pulled into the pitch-black driveway of St Nicholas. He rolled his car right under the building. Frankie was as pissed as hell because it didn't look like anyone was around. What the hell was Jason playing at? If this was some Mickey Mouse trip he'd make sure that the only food Jason got for the next week came through a drip.

*　　*　　*

Jason's struggles intensified at the same time as he heard a noise from the ground underneath him. Like the engine of a car. The sound cut.

'You know what they say, Jason. What goes around comes around.'

The hands around his ankle let go.

Frankie reached forward and pulled the keys out. He raised his head. Bang. The car rocked as something heavy fell onto it. Startled, he shuffled back in his seat as the car bounced. The alarm screamed. Shocked, he looked through the cracked windscreen at the contorted, bloody face of Jason Nelson staring with wide sightless eyes back at him.

'That ain't no way for a man to die.'

Finlay shook his head in disbelief as he stared at Jason's dead body. He stood on the right side of the car, Frankie on the left. The cool, damp air settled over them in the silent night. Blood seeped from Jason's smashed body, his limbs at a grotesque angle, apart from his hands, which lay flat against the car as if he were about to heave himself up.

'Shit, man,' Finlay said shaking his head.

Dazed, he pulled a spliff from his inside pocket. Lit up. Jacked in two quick puffs.

Exhaled, long and hard, the smoke dancing over Jason's body.

'What the fuck went down?' he asked, dragging his gaze to Frankie. He stretched his arm over the body, offering the joint to Frankie. Frankie took it. Inhaled, sucking in smoke and rage.

'This was a set-up.'

'How'd you figure that one out?' Finlay responded in surprise.

Frankie passed the dying spliff back to Finlay. 'I got a text from him. Told me to meet him here because he had some info. As soon as I park up he comes tumbling outta the sky.'

'You gonna let that Russian tit keep stamping all over your balls?'

Frustration hit Frankie because he knew he had to keep his eye on his trial. 'As much as I was Jason's mate I told him to look out for his own back. If he'd done that he wouldn't be pig fodder all over my windscreen now. So all we've got to do is keep our heads down, watch our backs until the trial is outta the way. Then we go looking for the Russian with as much firepower as we can find.' He gazed at Jason's body. Then back at Finlay. 'Dump the body. Meet me at the hotel tomorrow before the trial.'

He stared at the body one last time. From head to toe.

'I'll tell you this much, Jace, I'm gonna slaughter the fucker who did this.'

They entered the house using the spare keys. It was silent. Dark. Chilled. They knew where he was because all the lights were off. They stared up at the dark staircase. Turned to each other. Nodded. Crept slowly up the steps. Reached the landing. They moved silently until they found the door they were looking for. The door to the master bedroom was half open. Once again they turned to each other. Nodded. One of them pulled out a handgun. The other pushed the door. They stepped inside. The street light outside pushed slivers of light into the room so that their silhouetted reflections in the large mirror above the fireplace were visible as they moved towards their target. A man wheezing as he slept in the king-size bed. They reached him. Stood on his right side. The one without the gun half turned to the bedside table. Flicked the lamp switch on. The man on the bed immediately woke up. Shot upright. His body froze when he saw the gun pointed straight at his face.

Jackie and Ollie looked at the shock on Roxy's husband's face.

'What's going on?' he asked as he kept his eyes on the gun that Ollie held.

Jackie plonked herself next to him on the bed. 'I think you must've forgotten what I said the last time I saw you.'

While she spoke Ollie moved to the foot of the bed, keeping the gun aimed at him all the time.

Martin's terrified gaze swung between both women. 'I'm going to call . . .' he began to stutter.

'I don't think so,' Jackie cut him off. 'I mean, what would the twitchy-curtain neighbours think if they saw the Bill at your place twice in one day? So why don't you shut it for a change and listen.'

Ollie climbed onto the bed. Straddled Martin's legs. Eased down onto him. His harsh breathing filled the room. Ollie rammed the nozzle of the gun deep into his crotch. He whimpered, but didn't move.

'Let's have a little quiz,' Jackie said. His eyes darted to her face. 'Question number one. How many balls you got?'

His body began to tremble. 'Two,' he finally answered in a shaking voice.

Jackie shook her head. 'Wrong answer. You ain't got none because blokes who bash us girls around ain't got any.'

Ollie shoved the gun deeper into his crotch. His face screwed up like he was in the worst possible agony as tears swelled in his eyes.

'Question number two. What do you think my mate Ollie use to do before she turned sweet sixteen? Here's a clue. It involved working with her hands.'

'Leave me alone.'

'Wrong answer again. This is one you won't find in the jobcentre. She used to be a child soldier, which means she killed people.' Jackie swung her head towards the other woman. 'How many people you reckon you done?'

'I stopped counting after twenty.'

Jackie turned back to Martin and watched his Adam's apple bob as he swallowed convulsively. 'Last question. Let's hope it's third time lucky. I'm gonna make it easy this time and give you a multiple choice. Question number three. What are you gonna do when Roxy shows up at the house again? a) Calmly step aside so that she can get her gear. b) Start knocking her about again. c) Scarper, so she don't have to see your ugly mug ever again.'

'Scarper,' Martin yelled.

'The right answer.' Jackie leaned into Martin's face. 'As soon as the sun comes up you better get on the blower to a solicitor to arrange a divorce. And make sure that Roxy gets the house.'

Ollie cocked the trigger back. Martin started sobbing. Jackie gazed at him with disgust. She pulled herself back. Stood up. Ollie let him feel the power of the gun for a full ten seconds more. Then she eased off the bed. They both looked at the crying man in front of them.

'You're a sad excuse for a man,' Jackie said with revulsion. 'Roxy deserves all the happiness she can get. You better be gone by the time she comes back or else we'll be back and this time you really will be leaving here without a dick.'

They left, leaving Roxy's husband collapsed and sobbing on the bed.

Finlay stared at the fresh mound of earth. He knew he should've cut the body up and dissolved it in acid, but he didn't have time for that, he had a card game to attend. He checked his watch. Twenty minutes after two in the morning. The game would be in full swing by now. He'd got the call yesterday that a new game was being played in a venue he'd never attended before. In a backstreet near his music shop in Soho. He patted the ground with his shovel. 'Rest in peace, my friend,' were his final words to Jason. Then he jumped inside his motor, lit up a spliff and hit the street.

By the time he reached Soho, the adrenalin-fuelled anticipation of feeling a smooth pack of cards in his hands pulsed inside him. He parked the car near his shop. Whistled as he began to stroll away. He jerked to a stop when he heard the smash of breaking glass behind him. Swiftly he turned around to find a hooded figure standing next to his car. In their hands they held a baseball bat that they'd used to smash the windscreen.

'What the fuck?' Finlay yelled out as rage rushed through him.

The person next to his car raised the baseball bat and smashed it into the driver's window. Finlay didn't think, he motored forward. The figure didn't move; instead they remained defiantly by the car while Finlay rushed towards them. Finlay reached them. His hand moved into his pocket to get his gun.

That was when he felt it, a presence behind him. He swung around, drawing out his gun. But it was too late. A mighty force licked him in the face. He went down and didn't get back up.

*   *   *

Finlay came to. Felt disoriented. Drowsy. Shaken. Like some fucker had given him the kicking of his life. He winced, keeping his eyes shut, at the pain stamping on his face. Where the hell was he? A cloud of images started to swirl in his mind. They became clearer as he remembered. Remembered walking down the street on his way to a new poker game. Remembered . . .

His eyes screamed open. Breathing harshly, he frantically looked down at himself. He was sat upright, bound with tape in a chair. His gaze skated around the room. Bare floors. Microphones. A drum kit. He realised where he was. In his old studio in his record shop in Soho. That was when he felt the heat of someone standing behind him. Then he heard the voice.

'We understand that you like bringing girls here and throwing petrol over them.'

Bitch, the Russians had finally caught up with him. But how did they know what had happened here ten years ago?

'I ain't the man you're looking for.' His tone was desperate.

No answer. Then he heard the sound of something being turned. A pop. Then the acrid stench of petrol dominated the air.

'Look, man, I can help you . . .' Hs words were cut off by a splash of petrol hitting him on the back. Then on his right side.

'Help,' he screamed.

The petrol was poured over his head. It ran down his face. Into his wide-open, terror-struck eyes. Into his yelling mouth. He coughed as the liquid crawled inside his throat. He heard the click. Felt the flame of the lighter next to his skin.

'No,' he roared as the lighter was dropped onto him.

His piss ran down his legs as he ignited into huge flames.

forty-four

Three hours before his court appearance Frankie stared hard and long at his reflection in the hotel mirror. For a defendant, finding the right clobber to put on can be a delicate matter. For a bloke in the dock who's counting on an acquittal, something arrogant and flash can do the trick – a suit that says 'two fingers' to the beaks, briefs and boys in blue. Where a conviction looks inevitable, it has to be something apologetic. If a fine's on the cards, it pays to wear something smart but cheap, just in case the judge reckons you might be good for a large wedge. Frankie had gone for arrogant and flash. A single-breasted number with gold buttons and satin purple lining, with trousers grazing the top of designer Italian leather shoes.

He turned away from the mirror and approached Daisy's bed, where she was still as snug as a bug in la-la land. He stared down at her, choosing not to wake her up. He didn't need to see the forlorn, lost look in her eyes as she hugged and kissed him like he was never coming back. No, he wasn't going to do that to his Daisy. Besides, the only drama he wanted to deal with today was courtesy of being in the dock.

He checked the time on his watch. Swore. Finlay was late. He'd told him to be here a good forty-five minutes ago. He eased his mobile out of his inside jacket pocket. Punched in Finlay's number. Voicemail. Shit, where the hell could he be? He didn't need to be jerked around, today of all days. He gave it another fifteen minutes. Called Finlay again. Still no response. A chill descended on him because suddenly something didn't feel right. He grabbed his coat as he thought about where Finlay might be. Only one place Finlay loved more than anywhere else. Unless that murdering Russian cunt had nabbed him.

He shoved his gun in his waistband. Checked the time again. Two and a half hours left. Gave his daughter one last lingering look before he headed, tooled up, out of the door.

The man stepped inside Thornton Lane police station in London's West End. He wore a baseball cap pulled down hard over his face. He entered the reception. The area was deserted, except for a police-woman on the main desk, who stood in front of a mirror on the wall.

'Excuse me.'

The woman lifted her head. 'How can I help you, sir?'

The man raised his head, catching his reflection in the mirror behind the policewoman. He grimaced. For the second time in a week Misty McKenzie was back to being a fella.

His eyes shot back down to stare at the woman.

'I wanna report a crime, anonymously, in connection with the Frank Sullivan case.'

The smell inside Finlay's shop instantly confirmed to Frankie that something was wrong. Acrid and lingering, suffocating the oxygen in the air. Frankie drew his gun as he moved deeper inside. His gaze swung around, trying to find the source of the smell, but he couldn't. He pushed forward out of the main shop and into the back. The smell got stronger as he moved slowly down the corridor. He reached the studio. Stood still, holding back, listening for any sounds. None. Pushed the gun out as he kicked the door. The punch of petrol fumes and burnt flesh struck him in the face. He coughed, curling his finger around the trigger.

'Fucking hell,' he let out as he faced the charred remains of a body toppled on the floor, mixed with a burnt-out chair. He shivered as a strong chill ran through him. He knew the odds on the body not being Finlay were slim, but he had to make sure. He took slow steps forward. Ran his eyes quickly over the figure. Then he saw the two stud earrings stuck to a lump of black flesh.

'Bollocks,' Frankie swore with fury shifting his eyes away from the remains of his friend. If this was one of his men, not a trickle of emotion would have gone through him. But this was Finlay, for crying out loud. Finlay, who when he was nine years old had taught him how to play dominoes. He closed his eyes, trying to bite back the bitter taste of loss that rose up to swamp his mouth. First Jason, now Finlay. He knew who was next – him. That Russian slag was closing in on him. But he weren't going to get him, no fucking way. His eyes snapped open. He pushed his gun back into his waistband. Flicked up his arm to look at his watch. One hour to get to the court. He couldn't deal with Finlay or the Russians now. Retribution against the Russians would be his first action after walking free from court. And he would be free, he had no doubt about that. He gave Finlay's body one last look. 'See you in hell, mate.'

Then he calmly made his way out of the shop.

'Must be someone big today,' the middle-aged woman at the reception desk muttered to herself as she watched the press gather behind the glass door on the street outside the court. She put her head down, reading through the docket of today's cases.

'Excuse me.'

She lifted her head to find a man with a baseball cap staring at her. In his hand he held what looked like the shape of a bottle wrapped in pretty red gift paper and an envelope the size of a greeting card.

'Yes?' she said.

'I'm delivering this package for a Frank Sullivan.' The man placed the bottle and envelope on the desk.

The woman tried to think where she'd seen the name. She looked down at the list of cases. Stopped when she got to case number four. Frank Sullivan.

'I'm sorry, it's against our security policy.'

The man leaned over in a conspiratorial way and whispered, 'This is a gift from his girlfriend. They had a right old barney this morning. She ain't seen him since. Wants him to know that whatever happens she still loves him to bits.' The man winked.

'True love, innit.'

The woman smiled. 'Alright, I'll make sure he gets it.'

The man smiled and handed over the gift-wrapped bottle and card. As he whipped his hands away the woman frowned. She could swear he was wearing red nail polish.

'What do you think the verdict will be?'

'Businessman or villain, which one are you?'

'Think you'll get off, Frankie?'

The questions from the press gathered outside the court bombarded Frankie and Bell Dream as they tried to make their way up the steps. Frankie stopped, soaking up the questions. They made him feel important again. Made him feel that he was still a face that could pull 'em in. Made him feel that he was still a guy who could make this town sit up and take notice. London was his manor and he was going to make sure that no one in this town ever forgot it. He gave them his most charming expression. Spanned the crowd and touched each one of them with that blue magic twinkle in his eyes. One after the other, the faces of the press began to light up with a smile. That old magic never failed.

'Wish I could stand and chinwag with you all day, gents.' He dramatically cast his eyes towards the court building. 'But I think I've got a pre-booked appointment. Catch you later in the boozer for a jar, gents. Drinks are on me.'

'There'll be time for questions after,' Bell Dream interjected.

They walked up the steps and through the doors into a melee of leery defendants, anxious witnesses, bored officials and public gallery voyeurs. As they walked through the crowd, Frankie noticed three men sitting on a bench watching him closely. When he caught their eyes, they turned and looked into space. Frankie turned to his lawyer.

'What are they staring at?'

'Everybody stares at everybody here, Frankie. This is the public theatre of the law, they're probably just wondering if you're famous or not. We've still got ten minutes, so let's have a last-minute brush-up in here before the proceedings start.'

As she led him to a room Frankie looked back at the three men. They were deep in conversation.

'That was quite a scrum. You certainly are popular,' Bell said as they settled themselves at a wooden table in the otherwise bare room.

Frankie laughed, leaning back. 'Just hope they're there when I come waltzing back outside a vindicated man to take a picture of my smiling mug.'

'You seem very confident.'

'Let's just say I've got a funny feeling that the right honourable judge is gonna see the light and find in my favour.'

'I don't like the sound of that. I hope that . . .'

'Don't get your knickers in a twist, love, everything's kosher.'

'Do you still want me to do what you've asked regarding your daughter?'

'I don't think there's gonna be any need for that now.'

'No, you know exactly how to look after little girls,' Bell mumbled under her breath.

'What did you say?'

Before she could answer a tap sounded at the door. Before they could respond the door opened. A woman, who Frankie recognised as the person on the main desk in reception, came into the room.

'Yes?' Bell asked.

'Sorry to disturb you, but this was left at the desk for Mr Sullivan.' She held out the wrapped bottle and card.

'What's that?'

The woman beamed, like she was on a mission of mercy, as she moved towards Frankie. 'It's from your girlfriend. She wants to wish you luck.'

He didn't have a steady girlfriend. Alarm pricked the back of his neck. He took the items from the woman. As he set them on the table she discreetly left. Bell gazed at him curiously as he opened the card. Puzzlement and shock registered on his face when he saw the cover. The photograph of him and Daisy snapped years ago at Southend was stuck on a piece of folded white card. The photo he'd kept in his wallet. That is until the day he'd lost it. The day he'd surprised Jackie at the club. He opened the card. Big black writing. Three lines

Distraction and deception.
Revenge. Ain't it a bitch.
PS Have a drink on us.

The word 'revenge' slammed in his mind. What the fuck was going on?

Seeing the expression on his face, Bell urgently leaned forward. 'Are you OK?' He didn't answer. Instead he quickly set the card on the table and reached for the wrapped bottle. He tore the paper open. A bottle of vodka. Smirnoff vodka.

'What the hell?' That was when he knew who it must be. The only person who would send him vodka would be the Russian. But why? What the heck did this have to do with anything?

He ran his eyes over the bottle.

Smirnoff vodka.

He kept running his eyes over the label. Backwards. Forwards. Forwards. Backwards. As his eyes ran backwards over it for the third time the blood drained away from his face.

'No fucking way,' he muttered in absolute disbelief.

His breath caught in the back of his throat as he read each letter of Smirnoff Vodka one by one, starting from the end: a-k-d-o-v f-f-o-n-r-i-m-s.

'Akdov Ffonrims. Fonrims Akdov. Smirnoff vodka,' he said aloud. 'Frankie?'

He ignored Bell for the second time as the penny finally dropped with a shattering echo in his mind. He realised that there was no Fonrims Akdov. The name was just Smirnoff Vodka spelt backwards. If there was no Fonrims Akdov there was no Russian gangster.

In a stunned voice Frankie looked at Bell and said, 'He don't exist.'

'What's going on?'

Frankie's mind whipped back to the information he'd read about the mobster when he was on the boat. 'Have you heard of a place in Russia called Mugistan?'

Bell frowned at him. 'I don't claim to know the map of Russia inside out, but I can't say I've ever heard of such a place. Stan means land, so Afghanistan means the land of the Afghan. So Mugistan would mean the land of the mug.'

The land of the mug? That was when it hit Frankie – that he'd been played for a total mug.

Suddenly the door opened. A court official stood on the threshold. 'They're ready for you.'

Dazed, Frankie got up and moved in a trance, realising that he'd been set up. And there were only four people who could've done it.

forty-five

Ollie took her seat at the back of the court. Her job was simple – report the verdict back to the others.

'OK?'

The question made her glance sideways at Gio, who sat beside her. Misty thought it would be best if she took a bit of muscle along for the ride. They hadn't told Gio what was going on, but he'd grinned like he'd finally made it to heaven when he realised he was having Ollie all to himself. Ollie gave him a tentative, shy smile at the same time as Frankie and his lawyer stepped inside the room.

As soon as the judge opened her mouth Frankie knew that those four bitches had well and truly stitched him up. The courtroom was packed, with a few journalists and other spectators, all eagerly waiting to see if he would fry. But Frankie wasn't aware of them – all he heard was the voice of the judge. A voice that in no way resembled the one that Jackie had spoken to on the phone.

Shit.

He swore some more in his head. How the heck had the girls managed to set him up?

As the judge started the proceedings, flinging out legal and Latin words he didn't even understand, his mind scrambled back through the last two weeks.

He'd had the women carefully followed, watched their every move. Them getting the van, going to the school, finding a place to stash the kid, finally nabbing the kid . . . His thoughts screamed to a halt. Nabbing the kid. His mind ran over the scene he'd witnessed outside the club in Richmond.

Anna and Roxy following the boys, entering the club, walking the boys down a dark side street. The van screeching to a stop outside the mouth of the street. The back doors being flung open. The boys being dragged inside . . .

His mind screamed to a halt again.

Suddenly he knew exactly how they'd done it. The van's doors had been flung open alright, but one of the doors had obscured his view. Bollocks, he'd assumed that when the doors had slammed shut the boys were inside. Now he knew without a doubt that whoever the legs had belonged to that were visible under the van's doors, they hadn't been the boys'. Deception, wasn't that what the girls spelt out in the card they'd sent to him?

Shit.

So who were the boys he'd met on the boat? He didn't know, but what he did know was that one of them hadn't been the judge's son. And if that boy wasn't Danny, then the other boy couldn't have been his mate. Which meant there was definitely no Russian mobster. Distraction, wasn't that the other word the girls had flung in his face in the card? And they had distracted him alright, using the mythical Russian gangster as a way to keep him running around like a blue-arsed fly.

Shit.

So if Fonrims Akdov didn't exist, who'd killed Finlay and Jason? Who'd shot up the room on the fourth floor of St Nicholas? The girls couldn't have done it. Could they? No way would they have that type of fighting power and knowledge. He thought of the ways that Finlay and Jason had met their nasty ends. Who else but the girls would've known that Jason had hung Roxy out the window and Finlay had poured petrol over Ollie in his music shop? Would know about St Nicholas?

Deception and distraction. They'd used both to kipper him like a newborn kid. And who'd taught them the art and craft of both? he thought bitterly. Himself.

Shit. Shit. Shit.

'Frankie.'

He heard the whisper and realised that Bell was talking to him. He tilted his sweating head towards her. She raised her eyes towards the judge. He did the same. The look in the judge's eyes told him she was ready to pronounce her verdict.

'Boys, are you ready?' Jackie called out.

She nervously paced inside the main cabin of *Miss Josephine*. She knew the verdict on Frankie would be in soon.

'Come on, boys. We want to be back at the club by the time the verdict gets in.'

'We're ready,' a voice called from behind the kitchen door.

The door opened. Out walked two males. The actors, Whacky and Mojo.

Guilty.

The word battered the inside of Frankie's head as he angrily made his way through the court foyer with a grim-faced Bell Dream at his side. Plus the judge had also ruled that there was sufficient evidence to suggest Frankie made his dough from criminal activities, which gave the green light for the authorities to try to seize his assets. Only one place he was going now – to hunt down those four bitches and slaughter them one by one. He didn't care what plans he'd made for Daisy, Jackie Jarvis was gonna be a goner.

'We're gonna appeal, right?' he asked furiously as he walked past the three men he'd noticed earlier. As soon as they saw him they rose as if out of respect.

'Yes. But in the meantime they're still going to start proceedings to try to seize your assets. They want your wallet. They want the small change from your trousers and anything you might have lost down the back of the sofa.'

He reached the exit. Punched open one of the glass doors. A spark of light hit him in the eye as a camera flashed. A battery of reporters and journalists waited on the steps below. To him they look like birds waiting to pick at his carcass. If he was going down it weren't like no weeping dickhead. He set a glittering smile on his face. Started to descend. That was when he saw Ollie's face smiling at him through the crowd. By the time he was done with her she wouldn't have a face left, much less be able to smile. Her and her mates would soon learn the cost of making a public pussy out of him. He twisted his body in her direction. Took a rushed step forward. But she didn't move. Just watched him, smiling. As he took another step, hands grabbed his arms. Stunned, he twisted his head to find two of the three suited men from inside holding him, while the third stood to one side so the snappers could catch Frankie's face.

'Frankie Sullivan, I'm arresting you on charges of conspiracy to kidnap . . .'

The crowd below surged forward, cameras manically flashing.

Ollie and Gio walked away from the chaos of the crowd. As they moved briskly towards Gio's car Ollie pulled out her mobile.

'He's a finished man. We're on our way back now.'

Ollie took a deep breath as she took her place in the passenger seat. She tilted her head to the side to look at Gio as he switched on the radio. He looked back at her as the news report came on. Suddenly she grinned and punched her arms into the air.

'Yessss!' she shouted.

She reached over and hugged a startled Gio. His arms tightened around her. She pulled herself slightly back. Glanced up into his face. He looked down at her. Her heart did an unsteady jump. Suddenly her arms locked around the back of his neck as she pulled him down to kiss her. They tumbled backwards into her seat as their hands went into a frenzy over each other. As Ollie unbuttoned Gio's shirt the newscaster reported a new item:

'The bodies of two men were discovered in separate locations earlier on today. Sources close to both inquiries are saying that they may be associates of Frankie Sullivan . . .'

'Cheers, everyone,' Misty said.

She raised her champagne glass, which was filled with Smirnoff vodka, in a celebration. 'Never thought I'd say this, Roxy, but your long-established partnership with this remarkable drink was a lifesaver.'

The other people in the main room of the Shim-Sham-Shimmy Club raised their glasses. Jackie. Anna. Roxy.

And, of course, the actors, Whacky and Mojo.

'After what he did to us and our mums, did Frankie really think we were gonna roll over and kidnap somebody?' Anna said, stinging disbelief in her words. 'No way were we gonna put another fifteen-year-old kid through what we had been through. The only reason we're sitting here nice and tight and free is 'cos of Jackie's brilliant planning.' She raised her glass towards Jackie. The others nodded in agreement.

'You only ever told me and Whacky about our parts on a strict need-to-know basis,' Mojo said. 'So now we wanna know how you planned such a cool set-up?'

'You know what Frankie Sullivan said to me years ago?' Jackie asked. No one spoke, so she carried on. 'That life's all about distraction and deception. That's how we got Frankie, we played him at his own game every step of the way. It didn't take us long to figure out that that tit Finlay was on our tail twenty-four-seven. So our first deception was getting Finlay to believe we were getting ready to snatch the kid. So we did all the things they were expecting us to do – got a van, found an isolated place to keep the kid, made contact with the boy in the school. Then all we had to do was make Frankie think he saw us kidnap the boy.'

'How did you manage that?' Whacky asked.

Jackie grinned. 'We figured out that Frankie would most probably be watching our every move and was probably parked in a spot where he could see us. So all we had to do was convince Frankie that we'd snatched the kid. So we drove the van across the street and opened the doors so that Frankie couldn't actually see what was going on. The only thing he could see were legs under the van's door. And of course those legs belonged to Anna and Roxy. When the van door slammed the only people inside were Anna and Roxy . . .'

'But where did the boys go?' Whacky asked.

Anna took up the story. 'When we got Daniel and his mate in the street I told them that I was part of a special patrol set up by the government investigating underage kids in clubs. I told them that if they didn't go back to school ASAP I was taking them into custody. I said if they didn't believe me I had a van coming to get them. Just then the van swings into the street. The boys scarpered, but the reason Frankie never saw them come out of the street was because they went the other way.'

Jackie grinned at Whacky and Mojo. 'And that's where you two out-of-work actors came in because the next big deception was convincing Frankie we had the boys.'

Whacky started speaking with a large grin on his face. 'I must admit that when we came looking for work we never guessed in a trillion years it would be anything like this.'

Jackie's face became serious, her voice full of emotion. 'I can't thank you enough, boys.'

Whacky kept grinning. 'Don't get all soppy on us. If it weren't for you we'd most probably be following in our family tradition of doing a ten-stretch for a blag in the Scrubs. You helped us change our lives, Jackie, so we owed you one.'

'I still can't believe it.' Jackie shook her head as she toyed with the stem of her glass.

'There we are sitting in my gaff while Roxy talks us through the info she found on the Net about how to kidnap someone when you two come knocking at the door with Ryan. As soon as you two came into the kitchen my brain started going like the clappers. All of a sudden I start thinking, what if Whacky or Mojo pretend to be the kid? Didn't think you would do it, Whacky, but you were blindin'.'

'All I needed was some make-up, and once I was blindfolded and the tape was on my mouth you couldn't even see my face properly. I could've been mistaken for Prince Harry.'

'And my part,' Mojo said. 'Fantastic part to play, but how did the idea for the Russian gangster and his son come about?'

The grin was back on Jackie's face. 'When I was sitting with Danny and his mates teaching them rhyming slang, they started telling me about their family lives. One of them was real quiet. The others got all shifty. I knew what that meant, his dad was a businessman alright, but was well dodgy. And that's when I started thinking, what if Danny had a mate whose dad was a Russian kill-'em-all gangster? What if when we pretended to nab the boy we also had to nab his mate? What if this mate starts making a right load of noise about his killing machine of a dad flying into town the next day looking for him? Chuck a Russian gangster into the mix and all hell starts breaking loose in Frankie's life and we set up our biggest distraction. All we had to do was find a name for our gun-totin' gangster.'

'Smirnoff vodka, what a touch, Jackie,' Mojo said.

'That weren't down to me, that was our wonderful computer expert, Roxy over there, just like the Internet was.'

Roxy blushed as everyone looked her way. 'The only way that Frankie was going to believe that this so called Fonrims Akdov existed was to get information on the Web, which wasn't hard to do. So I created two pages, leaving one on the computer screen and the other on the toolbar. When he went over to the computer we were all sweating like mad, fingers crossed, praying that he wouldn't insist on checking the real Net.'

'Mind you, I thought everything was tits up,' Jackie said, 'when he put Mojo on that chair with that noose around his neck. Crikey, I nearly wet myself.'

Mojo rubbed his throat. 'Thought I was done for as well.'

'I tell you this much, I was ready to chuck the towel in. Just watching you swing in the air nearly give me heart failure.' She looked Mojo squarely in the eye. 'How did you have the guts to let him do it? You could've been brown bread.'

'There was no way I was letting some bloke who treats women the way he treated you lot get away with it. I ain't saying I weren't scared because I was shitting it. But you know what, I realised he was shitting himself as well. He weren't gonna do me.'

'Go on Anna.' Roxy giggled. 'Do your imitation of the judge again, it cracks me up.'

Anna swung her hair back over her shoulders, stuck her nose in the air, pressed her hand over her heart and in her best dramatic mock-posh accent said, 'Not my Danny. Please don't kill him. If you do, who am I going to leave the family silver to?' They all laughed.

'Doing the accent was the easy bit,' Anna started once the laughter had died down. 'Trying to figure out a way of getting out of *Miss Josephine*'s main cabin and outside so that I could be on the other end of Jackie's call was much harder.'

'So how did you do it?' Whacky asked.

'Well.' The word was long and drawn out as Anna looked at Roxy. 'Nothing a man hates more than seeing a woman cry. Frankie knew that Roxy is a bit of a waterworks merchant, so all we did was get Roxy to crack up in front of him. Roxy was bloody great. You should've seen their faces. They had to get her to shut up and short of whacking her they had no choice but to let me help calm her down. Once I was outta the room, bingo, my mobile's in my hand. Mind you.' Anna looked straight at Jackie. 'I nearly bloody well got caught out when you called that second time. I was in the club, music thumping in the background. I nearly blew it when I started by saying "You what?"'

'You should've seen my face when Frankie said that it sounded like the judge was in a disco. I thought the game was up.'

Whacky looked at Misty curiously. 'But how did you sort it so he gets arrested for attempted kidnapping?'

Misty looked at the women with a mischievous smile. All of a sudden, in unison, they began to sing:

> *Daisy, Daisy.*
> *Give me your answer do.*
> *I'm half crazy,*
> *All for the death of you . . .'*

The two actors looked at them as if they'd lost their minds. The women and Misty cracked up and started laughing.

When the laughter died down Misty explained, 'Let's just say that I took Frankie's motor for a spin and left him a few surprises. And I'll bet you ten bob the Bill are giving him a roasting about it right now.'

forty-six

'We have evidence to show that you were going to kidnap Judge Gray-Hammond's son,' the detective inspector confidently stated.

Frankie was down the nick with his brief, being given the third degree by the Bill.

'What evidence?' Frankie shot back.

'My client will not be making any statements until I've had the opportunity to speak alone with him.'

Frankie eyeballed the officer. 'They ain't got dick on me . . .'

'Mr Sullivan . . .' Bell tensely interrupted.

Frankie ignored her. 'The bastards have been out to get me from day one. It ain't enough that they're taking the livelihood way from an innocent man, now they've got to try and frame me for another crime as well.' He confidently leaned towards the other man. 'Go on,' he challenged. 'Show me this so-called evidence.'

The DI opened the file in front of him. Pulled out a few transparent A4 pockets, each of which had something inside it. He stabbed the first one with his finger. Twisted it around to face Frankie.

'Do you know who that is?'

Frankie looked at the evidence. A photograph of Daniel Gray-Hammond.

Frankie kept his face blank as he answered, 'Nice kid. But I ain't clapped eyes on him before in my life.'

'As you well know, this is Judge Gray-Hammond's son. We found two sets of fingerprints on it, one of which belongs to you.'

Frankie remained silent as his heartbeat increased.

'And this,' the next piece of evidence was pushed towards Frankie, 'is a detailed plan of the judge's son's school.'

The sweat formed over Frankie's lip.

'And I'm sure you know what this is.'

Frankie glanced at the next piece of evidence. Shit. It was his wallet. Displayed next to it was a white card. Nervous puffs of air entered Frankie's body.

'Doesn't take a genius to recognise that the gold engraved FS means this is your wallet. Next to it is a card with the address of the judge's son's school.'

The DI took out the next piece of evidence – four pieces of A4 paper stapled together. 'Now this,' the officer laid the papers in front of Frankie, 'is a blow-by-blow account of Judge Gray-Hammond's life. Address, schooling, what she does when she ain't handing down sentences to criminals like you. And of course information about her son. Once again, Frankie boy, this lot has your fingerprints all over it.'

'You could've got this shit from anywhere. You're just trying to fit me up.'

'Then how do you explain this?'

Frankie took a deep breath when he saw what was in front of him. Two photos of his stolen car. One showing the car in a lock-up and another showing the evidence that had just been shown to him strewn across the car's front seats. The officer sent him a triumphant smile.

'My client will not be answering any further questions.'

The celebration at the Shim-Sham-Shimmy went on for a good half-hour. Jackie still couldn't believe that Frankie was truly out of their lives. She felt like crying. She gave everyone a massive hug as they slowly started to leave. Finally it was just Misty and her, sat at the long table, polishing off the last drops of vodka.

'You need to go home so that we can get your hen night ready,' Misty said.

Jackie gave Misty an assessing look, feeling brave on booze and elation. 'I've always wanted to ask you a question, but I don't want you to take it the wrong way.'

Misty lifted an eyebrow. 'Only if you're gonna ask what colour G-string I wear every day of the week.'

Jackie chuckled. 'No.' The humour left her, replaced by anxiety as she watched Misty sip her drink. 'Are you my dad?'

Misty coughed and spluttered. 'What you trying to do, girl? Change the colour of my hair?'

Jackie nervously ran her fingers through her own hair. Misty quickly grabbed her hand as it came down. 'No I ain't. I don't know who he is, but if he was someone worth knowing Nikki would've told you.' She gave Jackie a bittersweet smile. 'I wish I were your old man because you know what, Jackie? Any bloke would kill to have a daughter like you.'

Jackie leaned forward. 'Can you keep a secret?'

'Cross my heart, hope to die,' Misty said playfully.

Jackie's voice dropped. 'I'm gonna have another kid.'

'Oh, sweetheart,' Misty said as she reached across to hug Jackie. 'Why didn't you tell me sooner? That bloody Schoolboy's gonna marry you now whether he likes it or not.'

Jackie eased back. 'I ain't told him yet or the others. So just between me and you for now.'

Misty squeezed Jackie's hand at the same time as Ollie stepped into the room.

'What is it?' Jackie asked, seeing the serious expression on her friend's face.

'It's just been on the news. The very dead bodies of Finlay and Jason have been found.'

Misty swung her stunned expression between both women. 'You lot didn't have nothin' to do with this?'

'Are you mad?' Jackie threw back. 'We might've hated them but we'd never kill no one. No way.' Jackie gave Misty a deep look. 'Was it you? You're connected. I know who your brothers are and everyone's shit scared of them.'

Misty shot up from her chair and turned away.

'My God, Misty, you never did . . . ?' Jackie shot out.

'No, no,' Misty reassured her. She slowly turned around. 'Alright, I'll admit that it did cross my mind to have my brother Charlie sort

Frankie out, but the night I came to *Miss Josephine* and you lot told me the truth I decided to do things your way. So I gave Charlie a bell and told him to back off.'

'It could've been anyone,' Ollie said. 'Frankie had more enemies than we've had hot dinners.'

Misty sent her a lukewarm smile. Her hand shook as she raised her glass. The girls might not have any idea who'd committed those murders, but she was pretty certain she did. Why didn't I see this coming when I got the phone call? Misty asked herself. When they grabbed me outside the club? Never in a million years did she think it was all going to get this out of control. And the girls were going to find out soon enough at the hen night because there were names on the invitation list the girls knew nothing about.

Daisy.

That was all Frankie could think about as he was jostled into the back of the security van on his way to some prison he'd never heard of. How many years was it going to be before he smoothed his hand over her hair again? Laughed with her as they watched the box together? Took her to stand at his mum's grave? It would be years, because however long they sent him down for he was never going to let her see him inside. Watching the respect fade from her beautiful eyes as the years went by was something he never wanted to see. There was him thinking that he'd sorted her future out if anything ever happened to him, when all the time that bitch Jackie was . . . He cut the thought off as his hands shook in the handcuffs. He needed a smoke like a prisoner craves privacy. Abruptly the van swerved to the left. His back punched against the wall, making one of his feet come off the ground. As he used his hands to steady himself he heard the screech of tyres. The van juddered to a halt. The sound of a slammed door hit the air. Then a bang. Frankie's body jolted straight. He knew that sound. A shotgun. Another blast. The van dipped on its right side as if a tyre had been blown out.

'Get out,' roared a voice.

He heard the front doors being harshly pulled open. Heard feet crunch onto the road and knew that the guards in the front were out of the van.

'Lie down.' The voice was ferocious now.

A few seconds later Frankie heard the key turning in the van's back doors. He pressed his back fearfully to the wall. The doors were flung back to reveal a black man standing with a shotgun. The man was huge and embodied the term badass.

'Get out.'

Heart beating like crazy, Frankie stepped forward. Jumped down.

'Come with me,' the man commanded.

'Who the fuck are you?'

'A friend from many years ago owes you a favour.'

He moved quickly with the man, past the petrified guards, who lay spreadeagled on the ground, towards an anonymous-looking car.

'In the back.'

Frankie jumped in.

The man got into the driver's seat. Slammed the door. Shoved the shotgun on the ground near his feet. Ignited the engine and took off.

'Who did you say you worked for?'

'Soon, my friend. Soon.'

It took the car over an hour to reach its destination. A cottage in Epping Forest. Frankie stared curiously out of the window as the driver killed the engine. The man got out of the car and moved to the back. He opened the door. Frankie stepped outside. He tripped and fell onto the man. His cuffed hands grabbed the man near his front jacket pocket. He shoved himself up, one of his hands curling tight, and said, 'Sorry mate.'

'Come,' the man said as he moved towards the front door.

Frankie followed him. They stepped inside. The air was cool, as if the house hadn't had its central heating system on for a long time. They moved down the hallway. The man reached a closed door. Held it open.

'Mrs Omote and the others are inside.'

Mrs who? Frankie thought as he moved past the man into the room. Omote? He knew that name. Didn't he? When he caught the faces of the three people inside he knew that the man had lied. These weren't friends. He stared at each one of them with shocked disbelief.

'Long time no see, Frankie,' said the one with the flaming shoulder-length red hair.

forty-seven

'You're all dead,' Frankie finally croaked as his body expanded with shock.

The three people who stood in front of him gazed at him with dangerous glints in their eyes. Nikki Flynn, Maxine Munro and Jasmine Craig. The women were all classily dressed, not a sign of grey hair, with a touch more living marked on their faces.

'He doesn't look very pleased to see us,' Nikki said.

'Well, you wouldn't, would you,' said Maxine. 'I mean, if you think you've topped someone then they turn up like a ghost ten years later it must be a proper shock.'

'The nerve of it,' Jasmine carried on. 'Not having the decency to remain dead.'

Nikki sauntered over to him on her four-inch heels, holding a filled champagne glass. She stopped two strides away from him. Stretched out an arm. 'Touch me,' she dared him. 'Feel me.' She took another step. This time he smelt her raging anger.

'Go on. See how dead I feel.'

The hand holding the champagne glass came up and he thought she was going to dash the contents in his face. Instead she drew it to her mouth. Took a deep sip.

'How did you fucking pull it off?'

'The power of the pussy, babe,' she replied in a tight quiet voice. 'See, that was the fatal flaw in your plan. Major Omote couldn't get enough of me. My boobs and butt were all he thought about morning, noon and bloody night. He got real attached to me calling him "big boy". Asking him to put me six feet under was like asking him to hack off his dick.'

She drained the last of the fizz. Turned away from him and went to stand with the others.

'So where have you been hooked up for the last ten years?' Frankie asked, the shock getting thicker in his voice.

Maxine stepped forward. A very different Maxine to the one he'd last seen ten years ago. She was composed, confident, head held high, and he would bet that the liquid in her glass was not champagne.

'See these?' She pointed to the diamond necklace around her neck. 'These are called Gates of Dawn. But of course you know that because you were trying to get your greedy mitts on them ten years ago. But what you didn't know was that they were going to save our lives. Unlike you, we're standing here because someone showed Nikki a great act of kindness.'

Nikki stepped forward. 'A young girl, same age as my Jade, is sharing a cell with me. She bribed a guard with a diamond. The night he comes to get her, instead of turning tail and leaving me, do you know what she does? She gives me one of her diamonds – I suspect the biggest diamond she has. She tells me to give it to the guard. At first I didn't have a clue what she was chatting about. Then I figured it out, so the next time Omote comes to see me I try to bribe him with the diamond to get us outta Sankura . . .'

'But he couldn't do it,' Jasmine cut in. 'The problem was that if we turned up back in England we'd have become an international embarrassment to the Sankura government because they'd told the world that they'd executed us. Omote said that we couldn't go free but maybe he could get us outta prison and take us somewhere else in Sankura. So he used Nikki's diamond to bribe a state official and took us away to live in his house in the mountains. Well, it was more like a palace really. From jailbirds to the lap of luxury, just like that.' She snapped her fingers.

'So you and your girls are in this together?'

'What are you talking about?' A bewildered expression crossed her face.

Realising that they knew nothing about his recent involvement with their daughters he grinned and dug the knife in. 'So you loved living it large in Sankura more than you did your little girls, or you would've come and got them.'

Nikki rushed over to him and delivered a stinging blow across his face. 'Don't you ever fucking say that to us.' He raised his head, his fingers brushing the trickle of blood at the corner of his mouth. 'Of course we wanted to fucking come back, but we couldn't. We didn't have passports, money, nothing. We lived in an area where everyone was shit scared of Omote, so no one was gonna help us do a bunk.' A soft expression covered Nikki's face. 'Strange thing was that big bastard Omote really started to love me. He knew I was missing my little girl, so after a couple of years he sent someone to London to check on our girls, only to find that they'd disappeared. Omote's man even went to see my mate Misty, but he couldn't tell Misty we had sent him because I needed Misty still to think I was dead. Misty didn't tell Omote's man anything because she thought Frankie had sent him. Every year Omote sent someone to look for them but no one could find any trace of them. You've got a little girl, Frankie. How would you feel if she disappeared off the face of the earth?'

Frankie said nothing.

Maxine said, 'Our girls were our only ties to London, so after a while we just settled into our new life.'

'Then a year ago two things happened at the same time,' Nikki said. 'Omote's missus kicks the bucket and his private army captures a diamond mine. One month later, guess who's the new Mrs Major Omote? Yours truly. Then last month there's a coup in the country and all hell breaks loose. When the dust settles Sankura has got a new government. A government who want Sankura to have a fresh start. So do you know what my husband does? He offers them his diamond mine in exchange for our freedom. You ever been loved by someone that much, Frankie?'

Frankie just looked back at her with scorn.

'The government agreed to set us free as long as we slipped away quietly. So Omote takes us to Switzerland, where his bank accounts are. But we had to try and find our girls one last time. So a week ago we arrive here and go to see my mate Misty. The first time I tried to see her was when she went to see this play . . .' Nikki's voice cracked. 'I had no idea that the woman and child with her were my daughter and grandson. Do you know what that feels like, not realising you're looking at your own flesh and blood? We finally caught up with Misty one night outside the club and that's when we found out what really happened to our girls.'

'You're scum,' Maxine spat. 'Total scum. How could you have treated children that way? Drugs, gun running, gem smuggling. The way we hear it is if the girl with them hadn't pumped you full of shit you would've tried to murder them as well. When I heard what you did to my little girl. Hung her out the window like she was a piece of crap . . .' Her voice cracked.

'You're gonna die, Frankie,' Jasmine said. 'Just like Jason and Finlay.'

'You killed them?'

'Did you like what we did at St Nicholas?' Nikki asked, ignoring his question.

'Frankie Sullivan RIP. Hope you liked "Ghost Town" because we thought it was a nice touch.' She threw her head back and laughed. 'Jason, what a fucking gullible prick. All we had to do was wave a bit of potential pussy in front of him for him to come running. Only one way he deserved to die, head first out of a window. And men who pour petrol over little girls deserve to arrive in hell in a blaze of glory.'

The image of Finlay burned and dead flashed into Frankie's mind.

'How should you go? That's the big question, Frankie,' Jasmine said, stepping forward. 'A man like you who's done so much evil. We had a real good chat about that one but we all agreed there's only one way for a man like you to go.'

Maxine walked to the door. Pulled it open. In came the man who'd taken Frankie from the van. This time he held a revolver in his hand.

They took him to the basement of the house. Unused, cold concrete. The man with the revolver pushed Frankie inside. His gaze ran over the room. Stopped when it hit one wall where another wall of bricks was starting to be built in front of it.

Nikki moved in front of him. 'We wanted you to die real slow to give you time to reflect on all the badness you've given the world.'

'What you talking about?'

'We're gonna prop you against the wall, eyes wide open, and then brick you up. Can you imagine that? Slowly dying of starvation.'

They turned around and headed for the door. He ran after them, yelling, 'You can't fucking do this to me.' The man with the gun shoved him back. He hit the cold floor. 'But we aren't cruel,' Nikki said. 'So we're gonna give you a couple of hours to remember your little girl. We'll be back tonight to say our final goodbyes. When my daughter gets married tomorrow I don't want you on the face of the earth any more.'

The door was bolted shut as Frankie lay on the floor. Fury and fright shot harshly from his mouth.

'Daisy, Daisy,' he mumbled over and over. His cuffed hands slammed against his pocket. That was when he felt the pen he'd picked from the pocket of the women's gorilla as he'd stumbled on him outside the cottage.

Nikki Flynn popped a Prozac into her mouth. Tilted the glass of water to her lips. Swallowed the chilled liquid in one gulp. They were back in the main room.

'You alright?' Jasmine asked.

Instead of answering Nikki gazed at her two friends. They'd all come such a long way since meeting as single mums aged eighteen, with no one to call their own except three babies with names the same as gems. The years hadn't been easy, but they'd stuck together like the family they had become.

'Yeah,' she finally answered. Then she shook her head. 'No. We're no better than him.'

'Don't forget what they did to us,' Maxine furiously threw out. 'They tried to kill us. Kill our girls. They got what was coming to them.'

Over the years Maxine had surprised them both. After she'd shaken off the drink, she'd become the strong one. The one who'd carefully planned Frankie's downfall.

Maxine pulled out her inhaler. Took a deep puff. 'The hardest thing we're gonna have to face,' she carried on, a forlorn quality entering her voice, 'is explaining to our girls why we're still alive.'

Jackie's hen night was in full swing. They were in the main room of the club, with dim lights falling across the curtain on the stage. Misty watched anxiously as her girls laughed, drank and fooled around. She checked her watch again. Shit, why hadn't she told the girl about their mums? She still couldn't believe it herself. Of course, the first time she'd seen Nikki had been outside Ryan's drama school, waiting by a silver Mercedes. Misty had thought her eyes were playing tricks on her. Then came the phone call with the person at the other end claiming to be Nikki Flynn. Misty had put that one down to a total wind-up. She shivered as she remembered the night she had stood outside the club, making the call to Charlie, when the hand grabbed her mouth. She'd nearly toppled over when she'd seen the women standing behind her, ghosts from the past. She'd whisked them into the club, where they'd explained what had happened to them. When she told them what had happened to the girls at the children's home the women had cried. She'd wept with them.

She'd told them straight to their faces that they should see the girls right away, but they'd refused. Said they had some business to take care of first. She should've sussed that the only way they were going to reveal themselves to their daughters was after they got Frankie good and proper. Misty didn't need a crystal ball to know it was them behind Finlay and Jason's deaths.

Misty's mobile rang. She didn't answer it. It was the signal she'd been waiting for. She knew it was time. With the electronic high energy of 'Tainted Love' pumping in the air Misty got to her feet. Took the stage. The spotlight hit her face. Instead of happiness, the light illuminated her anxious expression.

'Blimey, Misty, what you looking like a drowned rat for?' Anna shouted out, and then tucked her lips into her cocktail.

Misty said nothing. Instead she stretched her neck, making the tendons stand out like lifelines. Wet her lips. Her fingers did a nervous flapping jig in the air as she finally spoke. 'OK, ladies, we've reached the finale for the night.' She choked as the words caught in her throat. 'Shit,' she rasped out, clasping her hands together. 'I don't know how to say this girls, but . . .'

A raucous Jackie called out, 'Come on, Misty, it's not like you to have lost your flippin' voice.'

'Alright.' Misty's Adam's apple bobbed as she swallowed. 'I've got three very special people who want to meet you.' A noise came from the back of the stage The sound of feet moving behind the scenes. A silhouetted figure stepped onto the stage behind the curtain. Then another. And another.

'I told you I didn't want no strippers,' Jackie dragged out. 'I don't need any more geezers in my life.'

'I'm real sorry, girls,' Misty whispered. She stepped back out of the limelight of the stage. An uneasy hush fell across the room. The curtain moved. Eased back. The three silhouettes stepped forward as Marc Almond's forlorn refrain of 'Tainted Love' shook the air.

Jackie blinked. And blinked again. She convinced herself that she must be tanked out of her head because there were three women standing on the stage. And the one in the middle was a dead ringer for her mum. Below-knee black sequinned party dress, pale skin. And the hair. Jesus, the hair. Only Nikki had ever had that particular texture and density of red. This was a trick. That couldn't be her Nikki standing as bold as the living on the stage.

forty-eight

'Mum?'

It was Roxy's voice, all confused and bewildered. That was when Jackie realised who the other women were.

'Ohmygod,' Anna said. The muffled sound of her voice told Jackie that she had her hands over her face, cupping her mouth and nose.

As if a signal had been given, the girls shot to their feet. Instead of approaching the stage they huddled together, retreating back to being their own small family of terrified fifteen-year-olds. The only one who stood apart was Ollie. She moved towards the stage. Reached the front. Looked up at Nikki.

'I prayed for many years that the diamond had helped you get away.'

The women rushed off the stage, as Misty noisily cried, into the waiting arms of their daughters.

Nearly an hour later Jackie and Nikki stood facing each other in the private members' room upstairs. The last hour had been spent with the women explaining what had happened. Lots of crying and jubilation had followed. Then they naturally drifted into groups. Maxine and Roxy. Jasmine and Anna.

Nikki and Jackie. They stood alone by the floor-to-ceiling window, with the black-coated river in the background. With the ten years of life they had lived apart between them.

'What happened to my cuddly little girl?' Nikki finally broke the silence. 'You're all skin and bone.'

Jackie self-consciously folded her arms around her middle. 'I gave up on shoving all those puddings in my face because after you left life weren't so sweet.' As soon as the words were out of her mouth Jackie wanted to take them back. But she couldn't, just as she and her mum couldn't recapture the last decade. Nikki turned to face the river. Then she spoke.

'Sometimes I missed this city so much that I wanted to die thinking I was never gonna see it again. Funny that, because when I lived here most of the time I used to hate it. The damp, the rain, the dark winter evenings. But when I was locked in that prison cell sometimes I would dream about London and its muck and dirt sparkled like diamonds in my mind. But most of the time I'd dream about you. My beautiful little baby. Fifteen years old, a girl ready to step forward as a lady.' Suddenly her voice broke, clogged with remorse. 'I feel so ashamed. Of the life I lived. Of the life I made you live. Why couldn't I be a proper mum and have a job at the checkout at the supermarket? No, I had to be different. If I weren't taking my clothes off, I was ripping people off. Great mum you got, Jade.'

'Yesterday I didn't have a mum,' Jackie cut in quickly. 'Today I have and that's all that matters to me in the world.'

Nikki covered her mouth with the palm of her hand as racking sobs shook her body. Jackie rushed over and wrapped her arms around her in a firm hug. Nikki embraced her and cried like she never wanted to let her go.

'Please forgive me. Forgive me,' she chanted.

'I love you, Mummy, I love you,' Jackie whispered as her mum's hand caressed her hair.

The darkness embraced Frankie like he was already dead in his grave. He was on his knees, his breath ragged as his hands moved quickly with the sharpened end of the pen against the solid wall. He stopped, pulling damp air into his body with a deep breath. He brought the pen close to his eyes. Inspected his handiwork. The end had taken on the shape and sharpness of a knife. He'd learnt that trick the first time he'd been sent to a youth offenders' institute when he was thirteen. He knew that it wouldn't be much longer before they came for him, so now was the time to make his move.

He stood up and moved to the door. Banged on it, yelling. No one came. He kept banging until he heard footsteps outside. A voice shouted, 'Stop making that noise.'

'I need to take a leak, mate.'

'Go ahead and do it.'

'I don't think the ladies are gonna like coming back down here with the place stinking to kingdom come.'

Silence. Then the voice said, 'Step back.'

Frankie shuffled backwards as he shoved the pen up his sleeve. He cupped his cuffed hands close to the sleeves of his jacket. The door opened. The man who had brought him in the car stood in the doorway with his gun pointed at Frankie. The man signalled with the gun for Frankie to come forward. Frankie reached him. The man stepped to the side. Frankie took one step. Two. As he lifted his foot he twisted around and gripped the end of the pen at the same time. Lunged forward before the man had time to react. Shoved the sharpened edge of the pen hard into the man's neck. And twisted. The man groaned as blood spurted in the air, and crumpled to the floor. Frankie fell to his knees besides the man. Frantically felt in his pockets. He stopped when he found what he was looking for. The keys for the handcuffs and for the car. He freed his hands. Turned back to the man. Pulled the gun from his limp fingers. He kicked the man, rolling him until he was deep inside the basement room. Frankie locked the door.

Ran along the corridor, the gun alert in his hand. Reached the stairs. Slowly took them one at a time. Reached the door. With the tips of his fingers he pushed it open. He gulped down a deep breath. As he exhaled he quickly pushed himself outside, swinging the gun around. No one was there. He crept along the corridor towards the front door. He peered outside. No one. He rushed over towards the car. Pulled the keys from his pocket. Opened the door. Jumped inside. He dropped the gun in his lap as he ignited the engine.

*   *   *

Jackie leaned against the back of her front door as soon as she closed it. Exhaustion nearly pushed her to the floor. She was shagged out. Slowly she slid down the door. Hit the floor. She couldn't believe it, her mum was back. She wasn't sure whether she wanted to laugh or cry. She gulped as she pressed her hand against her mouth, thinking of all the years together they'd lost. Then she started to laugh, huge waves of happiness tumbling in the air. She thought about that totally over-the-top white wedding dress she was going to be wearing tomorrow with her mum sitting in the front pew. Finally Jackie Jarvis was getting married. And now nothing and no one was going to stand in her way. No Frankie. No past. No Jade.

She picked herself up and moved towards the main room. She twisted the handle. Pushed the door. Took one step inside. That was when she felt it; another human being was in the room. She flicked the light on.

'Schoolboy,' she breathed with relief.

'I got back early, so I told the babysitter to take the rest of the night off.' He peered hard at her. 'You alright, babe?'

She watched as he picked himself up from the sofa. Suddenly the tiredness came back. The lies she'd told him came back. She knew the time was right. She had to tell him.

She looked him squarely in the face. 'A man's got a right to know who he's marrying. My name ain't Jackie Jarvis. It's Jade Flynn.'

Twenty minutes later Jackie stopped talking. She bit her lip as she anxiously looked at Schoolboy across the kitchen table. During her tale he'd said nothing, and hadn't betrayed what he was feeling through his expression.

'So.' He finally spoke. 'What you're trying to tell me is that I'm getting hitched to someone who's got brown hair, not red.'

Jackie gave him a stunned look. 'You still wanna marry me after what I just told you?'

Instead of answering her he stood up. She felt the tears bubble in her eyes because she knew he was getting ready to go. Why didn't she just keep her soddin' trap shut? Now her future was getting ready to waltz out the door.

'Please don't . . .' she began to beg.

'Get your coat.' His soft command cut across her.

'You what?' she answered in surprise.

'We're going for a little walk.'

'Are you trying to get us shot?'

Jackie flung out her incredulous question in the one place the general population of Hackney made sure they weren't anywhere near come midnight. Cinnamon Junction. The place whose logo was gunplay and death. People used it to quickly hustle from Hackney to Islington, Islington to Hackney. Tonight the junction was deserted except for the occasional car that blew past. Jackie stood with Schoolboy underneath the weak light of a street lamp.

'What are we doing here?' Jackie continued.

'Over here,' Schoolboy answered as he grabbed her hand.

He steered her towards the bus shelter as her eyes darted fretfully around her. Schoolboy sat down on the red plastic bench provided for passengers waiting for the bus. He tugged her hand, making her sit.

'When I needed somewhere to think I used to come here in the early morning. No one, apart from me, had figured out that at that time of the day this place was always quiet. Restful.'

'Well, I don't feel restful,' Jackie said, moving her body defensively closer to his. 'So whatever it is we're doing here let's get it over with and get the f'ing hell outta here.'

'You're not the only one with dirty secrets. You know what type of life I used to live. What I'm about to tell you only my sister and her man know about. Do you remember all those rumours going around about why I had to leave town three years ago?' Jackie nodded. 'The truth is early one morning I came down here to do some thinking. I wanted out of the ugly life I was living and a mate of mine was giving me a golden opportunity to do it. The only problem was I needed some cash and I didn't have none. So I'm walking down here, brain ticking, and do you know what I found over there?' He pointed to a patch of pavement a few metres away from the bus stop.

'A bag of dosh?' she ventured in a small voice.

'A dead body.'

Jackie's indrawn breath slapped against the air, but she said nothing.

'Turkish bloke, mashed up real bad from a mega-beating. Two things I could've done – hightailed it outta here or called the Bill. Do you know what I did instead?' He slid his head sideways to look at her. Their gazes caught and held. 'I went over. Looked him up and down like he was a rival dealer. Then I noticed that one of his trainers had come off. So I was feeling so fucked off with life I booted the trainer. And out bounces this mobile phone. I should've put it back, got on the blower to the cops, but I didn't. All I kept thinking about was selling the phone to make some cash. I kept telling myself it wasn't like that bloke needed it where he was going. So I turned my back and walked away with some dead guy's mobile phone in my pocket.' He switched his face back to the road. But he kept on talking. 'I haven't even got your excuse, no one made me do it. You don't have to ask for my forgiveness. You were a teenager who lost her mum because some villain, who thinks he's an extra in *The Long Good Friday*, decides to set her up. Instead of looking out for you, the authorities let some dodgy social worker dump you in the hands of this gangsta. It ain't your fault you ended up packing drugs and all the other shit you was made to do. And when you scarpered with your mates not one of those people who were meant to be looking after you gave a toss. The only thing I'm angry about is that Ollie didn't blow the balls off this scumbag Frankie Sullivan.'

He picked up her cold palm. Enveloped her fingers with his.

'You're my girl and no matter what happens you always will be. But am I your guy? You sure you wanna hook up with someone who robs dead people?'

She reached her other hand across and rubbed her thumb over his cheek. 'Did you ever go to church when you were little?' she asked him.

'Yeah. My mum used to take me. Why?'

'At the church I went to we always used to light candles underneath the statue of a saint so they could pray for someone you loved. I used to do it for my mum. There ain't much of it left, but I've still got the same candle. I know you ain't no churchgoer any more, but when we get back to my place will you say a prayer with me asking for everything to be alright at our wedding tomorrow?'

Schoolboy let out a long breath. Leaned over and kissed her. He pulled her up and put his arm around her. As they began to walk he asked, 'You know what really frightens the living shit outta me?' She shook her head, her features becoming all serious again. He whispered, 'I'm gonna have a mother-in-law.'

She tutted as she hit him playfully on the arm. Then they both laughed as they melted into London's shadows.

Nikki, Maxine and Jasmine got back to the house in Epping Forest minutes after midnight.

'Are we all agreed that we still wanna do this?' Nikki asked as she cut the engine.

The other two nodded. They all got out of the car. Moved towards the house.

'Look, the door's open,' Jasmine cried out, making the others stop.

'We told Ibrahim to keep everything closed,' Nikki said.

'Something's up,' Maxine added.

They ran towards the house. Bolted down to the basement once they got inside. Their harsh breathing echoed inside the basement corridor as they neared the door. Nikki moved forward to open it.

'Be careful,' Maxine cried.

Nikki twisted the handle and slammed the door back. 'Oh no,' she cried out as she rushed inside. The others quickly followed her in. They all stared, horrified, at Ibrahim's body on the floor. Nikki began to sob as she dropped to her knees beside him. She winced when she saw the pen sticking out of his neck. She felt his pulse.

'He's dead.'

Their collective sobbing filled the air. Ibrahim had been with them almost from the beginning. They had found him begging in one of the crowded marketplaces in Sankura. They had taken him in and he'd become their official bodyguard. When they left Sankura he'd come with them.

'We should've killed that bastard when we had the chance,' Maxine railed.

'What we gonna do?'

Jasmine answered Nikki's question. 'We can't look for him now, we'd never find him. We're gonna have to use some of our contacts here and arrange a hit.'

'But say he turns up at the wedding tomorrow?' The thought that Frankie would turn up at her daughter's wedding pushed the terror deep into Nikki's eyes.

Maxine grabbed her hand. 'Not even Frankie would be stupid enough to pull a stunt like that in a crowded place.'

forty-nine

Frankie knew it was a stupid thing to do but he couldn't help it. Instead of hiding in the car somewhere safe he'd come to the hotel to get one last glimpse of Daisy. He lay low in the driver's seat as he peered at the hotel across the street in the rear-view mirror. There were two other cars stationed outside, which he suspected were the Old Bill waiting for him to pop up. He clutched the gun in his chilled fingers. One last glimpse of Daisy, that was all he needed. Then he would be ready to sort out those bitches once and for all.

Jackie was woken up on her wedding day by a soft, insistent knock at the front door. Drowsily she reached for the clock. After nine. Shit. She leapt out of bed. She should have been up hours ago. Why the hell hadn't Schoolboy woken her up when he'd left, taking Ryan with him, earlier? The knock at the door came again.

'Hold your horses,' she yelled as she jammed her feet into her pink slippers and pulled a long T-shirt over her head. Still struggling with the shirt, she headed for the door. Pulled it open. Stopped dead when she saw Nikki standing there.

'Mum,' she said, flustered. She still couldn't get used to saying it.

'Jade, don't tell me you've just got up?' Nikki said as she bustled inside.

Jade. The name rang in the hallway. She closed the door slowly. She didn't feel like a Jade. Hadn't for ten years. She didn't want to burst her mum's bubble but she was going to have to say something. 'Mum?' she called. Nikki turned to face her. 'I know I'll always be Jade to you, but for today could you just call me Jackie. People might find it funny that you're calling me something else.'

'Oh,' Nikki responded, looking deflated. 'Alright. No problem.'

The years during which they hadn't seen each other stretched uncomfortably between them.

'I blame myself, you know,' Nikki started. 'If only I . . .'

Jackie rushed forward and grabbed her mum's hands. 'We can't go back, Mum. What we've got to be thankful for is that we're back in each other's lives. And nothing is gonna tear us apart again.'

Nikki pulled her into a tight embrace. 'When did my girl get so wise?' she asked against Jackie's neck.

Jackie gently eased back and shyly said, 'Mum, I've got something that I've been hanging onto for you for ten years.'

Ignoring Nikki's puzzled expression, Jackie slowly unclasped her mother's necklace from her neck. She held her hand out, saying, 'Mum, will you wear this today at the wedding?'

'Bloody hell,' Nikki whispered as she stared at the gold chain in Jackie's hand. Her chain with the heart-shaped locket that had been ripped from her throat a decade ago in Sankura.

'I got it repaired and wore it just like you always used to do.'

Nikki slowly took it from her. Her hand curled around it as she said, 'You bet your life I'm gonna be showing it off today.' She swung a happy gaze at her daughter. 'Right, young lady, you are getting hitched today. And I'm gonna make sure that you look like the most beautiful bride there is.'

'But the others are gonna be here soon to get me all ready.'

'No they ain't. Everyone's waiting at the Shim-Sham-Shimmy to spruce you up. Now get your skates on, girl.'

Laughing like a giddy schoolkid, Jackie ran into her bedroom.

Frankie knew if he didn't get out of there soon he was going to get caught. He shifted up. Caught his reflection in the mirror.

Bloodshot eyes, tired skin, the face of a man who hadn't got a wink of sleep and was on the run. He'd stayed awake all night, hoping, just hoping. But he'd seen no sign of Daisy. He wiped his hand over his mouth. Checked the time on the radio clock. Two minutes to eleven. Put the radio on. Hard-hitting techno music boomed in the car. Quickly he turned the volume low. Twisted the dial until he came across a national station that would have the news on in just over a minute. He eased back down. Kept his ear on the radio, his eyes on the hotel through the rear-view mirror. The news flashed on. His breathing pumped low, as he waited to hear if his name was mentioned.

Teenage shooting.

Train strike.

War in the Middle East.

Him.

His breathing switched to shallow gasps.

'Police are warning members of the public not to approach escaped criminal Frankie Sullivan as he is believed to be very dangerous. Frankie Sullivan escaped after . . .'

He jerked his hand through his hair. Knew it was time. Time to get cleaned up so he could attend a wedding.

Stunned silence. That was what greeted Jackie when she walked nervously back into the room on the middle floor of the club. She stared at the people looking at her. Misty. Anna. Roxy. Ollie. Maxine. Jasmine. And Nikki. They all stared back as if this was the first time they'd laid eyes on her. Self-consciously she smoothed her palms down the side of her wedding dress.

'What's the matter? Do I look like mutton dressed up as lamb?'

Nikki stepped towards her. Tears shone in her eyes. She gently grabbed Jackie's hands. 'You look like a princess.'

As if at a signal all the others gathered around her and congratulated her on how she looked. As they laughed, the door opened. Gio came in, dressed in his finest, ready for the wedding. But his face looked serious.

'Miss Misty,' he called.

Quickly Misty moved in her figure-hugging-floor length dress in West Ham Utd colours. Gio whispered in her ear. Misty faced everyone with a skin as pale as Jackie's dress.

'It's just been on the news. Frankie escaped. Someone bailed him out.'

Ollie, Roxy, Anna and Jackie gasped. No one noticed the look that passed between Nikki, Jasmine and Maxine.

'Shit,' Jackie said, her knees feeling weak. 'What if he comes . . . ?'

'He won't.' Misty moved towards Jackie. 'He wouldn't dare. That little toerag is either on a plane to Brazil or under a stone somewhere. They'll pick him up. Now come on, we've got a wedding to go to.'

Jackie glanced quickly at her three friends. 'Me and the girls just want a couple of minutes together.' She rushed over to her mum and gave her a gentle kiss on the cheek. 'I'll see you at the church. Misty, why don't you check that the limousine's on its way. Let us know when it's arrived.'

A few seconds later the four women were alone. They stared at each other, the silence growing like an uninvited guest in the room.

Ollie broke the silence. 'He's coming after us.'

Frankie parked the motor on the street running adjacent to St Matilda's church. Checked over his appearance in the overhead mirror. He'd managed to clean himself up in a public toilet earlier on. Next he checked the number of bullets in the magazine of his gun. Jammed it back into place. Got out and began to walk. As he passed a pretty, well-kept house, he plucked a rose from its hedge. Fixed it into the buttonhole of his jacket. The church was open with people already going inside as he reached it. He kept his head down as he entered. The church was packed. He found a seat in the middle row, at the end, next to a pillar. Picked up a hymn book resting on the pew. Opened it up and concealed his gun inside.

*   *   *

Suddenly Ollie started to move towards a cupboard in a corner. She bent low as she opened it. She pulled out a black rucksack. Dave's rucksack. Dropped it onto a table.

The others gathered around.

She unzipped the bag. Tipped the contents onto the table.

Four guns.

now

JaDE & JacKiE

fifty

Jackie and her bridesmaids stared at their guns.

Uzi.

Pistol.

Revolver.

MAC-10.

Jackie dragged her gaze away from the weapons. Stared directly at her three friends. Roxy. Anna. Ollie. Finally broke the silence.

'Ollie's right, he's coming to get us, I know he is. And we can't take the chance that he might not come to the church.' She stopped. Her tongue did a nervous flick across her lips. 'If you want out, now's the time to say it.'

Once again, she gazed at her friends.

'I'm in,' Ollie said calmly.

'So am I,' Roxy added.

'You know me, girl.' Anna gave Jackie a half-smile. 'I'm always in.'

Jackie nodded. 'OK, this is the set-up. Anna and Roxy, there's no need for you two to be tooled up. But as soon as we hit the church you both become our eyes. Check the place over, up and down, to see if he's there.'

'And if he is?' Anna cut in.

The glow in Jackie's green eyes became grim. 'If that bastard has the brass balls to gatecrash my wedding . . .' She stopped. Eyeballed the guns. 'Me and Ollie will have no choice but to blow him away.'

They all looked at Ollie. She ran her gaze over the guns. Reached over. Made her choice. Picked up the double-action pistol. Shoved it inside the bouquet she held in her hand. Now they all looked at Jackie. She took a deep breath. Leaned forward. Made her choice. Plucked up the compact revolver.

'Anna, hide the other shooters,' Jackie commanded as she stepped back from the table. She moved quickly. Towards a chair. Lifted her right leg. Placed her white satin shoe on the seat. Her dress made a whooshing sound as she bunched it up. Past her ankle. Over her calf muscle. To the top of her thigh. Until her white stockinged leg and electric-blue garter gleamed in the midday light. She stretched the garter with one hand. Placed the gun between it and her thigh. Shivered as the coolness of the metal settled against her skin.

'Sweet Jesus, Mother Mary and all the saints,' she whispered. Then she gently placed the garter back in place.

She moved towards the free-standing mirror, walking in the shaft of sunlight that hit the room. She gazed at her white reflection. Sighed. This should've been the happiest day of her life. The others quickly gathered around her. Stared tensely at their own reflections. They wore sky-blue A-line, above the knee, bridesmaids' dresses, and claret heels, the colours of Jackie's favourite footie team, West Ham United.

'Whatever happens,' Ollie said as her hand tightened on her bouquet. 'Always remember that we're family. We came into this together and we'll come out of it together.'

They remained silent as they stared at their collective reflections like it was the last picture they would ever take together.

'OK, ladies,' Jackie said. 'It's time to rock 'n' roll.'

They moved. Towards the door. The door opened just before they reached it. In the doorway stood Misty. She gave Jackie an ecstatic, proud smile. 'Sweetheart, you look like a flamin' angel.'

Jackie's wedding dress whispered as she moved to meet Misty. Misty crooked her arm. Jackie slid her arm into Misty's. Smiled. Misty kissed her on the cheek. Then they turned. Stepped out of the door. The gun on her thigh began to warm up against her skin.

*   *   *

'Ready?'

Jackie nodded at Misty as they stood on the threshold of the church where the packed crowd waited inside. Her right hand tightened on Misty's sleeve. Her left hand smoothed along her dress, feeling the outline of the gun. She took a deep breath. Held it. Stepped forward. Exhaled. The organ started to play West Ham United's theme song. The congregation turned around, watching Jackie coming down the aisle, as they began to sing.

> *'I'm forever blowing bubbles.*
> *Pretty bubbles in the air . . .'*

The song bounced with a rowdy, jubilant quality that any Hammers fanatic would be proud of. Ryan, decked out in claret trousers and jacket and blue waistcoat, blew bubbles at his mum at she passed by. Jackie gave him a reassuring, shaky smile as a wet bubble burst against her veil. She quickly looked away, her gaze searching the crowd. For him. Frankie.

She checked the faces of the crowd on the left as the pulse of the singing swayed higher.

> *'They fly so high, nearly reach the sky . . .'*

Checked right.

> *'Then like my dreams they all fade and die . . .'*

She blew out a deep, low breath because there was no sign of him. Her face lit up into a cheek-popping smile. She fixed her eyes straight ahead. Onto the man she was about the marry. *Everything's gonna be alright; everything's gonna be alright*, she chanted in her head as she moved. Finally she reached Schoolboy, as the crowd raised the roof with the song's final line.

> *'Pretty bubbles in the air.'*

Schoolboy lifted her veil. Touched her face. His hand fell away as Father Tom began. 'Dearly beloved . . .'

Yeah, everything was gonna be alright.

Fifteen minutes later the priest announced, 'I now pronounce you husband and wife.' Jackie stared up at Schoolboy, the gun at her thigh forgotten. His hand slid to her face. Pulled her forward. Gave her the biggest smacker she'd ever had. The crowd wolf-whistled and clapped. A camera flashed.

Bang.

A gunshot ripped through the air.

Someone screamed. Jackie knew it wasn't her. Schoolboy clung to her. Pressed her close. Then his arms fell away. He staggered back. Her head flopped down to stare at her wedding dress. To stare at the blood splashed across it. Her knees began to buckle as the blood began to spread.

Chaos erupted inside the church. Screams echoed as people leapt over the pews and began ducking and diving in a desperate attempt to get outside. Jackie straightened, transfixed by the blood on her dress. She felt no pain, which was really strange if she'd been shot. Her head came up to find Schoolboy looking at her. Instead of moving towards her he swayed. Then she caught the shock and surprise bulging in his eyes. He began to fall at the same time as she realised the truth. The blood on her dress wasn't hers, it was his. Schoolboy hit the floor. That was when she began moving towards him.

A whoosh of air swept inside as the doors were finally opened, allowing the terrified congregation to make their escape. As Jackie crouched by Schoolboy she desperately searched the fleeing crowd, trying to find Ryan. She looked left, right, up, down. She couldn't find him.

'Jackie.' Two voices screamed the warning at her in unison. Quickly she turned to find Misty and Nikki shouting at her. Another shot cracked in the air, making them stop in their tracks. Misty grabbed Nikki's arm and dragged her behind a pew.

'Get Ryan outta here,' she shouted back. She saw Misty and her mum rush towards the door as she jerked around to look at

Schoolboy. His chest was barely moving. No way could she leave him. She heard another shot. Flicked her head up to find Ollie holding her gun with both hands aimed at a pillar. No one needed to tell Jackie who her friend was aiming at. Frankie. She saw his head dart out. Then back in. The nozzle of his gun peeped out. aiming straight at Ollie.

'Ollie, for fuck's sake get down,' Jackie yelled.

Ollie dropped down at the same time as Frankie's shot rang out. Jackie hiked up her dress. Found the gun at her garter. As she raised the gun Schoolboy moaned. Breathing hard, she turned back to him. Felt the pulse in his neck. Faint, and she suspected fading. She knew she had to make a decision – whether to use her gun to try and wipe Frankie out or to help her new husband. Schoolboy let out a long, tortuous groan that made the decision for her.

She dropped the gun on the floor. Crawled on her hands and knees towards his head. Locked her arms under his armpits and began to drag him. She grunted, strained, as the burden of his dead weight was almost too much to bare. She stopped, her head dipping as more shots tore up the air. Suddenly the shots stopped coming from Ollie's direction.

'Jesus, Mother Mary and all the saints, please, not Ollie,' she whispered in prayer. She dragged Schoolboy with renewed anger and desperation. Silence. Then she heard them. Footsteps. Coming towards her. Like a madwoman she kept dragging Schoolboy. The footsteps got closer. She kept moving. The footsteps stopped. A shadow fell over her. She stopped moving. Her breathing came in shattered shallow beats as her gaze staggered up the figure looming over her. Frankie. She gasped when she realised that his gun wasn't pointed at her. It was pointed at the person he held tight against his chest.

Ryan.

'Mum,' Ryan sobbed.

Jackie shot to her feet, almost tripping as the shock unbalanced her. Frankie pushed the gun harder against the boy's skull.

'Don't do it,' Jackie begged.

'Revenge. Ain't it a bitch.' He echoed the words she and the others had written on the card Misty had delivered to the court. 'I told you who was gonna have to pay the price if you tried to fuck me over.' Ryan whimpered as Frankie's arm tightened around him.

'Please.' Jackie's arms stretched towards her son.

Frankie smirked at her. Suddenly he dropped Ryan from his arms. The boy scrambled to his mum. She enfolded him in her embrace, shielding his head against her bloody wedding dress.

'Nothing like seeing a happy family. Mum, son, hubbie, although the way he's leaking he'll be brown bread within ten minutes. Now all we're missing is granny . . .'

'Put it down,' a voice yelled.

They swung around in the direction of the command to find Ollie pointing her gun at Frankie.

'You heard what I said.' Ollie stepped out from behind the pew.

'Go ahead, shoot me,' Frankie taunted her.

Jackie gripped Ryan's hand. She watched Ollie as she took another step towards them. But she didn't press the trigger. Instead her hand shook.

'You can't, can you?' Frankie said. 'Because you've run out of bullets. That's why you stopped shooting at me.'

Ollie gulped as she slowly lowered her gun.

'I should really pay you back the compliment you paid me all those years ago.' His gun shifted down, aimed at her right leg. 'But I'm gonna let you use your legs to walk out of here. Find Nikki Flynn and tell her that her presence is requested at our special family reunion. Tell if she doesn't attend the next time she sees her precious daughter and grandson they will be riddled with holes.'

But Ollie didn't move. She stood her ground. Frankie swiftly turned and aimed the gun at Ryan's head.

'Do what he says,' Jackie shouted.

Finally Ollie followed his instruction.

'Who's gonna burn a candle for you when you're gone?' Frankie taunted Jackie.

'Let my boy go.'

'And miss our little intimate party? I don't think so.'

'Please.'

Frankie widened his stance. 'That double-cross you lot did with the kidnapping was clever. But stupid because I'm the one now standing here with the gun pointing in your face . . .'

'You're a dead man, Frankie,' a voice said behind him.

Swiftly he turned around as Jackie looked over his head to find Nikki walking calmly and empty-handed down the aisle.

'Well, well, well, if it isn't the very dead Nikki Flynn,' Frankie taunted as he trained the gun on her.

He waved the gun at her, indicating she should stand with her daughter and grandson.

'You alright, baby?' Nikki whispered to Jackie once she reached her.

Jackie gave her a curt nod.

'There ain't any Old Bill here yet, Frankie,' Nikki said softly. 'You can still get away.'

'What, and miss the party with my two favourite girls?' He let out a humourless laugh.

'I don't think so.' He fixed his gaze directly onto Jackie. 'You wanna know how I managed to escape yesterday, why don't you ask your dear old mum.'

Nikki said nothing.

'Well, it looks like I'll have to tell you, then. After she and her mates topped Jason and Finlay,' Jackie gave him an incredulous look, 'they still had to deal with me. Not trusting Her Majesty's justice system they busted me out so that they could administer justice their own way . . .'

A cry from Schoolboy made them all look at him. Ryan pulled himself away from Jackie and before she could stop him he had run over to his new stepfather. He crouched down by Schoolboy and held his hand. Sirens ripped the air outside.

'I think the time for talking is over,' Frankie said. 'It's time to make sure you two never interrupt my life again.'

Frankie raised the gun. Pointed it at Nikki. He smiled. His finger curved around the trigger. A blast shook the church as a bullet slammed into Frankie's chest, spraying blood across the pews behind him. As he toppled, Nikki and Jackie twisted around. The blast of the gun he held in his hands, which he'd found on the floor next to Schoolboy's body, had laid Ryan flat on his back.

fifty-one

'I've already told you, I don't know nothin' about that dead guy at my wedding.'

Jackie sat, hand tense around a lukewarm cup of coffee, opposite the plainclothed policewoman from the murder squad. She still wore her bloody wedding dress, but with a jacket someone had draped around her to keep her warm. Jackie couldn't remember the policewoman's name. Couldn't remember how long they'd been sitting in the tiny room. All she could remember was Frankie's gun, Schoolboy's blood and her son lying on his back with a smoking shooter in his hand. Her son had killed Frankie. The pain tore inside her chest. This was all her fault. Schoolboy was going to die because of her. Ryan was going to be . . . Jackie squeezed the thought back. The policewoman sent her a reassuring look. 'I don't believe that any more than you do, Mrs Campbell . . .'

'It's Jarvis. Ms Jarvis. We agreed that I wouldn't change my name. Mind you, that ain't gonna matter soon, is it, because I know that Schoolboy's gonna die . . .' The sobs erupted from her. Her hand left the cup to cover her mouth.

The policewoman gave her a few minutes to compose herself. Then stretched her hands across the table. 'It's just me and you, Jackie. I haven't got a tape on. You're not under caution. I've been in this game for twenty-odd years and I know when someone's holding back on me. So why don't you tell me what really happened.'

Jackie took an unsteady gulp from the cup. Kept her hands tight around it as she began to talk. 'Alright, but you ain't gonna believe the truth either. Ten years ago I was fifteen years old. My mum and two other women were on death row in Sankura. I ended up in a home called St Nicholas, with three other girls. That's where I met this geezer called Frankie Sullivan . . .'

For the next half-hour she haltingly told the policewoman everything. Well, almost everything. The diamonds and her mum's resurrection were strictly no one else's business.

'That's the God honest truth,' Jackie finally finished.

'If I remember right, there was an investigation at the St Nicholas care home in Chingford after the director was arrested on child abuse charges. Why didn't you come to us?'

'We were frightened. I've been beaten, half suffocated, had a gun put to my head, watched as a mate was hung out of the window when she was fifteen years old. When we did a bunk ten years ago, you wanna know who came looking for us? No one. Not anyone from my school, the social services, the Bill.'

Embarrassment stained the policewoman's face. Jackie carried on talking. 'No one gave a bollocks if we were alive or dead. But you know what, I think we were the lucky ones. Children were beaten and abused in that home. We managed to get away, they didn't. We were on our own and that's how we've played life ever since. We ain't done nothin, but . . .' Her mouth wobbled. 'My Ryan has. All I wanna know is whether you're gonna charge him with . . .' The words stopped as the tears gushed out again.

'Jackie, I . . .'

The door opened, stopping the other woman's words. A male doctor stood in the doorway of the hospital room. Jackie shot to her feet when she saw the expression on his face.

'Schoolboy?' she pushed out.

The doctor's face became solemn. Jackie rushed past him, out of the door.

'What you trying to do? Turn my hair white overnight?' Jackie grasped Schoolboy's hand as she sat on the edge of the bed. An avalanche of tears streamed down her face. Her new husband lay on the bed, looking weak and drawn. But alive. His hand squeezed hers back.

'I wish I could sit up and wipe the tears from your eyes,' he told her in a weak voice. Her open palm wiped her face. 'This is all my fault . . .'

'You put a sock in it right now. Only one person who's to blame and he's brown bread. He can't hurt you no more.'

'You're gonna be alright. The bullet didn't hit any vital organs, so hopefully you can come home soon.'

'What did you tell the cops?'

'It was time for the truth. No more lies and deception. But I never told them about our mums, so as far as they're concerned Nikki was just a woman who was in the right place at the wrong time. All I can do is pray that everyone keeps their mouth shut about Ollie and the gun. But Ryan . . .' The tears started falling again from her crumpled face.

'Come here,' Schoolboy said softly.

He wrapped his arms tight around her as she cried against his chest. 'Sh. Everything's gonna work out, babe . . .'

'We're gonna have a baby,' Jackie gushed out between her tears.

Schoolboy said nothing, but his arms tightened around her. They stayed like that, holding each other tight, until they heard footsteps next to the bed. Jackie pulled herself straight when she saw the policewoman.

'I've spoken to your three bridesmaids who confirm your story, so this is what I'm gonna do.' Jackie held her breath. 'Frank Sullivan was on the run, a desperate man. As you know, we've been after him for a long time and now he's gone. Case closed.'

'Ryan?'

'Was placed in the terrible position of seeing an escaped criminal attacking his mother. He picked up the gun with only one intention – to save his mother. And that's what happened. So I don't see the need to investigate this any further. But when you've finished here, if you and your son could come to the station to make a statement . . .'

Jackie rapidly nodded. The policewoman turned around, heading for the door. As she reached it she stopped. 'Just out of interest, how is it that you all own that club in Wapping?'

Jackie gave her guarded look. 'Misty won the lottery ten years ago.'

'Ten years ago? What a coincidence.' She gave Jackie a small smile. 'Let's hope her luck rubs off on me when I check my numbers tonight.'

She left them. Jackie swung back to Schoolboy. 'Shit, do you think . . . ?'

'All the cops have ever wanted was Frankie Sullivan. Now they've got him. Game over. Why don't you tell everyone else to come in?'

'I love you,' Jackie said before she rushed for the door. The first person inside was Ryan, who flew into his mum's arms. Soon the room was spilling over with people. Misty. Ollie. Roxy. Anna. Nikki. Maxine. Jasmine. All the people Jackie loved most in this world.

fifty-two

A week later Jackie sat with Ryan and Schoolboy watching Whacky and Mojo on the box. It was a repeat of the series about a girl with magical powers in which the men played two time-travelling gangsters. She smiled at her new family unit. Schoolboy's wound had healed very quickly but he still needed heaps of bed rest. The policewoman had kept her word and left them alone after they'd made their statements down the nick. Sometimes she still couldn't believe that Frankie Sullivan was finally out of their lives.

The doorbell rang, interrupting her thoughts. She shoved her hand through her hair as she headed for the door. A huge smile danced on her lips when she saw who it was.

'Mum.' She launched herself into Nikki's arms.

They'd both spent the last month finding time to get to know each other all over again. Nikki stepped inside.

'I'm not stopping,' she said.

The smile fell from Jackie's face. She knew that it was finally time for her mum to go.

'Hey,' Nikki said, caressing Jackie's cheek. 'Don't give me that sad look. Switzerland isn't that far away. Come over anytime.'

'I wish you could stay here.'

Nikki shook her head. 'England ain't my manor any more. Besides . . .' Nikki gave her a timid grin. 'My husband is desperate for me to come home.'

'You sure you wanna stay with this Omote fella?'

'He loves me and I love him in my way. We just understand each other.'

They stood there is silence, looking at each other.

Suddenly a serious look swept over Nikki's face. 'I've got to tell you about Jason and Finlay and why we . . .'

Jackie stretched across and placed a finger against her mum's lips. 'You ain't gotta tell me nothin'. If anyone had done to Ryan what they did to me I would've done the same thing in your place. All that matters is that we're a family again.'

Nikki's hand slipped over Jade's still-flat tummy. 'You know why I called you Jade? Because you were the brightest and most precious thing in my life. And you still are.' Her hand dropped away. 'Where's that other grandchild of mine and Schoolboy?'

Smiling, Jackie led her to the main room. 'Look who's here.'

Jackie's mobile rang on the table as Nikki walked into the room. Jackie took her mobile out of the room. 'Yeah?'

'It's Bell Dream.'

Jackie's heart jumped. 'Is Anna alright?'

'She's fine. I just wondered if you've got some time to come to my office today.'

'Sure,' she replied with unease. 'What's going on?'

'Here's my address,' the other woman replied, not answering Jackie's question.

Jackie got to Bell Dream's office later that afternoon. The only person there was a woman who Jackie assumed was Bell's PA.

'Ms Jarvis,' the woman said as soon as she saw Jackie, standing up.

She shook Jackie's hand. 'What's all this about?' Jackie asked as soon as she got her hand back.

'Let me take you through.'

The PA led Jackie into a smart-looking room with fantastic views across the city. Bell sat behind her desk.

'Jackie,' she said, extending her hand.

As Jackie took it she thought there was a whole lotta shaking hands going on but no answers to her questions. Bell waved for Jackie to take a seat.

'How's your son and . . . ?'

'What's going on?' Jackie cut across her.

Bell pulled open her drawer and drew out a tan-coloured document wallet. She flipped it open. Pulled out a white envelope. 'This is for you.' She leaned over the desk and held out the envelope. Jackie looked at it suspiciously. Then took it. Looked at it again. No writing on the front.

'Who's it from?' She lifted her eyes back to the other woman.

For the first time Jackie saw Bell rub her lips together in a nervous gesture. Then she composed herself. Linked her fingers together on the desk. Finally she answered Jackie's question.

'Frank Sullivan.'

'You what? You think I look crackers or something?' Jackie stormed, letting the envelope fly onto the table as if it had been burning her skin. She jumped up, picked up her bag and said, 'I'm outta here.'

'Jackie, please.' The solicitor's plea stopped Jackie in her tracks. Left her shaking one inch from the door. One inch from giving Frankie the finger one final triumphant time. 'Just read it and then if you decide you want to go I won't stop you.'

Jackie remained immobile. Felt the beat of her heart all over her body. Then she turned back around. She wasn't sure what made her do it. Curiosity? The desperation in Bell's voice?

'Alright, I'll read it, but remember this, whatever it says I ain't stopping after I've read it.'

She sat back down. Picked up the envelope. Slid her finger along the top. Tore it open. She pulled out what was inside. A single piece of A4 paper, folded three times. She unfolded it. A letter. Black ballpoint ink against a white background.

Dear Jade

Don't know if I ever told you about my little Daisy. She's 15 years old, has dimples, loves bubbles in her bath and first wrote her name in joined up writing when she was 6 years old. She don't have no one left in the world. Now I don't need to tell you what that means. If they get their mitts on

*her, they'll put her in the system. Just like me and you. I
know that you hate my guts, I would in your position. But
don't let them take her. Don't let them do to her what they
did to me. Only one person can stop that happening and
that's you.*

*Don't tell Daisy too much about me. The only thing I ask
is when you think she's ready get her to light a candle for
me.*

Frankie

Only when Jackie noticed the tear stain on the letter did she realise
she was crying. She shook her head, using one hand to wipe the tears
from her face, and said, 'The world's a better place without Frankie
Sullivan. I can't do this . . .'

'After what he did at your wedding I nearly threw his letter away. I
didn't want to bring any more trouble to your door. But then I
realised that this isn't my decision, it's yours.'

'He tried to kill me and my mates, including your girl. Kill our
mums. Kill my fella. Made a killer of my son. No.' She shot to her feet
and began backing away from Bell 'He ain't gonna control my life
from beyond the grave. I'm sorry.'

Bell gave her an understanding nod. Her mind twisting in turmoil,
Jackie opened the door. As soon as she stepped outside it wasn't the
PA's face she saw but that of a girl sitting still on a sofa. She knew
who the girl was instantly, remembering her face from the photo
she'd nicked from Frankie's wallet. Even if she'd never seen the
photo she would have known the girl anywhere. Frankie's blue eyes
stared back at her. Daisy sat there, looking pale and drawn, her face
the mask of someone who'd lost someone close to her. The look of
complete abandonment on the child's face reminded her of being
fifteen years old.

'Miss, do you wanna tissue?' Daisy asked.

Jackie touched her face and realised that she was still silently
crying. Daisy dug into her pocket. Pulled out a small packet of
tissues. Held one out to Jackie.

'You can have it. I've got lots more left.'

Jackie said a quick silent prayer. She wanted to turn her back. Keep walking. But she couldn't. She walked over. 'Thanks,' she said, and smiled as she took the offered tissue. 'You look like you've been crying as well?'

Daisy shrugged. 'Yes. My dad ain't coming home any more. I've been staying with Ms Dream, but she says that I'm going to live somewhere else soon.'

Jackie's heart did a painful lurch. She turned to look at Bell, who stood in the doorway. 'If I took her, what would I have to do?'

'Just sign some documents which make you her legal guardian.'

'Can me and Daisy have a couple of minutes on our own?'

Bell signalled for her PA to join her in her office.

Jackie sat down gently beside Daisy. The girl looked at her with tears brimming in her eyes. 'I ain't got a mum and my dad ain't coming home.'

Jackie slid her arm around her. Let the girl lean her head on her shoulder. 'I know. My mum was gone for a long time and I missed her so much. My name's Jackie and Ms Dream wants to know if it's alright to take you home?'

As Jackie carried on talking, neither of them noticed when Bell quietly closed the door.

A Dark Redemption

Stav Sherez

It's not always easy trying to decide what to read when you've finished a book you've loved.

So we asked Dreda Say Mitchell to recommend a book she loves and that you might enjoy next – *A Dark Redemption* by Stav Sherez.

Simply turn the page to start reading the first chapter...

A Dark Redemption introduces DI Jack Carrigan and DS Geneva Miller as they investigate the brutal rape and murder of a young Ugandan student. Plunged into an underworld of illegal immigrant communities, they discover that the murdered girl's studies at a London College may have threatened to reveal things that some people will go to any lengths to keep secret...

Unflinching, inventive and intelligent, *A Dark Redemption* explores a sinister case that will force DI Carrigan to face up to his past and DS Miller to confront what path she wants her future to follow.

They came more often now, the headaches. Raging storms within his skull, crippling pain, flashes of light. There was nothing to do but shut his eyes and lie back, let the pain and visions take over.

Memories and flashbacks trailed the headaches. Jack would close his eyes and see blue sky, green jungle, red road. He would try to watch the trees outside his window divesting themselves of leaves, the slow spinning fall of September, but instead he saw the leaves of the jungle, leaves so big you could sit inside them and be wholly encased, leaves which vibrated and twitched and reacted to your presence as if sentient beings.

They'd arrived in the middle of a heat wave. David buckled as he exited the plane, feet planted on the stairway, the sun leaching all colour and breath from his face. He stood there and took in the burned yellow country in front of him then turned back into the plane as if the pilot had made a mistake, but Jack was right there, taking his arm, leading him back out into the light, whispering in his ear *We're here*.

They deplaned onto the gleaming cracked tarmac, the customs hall five hundred feet away, shimmering like a mirage in the heat. The other passengers rushed past them, pushing, elbows out, as if there were a prize for the first to get to the hall.

They walked as slowly as they could, savouring the air, the unfamiliar sky – those first moments when you land in a new country and feel a sudden quickening, a snapcharge rattling through your bones.

Their friends were in India, Peru, Vietnam. They were sitting on beaches, cocktails in hand, watching the surf break against the sand, waiting for the night, the drugs, the screaming music and torrential sex.

'Everybody goes there,' Jack had protested after David suggested a trip down the Ganges. 'We'll be on a boat in the middle of nowhere and we'll bump into everyone we know.'

It had been the afternoon of their graduation. They still wore the robes and mortars, still wore the smiles they'd flashed for the cameras, degrees in hand, or parents held close, each trying to outgrin the other. Now the parents were gone, the degrees stuffed into a desk somewhere, the beer and cigarettes flowing.

'Jack's right,' Ben replied, sipping a pint, his fingers playing with an unlit cigarette. Unlike Jack and David, Ben had worn a proper suit underneath the gown and now seemed out of place and out of age in this noisy student pub. 'We might as well stay here as go to India.'

'Just because everyone goes there doesn't mean it's a bad idea.' David slumped back into the booth, his hair draped like a shawl around his shoulders, the button-down shirt and drainpipe jeans a strange contrast with those long black locks.

'Doesn't mean it's a good one either,' Ben replied as he spread out a map of the world in front of them.

Jack moved the glasses away so they could have more room. 'Uganda.' He pointed to a bright orange square halfway up the map. 'Cheap, safe, guaranteed sun, and no chance of bumping into anyone we know.'

2

They stared at it as if ensnared, the mass of multicoloured land that delineated the African continent, the regimented lines of borders, the names of countries they hadn't even known existed until they saw them printed on the map.

That was all the decision there was to it. David, as usual, acquiesced. That they would be together was more important than where they went. They all knew this would be the last time. Summer was approaching fast and then would come autumn and jobs and careers and the beginning of something, the end of something else.

They went through customs without a hitch. They caught a cab and threaded through sunburned fields, the driver speaking English so fast and fractured he sounded like a man drowning. They nodded their heads, mustered an appropriate *yeah* every now and then, but their faces were turned away, staring through the grimy windows, watching the plains of East Africa roll by, a landscape of tall grasses and spindly trees, skeletal cattle and dark beckoning mountains punctuating the distant horizon.

Jack rubbed his head and stared out into the London night remembering the tumult of sense and smell and noise as they entered Kampala. His headache began to recede as he let the memories flicker and spin. He remembered David exiting the taxi, bending down and vomiting in the street, his skin pallid as a corpse. Jack had crossed over to a stall, kids instantly surrounding him, their little hands waving and clutching cheap plastic objects he couldn't make sense of, old boxes of matches and photocopied pictures of Michael Jackson. He bought three warm Cokes and came back to find Ben handing out crumpled banknotes to the bright-eyed and smiling children.

They sat on their backpacks and drank the Coke, warm and sickly sweet, and it was the best Coke they'd ever tasted.

The kids delighted them even though they could see beyond the smiles and welcomes to the grinding poverty which underlay their lives. There were always more kids, more hands outstretched; what they asked for was so little in English money that it seemed mean to deny them, but then you found all your time being taken by handing out money and you forgot to look up at the buildings, the sky, the trees, the surly young men lounging on every street corner.

They all went through it once: tears, jags of self-pity, wanting desperately to go home – even Ben, who'd travelled almost everywhere by the time he'd got to university. 'Just good ol' culture shock,' Jack quipped after Ben had come back from the hostel toilet having found it overflowing, an army of cockroaches big as baby shoes swarming over the bowl. When they lay down on their pillows that evening they could smell other men's nights, puke and booze and blood.

'I think we should pick up the car and get out of here,' Jack suggested on the third day.

They paid twice what they'd agreed for the car back home but it was still cheap – they still thought in English money – and though the car, an old white Honda Civic, looked like it would fall apart at the first kick of the engine, it managed to glide effortlessly through the cracked and teeming streets of the capital.

They took the Masaka–Kampala Road west out of the city. In less than ten minutes the concrete gave way to flat pastureland, dry and cracked, small villages everywhere, circular patterns of daub-and-wattle huts just visible on the side of the highway. The road was empty apart from army vehicles blazing down the fast lane, young soldiers bumping along in the beds of open-backed trucks, their eyes lazily drifting to the three white boys and then back to their cigarettes.

They made a detour down to the shores of Lake Victoria and ate fruit and crackers as the sun flashed along the calm surface of the water and Ben explained the history and naming of the lake, the great foolish Victorians with their hats and pomp and retinue of carriers and servants.

Jack suggested they head for Murchison Falls national park, the name a siren song to him, its grandiloquence and archaic quality like something out of a Sherlock Holmes novel.

'We could just stay in Masaka and check out the Ruwenzoris.' Ben was consulting their second-hand guide book. 'What's so special about Murchison Falls?'

'I love the way it sounds,' Jack replied, seduced as always by the poetry of place names, the worlds conjured up by phonetic accident.

'That's why you want to go there?' David had the gift of always sounding flabbergasted, surprised at the world in all its variance, an antidote to their measured and unearned cynicism.

The waters of Lake Victoria glowed like polished glass. 'Forget the guide book,' Jack replied, staring out towards the dark shadowed rim of the horizon, 'let's just start driving.'

Ben and David exchanged a glance that reflected years of growing up together, sharing hidden jokes, conspiring against parents – and agreed, but Ben kept the guide book safely in his bag just in case.

They backtracked and took the highway north, watching the land change. The fields and crops and empty plains gave way to more rugged terrain; mountains loomed out of the sky and disappeared; the road deteriorated until it was only a narrow lane. The heat became worse, not just sun striking the roof of the car, but a deeper denser heat, a humidity they'd never experienced before, a rottenness in the air that crept into your bones and brain, making your eyes water and the breath die in your throat.

Sweet potato and maize fields stretched out either side of them, dry and willowy in the early-evening heat haze. Termite mounds stood ten feet tall, skyscrapers among the cornstalks and grasses, like totem poles from another race, the tenements of a forgotten people.

The town of Masindi appeared out of nowhere. One minute they were driving the dirt road, yellow fields bordering them on both sides, and the next they were on a dusty corrugated street with white single-storey buildings, women carrying baskets on their heads, kids and more kids, the whole African movie-trailer cliché right before their eyes.

They stopped for beer and food at a tiny stall still bearing the name of the Asian proprietor who'd established it before being expelled by Idi Amin in '72. The old man, the new owner, served them warm Niles, the slogan 'The true reward of progress' making David chuckle as he swigged the sweet beer.

They watched cars go by leaving trails of dust in the air. Far-off volcanoes shimmered on the horizon like things unsubstantial and contingent. Children came and held their palms out, smiled, laughed and danced on the spot as Ben handed them money.

They sat in the rear of the cafe washing the dust and heat from their bodies, glad for the stillness after eight hours of bad road. Murchison wasn't far, another few hours' drive north; they'd stay in Masindi for the night, it was decided, and head there tomorrow.

'I still can't believe it.' David was sitting under a palm tree, peeling the label off a bottle of Nile. 'Being here, I mean.'

'Remember how much we talked about it?' Ben leant forward, spilling ash over the table. It had been their only topic of discussion these last few months, cramming for exams, finishing their dissertations, the horizon of the holiday the one bright thing to look forward to, the question of where to go burning in their minds.

David finished off his beer. 'The three of us here, together.' He paused so they could all savour this. A shadow briefly crossed his face. He stared at the thin tapering road. 'Who knows where we'll be this time next year.'

'I think Jack's got a pretty good idea,' Ben smiled, his teeth shining white in the sun.

Jack looked off into the distance, the volcanoes smoky and out of focus like cheap back-projections in a pre-war movie. 'I wish I did,' he replied, thinking back to the day, three weeks ago, when he'd broken the news. At first, he'd wanted to keep it secret, alternately proud and a little ashamed of his good luck, the way you always are with close friends. But they'd got drunk one evening, another in a long line of housemates' birthday parties, and he told them about the deal: three albums, a decent amount of money, a cool London-based record label.

'I wish it felt real. I wish it felt like something I could celebrate, but I keep thinking I'll come back and find a letter apologising for the mistake they've made.' Jack focused on the table, the empty green bottles like soldiers standing silent sentry.

Ben clapped him on the back, gave him one of those Ben smiles they all knew, the smile that had got them girls, entry to parties, whatever they'd desired. 'Nonsense. Too late for that, it's coming out next month.'

'September,' Jack corrected him, his legs shivering despite the humidity. Only a couple of months to go until the album was in the shops, on the radio. It felt too surreal, too weird, to accept as fact. It had been only a dream for so long that its reality seemed conjured from nothing but wish and desire. He'd made the album, just like he'd made the ones which preceded it, in his room on a four-track. He'd laid down the guitars, vocals and drum machine himself. He'd sent it out like he'd sent the countless tapes before, but this time the record company had got back to him; a man with a silly accent raving and ranting about how Jack was going to be the next big thing. He'd travelled down to London, signed the deal in a Soho restaurant and was back in Manchester in time to finish his exams.

'To *Top of the Pops*!' David held his bottle up, Jack and Ben crashed theirs against it, the clink and scrape amplified in the still air.

'Yeah, as if . . .' Jack finished off his beer. He got up and went to get the next round. He thought about his songs on the radio, tentacles reaching out of the speakers and into the ears of listeners – and then he shut the thought down, knowing the dangers that lurked in daydreams. It was just a small release on a tiny label, nothing to get excited about, the first rung of many.

Still, as he took the beers, the cool glass sweet against his palms, he couldn't help but feel that things were coming together for the first time, that his life was at last taking some kind of shape and that he was here doing exactly what he wanted to be doing with exactly the two people he wanted to be doing it with.

He noticed that something had changed when he came back out with the drinks. Ben and David were sitting silently, their eyes fixed on the opposite side of the road. He sat next to them, doled out the beers, was about to say something when Ben's expression stopped him, made him look across the street.

Two policemen were leaning over something. They were tall, young, dressed in dark blue. They held black sticks in their hands, like truncheons but longer and skinnier. Jack squinted, trying to focus through the heat haze, and noticed the heap of clothes lying on the ground between them. He watched as the heap moved, gradually revealing a face, eyes, hair. The soldiers swung in long deliberate arcs. The crunch of truncheon against bone echoed all the way across to where they sat, a thick heavy stuttering splitting the air. They watched silently as the policemen started kicking the man, passing around a bottle of clear liquid, wiping their mouths, then wiping the blood from their shoes on the crumpled man's clothes.

'No!' Ben grabbed David the moment he stood up, held him firmly by the arm. 'It's not our business.'

David swayed and shuddered in his grip. The soldiers had regained their momentum and were swinging on the man as if breaking rocks. Jack shook his head. 'Sit down before they notice us.'

David pulled away. 'They're going to kill him,' he said, his voice pinched. 'Of course it's our business.'

'David!' A thin line of sweat broke out on Ben's forehead and his voice caught in the sticky air.

Jack sat and watched the soldiers beat the man. His legs felt like they were on fire, as though the only thing that would make them better would be to get up, cross the road and stop this terrible thing, but he couldn't move. The heat and dread sealed him to the spot. With every blow he felt something inside him rip. He gripped the rough splintered edges of the chair until he felt a warm trickle of blood covering his fingers.

Suddenly the policemen stopped, noticing their audience for the first time. They turned towards the three white boys drinking at the bar and started clapping their hands as if they were the ones watching and not the other way round. Jack stood up.

'No!' Ben was almost shouting. 'What the fuck do you think will happen to us if we interfere?'

Jack looked at David, saw his own thoughts and fears wheeling through his friend's eyes, the space between them, the time it would take to cross the road. He sat down. 'Christ!' he ground his feet into the dirt below him, beetles cracking like eggshells under his heels.

David stood for a few seconds staring at the policemen, then shook his head and sat down too. They opened their beers and drank them without saying anything. The policemen eventually stopped and walked off. A woman came and knelt by the bleeding man, crying and shouting at the empty road. They finished their beers and headed upstairs to their rooms.

'IF YOU SEEK REVENGE, DIG TWO GRAVES'

Want to read more?

That's great! We were hoping you would do. We've put some more suggestions for amazing reads on
worldbooknight.org

You can also join your local library – for FREE – if you've not already done so. It's stuffed full of brilliant books with librarians who can help you choose what to read next.
findalibrary.co.uk

Reading groups are great for encouraging you to read new books. Go on your own, with a friend or take the family. At The Reading Agency we run a website where you can find your local reading group and get free books from publishers.
readinggroups.org

And check out your local bookshop. They're filled with books waiting to be discovered and staffed by experts who will help you find your next read.

Other annual reading celebrations

Along with World Book Night, World Book Day and Quick Reads are yearly campaigns in the UK and Ireland that aim to help more people learn to love reading.

World Book Day gives £1 book tokens to every child in primary school, which they can exchange for a World Book Day book or help buy a book of their choice.
worldbookday.com

Quick Reads are short new books written each year by bestselling authors and celebrities to encourage more young people and adults to read, and read more.
quickreads.org.uk

Partners and Supporters

World Book Night is run by The Reading Agency, a charity whose mission is to give everyone an equal chance in life by helping people become confident and enthusiastic readers.

World Book Night is supported using public funding by Arts Council England

Supported using public funding by
**ARTS COUNCIL
ENGLAND**

World Book Night would not be possible without the donors who have given so generously to support us, from the givers and readers who have given a few pounds to major funders who have given thousands.

You can join them and help get more books to more people, just **text* READ14 £3 to 70080**

Or for a full list of funders and to find out how you can support us further visit **worldbooknight.org/support**

World Book Night's primary partners are:
The BBC
The Publishers Association
The Booksellers Association of UK and Ireland

We are supported by the generosity of among others:
The authors, agents and publishers who waive their royalties and fund the printing of the books.
The libraries and booksellers across the country who promote reading every day and participate as collection points.
The volunteer givers, who give their time, energy and passion to promote reading in their communities.

Printing:
Clays
CPI Group (UK)

World Book Night is run by the charity The Reading Agency (registered charity number 1085443, registered number 3904882, England & Wales) Registered Office: Free Word Centre, 60 Farringdon Road, London, EC1R 3GA. *Text costs £3 plus network charge. The Reading Agency receives 100% of your donation. Obtain bill payer's permission. Customer care 08448479800.